Harriet Hudson was born in Kent. After taking a degree in English literature, she was director of a London publishing company and is now a freelance editor and writer. She is married to an American, and they live in a Kentish village on the North Downs. She also writes crime novels under the name of Amy Myers.

Also by Harriet Hudson

Look for Me by Moonlight

Under the name of Amy Myers

Murder in Pug's Parlour
Murder in the Limelight
Murder at Plum's

When Nightingales Sang

Harriet Hudson

KNIGHT

First published in 1990
by HEADLINE BOOK PUBLISHING PLC

First published in paperback in 1991
by HEADLINE BOOK PUBLISHING PLC

This edition published 1997 by
Knight an imprint of Brockhampton Press

10 9 8 7 6 5 4 3 2

ISBN 1 86019 6136

Typeset in 10/12¼ pt English Times
by Colset Private Limited, Singapore

Printed and bound in Great Britain

Brockhampton Press
20 Bloomsbury Street
London
WC1B 3QA

For Mary,
who taught me so much.

Acknowledgements

Many of the places and airfields that form the background to this novel are real, but some like West Forstling, Tregeddra and Wilburton, and the village of Frittingbourne are fictitious. Although escape and evasion lines were responsible for returning thousands of Allied servicemen to Britain during World War II, the St Jacques line itself is fictitious. During my publishing career I had the privilege of knowing many pilots of both the First and Second World Wars, in particular Lt-Colonel James Goodson of the USAAF, author of *Tumult in the Clouds*; but for technical advice I owe an enormous debt to the aviation historian Norman L. R. Franks who kindly vetted the typescript of this book for me. Any errors that might have crept in would have done so after his eagle eye had reviewed it, in my efforts to amend it to meet his criticisms. The typescript would never have reached that stage at all, however, had it not been for the patience of my agent Dot Lumley and editor Jane Morpeth; their expertise lit the flarepath and I am so grateful to them. I would also like to thank Mr Roy Atkins at the St Ermin's Hotel; Mr David Johnson of the House of Lords Records Office; Mrs Marian Anderson; Mr Peter Gent; Monsieur Emil Arcé of the Hotel Arcé,

St Etienne; Monsieur Reynier at the Hostellerie de la Loire at Gennes, and, in particular, Monsieur Miton at the Auberge du Pont, Londinières. The latter two inns have their place in the story, but the inhabitants of both in this novel are fictitious.

Part One

Don't You Hear the Fond Tale?

Don't you hear the fond tale
Of the sweet nightingale
As she sings in the valley below
As she sings in the valley below.

– *The Sweet Nightingale*,
old Cornish folk song

Chapter One

'I won't be there.'

'What?' Cicely Gray's voice rose, shrill and unbecoming, as she faced her wayward daughter. 'But you must. I told you, he's coming to meet you. I told him—'

'Then you'll have to untell him, Mother,' replied Jessica lightly. Stay calm, she told herself. You must keep calm. 'I've helped you prepare for the party and now I'm going.' Ignoring her mother's shrieks she strode away, trembling slightly as she still did after every confrontation. The famous 'Bubbles' Gray was not always the sunny, sweet-natured lady who had graced the musical stage for so long. Not when crossed.

'Don't you want to get married?' her mother hurled after Jessica as she hurried down the terrace steps.

She did not reply, there was no need. She tried not to break into a run as she crossed the gardens of Frittingbourne Manor, aglow with flowers on this early July Sunday, but her quick steps betrayed her eagerness to be away.

Married? Her sense of humour came to the rescue. Cue for happy ending: song with full chorus in white organdie (bouquets to be tossed twelve inches in the air).

Who but her mother could think of the marriage market when England was poised on the brink of being invaded, and Kent in the front line; when German troops might be crashing through the narrow lanes within days and every serviceable fighter aircraft in the south-east was keyed up awaiting the battle with the Luftwaffe that must surely precede invasion? Indeed, the battle for supremacy over the Channel had already begun. Yet ever since West Forstling aerodrome had opened on the North Downs at the beginning of the war, as a satellite to Biggin Hill, her mother had been busily trying to marry her off to a fighter pilot; partly because the excitement of playing gracious hostess to so many young men added lustre to her own social life now Cicely Gray no longer found parts so easy to find in London, and partly in determination to marry off her obstinate daughter, with or without white organdie. Not, thought Jessica somewhat grimly, in that daughter's own interests, however. Her mother's hopes had at first seemed doomed to disappointment since only a squadron of Anson pilots had been stationed at West Forstling. Now though, with Dunkirk past and invasion imminent, two fighter squadrons had been flown in, one of Spitfires and one of Hurricanes, and Cicely 'Bubbles' Gray's parties immediately acquired an added glamour.

Don't you want to get married? thought Jessica wrily, pushing the meadow's wicket gate hard in a spurt of desperation. There was only one thing she had ever wanted from life – the thing that now seemed denied to her forever. To sing: not as her mother sang, tinkly, bubbly songs in musical comedy, but from the heart, straight to the emotions of her audience. Nearly two years ago, when she was eighteen, she'd been offered a chance that would have given her all she'd ever dreamed of – the opportunity to sing with Ken Peters and his band. She'd worked so hard for it: the lessons she worked to pay for herself, the local concerts, the encouragement from her teachers, finally the introduction to the famous band leader. The audition had gone well, then a second audition, then 'I'm going to get some songs specially written for you, Jess, that voice—' And then nothing. Nothing until the final bleak communication.

Her voice was not good enough.

But what else was there in life for her but to sing? To sing aloud to the heavens, to reach people's hearts and speak to them in a way that mere words could rarely do, to sing of life's joys, of its sadnesses, and now that war had come, of its hopes and tragedies. When she sang, her strong voice, an almost husky rich contralto, sounded at times ready to wrest itself free of Jessica's slight frame, charged with all the passion of her emotions. Her copper-coloured curls seemed almost to share her body's tenseness, while her eyes remained dark, soft, fathomless. When she sang the awkwardness and gaucheness that earned her the nickname of 'Brickie' from her parents as a child, because she dropped things so much, left her as body, spirit and voice worked as one in a harmony.

'Phew.'

Jessica closed the door of her oasthouse home firmly behind her and sank against it in relief. She could hardly believe her own reprieve. Usually at these late Sunday afternoon gatherings, she was forced to take part in the general chatter. Before the war, she had amused herself by murmuring polite nothings while inside she was busy casting the guests into a Gilbert and Sullivan comedy of their own. Now a more sombre chorus line replaced it as one pilot after another was paraded in front of her, no doubt often feeling equally as out of water as was she, murmuring their 'Good shows', and 'Wizards', and talking of prangs, circuits and bumps, and having a crack at the Hun. And all the while everyone ignored the sound of overhead aircraft engines, the only tangible sign that England really was at war, in fighters flown by pilots such as these. Boys almost, many no older than she was herself.

But today she was safe in the old oasthouse that belonged to Manor Farm. In earlier days the Manor had been the centre of a large estate chiefly given over to hop growing. On the death of the old squire, Michael and Cicely Gray had moved in on their marriage twenty-two years earlier, to the initial disapproval of the village. London folks, especially stage folks and artists, were objects of suspicion. In time, they found their presence added glamour, and their visitors a never failing source of gossip. But farming interested the Grays not at all. The farm was rented out to Joe Barnham. Now that, in common with so many farmers, he had got out of hop growing, the old Kentish ragstone oast was superfluous until Jessica converted it into a home for herself. It had been the one good thing that had come out of that terrible rejection two years ago. She had thrown herself into technical discussions on beams and tiles, since the cooling and storage rooms of the oast had been converted from a timber-framed barn. Much of the practical work she had done herself; anything to overcome that ache of disappointment.

She had continued teaching at the village school, at first numb with shock. Then as the future stretched bleakly before her, she had resolved to leave home, do anything, provided she could use her voice – teach singing perhaps – even if she could not sing well enough to turn professional. But she had made the mistake of saying so, and Cicely Gray had intervened. She fiercely resisted Jessica's plans, throwing one of her famous tantrums, coupled with copious tears. Jessica's father, Michael, who longed only for a quiet life in which to paint and was devoted to Cicely, capitulated at once with a humorous shrug at Jessica, withdrawing his support for her plans.

'I need you *here*, Brickie,' her mother had insisted between sobs. 'My old trouble. It may be serious this time.' Cicely gave a brave smile. It was blackmail of the sort she specialised in.

In her childhood, Jessica had believed her. Only as she grew older did she slowly realise that Cicely's fragile health was a fiction, indulged by her husband, and exploited to full advantage. Maggie, their Scottish housekeeper, had looked after Cicely as a girl, and, knowing her wiles, kept a watchful eye. But she was powerless – and too loyal to Cicely – to shield Jessica from the loneliness she endured as a child, between a mother who lived for public applause on stage and off, and a father who, immersed in his painting and his ambitions, fostered by his wife, retreated from conflict.

Now Jessica was no longer taken in by her mother's plots and plans. Indeed she could often tolerate them with an affectionate amusement. But even so she was in no doubt as to Cicely's mischief-making powers. Even the use of the hated nickname was calculated to sap her resistance. When Jessica was a child Cicely had encouraged her to sing, but as it grew obvious that the girl's voice was not in the same mould as her own light soprano, which almost as much as her blonde curls had earned her the nickname 'Bubbles', her attitude subtly but surely changed.

'Very well,' Jessica had said, tired of the battle. 'I'll stay.' On one condition: she wanted the old oast to live in. No longer would she endure the frippery way of life at Frittingbourne Manor. Much as she loved the old red-brick house itself, in the rarefied atmosphere her mother created there, Jessica felt like a fish out of water. Since Cicely had won her way over Jessica's not leaving home, she was at first puzzled as to why the idea of marriage was quite so eagerly promoted. Then slowly she had realised. It would probably put paid to any idea of her pursuing the singing career to which her mother had been so opposed. She need not have worried, Jessica gloomily reflected. There seemed precious little chance of that now.

She walked slowly into the roundel room of the oast, with its two small windows, cool after the afternoon sun outside, peaceful, and smelling of over a century of history under the red-tiled roof topped with the huge white cowl so carefully restored for her by the village wheelwright. This was her special room, the core of her life. She sat down at the piano and began to play, nothing in particular, her fingers running over the keys and drawing from them the sense of relaxation and comfort that they always gave. Then she began to sing softly. Two years ago she had thought she would never sing again. But of course she had to. Inside her song and sound surged continuously and had to have their outlet. To sing was the reason for her living.

'We'll meet again . . .' Everyone was singing it. Songs of parting were what people responded to now. Simple straightforward messages of love and longing. She ran her fingers over the keys. 'A nightingale sang in Berkeley Square . . .' She finished the verse, but as usual she was dissatisfied with it. Not a song for her. She could not quite get it right. Perhaps it was because she'd never been in love. She supposed she loved Tom, might even marry him one day, but that sensation of seeing a stranger and knowing that love hovered nearby, to be grasped with grateful heart – ah, that she'd never felt. And was never likely to in Frittingbourne. She needed to be away with some young Lochinvar, riding in from the West to sweep his lady from the fate awaiting her and carry her off to freedom.

'No such luck for me,' muttered Jessica ruefully, crashing her fingers down on the keys. Freedom . . . How could she think in these terms when no one could be sure of freedom any more? She shivered. Yet no one seemed to take the very real threat of invasion seriously. The local papers were still dominated by front page wedding reports with hardly any mention of war.

'Jess?'

Crash! Her fingers came down again. She hated the diminutive of her name, almost as much as she hated 'Brickie'. Scowling, she spun round on the stool. She hated anyone coming in here, even her cousin.

'Jess, do come,' pleaded Vanessa. 'You know how edgy Cicely gets when you're not there.' Jessica smiled at the omission of 'Aunt' before Cicely's name – too ageing, her mother always protested. 'You'll enjoy it. Don Field is there.'

'Really?' Jessica's interest was aroused. Don Field was a Denmark Street publisher of popular songs. She'd heard of him, but never met him. Still . . . what was the point? She needed no new songs. For her local concerts she sang folk and semi-classical songs, and established popular favourites. But she wavered. Seeing this, Vanessa slipped her arm persuasively through her cousin's. 'Come on, Jess, you needn't stay long.'

'What about those ghastly fighter pilots?' said Jessica mutinously.

'You know me, I'll take them off your hands.'

Jessica laughed. Vanessa, with her long blonde hair and happy, bubbling infectious laughter, would have all their attention in seconds. They wouldn't cast a second glance at Jessica with her unruly dark copper curls, and slim boyish figure that seemed all awkward, jutting angles – until she sang. Then her hands and feet seemed to know where to go of their own accord, as she lost herself in music.

'Very well, sweet coz let us go to meet my fate,' she said melodramatically. 'Maybe I'll find a Lochinvar to sweep me off in his Spitfire.'

'Lucky you,' remarked Vanessa. 'I'd do anything to get away from this dump.'

'Dump?' asked Jessica curiously.

'Not the Manor,' said Vanessa hastily. As the only daughter of Michael's brother, she cherished her association with the Manor as the only path to luxury open to her, now that her father was dead and her mother, proud and determined to ask for no help, struggled to make a living in the village dairy. 'Frittingbourne. It's so tiny, and I want – the world.' Her eyes shone. 'Furs, travel, Hollywood – the lot.'

Jessica was silent for a moment. They were worlds apart yet she was fond of her cousin.

'It's the Manor that I want to leave,' she blurted out, then regretted it. Vanessa had too easy a relationship with Bubbles for Jessica to confide in her about things that mattered deeply. Only Tom did she trust completely. She'd run to his family for the warmth and affection missing from her own, and taken his steady protection, and companionship for granted, always at ease with him although he was so much older than she.

She loved the village with its early white clapboarded and beamed cottages, its mellow red-brick Victorian houses, its pretty gardens, thirteenth-century church and the picturesque pub. If she could only get away, perhaps she'd see the Manor too in its proper perspective, as the mellow, seventeenth-century mansion she loved. Who but her mother could have wheedled her way past officialdom to ensure that it remained unrequisitioned at the outbreak of war, charmingly offering to take however many evacuees were billeted on her, and somehow in the event avoiding having any at all?

Sometimes when her parents weren't there, Jessica relaxed in the sunny drawing room, sensitive to the atmosphere of the house itself, imagining the generations of families whose hopes and loves, dramas and tragedies, had all been played out within those walls, leaving something of themselves enshrined forever within; the voices that had filled the rooms with song over the years, the music that haunted its halls. Then her mother would sweep back in and – no, she wouldn't think of that. Exasperating though her mother was, Jessica was fond of her. Exactly when the childhood adoration of her mother had turned to fondness, she wasn't sure. Perhaps when Jessica's observant dark eyes first realised her mother's essential superficialness. Since then there had been a tacit understanding between Jessica and her father that it should never be acknowledged between them.

As they walked back through the gardens, the strains of 'Run Rabbit, Run Rabbit!' blared out from a gramophone. Later the music would be dreamier and Michael Gray would take Cicely in his arms and begin to dance. It had happened a hundred times before and would happen a hundred more. Or would it? thought Jessica, in sudden alarm. Would this be the last time? Would next week bring invasion – huddling in the concrete shelters built in the garden, hoping the makeshift tank traps, the barricades of old junk and the army of farmers bearing pitchforks, would repel the highly trained Wehrmacht?

'Ah, there you are, darling.' Cicely beamed, for all the world as if her daughter had been there all the time. But Jessica did not miss the conspiratorial wink her mother directed towards Vanessa. 'He hasn't arrived yet.'

'Who, Mother?' Jessica innocently enquired.

'Johnnie Gale, the fighter pilot I told you about, darling,' said Cicely exasperatedly. Nuances were always beyond her. 'He's got the DFC,' she breathed.

'Tell me when the inspection parade is, Mother, and I'll dance in right on cue.'

'Don't be silly, darling,' said Cicely vaguely, and floated away in a waft of chiffon.

Would the drizzle hold off? Would the Germans invade? The prospects were equally threatening to her mother, Jessica thought in despair, glancing after her retreating figure.

'Here, Jessica,' Vanessa caught her arm, 'this is Don Field.'

Field was a comfortable, middle-aged man with glasses who looked more like a benign grocer than an astute and successful song publisher. He listened silently to Vanessa's chatter, but it was Jessica who held his attention to the point where her cousin lost interest and wandered off.

'You're the girl Ken Peters thought so highly of, aren't you?'

Two years disappeared in a flash as the horror of his ultimate rejection flooded back. 'No,' she said stiffly. 'He didn't think highly of me at all. My voice wasn't good enough.'

'It was good enough for him to sound me out on some songs for you,' commented Field slowly. 'I had my best song-writers working on it. Then it fell through. I was pretty annoyed. Why'd you back out?'

'Back out - *me*?' Her head began to swim.

'Changed your mind, so he told me.' Field eyed her keenly. 'Not so, eh?' he added as he saw her expression. 'Ah, confirms what I thought.' He paused, fingering his glass pensively. 'Ken Peters is a friend of mine, and he's a good man. But it's a tough world, Miss Gray. I think you've got a powerful enemy out there.'

'That's not possible,' she managed to say. 'Apart from Mr Peters I don't know anybody in the song world.'

'Somebody knew you,' he said flatly. 'I heard a rumour – put two and two together. Band leaders are dependent on their bookings like anyone else, however popular. Radio, theatre bookings . . . Do you know who Bill Rolands is?' Everyone knew who he was for he owned a chain of theatres and cinemas in London. 'Rumour goes he stepped in and said he didn't want you at any price.'

'But I've never met Bill Rolands!' she cried. What was all this? She didn't know him. Then something seemed to hit her in the pit of her stomach. *Her mother did*. Her mother appeared exclusively in Rolands' theatres. She pushed the sickening thought aside, hardly conscious of what Field was saying now, and with a muttered excuse, ran out of the room and round the corner of the house where no one could see her. She must think, *think*. Surely no one, let alone her mother, would do such a thing? How could Cicely hate her so much that she would wreck her whole career? Surely not even Cicely would have gone as far as that? She'd said that she didn't want to see Jessica hurt, continually disappointed by a second-rate singing career now that she knew she had no hope of reaching the top. *Could* it be that Cicely herself had somehow prevented her from getting there? She tried to think calmly. In 1938, the year of Jessica's big disappointment, her mother had appeared in *Hearts and Diamonds*, her last big role. Had she been determined to see that her daughter would never find the acclaim that afterwards slipped from Cicely herself? Jessica swallowed. Sick anger mingled with pity – for herself and for her mother. But *could* she do such a thing to her own daughter? Yes, she could, Jessica slowly decided.

'Darling—'

Jessica looked up and studied her mother dispassionately. She was still pretty with her baby blue eyes so innocent under the frizz of curls, still blonde but lacking the radiant youthful gleam of Vanessa's.

'You did it, didn't you?' Jessica said flatly.

'What, darling?'

'You put pressure on Ken Peters to turn me down for that job.'

By the trapped look on her mother's face, she knew she was right.

'How could you?' Jessica burst out, bewildered more than angry. 'You knew how much it meant to me. Not only did you stop me getting the job, but you made him tell me my voice was no good.'

'I don't know what you mean,' laughed Cicely shrilly. 'You can't sing, that's all. Ken Peters told you so.'

Jessica's heart sank. She had hoped against hope that she'd been wrong. Now she knew.

'How did you know that?' she asked slowly. 'I never told you what Ken Peters said in his letter to me.'

'Well, if he didn't want you, it must have meant that,' Cicely came back weakly after a moment's pause.

Jessica said nothing, but the look on her face goaded Cicely into saying: 'What if I did talk to him? I was right. That's not a voice you've got, that's just a husky drawl, a freak. Did you think you were going to be a singer with that? You'd be laughed off the stage.'

'You didn't want me on the stage, rivalling you,' said Jessica bluntly, chilled with horror.

'How can you be so cruel?' cried Cicely, tears beginning to pool in her blue eyes.

'Cruel?' echoed Jessica. 'Mother, you don't know

what cruelty is. Two years, *two years*, you've let me believe I couldn't sing. Two years when I could have been away from all this, singing to people.'

Cicely's furious face was almost ugly. 'You? You haven't the presence. You're clumsy, ungainly—'

'I'm your daughter,' cut in Jessica unbelievingly. She had never seen this side of her mother. She had thought her merely silly. But now . . . 'Don't you have any feeling for me?'

'Yes,' said Cicely, summoning up her hurt look. 'I have. I want you to be happily married. You're too thin-skinned to go on the stage. I wanted to protect you. Oh, you don't appreciate what I want for you.' She flounced away, almost running.

'And what about what *I* want?' said Jessica quietly to her retreating back. She leaned her head against the old red brick of the house, trying to control the sense of bitterness, frustration and loss. Two years had gone by. It was useless to bemoan what was irreparable now. Yet how could she stay here after her mother's betrayal? She must volunteer for the services, be a Land Girl, *anything*. But could she leave, with the county about to be invaded? She couldn't abandon the school just like that. She had a duty to her pupils . . . There had to be something! An audition at the BBC? She must *sing*. Deep within her a tiny fanfare of music was swelling into a triumphant march of freedom. She wanted to shout, to sing, to dance away the anguish of the last two years. Most of all to *sing*. She was free at last.

She heard the scream of the motor cars' brakes first as they came to a halt outside the house, a Lagonda and a Bentley, each carrying perhaps half a dozen pilots. Then uniformed figures were climbing out, shouting to each other, marching in a phalanx towards the porch where she could hear her mother's voice as, miraculously recovered, she stood beside Michael to greet the new arrivals.

So, *they* were here. Well, she wasn't going to stay. Not now. Her thoughts in turmoil, she ran back to the terrace and was descending the steps to make her way back home when Vanessa grabbed her arm.

'Where do you think you're off to?' she said laughingly.

'Let me go, Van,' Jessica said wildly, pulling away. But Vanessa only held on the tighter.

'Oh no, you don't. What would Cicely say if I let you get away again?'

Jessica wrenched her arm away. Impossible to explain. Impossible to leave. She gave up and allowed herself to be led on to the terrace. She looked round for someone to talk to, someone other than fighter pilots.

'Miss Gray?' a deep voice enquired behind her.

'Yes,' Jessica and Vanessa said in unison.

Two amused eyes looked at them quizzically.

'The terrible twins, eh? I was told I'd find one beautiful daughter, not two. Jessica?' His grey eyes travelled hopefully towards Vanessa. Naturally, thought Jessica, unresentful and resigned.

'I'm Vanessa Gray, the impoverished cousin,' she laughed, her eyes lighting up as only they could when there was a handsome man around.

'I'm Jessica,' she offered, feeling suddenly all too conscious of her skinny arms and legs, and the shapeless mauve cotton frock, beside Vanessa's blonde stylishness. She glared at the newcomer defiantly, looking at her mother's choice for the first time. A shock vibrated through her. Dark hair, now that he had removed his hat, craggily handsome features, dark eyes . . . she didn't take in any of these for what they were. For one fleeting second it flashed through her mind that this was much as young Lochinvar might have looked. Then he laughed, and the illusion vanished. He was no Lochinvar, just a cardboard cut-out from a musical. A Ruritanian all-singing, all-dancing hero!

'Stupid of me,' he said easily. 'I see the resemblance to the lovely Bubbles Gray now.'

Idiot! she thought scathingly. Nobody could really identify her as Cicely's daughter; she looked more like her father and had inherited his awkwardness, if not his height. Vanessa was the daughter Bubbles should have had.

'John Gale at your service, ladies – and this is Graham Macintosh,' carelessly indicating a nervous-looking thin dark man who had just joined them.

'How do you do, Johnnie?' smiled Vanessa, wasting no time on non-commissioned officers like Graham. She knew her uniforms, and turned her charm full on John. But even her propinquity seemed to bowl Graham over. Indeed, in her square-shouldered, cream-coloured cotton dress, with a scarlet belt adding a splash of colour, she looked stunning. Only Jessica knew that the belt had come from a rummage sale, the material for the dress from an old sheet. Vanessa had a knack with these things, something Jessica sadly lacked.

'I'm so glad you've met Johnnie, darling.' Cicely came up to them, beaming. Not a sign on her face that anything untoward had happened, marvelled Jessica. She sometimes wondered whether anything registered for long with her mother. Cicely looked knowingly from one to the other. 'Why don't you two run along and dance?' she suggested archly.

Jessica writhed in embarrassment. It was too much – as though she were some piece of merchandise to be disposed of. She noted the momentary flash of disappointment on John's face as he glanced at Vanessa.

'I was just about to do that, Bubbles,' he replied gallantly. 'Now I'm torn between the three of you. Jessica?'

'I don't want to dance,' she replied violently, her voice sounding too loud and ungracious even in her own ears. They all seemed ranged against her – her mother, her father, now this fighter pilot, even Vanessa seemed an enemy. She saw the astonishment on John's face, opened her mouth to explain and could not. Caught between them, an exhibit on display, she turned and walked quickly across the lawn, shoving her hands deep inside the patch pockets of her dress, striving to contain her feelings lest she shout out to the world what her mother had done.

Even her home seemed to stifle her this evening, its lingering smell of dried hops cloying in her nostrils. She went through to the back door of the oast, out on to the small paved area she had created, and sat down on the bench. The sun was setting now, heralding another week. What would it bring? And how suddenly immaterial it seemed compared with the turmoil raging within her. Yet mixed with her rage was that spark of triumph. It hadn't been true what Ken Peters told her: her voice *was* good. It must have been, if he had taken the trouble to commission songs for her. There might still be a future ahead of her. Perhaps it wasn't too late.

Then she remembered. Britain was at war. Who knew what would happen in the next weeks? If the Germans invaded she'd be lucky if she could keep this house, and she would have to stay a teacher. No singing then, in concerts or anywhere else. If the war continued, they might call women up. At least that would bring escape of a kind. But still within her was that glimmer of happiness: she could sing. Not just in local concerts, or to friends, or herself, but to everyone. Her voice could reach out to people's hearts if only she could find the way.

'Jessica?'

She started, and turned to see Flying Officer John Gale lolling against the doorpost.

'What are you doing here?' she said belligerently.

'I'm sorry – the door was open so I came through.' He smiled, the friendly expression lighting up his eyes, she noted for some reason.

'Why?' The monosyllable was abrupt, ungracious, but she did not care.

'I—' John hesitated. With the Vanessas of this world, he was very much at home, but not with this odd girl Jessica. 'I suppose I'm not used to being turned down,' he replied truthfully.

She looked hard at him, this intruder from her mother's world, her mother's choice, and tried to be fair. It wasn't his fault she'd mentally cast him as the Student Prince. She had a sudden vision of his carolling the famous Drinking Song. 'It wasn't your fault,' she said at last. 'I was—'

'In the middle of a row with your mother, by the look of it,' he interrupted cheerfully.

'How did you know?' she asked, amazed.

He shrugged. 'When she arrived, there was an atmosphere I wouldn't have cared to have flown my Spit through.' He didn't say that he recognised of old the signs of family feuding, the hurt desperation on Jessica's face, the bland smugness on Bubbles'. Parents were all the same, famous West End stars or country vicars.

She gave a reluctant grin, and then laughed, rather to her own surprise.

'Why don't you come back now and make it up to me?'

'No, I—' She cast round for an excuse. There was no way she was walking back into *that*. 'I have to feed Astaire.'

'Who?' he asked, startled, then followed the direction of her eyes.

In a large roomy cage in one corner of the paved area there were two birds.

'Good Lord,' he said, astonished. 'Who are those little fellows?'

'They're permanent guests,' she said defensively. She didn't want to have to discuss her home or herself with this emissary of her mother's. But he was looking at her expectantly. She had to say something. 'Both of them have broken wings that will never heal well enough for them to fly again. I sort of acquired them.'

'You sound like the Artful Dodger,' commented John. 'What are they?'

'Astaire's a wagtail and Lind's a nightingale.'

'Nightingale? Like the ones that sing in Berkeley Square?'

She glanced at him, sprawled on the garden seat.

'Something like that.' Inside her the tune welled up, catching her in its toils, as across the gardens, faintly in the distance, the gramophone began to play.

'There you are, you see,' he teased. 'They're playing our song.'

Chapter Two

'What's new, Gerry?'

Flying Officer the Honourable Gerald Rhodes was deep in the *South East Gazette*. Literally, for he was reclining in a deck chair, apparently peacefully sleeping, with it spread over his face.

'The Pink Knicker thief is at it again. Maidstone's Phantom Clothes-line Raider,' he intoned gravely, the newspaper rising and falling with his words.

'Perhaps it's Göring,' commented John Gale, sprawling on the steps at his side.

'More likely you on the scrounge for one of your girlfriends, dear boy. Making good the damage.'

'Scoreboard's even now.' John pointed lazily to the chalked figures on the blackboard that kept tallies of kills on the ground as well as in the air.

'Three cows killed in a hit and run raid,' intoned Gerry gravely, ignoring this riposte.

'Throwing everything they've got into the battle now.'

Outwardly the scene was peaceful – twelve men apparently lazing. In fact every nerve was tensed, every heart beating in anticipation, ever since the tannoy had called them to thirty minutes' readiness. Ten to one it was a false alarm again. Always waiting, waiting for

Göring to make a move, but nothing of consequence to mix with yet. Attacks in the Channel, the odd sneak raids over Kent, Lenham Chapel destroyed, a bomb last week at Bekesbourne, a few more bombs over Canterbury. England was finished, the raiders would report.

Only they knew differently. In 11 Group, defending South-East England, squadrons like theirs from Kenley, Croydon, Biggin Hill, Tangmere and their satellites, scenes like this were enacted daily; men sat around at Dispersal, smoke haze everywhere, the gramophones everlastingly churning out the same songs, often in makeshift airfields.

There was no sign yet of the awaited invasion. But they were waiting . . . waiting . . .

The harsh ringing of the telephone split the silence.

'Scramble, chaps.'

Flying Officer John Gale, DFC, section leader, was first out of the door, running towards Spit L-Lion, *his* Spit, Mae West on, closely followed by the other eleven. Greet the ground crew, strap in, straps and parachute harness, check the trim and flaps, signal to the mechanics, 'Contact!' and the comforting exhilarating sound of the Merlin engine would roar into his ears, chocks away – it was all routine now, but still the familiar flare of excitement would ignite in the pit of his stomach as she lifted into the blue. Any aeroplane, any place, but above all the Spitfire. They'd only had them a few weeks, but already he knew there was no other aircraft for him.

He'd flown Hawker Furies in his first squadron, a sprog pilot who'd joined the RAF with many of his contemporaries from Oxford in the autumn of 1938 in protest against the misguided pacifism of Munich. A few years earlier, their predecessors at Oxford had voted in the famous debate that in no circumstances would they fight for King and Country. King and Country? That was a concept he had doubts about. But he had no doubts about freedom. No doubts about the rights of Poles and Czechs to their own land. No doubts that the same fate might befall Britain. He intended to be ready for it.

But when war came, his squadron was kept in Scotland, while many of those he'd trained with flew to France to be sitting ducks when they flew reconnaissance missions throughout the 'Bore' War, and to be decimated when *Blitzkrieg* came in May. Jacob Adams, who took a first in Classics, Pat Marwick, rowing blue, and Quentin - no, he couldn't think of Quentin, even now. John had pestered, cajoled and generally made a nuisance of himself, but his squadron was kept firmly in Scotland which up to the outbreak of *Blitzkrieg* had been thought to be Hitler's first objective. When the War Office finally conceded they were wrong, John Gale's squadron, now flying Hurricanes, was posted south - just in time for Dunkirk.

He'd won the DFC at Dunkirk, despite the Army saying that the RAF was nowhere to be seen. He knew all too well it was; he, and scores of others, fighting the Hun like blazes, too far inland, too high for the soldiers on the beaches below to see, too high for anything save concentrating on who was on your tail, trying to see all around you and watch the horizon as well. He'd been lucky in his blooding. Mickie Wilson, his section leader, had protected him - otherwise he'd have been a goner. He'd gone on to win a gong and Mickie Wilson, veteran of the Battle of France, had been shot down on his next sortie. That was less than six weeks ago, yet already it seemed ancient history. It had changed him, though. He'd come down from the North confident and ready to blow the Hun out of the sky. Now there was a small residue of doubt. What if they didn't succeed? But they must not think that way. And so they drank at nights, they womanised, they danced, they slept, and the next day they'd be at dawn readiness – waiting for it to begin all over again. Perhaps this was it today; the beginning of Armageddon.

His Spit bumped over the grass, taking off into the air like the lady she was. This was the only woman he wanted, all grace, all light, all charm, responding intuitively to his touch, moving with him. Up here he could forget the Vanessas of this world. On the ground they were necessary, but up here, in the skies, it was different. For some reason the image of that odd girl Jessica came into his mind. Funny her bird being a wagtail when that was the squadron call-sign. Lucky omen perhaps. He was glad he'd invited her to the dance now. Though she didn't like him much – which only intrigued him. Girls normally did like him. But she couldn't dance – no rhythm. Too awkward. Not like his Spit.

'Come on, my beauty, love me,' he whispered, exhilarated, as she rose high into the sky, his Red Section on the CO's left wing. Graham Macintosh was behind him, the newcomer Maxwell tucked in between them. He'd be all right. Newcomers had to be protected. They'd be needing them . . .

Below them the cliffs of Dover, grey rather than white today, beyond them the Channel, blue-grey and evil-looking, as the flight soared to meet whatever was in store for them on this patrol. Thirty plus bandits, control was saying. Plenty of yellow-nosed 109s probably, guarding the bombers. Spitfires could dart around the bombers like fireflies, but the 109s were a match for them. He remembered what his uncle, a First World War pilot, had told him: the pilot that sees furthest lives longest. You became attuned to seeing them in the distance that split fraction of a second before they saw you; those that didn't learn that, died.

'This is Wagtail Red Leader. Tally ho! Snappers two o'clock above! Here we go, chaps.'

'Roger Red Leader,' Graham acknowledged, Maxwell after him. Then they were climbing before the 109s could swoop. That was their strength, the one thing a Spit could not excel in. Dive. Not a moment too soon. Then the noise, the confusion, the smoke, the Brownings in action – all the time trying to keep an eye on Maxwell. The rattle and thud of hits scored hardly registered; he was too busy to worry about what damage they might be doing. Just keep flying, keep turning, my beauty, my love. Blue Leader had scored a kill judging by that spiralling black plume of smoke. Where was Maxwell – where? He took a second too long to look, disregarded his tail and only keen-eyed Macintosh swooping in behind the bandit with all Brownings blazing saved his bacon.

They landed within two minutes of each other. 'Thanks, Mac,' John said nonchalantly. 'I owe you a pint.'

But it would have to wait. Flight Sergeant Graham

Macintosh was non-commissioned. They didn't share the same mess. Only the same danger.

'Blast,' muttered Jessica as she dropped the pile of books on the floor and bent down to pick them up.

'Here, let me.' A bony hand stretched down. Tom Ackroyd was firmly pushing her out of the way and picking them up as though to demonstrate that his game leg might keep him out of the Army, but it didn't make him entirely helpless.

'Thanks, Tom. Why you should have to suffer for my clumsiness, I don't know.'

'Brickie,' he said, grinning at her.

She threw an exercise book at him.

'Ow,' he said, 'that hurt.'

'Good,' she said. 'That'll teach you to taunt me.'

'The privilege of having grown up with you.'

'You didn't exactly grow up with me,' she pointed out. 'You were eight when I was born.'

'That's why I'm headmaster and you're my subservient menial.'

She laughed, somewhat to his relief. He'd thought his joke had gone too far. He was the only person who knew how she had felt about what had happened two years ago, and realised that however good a teacher of children she might be, it was not her real vocation.

'Tom,' she said, more seriously, 'something happened. I want to join up. Do you mind? Could you get a replacement over the school holidays?'

He looked at her closely. 'I knew something was wrong. Yes, Jessica, I would mind. You're a good teacher, and you're needed here, especially now most of the men have been called up. There's going to be a future whatever the outcome of the war and the children are it. There's no spare teachers worth their salt in Kent at the moment. Tell me what's wrong.'

She paused. 'I've got to get away, Tom.' She ran her fingers through her curls so that they were even more on end than usual. 'I'm all fenced in. I've got to sing. If I joined up . . .'

'Don't do anything in a hurry, Jessica,' he said quietly. 'After the holidays—' He stopped. There was no need to say anything more. After the holidays the school could be controlled by the Germans.

'I can't wait that long. Even if there's hop-picking to look forward to,' she tried to joke. 'So please try to get someone.'

'If life at home's difficult,' he said lightly, guessing, 'you could always marry me.' He fiddled with the exercise books.

What on earth did she say to that? Tom had been an undemanding friend, then boyfriend, then tentatively aspiring lover. Her mother couldn't stand him, which did more for him in Jessica's eyes than anything else before she learned to appreciate his worth. Now twenty-eight, he was tall, lean and academic-looking, with a humorous twist to his mouth, that suggested he took life easily. Only Jessica knew how hard his rejection from enlisting in the Army had hit him. Now he took his local defence volunteer duties half seriously, half mockingly, referring to himself as 'Pitchfork Percy'. She owed so much to him – including her job.

'That's not the answer,' she said quietly. 'You do understand, Tom? I would if I could.'

He did understand. Better than Jessica herself. Picking up the books without a word, he left her.

'Damn,' she said again under her breath. 'Damn *everything*.' She hated hurting Tom. It was like punching a defenceless teddy bear. He wasn't like John Gale. She'd been as offputting, even rude, as she could to him, but still she hadn't managed to get past that smiling armour of charm. Her mother had picked a good one this time, she'd say that for her. So much so that she'd been left with no excuse for refusing when he invited her to the mess dance this Saturday. Afterwards she'd fumed at her stupidity but now found the prospect exciting, for an idea was beginning to form in her mind. There'd be a band there, John had said. A station band.

The next day she was regretting it once again. Whyever had she said she'd go? she berated herself, tugging a comb almost viciously through her curls. Ten to one the band would be useless. Only the thought that it would get her away from Frittingbourne stopped her from backing out. She couldn't endure her mother's constant visits to the oasthouse as if to assure herself that nothing at all had happened between them.

'I look like a pile of mince,' she sighed, frowning into the mirror.

'Nonsense,' said Vanessa valiantly, tying a pink ribbon round Jessica's hair. 'There,' she said encouragingly.

'Now I look like mince with a ribbon round it.'

'You look very nice,' said Vanessa firmly, and indeed Jessica didn't look too bad, after she'd been persuaded not to wear the bright green dress but the brown which highlighted her dark copper-coloured hair. 'Here, put some of my lipstick on.' There was a short silence.

'Grimaldi?' ventured Jessica, gazing fascinated into the mirror at the result.

'Now, Jessie, you look splendid. Let's just add something - this sash to match the ribbon. Perfect.'

'But not like you.' No one looking at Vanessa's figure-hugging red lace dress with its swirling skirt would ever guess it was made out of dyed old net curtains. Occasionally she was envious of Vanessa's flaunting beauty. No one was ever going to call Jessica beautiful or even pretty for all her heart-shaped face and lively eyes.

The mess dance was being held in Kippen Hall, the home of Lady Manton, which had been requisitioned firstly for the Royal East Kent Regiment and then, with the invasion threat, by West Forstling airfield for its headquarters and officers' mess.

Vanessa drove Michael's old Packard. He would not let them near the new Rover. Driving with Vanessa was an unnerving experience. She was all too apt to take her hands off the wheel and her eyes off the road while she described a particularly attractive man, and at night with the blackout and masked headlights, country lanes assumed terrifying proportions even at the low speed all civilians had adopted to conserve petrol. Fortunately there was still just light enough to see. A near collision at the gates with a motor car full of nurses from the nearby hospital sobered Vanessa and she drove up the drive in sedate style for her, even avoiding the large fishpond which was inconsiderately placed at the top. Not a chink of light from the blacked-out windows betrayed what was going on behind; only the sound of a band playing and the hum of voices betrayed the festivities within. But the door was flung open with a fine disregard for the blackout restrictions as they ran up the steps.

I'll be nice to him, Jessica decided, feeling suddenly in a party mood. It's not his fault my mother fastened on him, after all.

Inside, she blinked. The ballroom, once Lady Manton's drawing room, was cleared of furniture for the occasion, rugs rolled back, and at the far end a rostrum erected for the musicians. Not that she could see that far for the dim light and mass of bodies. She craned her neck to assess the band. Small. Five-piece only. But she could barely hear the music for the racket going on. A haze of smoke hung over the room, clouding even this entrance. A few couples were pirouetting on the terrace in the fading light. Exactly like an Astaire and Rogers film, Jessica decided, 'Dancing Cheek to Cheek' running through her mind.

'He-llo,' drawled a tall, languid officer, sporting a monocle and a fine moustache. 'Girlies, I do believe. New birds, lovelies too. It's Gerry's night tonight.'

'This I don't believe,' muttered Jessica, brought down to earth. 'Is this really happening?' But Vanessa seemed to notice nothing funny. She took off her jacket, her body arching sensuously as she did so.

'Not so, Gerry. My guest.' John Gale, glass in hand, firmly pushed him aside.

'Come now, you don't need 'em both, dear fellow – or do you?' drawled Gerry plaintively, emptying his beer mug at a gulp.

John cast him a furious look. 'Ah,' said Gerry thoughtfully, interpreting the look, and detaching himself from the balustrade supporting him, lurched back into the dancing room.

Jessica took half a pace towards John to greet him, but before she could speak he had taken Vanessa's hand. God, she was looking even better than he remembered, John thought hazily. He had already had several drinks. What a figure. All he could register were those eyes and those . . .

'Vanessa, my lovely, and—' he looked round vaguely, '—Jessica. You came.' The smile flashed. 'Good of you. Enjoy yourself.' He waved a vague hand in the direction of the dance floor and focussed again on Vanessa, putting his arm round her waist and sweeping her off.

Jessica was left standing alone, at first stunned then furious with herself. She might have known it. He was just another of her mother's protégés, that was all. Another damned fighter pilot. What on earth was she doing here like a wilting wallflower? She could have been in the oasthouse singing, playing the piano, reading, even listening to the wireless. Or out with Tom. A thousand things, instead of standing like a damned fool in the middle of a scene from a propaganda war film.

That was that for John Gale, plan or no plan.

'Handsome couple, aren't they?' Graham Macintosh was standing by her side, and she saw his eyes fixed on Vanessa as she whirled round in John Gale's arms, like a red flame in her bright dress. As he cupped his hands to light his cigarette, she noticed they trembled slightly.

'Couple?' she echoed, still annoyed.

'Of course, Johnnie doesn't really need someone like Vanessa, but I—'

'Come on. We can dance, too,' cut in Jessica firmly.

He flushed. 'I can't, I'm afraid,' he said awkwardly. 'It's an officers' mess dance and I'm not commissioned. I'm only here to deliver a message to the CO.'

'But you're a pilot, too,' she said, amazed.

He grinned. 'Makes no difference. Anyway, I'd rather be in the sergeants' mess than with this lot.' With an expression of distaste he watched Gerry stumble by.

'Well, if we can't dance, you can tell me about the band,' said Jessica determinedly. To hell with John Gale! She'd been wrong about another thing too – the band wasn't useless. Far from it. 'Is it a station band? Do they have to be officers to be in it?'

Graham laughed. 'Good lord, no! Officers wouldn't demean themselves by playing in a band. They're airmen. Pre-war professionals of a sort. The trumpet player is the best, Art Simmonds. He's the keen one; he and the saxophonist are cooks, the other three mechanics. It's a real mixture but it works.'

'Do they have a singer?' she asked eagerly.

'I've never heard one. They play for the dances here, in between their other duties.'

'Do you think I could sing with them?'

'You?' His amazement was obvious. 'Well, I—'

'Could you introduce me?'

He looked uneasy. 'I think you'd better have a word with John – he's responsible for the entertainments side. It might have to go to the CO – he's keen on the band, though. If you were a WAAF it would be different, but—' He broke off with relief. He was getting out of his depth. 'Here,' he said, catching a passing sleeve, 'let me introduce you to Pilot Officer Cartwright.'

She began to relax and even enjoy the evening, despite the band's increasing volume and the flowing beer. She found herself clamped to one uniform jacket after another, whirled into dance after dance until the heat began to overwhelm her. Murmuring an excuse, she found her way on to the terrace.

She looked at the tranquil sky and it seemed impossible that across the Channel invasion forces were building up, that such a peaceful night might be shattered by the instruments of war. Yet for what other reason were all these young men here, but to face that challenge? The John Gales of this world might be cut down one by one, just as in the battle for France. Tom had told her about his brother, a Hurricane pilot, who when *Blitzkrieg* had been unleashed across Belgium and France had been one of the handful of fighter pilots left there to battle against the Luftwaffe, with pitifully uneven odds. Now he lay in hospital, blinded, burned, and with little future ahead.

Inside the hall the noise of the band grew ever louder as if to drown the dogs of war. 'Care to dance, sweetheart?' A pair of hands grasped her round the waist from behind.

She pushed them off indignantly and turned to find the tall, pretentious Gerry who'd greeted them on their arrival, now several degrees drunker. He did not wait to go back to the dance floor, but seized her in his arms so close she could scarcely breathe, his beery breath steaming over her, his hands moving slowly down well below her waist. She dug him sharply in the ribs with her elbow, so that he backed off with a surprised yelp of pain, then as he reached for her again, she slapped his face hard.

'Having fun, Jessica?' enquired John Gale, arriving

just as Gerry lurched forward once more, and pushing him away with one hand.

'Tremendous fun, thank you,' she replied sweetly.

'Your mount, eh, Johnnie?' asked Gerry.

'You're drunk, Gerry,' said John amiably.

'Yes,' he agreed and lurched off. A few moments later she could see him whirling Vanessa round the floor.

'All right, Jessica?'

'Of course I am,' she replied, nettled. 'I'm hardly a damsel in distress.' Then she remembered that he was in charge of entertainments. She swallowed her pride. 'John, I wanted to ask you about the band.'

'Yes,' he agreed. 'Come and dance with me.'

'But—'

'They're playing our song.'

Charmer, she thought crossly. 'Look, the band—'

'How's old Lind doing?' But he seemed as little interested in Lind's welfare as in the band, for he bent his head over hers, humming in her ear and singing softly. Part of her told herself that he had barely remembered her when she arrived, that this was just charm. But the other half began to move in step with him. She could talk about the band later. For the first time she was not falling over her partner's feet but lost in the dance, the music, and the sudden stabbing enchantment of a July night.

'Do you like Ginger Rogers?' he asked prosaically, breaking the silence.

She raised her head. 'Yes, but—'

'Good. "Euphelia serves to grace my measure, but Chloe is my real flame", as the poet says. For Chloe read Ginger. She's on at the Granada next week with James

Stewart. *Vivacious Lady* together with Ray Milland in *Untamed*. We'll go.'

'But—'

'Can you think of one good reason to refuse me?'

'No, but—'

'Do you ever say anything else but but?'

'Occasionally I say yes,' she replied gravely. Inside she was leaping with excitement. It would be one way of talking to him alone. *Then* she'd ask him.

It was an uneventful patrol. Constant showers and cloud were keeping the numbers of raiders down at the moment. By 18th July, the expected onslaught on mainland Britain still had not begun, but battle raged over the Channel. The Spitfire droned on in a grey sky. John Gale could hardly see his number two, let alone the rest of the flight.

Tomorrow he'd said he would take Jessica Gray to the pictures. Whatever had made him offer? Not just because Bubbles had been pushing, that was for sure. Pique because Vanessa had turned him down, he supposed. But there was something about the girl . . . Why was she so prickly? He'd enjoyed the game of getting her to go out with him. He knew she would in the end. Obviously a virgin though, so no joy there. Still, he wouldn't mind seeing more of Frittingbourne Manor. There must be a few pennies around there. It was a way of life that fascinated him, odd really when he felt this overpowering need always to help the underdog – the NCOs, Poland come to that. Now Britain herself. He wondered if that was what intrigued him about Jessica, that hunted look of desperation he'd seen on her face, which had made him remember his own family struggles. Though Frittingbourne Manor was a far cry from the vicarage, that was for sure. He wondered what his mother would make of Jessica.

He thought of her in the huge flat-stoned kitchen of the vicarage, trying for the umpteenth time to get the range lit while Dad wrote his blessed endless sermons up in the study. He couldn't have had better parents, but theirs wasn't the life for him. They wanted nothing more than for him to follow them into their church, waited patiently and in vain for him to receive the call. He hadn't. Then the rows had started, rows in which he ended up the victor by logic, but the moral loser. Parents – what they wanted for you and what you wanted were rarely the same. But once he'd got to Oxford that was the end of it. There were more religions to choose from than he'd ever heard of, and so far he'd chosen none. He had more immediate concerns.

He grimaced. He'd let Vanessa stew in her own juice for a few days.

Jessica dashed through the shower towards her oasthouse home. Thank heavens tea was over! She'd had to force herself to go to the Manor after the scene with her mother. She had to go on living here, for the moment at least, so for her father's sake she must struggle to put the fact of her mother's treachery to the back of her mind. Not to be forgotten, but to be mulled over until the chance of a reckoning appeared. But this knowledge hadn't made tea-time at the Manor any easier.

With another stab of irritation she thought over what had happened last Sunday, after the dance. She had said nothing about it, nothing about John Gale. Then Vanessa had swept in, effusively kissing Michael and Cicely and plumping herself down on the cushions.

'I'm all in today, after last night, aren't you, Jess?'

'Last night?' enquired Michael. 'Late night oasthouse session, was it?'

'Yes,' said Jessica instantly, simultaneously with Vanessa's: 'No. Didn't she tell you? You are a secretive old boots, Jess. We went to the squadron dance.'

'How sweet of you to take Brickie along, Vanessa,' Cicely beamed.

'I don't know what Johnnie Gale would have said if I'd left her behind. He invited her, after all.'

'What?' Cicely's look of amazement was instantly replaced with sugary charm. 'Oh, Brickie darling. I just knew you two were meant for each other.'

'We're not meant for each other, Mother,' Jessica replied steadily. 'He needed extra girls for the dance, that's all.'

'But you made an impression all right,' Vanessa said archly, oblivious to Jessica's glares. 'He's asked you out.'

'Really, darling?' Cicely breathed.

Jessica stood up, fighting for patience when she saw the cock-a-hoop look on her mother's face. How on earth had Vanessa known? 'Yes, really,' she replied. 'I must have been drunk at the time to agree.' It wasn't a particularly convincing exit line, she realised from the look of triumph on her mother's face.

Perhaps she'd been wrong to accept John Gale's invitation, however strong her reasons. He might be good-looking and fun to be with, and he was the way of approaching the band, but he was part of her mother's entourage, she reminded herself firmly. But somehow that didn't seem so important now. People were people, weren't they? It wasn't his fault Cicely had picked on him. She wondered if John were up there even now in the clouds, waiting for the Luftwaffe. Or would they be stood down because of the weather? Only drizzle and grey skies for the last few days. Still, that meant the Luftwaffe were as hampered as the RAF. It was tomorrow she was going to the pictures with John, provided the squadron was released in time. A sudden jab of excitement. Let it rain, rain, *rain*, and then they would be stood down by afternoon perhaps.

Jessica was glowing with hope, alive inside as she had not been for two years. The excitement grew and now her thoughts tumbled over themselves. Songs filled her head, colouring the days with the glory of her secret music. If, *when*, she persuaded John to let her sing with the band - being an officer they'd have to listen to him - she might become known for her singing. They were professionals, they'd have contacts, they might play at other stations, maybe broadcast like Bert Ambrose's band, and Lew Stone's. And Ken Peters' . . . Even that thought had no power to hurt. Her mind ran wild over the possibilities, then returned to John Gale. Some turnaround, she laughed to herself, from swearing she'd never go out with a fighter pilot! Even if it was just a means to an end. Would he kiss her? Would she mind? A thrill of excitement caught her. She wouldn't mind at all. The thought of being in John Gale's arms made her feel alive, as though her senses were on tiptoe.

When she left the dance on Saturday night, he had brushed her cheek with his lips and the thought of Lochinvar returned to her. And this time did not vanish.

Chapter Three

There was a sudden lull in the conversation, then a back was ostentatiously turned. Other backs followed suit. John Gale strode up to the mess bar. 'Two pints, Charlie.' He stuck out his chin aggressively. 'Have one, Seb?'

'Not thirsty, old man.' Pilot Officer Seb Cartwright, stocky, determined and red-headed, didn't turn round, merely took another gulp of his pint, draining it to the bottom of the glass.

'Gerry?'

'My dear fellow, mustn't interrupt your twosome, eh?'

Graham Macintosh flushed. 'I'd better go, Johnnie.'

'My guests don't *go*, Mac,' said John broadly. 'They stay.'

'Yes, sir,' muttered Graham, as ill at ease as any of the twenty or so commissioned pilots gathered in the officers' mess at Kippen Hall. In theory any guests were welcome; in practice it was different. Graham would much rather have been in the convivial sergeants' mess where there was none of this protocol, but Johnnie had got this bee in his bonnet. He was a strange chap. Mac had set him down as yet another university twit-type when he first met him at Initial Training, with his overt good looks, his confident almost arrogant walk, his at times affected drawl, and scarf worn ostentatiously long. But there was more to him than that. He was a good section leader, with no disputes as to his ability as a pilot or his bravery in the air, and he had an easy authority that made him popular with everyone from the CO down to the erks. But he was almost *too* popular with the erks. It wasn't that they didn't respect him, they did; but he made almost a point of singling them out and chatting with them, and it was making the other chaps wary of him. Graham sometimes thought he was more of a symbol to Johnnie than a mate. Not that one could be too matey with an officer. He'd been all ready to drop out after training when Johnnie went to officers' training school. But Johnnie would have none of it.

'I don't believe you've been introduced to Flight Sergeant Macintosh,' John buttonholed Roddy Maxwell. A newcomer was easy game. The youngster was unable to deny his section leader, but glanced uneasily at the turned backs.

'No, sir. Thank you, sir. How do you do, Macintosh?'

'Good hunting today, Gerry. Congratulations.' John raised his voice.

Even Gerry could not ignore a second summons.

'You call that good?' he drawled. 'Jesus, have you got low standards! The sergeant here can knock spots off anything I can do, I'm sure.'

Graham grinned awkwardly. He had indeed more victories to his credit than any of them - and a DFM to show for it.

Retribution for John arrived swiftly in the morning with a summons to the CO.

'Flying Officer Gale, sir.'

Squadron Leader Bill Walding did not look up from his desk, but continued writing. Let the fellow stew.

'All right,' he barked eventually. 'Sit down, Gale. I hear you've been at your bloody commie games again. Been entertaining sergeants in the officers' mess.'

'Nothing in the regulations against it, sir,' John replied woodenly. 'He was my guest.'

'Nothing in the regulations says I can't demote you to the sergeants' mess where you seem to want to be. I won't have my officers' mess used as a testing ground for your commie theories. Understand?'

'Macintosh saved my life, sir. I owed him a drink.'

'Then you owe him more than putting him through that.'

'Can you give me a reason, sir? I don't see what's communist merely—'

'Yes, I bloody well can.' The CO went red in the face, then calmed down. 'Look, John, the big show's coming any minute now.' He went to the window and looked out over the field where fifteen Spitfires were lined up facing towards the Channel. 'Why do you think the Führer is keeping so quiet, eh?'

'He may be deciding to go for the Eastern Front. I think he'll go for Russia one of these days for all—'

The CO snorted. 'Come on, John. Would you leave a hornet to sting your arse the moment your back's turned?'

'Perhaps he's trying to negotiate peace, sir.'

'He's building up his forces over there,' the CO said decisively, staring out over the field. 'You know the tales they're bringing back from recce. More and more craft in every port from Le Havre round to Rotterdam. But before they can set sail, he has to put us out of action. My guess is he's trying to lure us out over the Channel now so that he can pick us off one by one. And when that fails and when he's settled into his new airfields and so on, then he'll hurl everything he's got at us over here. Bombers, fighters, the lot. You won't see the sun for little black dots flying out of it, every one hell bent on knocking us out of the skies.' He swung round. 'Understand?'

'Yessir, but—'

'But nothing,' he interrupted. 'You're not going to upset any apple carts with your pseudo-intellectual Oxford clap-trap. I want my officers working together, not at each other's throats in the mess each night. It's up to you, Gale. Any more difficulties like last night's and I'll have your rank braid off quicker than a barmaid's knickers and post you to a training unit. That what you want?'

John Gale went white. 'No sir.' Posted away from the action? Away from 11 Group? Now, when every nerve was tingling, tensed for what was coming? This was something he had to be part of, even if only to stop that irrational guilt inside him at leaving his father's world behind. And if that meant kow-towing to a lot of outdated class divisions, that's the way it had to be.

Jessica fidgeted impatiently while the children packed their satchels, found their gas masks and were despatched into the late afternoon sun, hurrying away from the solid grey stone school building. At last she was free to think about the evening.

For once she found herself relishing the ritual of

preparing to go out. In the bedroom she had created on the first floor of the oasthouse storage room, she sat at the dressing table and with a magazine picture in front of her tried to get her curls into some passing resemblance of the simpering model's. Finally she gave up in despair.

Making a face at her tousled reflection she stuck a tea rose in her hair, then laughed. Who on earth did she think she was, Vivien Leigh? Thank heavens she didn't live in the Manor so that before her date she would have to undergo an inquisition from her parents, see her mother's smug smile. Tonight was it. Tonight she'd be side by side with John in the Lagonda with the chance to broach her plans. Convince him that she deserved that introduction, that a vocalist – a *female* vocalist – was what the band needed. All the best bands had them. Look at Bert Ambrose and Vera Lynn. She, Jessica, would be an asset for the West Forstling band. She couldn't wait to get started.

'Going to see Ginger tonight,' she told Astaire cheerily, as she gave him some crumbs of cheese for a special treat.

He gave an approving 'too-reep'.

'Not late, am I?' Vanessa had suddenly appeared in the doorway, exuding wafts of lily of the valley perfume.

Jessica stared at her blankly.

'Don't look so surprised,' said Vanessa carelessly. 'Didn't Johnnie tell you we're going as a foursome? You, me, Johnnie and Gerry. The *Honourable* Gerald Rhodes. He's the younger son of the Earl of Woodbridge.'

'No,' managed Jessica as coolly as she could. 'No, he didn't mention it.' Her heart gave a sickening thump.

'They'll be here shortly. The squadron was released two hours ago,' said Vanessa. 'You look nice.' She meant it kindly, but it sounded patronising. Jessica had never been less fond of her. She damned well should look nice, she fumed to herself. She'd taken hours to get ready, only to discover the evening wasn't going to be as she had hoped. Then she calmed down. It wasn't Vanessa's fault, she supposed, but began to have forebodings. It was going to be all too much like an evening her mother might have planned. She was being fitted in, a useful cog.

Her fears were justified. The Lagonda arrived with John driving and Gerry in the back. He leapt out, kissing Vanessa's hand with exaggerated courtesy, then turned to Jessica. An ironic gleam of recognition in his eyes, he smote his forehead stagily. 'The Ice Queen,' he cried. 'Of course. Beautiful Ice Queen Jessica.'

'Gerry,' said John warningly, turning to Jessica and saying easily, 'It's your lovely fiery red curls. Makes him think of the opposite.' It was the best he could do on the spur of the moment. 'This passes for a sense of humour with him.'

'With me he passes for a sub-standard clown,' she replied sweetly.

'Dear lady, don't be upset,' pleaded Gerry unabashed. 'I abase myself, I am contrite . . .' And buried his head in Vanessa's shoulder, as she giggled in embarrassment.

If she could have escaped, Jessica would have, but there was no way without putting herself in the wrong.

John was ushering her into the front seat, saying to her almost in reproof, 'He's a pretty good pilot, you know.'

The drizzle had stopped, and the scents of greenery, strong after the rain, filled her nostrils as the Lagonda wound its way through the lanes. Jessica was in no mood to appreciate them. She was furious with herself for having expected so much. The horrible scenes of last Sunday week must have affected her more than she realised. She was grasping at straws, anything that seemed to offer her an escape from coping with her heartache. There were other bands, other avenues she could explore, avenues not tied up with John Gale. She would find her own way.

She was being unfair, she realised. After what they endured every day in the air, how could she expect normal standards to apply? Perhaps there was excuse even for the awful Gerry. And, she kept reminding herself, it wasn't John's fault he had such mesmeric eyes and easy charm.

In the cinema Gerry called loudly for seats in the back row, and she felt her cheeks burning as eyes turned to look at them. She was a local teacher after all. Muffled giggles came from Vanessa throughout the two films, and when the lights went up at the interval her cheeks were flushed. Jessica's hand lay in John's like a lump of suet pudding, she thought, and soon he dropped it and sat gazing ahead, apparently wrapped up in the film. She didn't care for *Untamed* but enjoyed *Vivacious Lady*, and was almost forgetting her annoyance by the time they came out into the twilight.

All the same, she was counting the minutes till she could escape. After what seemed an interminably long time she realised they were near Frittingbourne, masked headlights picking out the way by the turn of the lanes now that darkness had fallen completely. But escape was not possible yet.

'Stop the car, dear fellow. Vanessa and I wish to pick some flowers.'

The Lagonda halted abruptly; she heard John swear under his breath and watched with sinking heart as Vanessa and Gerry, arms wrapped round each other, went off laughing into the dark field. Surely Vanessa wasn't such a fool as to - not with a man like Gerry, thought Jessica in alarm. Or would she, with the chance of snaring an Honourable before her? Jessica was aware of her cousin's failings as well as her strengths. Vanessa would know how to take care of herself. She could ask John about the band now. But somehow all her desire and eagerness had evaporated. This was not a man to whom she could talk, who would understand, share her enthusiasm. This was simply a friend of her mother's.

The minutes stretched into five, then ten . . . and all the time John sat silently beside her in the gloom, his dark hair almost merging into the darkness all around them. The atmosphere between them grew oppressive. Then it was broken, suddenly and unexpectedly.

John turned to her and took her fiercely in his arms. His lips pressed hard on hers but she could not respond, did not want to. His lips felt hungry, demanding, and completely alien. What he demanded, he demanded of a woman who did not exist. She began to struggle, to push him away, but felt his hands seeking her breast.

'Don't,' she cried sharply, and pulled away so forcefully that he let her go.

'You're not much like your cousin, are you?' he said jerkily, after a pause, lighting a cigarette.

'No,' she said crisply, watching his face in the light of the match and wondering how she could ever have thought it attractive. 'I'm not like Vanessa. Sorry if that disappoints you.' Why had she said that? she wondered hazily.

'What the hell's that supposed to mean?' He turned on her angrily.

'It means if you want to go out with her, then do so. But I'm *me*, not Vanessa.'

'If I wanted to, I would,' he glared, furious because she had hit on the truth. But Madam had preferred Gerry . . . 'What have you got against me, anyway?' he asked. 'Every time you see me you're as spiky as a porcupine.'

'I didn't ask you to take me out,' she shouted, faintly surprised at her own childishness. 'Even if my mother did.'

'Your mother? How on earth did Bubbles get into this?' *He* decided who he'd take out and no one else, no matter how hard she pushed.

'Bubbles,' she said scornfully. 'There you are. You've been sucked into her whole false, rotten circle. And I want no part of it. Or you.'

'Suits me,' he said swiftly.

'Having fun, dear people?' Gerry and Vanessa had returned after half an hour, draped round one another. John did not even glance at them as they climbed in, merely started the Lagonda and set off, grinding the gears unmercifully.

'Are we going to the Manor?' Vanessa called out brightly. 'Cicely invited us back.'

'Why not?' said John. That would fix Miss Spark-Plug here, he thought in satisfaction. Her and her petty feuds.

Jessica said nothing.

When they reached the Manor House she got out of the Lagonda and walked away, trying not to stumble in the darkness.

'Aren't you coming in, Jess?' called Vanessa, puzzled.

She turned and looked at the three of them.

'I live in the oasthouse,' she said steadily. 'Not here.'

Well, that was that plan well and truly dished, she thought ruefully, regretting her own pigheadedness in walking back in the dark and tripping over every tussock. She'd be dammed if she'd even ask John Gale the time of day, let alone for his help.

'It's coming then.'

'The only thing that's coming is my next pint, old chap,' said Gerry. Young Maxwell stood rebuked.

No talk of that thing called war in the mess, thought John Gale. No mention of the raid there had been on Dover Harbour last Saturday with one hundred and twenty German aircraft soaring in to sink one destroyer and damage two others. Still, they'd seen seventeen of the bastards off in twenty minutes for the loss of only one. But no one was going to shoot a line about it.

'Grouse season's been brought forward to the fifth.' Only he was aware of the tremble, the effort it took to keep that glass steady, to preserve the façade he needed in order to go on. Bloody war, bloody politicians, bloody Americans. Weren't going to lift a finger to help out. Waiting to see which way it went, just like the last time. Why'd this bloody war have to come along and mess up his life? There wasn't much to it anyway. His brother had got the lot; heir to the title, and estate, exemption from war service, married at St Margaret's into the right sort of family, about to produce the right sort of kids. He crashed the glass down on the bar, and sneered when he saw Maxwell looking at him in astonishment. Kids – some chance of that. That was another thing this bloody war had done to him. He quickly swallowed the pint and called for another. Tonight he deserved to get drunk. They all did.

'Only five days to go, and then I'm off,' drawled Gerry, glass in hand.

Scrambled again. Three times today. John couldn't drag his mind away from it yet. The Luftwaffe had decided to have a bash at the balloon barrage at Dover as well as shipping. Yes, it was coming all right. They're getting bolder, 'Spy' had said with relish at debriefing just now. Fine for Spy with his statistics and his forms. He didn't have to climb into that cockpit. All Spy had to do was put in his reports and figures, on the basis of which perhaps they'd all get medals. Unless they were dead, of course. Then it was merely a matter of someone rubbing out a cross on the mess blackboard and a pint in your honour afterwards. If you were lucky.

Tonight's turn for the pint of honour was Jack Preston's of B Flight, their flight commander and one of the best. He'd last been spotted through the haze on the end of a parachute heading for the Channel. So far he hadn't been picked up. They'd go on looking, but there'd been something about the way he'd dangled from the 'chute that told John that even if they picked him up, Jack wouldn't be back any more. One more set of belongings to be packed away and then returned to next of kin, one more temporarily empty bed. Jack's desk wouldn't be empty, though, for John Gale would be acting flight commander until his replacement arrived, so the CO had told.him just now. What a way to promotion, thought John grimly, draining his glass, occupying a dead man's desk.

'I see the old Aphis is getting the hops then,' remarked Gerry brightly.

'I think it's got at this beer, already,' commented John morosely, gazing down into the weak brew and then with some care tipping it over Gerry's head. His answering howl brought the entire mess into the conflict. For once opinion was on Gerry's side. The offender was upended and hoisted in the air till his shoes were touching the ceiling.

'Sing us a song, Johnnie.' A record was put on the gramophone turntable and 'Umbrella Man' roared out over the mess. Above the music, John Gale's voice struggled for supremacy, shouting: 'A poor aviator lay dying—' From his upside down position he saw the door open and the newcomer's arrival. The man was tall and lean, in his early twenties, with light brown hair and the thin single braid of a pilot officer on his tunic. Unruffled by the noise that greeted him he waited there till the record blared to a halt.

'Any of you guys know where I get to find Flying Officer Gale?'

At the sound of his accent, the attention of the whole mess was riveted on him. Especially Gerry's. Bloody Yanks! It was all their fault.

'I'm Gale,' announced John thickly.

'Pilot Officer Donaldson, sir,' said the newcomer, as though it was perfectly normal to be addressed from John's inverted position. 'Told to report to you, sir.'

'Let me down,' John demanded, and his request was greeted with more haste than ceremony.

'The replacement for Willis?' he asked bluntly, restored to full alertness. Willis had been shot down in the Dover raid.

'I guess I wouldn't know about that, sir.'

'A Yank,' said Gerry disbelievingly. 'They've sent us a bloody Yank. One out of one hundred and fifty million chickens. One bloody Yank to assist the war effort. They know we'll be okay now.'

The newcomer regarded him steadily from bright brown eyes. 'I guess I wouldn't know about that either. I'm RAF.' Only a muscle twitching in his cheek betrayed emotion.

John held out his hand. 'Glad you're with us, Donaldson. You're in B Flight. I'm acting flight commander, till they fly in a new one.' Then said hastily – no need to dwell on the losses – 'Where have they put you?'

'C-Hut, sir.'

Gerry groaned. 'They've sent me a dough-boy.' Christ, so he was even sharing with the bastard.

'No substitute for crumpet, I guess,' said Donaldson nonchalantly. He had seen Gerry's highly individual and flamboyant decorations to the hut.

There was a split-second pause, then the mess collapsed into helpless laughter.

Only Gerry did not join in. 'If you don't like our ladies, Yank,' he said pleasantly, 'how do you feel about our beer?' And flung the contents of his pint in Donaldson's face.

The mess was suddenly still. This was not the accepted tomfoolery of John Gale's gesture, and no welcome for a new pilot, even a Yank. But it was knight's move.

Beer dripped from Donaldson's cap down his face on to his uniform. He did nothing. Just stood, letting it drip. Then he put out his tongue, licking the dripping liquid experimentally.

'Don't you guys have any ice round here?'

The general laughter that followed broke the tension, and the mess returned to its own concerns. Furious with Gerry Rhodes, John brushed past him and made to apologise, but Gerry interrupted him: 'It's not finished yet, Yank,' he said softly.

'It's over, Rhodes,' said John sharply.

Will Donaldson shook John Gale's outstretched hand, then turned to Gerry Rhodes and said coolly: 'I guess it's never over till the fat lady sings, fella.'

The Pilgrims Arms was crowded that night. Frittingbourne was a close-knit village and it guarded its privacy. The opening of the airfield had been regarded with deep suspicion by the villagers and local farmers, already antagonised by the noise and requisition of good farming land. The Anson squadron had been undemanding and a truce had been struck whereby their presence in the pub was tolerated. These new fighter pilots were a different matter. Extrovert and often brash, top tunic buttons left ostentatiously undone, they did not endear themselves to the usual clientele. Officers with good supply lines to illicit supplies of petrol had taken over a pub in the neighbouring village of Doddingham, leaving the field clear for the NCOs and erks.

Graham Macintosh, already nervous in Vanessa's presence, was further discomposed by the hostile stares that greeted their arrival. The son of a Sheffield engine driver, he still wasn't used to country ways, despite his RAF apprenticeship up in Lancashire.

'What will you have, Vanessa?'

'Gin-and-it, please, Graham.' She flashed a smile at him which almost compensated for the expense. An NCO's pay was low.

Settling herself in a corner, she took out a mirror and examined her lipstick. It promised to be a boring evening but then, for once she had nothing else to do and if he wanted to make sheep's eyes at her all evening, why not? Provided neither Gerry nor Johnnie ever knew.

'That-en my seat.' A burly farm-worker seized the chair that Graham had drawn up to the table.

'I'm sorry - I didn't—'

'You lot all the same. Reckon you bloody well owns the place.'

'Look here, I said—'

'Someone ought to teach you a lesson, I reckon. So you knows what's what.'

'Dave, do give over,' said Vanessa impatiently.

'Oh, so now Miss Vanessa's in their pocket, eh? We ain't good enough for the likes of her.'

A brawny hand shot out and pushed the slightly built Graham towards the door. Caught off balance, he fell, then was up like a terrier and on to his assailant. Someone screamed, the barman shouted, and Tom Ackroyd, alerted by the noise, pushed his way between them. Dave stepped back. Tom Ackroyd was respected by all of them. He'd stayed after all, was one of them, for all he was the local schoolmaster.

'Enough, Dave,' he said quietly, then turned to

Graham. 'I apologise for Frittingbourne's bad manners. But if I were you, I'd go into Maidstone next time. The village doesn't take kindly to its girls going out with strangers.'

'Oh, Tom, *really*,' said Vanessa, tossing her head. 'You are an old fuddy-duddy. No wonder Jessica's so fond of you.'

He flushed and was about to say something when Graham spoke.

'Very well,' he said slowly to the pub at large, 'I'll go. But let me tell you this, you turnips. Unless you get off your backsides and start giving us a hand, there's going to be a hell of a lot more strangers in here: German ones.'

'You told me to report to you, sir.'

'Come in, Donaldson.'

The flight commander's small office was comfortably untidy, but without its previous owner, depressing. John Gale sat behind the desk uneasily, the American's records and log book before him.

'Settle in all right?'

'Yessir.'

John looked at him. 'No more trouble?'

'No, sir.'

'You're a bad liar, Donaldson.'

'Yessir.'

'Rhodes is all right, you know.'

'Maybe, sir.'

'Give it time. William Donaldson, isn't it?'

'They call me Will, sir.'

'How come you're in the RAF? There aren't many of you. Only half a dozen or so, aren't there?'

Will paused, assessing the man in front of him, wondering whether to speak out or return some noncommittal answer. But something about John Gale set him apart from the usual run of mess clowns. 'I did a year at Cambridge, then some travelling round Europe, sir. I didn't like what I saw. You folks over here seemed to be shutting your eyes to it, so after Munich I went back home to Massachusetts.'

'I don't blame you. I felt pretty sick about it myself,' said John wrily.

'Then I got to thinking, what's the use of running out on things? You can't change 'em that way. So I learned to fly and started spreading the word about the Nazis and the Führer. But when I heard about Poland and then the torpedoing of the *Athenia*, when all those innocent people drowned, I went right over the border into Canada to join the RAF. It sure wasn't easy. You folks are mighty keen on stopping guys who want to help you. But I made it.'

'How many hours on Spits?'

'Trained on Hurricanes, sir. Three hours only on Spits.'

John groaned. 'The war's heading right this way, Donaldson. Three hours? And no operational experience. Stay close to me, for Christ's sake. Don't move an inch without my say so. Understand?'

'Yessir.' Will Donaldson stepped back, saluted and departed. This, he thought to himself as he left, is one helluva long way from New York. Massachusetts seemed a mighty long way away too. What the blazes was he doing here anyway? Here to fight someone else's war. A crazy idealist, like the commies who'd gone to fight against Franco in Spain. And half the guys here didn't want to pass the time of day with him, shut off in their island superiority. Not for much longer, though. At least he'd arrived in time for the big picture!

Michael Gray looked up from his canvas as his wife broke the silence.

'I've an idea.'

'Cicely, you've had twenty ideas already today,' he said a trifle impatiently. He didn't like her hovering while he was working.

'This one's important. It's about Jessica.'

Michael Gray slumped. 'Jessica is much better left to herself, darling.'

'You never see a thing,' Cicely said crossly. 'That pilot whom I thought was so interested in her hasn't come again. And I think she's pining.'

'Pining!' Michael laughed. 'How on earth do you deduce that?'

'A mother knows these things,' Cicely Gray said mysteriously, fiddling carelessly with a tube of oil paint.

Something was wrong, she could see. She didn't like Jessica shutting herself away in that oasthouse. Particularly since that unfortunate episode at the party. Who'd have thought Don Field would have known anything about it? It was very bad luck. Jessica had been very quiet; Cicely hoped she wasn't brooding, getting any ridiculous ideas about trying again to make a career for herself in singing. No, she'd be much better off married, not to that dull old Tom Ackroyd but to someone who could give her a good time, exciting, adventurous . . . Away from Frittingbourne. If she stayed here goodness knows what ideas she might get in future. Whereas married, with a family – of course, it was the worst possible time, with the war occupying everyone, but nevertheless Cicely would try.

'So I had an idea – why don't you offer to paint some of these fighter pilots? The squadron personalities? It would be wonderful publicity for – for the war effort,' she ended.

'And for me, too?' Michael laughed resignedly. 'My own publicity agent. All the same,' he said thoughtfully, 'it's not a bad idea.'

'And then they could come here to be painted,' she said eagerly, pleased with the success of her idea.

'Drawings, I think,' Gray said, seeing in his mind's eye a row of determined young faces. 'For one of the illustrated magazines.'

The sounds of the piano, playing something he could not quite identify, greeted John as he crossed the field to the oasthouse. The music brought memories of home and Sunday evening gatherings in the vicarage parlour. Suddenly he felt weary, unequal to the struggle in the air that lay ahead. He couldn't be bothered with complications on the ground. Why had he come? He hadn't had any desire to see the girl again after that fiasco. He nearly turned back, but something, perhaps the sound of the voice that now soared above the piano, changed his mind for him and he continued over the field, regardless of the thick mud after a recent rain fall.

The front door was open. He walked through following the sound. Jessica was in the roundel room of the oast, her back to him, her thin shoulders hunched over the piano as she played. Now he could identify it. Something from the *Messiah*, wasn't it?

He stood there for some minutes, watching the way the sunlight played upon her hair, before something made her aware of his presence.

'What are you doing here?' she said fiercely, spinning round on the stool.

He was taken aback. 'I don't quite know,' he answered truthfully. 'I suppose,' he said hesitantly, 'I came to apologise.' Had he? He hadn't realised till then he had anything much to apologise for.

She looked at him suspiciously. 'No,' she corrected reluctantly, 'it's me who should apologise.' How stupid it had been to attack John. He had enough on his plate without hysterical girls shouting at him. It wasn't his fault he'd come along when he did that Sunday afternoon. Bubbles had lured him into her charmed circle with her parties and introductions and invitations.

'It was a rough evening, wasn't it?' John tried. 'Gerry's not everyone's cup of tea, I'm afraid.' Just Vanessa's, the thought came to him unbidden. Yet he could have sworn—

'I'm sure he's perfectly splendid,' Jessica responded, trying so hard that he laughed, forcing an answering grin from her.

'That's quite a voice you have. Is it trained?'

'You heard?' she said, abashed, then: 'Oh, John, I wanted to ask you – the band, the band that played at the dance. Do you think I could sing with them at dances? Perhaps concerts, if you have them. Could you introduce me?'

He looked embarrassed. 'I don't think—' he said

awkwardly, '—um, the fellows aren't too keen on the *Messiah*.'

'Oh, I sing everything,' she said eagerly.

Thoughts raced through John's head. Why not let her sing with the airmen? Let HQ and the outdated hierarchy see that the lower ranks counted for something. That Bubbles Gray's daughter wasn't too proud to sing with an other ranks' band. 'Yes,' he said with his charming smile, 'I'll introduce you.'

She relaxed in relief. 'Thank you,' she breathed. 'I wanted to ask you the other evening, but it went wrong.'

'You could say that.' He grinned. 'Is that why you went for me the way you did?'

She felt trapped, then she took the bull by the horns. 'My mother has plans for my future,' she said steadily. 'Excluding singing, and including—'

'Including what?'

'Marrying me off to a fighter pilot,' she blurted out.

There was a split-second pause. Then he began to laugh, long and hard. He came up to her and gave her a quick hug. 'Is *that* why you're so prickly?'

'Yes,' she answered, beginning to laugh herself.

'You don't have anything to fear from me,' he said, still shaking with mirth. 'I'm only too anxious not to get married myself. Other chaps feel differently, I suppose. Take Graham now, he'd marry Vanessa tomorrow. He's the sort who needs to settle down, feel he has roots. But me – listen, Jessica, you don't know what it's like up there. It's another world, a world where you're your own master, free. Sure, a Hun can come out of the sky and you're a goner. But that's something you reckon with alone. You don't need a wife cluttering up the scene, grieving for you when you don't come back. Down on the ground it's different.' He paused, not knowing better how to put it.

'You cry for "Madder music and for stronger wine" – and a woman or two,' she helped him.

'Yes.' He looked at her gratefully. 'Yes, to escape. You feel a need. That's why that evening I—'

'Did your Tarzan act, Johnnie Weissmuller.'

'Don't be cheeky, young Jessica,' he warned, pulling one of her curls. 'I'm an important part of the war effort.'

'You sound like a blackout curtain.'

'Any more of that and old Lind out there will be singing for his supper a long, long time.' And he grabbed hold of her and kissed her lightly. It was very light, but she'd never before felt like that after a kiss. Never so aglow, never so expectant, as though her whole body could burst into song.

'Now, what do I tell the band?' he asked, as he released her. 'That you're another Vera Lynn, Ray Eberle? That you'll be singing our song for the men?' He kissed her again. 'Do they really sing in Berkeley Square, do you think?' he said idly.

'Nightingales sing everywhere for those with ears to hear them,' she said, laughing. 'Those in Berkeley Square just have golden beaks, that's all.'

'They'll be melted down for the Spitfire fund, if they don't watch out. You know,' he said suddenly, 'my mother used to sing a song about a nightingale. And valleys or something.'

'I know it. Listen, I'll sing it for you.'

'My sweetheart come along,
Don't you hear the fond song
The sweet notes of the nightingale flow . . .'

Will Donaldson, crossing the field in search of his flight commander, was suddenly still, as there floated across the grass meadow the husky magic of a girl's voice.

'No more is she afraid
For to walk in the shade
Or to sit in the valley below . . .'

Simple, clear, vibrant, the song carolled into the summer sky, putting to flight all thoughts of war and leaving in their place a triumphant message of life. Involuntarily, Will began to run, seeking the source of the song, transported as only music had the power to do for him. He came upon the oasthouse, cowl pointing to the heavens, timeless and English, set in a tranquil corner that seemed never to have heard of Dunkirk, of the Fall of France, of the evil of Fascism. He burst in, oblivious of anything save the need to find the song and its singer. Before him was the roundel oast room. He went towards it as to his Grail – and there he found his flight commander.

'Some voice, eh, Will?'

'Yessir.' The magic was broken, the spell stilled.

In front of him was a girl in a summer frock with lively intelligent eyes, a mass of curls and a heart-shaped face, a fierce impatience about her as if she were waiting for life to happen. Only one thing made no sense to him. Those eyes were fixed on John Gale.

'Meet Will Donaldson, Jessica. He's new to my flight.

An American. Jessica Gray. She wants to sing with the station band.'

'How do you do?' Jessica put out her hand.

'My pleasure, ma'am,' said Will formally.

The CO was keyed-up. Nothing much had been happening for the last week or so, which was hardly surprising for traffic in the Channel had virtually ceased. Now, on 8th August: 'The balloon's going up, John. Peewit convoy was attacked by U-boats early this morning in the Channel. I'm flying B Flight off to forward base for instant readiness. The Luftwaffe will be back for another crack. Well, the bastards are going to get more than they bargained for.'

And they came, Stukas in huge numbers, just after midday. By late-afternoon few ships remained untouched and nineteen had been lost, but the RAF claimed sixty German aircraft. These were but figures; what led to them was a desperate battle for survival.

'Wagtail Red Leader. Tally ho. Red Two, keep on my tail at all times.'

'Roger, Red Leader,' Will acknowledged.

John Gale peered into his horizon. Donaldson would be all right, provided he survived this op. But he was going to need protection from this lot. The familiar excitement gripped him as he saw the 109s approaching, like a cloud of hornets. He was coming out of the sun, down on to them; his prey didn't stand a chance, spiralling into the sea in flames.

On his tail, Will picked out a straggler, got him in his sights, and let loose with the Brownings. 'What a beaut,' he said to himself. He watched it disappear for one second too long, and lost John Gale in the mêlée. Looking round frantically, he failed to see the 109s above him, one diving towards his tail. But John Gale did. The Messerschmitt whistled past Will in flames to crash in the fields below, but he did not see it. All he saw was John Gale's Spitfire spiralling down after it, a winged bird . . .

The squadron remained on call for an hour after Will landed back at West Forstling. John's name was rubbed off the blackboard and replaced by another. Still numb with shock, after the squadron was released, Will walked into the mess. The first person he saw was John Gale, lounging over the bar.

'Jee-sus!' Will whistled, his face white with shock, relief flooding over him. 'I thought you'd bought it.'

'Baled out, Donaldson. Landed in a field. Persuaded the gentlemen who advanced on me with pitchforks that I wasn't Herr Hitler arrived in person, and hitched a lift back to base. You owe me a pint, and the next time I say stick to my tail, Will, *stick to it*.'

John didn't seem to want to talk about the war, nor of baling out of the aircraft which he'd only mentioned briefly; in fact Jessica didn't know quite why he'd asked her to come on this walk on the downs after he'd come for a final sitting for his portrait. He seemed strained. With great self-control she held back on the questions she was bursting to ask him. The band – what about the band? Had he spoken to the leader yet? Did she stand a chance?

'What have you been doing with yourself?' he asked idly as they clambered over a stile into the meadow.

'Oh, a riotous time today.' Jessica flourished a sorrel

stem seized from the bank of a ditch as she walked. 'Food demonstration day in Maidstone. How to cook a parsnip in a hundred different ways. How to grow a ton of potatoes in a window box. How to make delicious sorrel soup.' She had whiled away the time mentally setting tunes to the recipes. 'Take a pair of radishes,' she was silently carolling, 'and a heart of lovely lettuce . . .'

'Sounds fun,' he said idly.

'It's part of The Effort,' she intoned primly.

'The kitchen front? Yes, I suppose so. It doesn't seem much to fight Hitler with.'

'That's alarm and despondency. Look,' she said, spreading her arms wide, 'how can you think we'd let all this go? In the valley down there, those roofs, the spirals of smoke, fields glowing yellow ready for harvest, hops waiting for the hop-pickers to arrive, flowers which have grown here for hundreds, thousands of years, this tiny scarlet pimpernel, that nut tree there. Do you think all this can change? Do you think we men of Kent can be wiped out so easily? Cue for song,' she ended self-consciously.

'Have some chocolate,' he said.

The change to the prosaic made her laugh. 'There I am in the middle of my big speech and you offer me chocolate.'

'It's very good chocolate,' he said. 'Will Donaldson gave it to me.'

'He's rather nice. Not what I expected of an American.'

'Not exactly Clark Gable.'

'No.' She thought about him. 'Nice-looking, though. More a Gary Cooper.' Then she considered further. No, that wasn't right either. Gary Cooper didn't have that quiet alertness, that air of being interested in everything, yet remaining detached. Nor, she supposed, did Gary Cooper do bird-song imitations through his cupped hands, a talent which had impressed both her and Astaire greatly, judging by the latter's excited twittering.

'He's quite a comedian too,' John was saying. 'You should have seen him at the Squadron dance last Saturday. Where were you by the way?' as if just realising her absence.

'You didn't invite me,' she said, trying to sound casual.

'You don't need an invitation. You know the ropes now. You'd have enjoyed it. It was in the hangar. The band was in great form – oh, hell, I forgot! You wanted an intro, didn't you?'

'Any time will do,' she said stiffly.

'No, it won't. It was important to you – and stupid of me. You know, Jessica, nothing's quite real at the moment. It's like another world at the station – the minute you're inside those gates, there's no room for anything else.'

'Except Vanessa,' she muttered mutinously before she could stop herself.

'Damn it, Jessica, will you forget Vanessa? She's nothing to do with us.'

'But—'

He meant to take hold of her and stop her buts with a light kiss. That usually stopped women's fussing. Instead he found himself folding her into his arms, and amazed himself with the tenderness of his embrace.

Chapter Four

'Perhaps that's him now, that one there.'

Jessica lay on her back in the meadow, squinting into the sun. It seemed all wrong that she should be lazing here doing nothing when John might be one of those black dots, part of the continuous drone of aircraft engines that had replaced the drone of bees on this summer day. 'The Glorious Twelfth' they called it – but only the sun after days of cloud was glorious this year.

Was there nothing she could do to help? She found it so frustrating collecting for the Spitfire Fund, growing vegetables, always making do, cutting down, taking down signposts. Yes, it was all part of the war effort, but somehow futile compared with what was happening up there. None of it would save John if a Messerschmitt had him in its sights.

John, a sudden thrill of excitement, a guilty pang of happiness, shot through her when she thought of him – which was nearly all the time, she suddenly realised. Now she sang spontaneously for the first time in two years, instead of grimly going through exercises in the hope of a tomorrow that had never come. Now she was certain it would. Impossible that even Hitler might stand in the way. She had met the band. It hadn't gone easily at first, the airmen wary and resentful of having someone they clearly thought of as just another girlfriend of John Gale's thrust upon them. They might respect him, but that tolerance didn't extend to his girls, was the clear message.

But when she'd sung – oh, that was different. She basked in the memory again. Instant attention, looks passing involuntarily between them, and finally Art Simmonds heaving himself off the upturned beer barrel which served as his seat. 'That'll do for starters,' he'd said, carefully non-committal. 'Now sing with us.' Then a look passed between the band members, which plainly said: 'Everything you've got, lads.' They'd tried every trick to throw her, even deliberately changing tempo to swing. But she'd stuck with them. At the end Art Simmonds laid down his trumpet, wiped his mouth and said, 'Okay, Miss Gray, you're in. We'll give it a go.'

They weren't bad, not bad at all, she thought, as she lay in the meadow. Not Ken Peters yet, but what they might achieve together – her mind roved over the possibilities. They were her passport to the future. Even her mother's betrayal had receded into the background, now life was a kaleidoscope of such unexpected colours and left everyday routine behind. Would it ever return? On this day, it was impossible fully to comprehend the perilous position the country was in. John – and singing – blotted out everything else.

'Jessica.'

She opened her eyes, startled to see Tom Ackroyd looming above her, a black figure against the sun. He plumped himself down on the rug beside her.

'I haven't seen much of you lately,' he said, a slight

note of inquiry in his voice. Indeed he hadn't. On only one occasion when she'd been with John in a pub early one evening when he was stood down for a rare day's rest. She'd introduced them awkwardly, John's easy charm had reduced Tom to a morose silence, which ended in his swallowing his drink and hurriedly departing.

'I've been quite busy,' she replied, trying not to sound defensive. Usually during the summer holidays they spent a lot of time together, but there was no reason she *had* to see him.

'So I imagine,' he said coolly. 'Is it the Spitfire Fund or the pilots you're more interested in?'

She stared at him aghast, taken aback at his uncharacteristic outspokenness.

'I—' Then she became angry. It was her life, her concern. Tom was reducing it to something tawdry, tarnishing the special something between herself and John. 'If it's any concern of yours, it's to do with my voice. I'm going to sing with the West Forstling band,' she flashed, knowing she was being unfair.

'It is of some interest,' he replied matter-of-factly. 'I've some right to be disappointed seeing you swept away by a midsummer madness. Although I can understand it.'

Her cheeks were pink. 'I'm singing, that's all,' she said steadily. 'Don't you see, it's a start for me? They've got contacts in London.'

He ignored her. 'The same thing happened to me once, Jessica. You never knew about it. It was when I was at college, and you were just starting at that posh boarding school of yours. I was at the age you are now. That's how

I know. She was everything that was wrong for me and I loved her like Abelard did Heloise – or so I imagined. The sun shone brighter when she was there, the birds sang louder, I wrote poetry – all that stuff. Then she vanished. Just as this fighter pilot of yours will. I realised – as you will – it's a passing phase we all go through.'

'He's nothing to do with it! And what do you mean – vanished?' she demanded, curiosity momentarily outweighing anger.

'Thin air. Wave of the wand. All that stuff. Not literally unfortunately. She—' he hesitated – 'she fell for a sailor lad, if you must know, and three years of my life went with her. I realised it had all been a dream. Dreamed by me, not her. The person I'd loved had never existed. Like your fighter pilot.'

She started to retort angrily but he continued inexorably: 'You don't know the sort of man you want, you see. You've latched on to this Gale fellow, seeing him as an escape route from all your problems.'

She had no answer except that he was wrong, wrong, *wrong*! 'You're jealous.'

He smiled sadly. 'Come, Jessica. You can do better than that. Of course I'm jealous. But that doesn't make me wrong, does it?' And he got to his feet and ambled off, only a certain rigidity about his shoulders displaying the strength of his feelings.

This is some crazy way to fight a war, Will Donaldson was thinking with one part of his brain. Flying should bring peace, a feeling of being at one with the heavens, not wheeling black dots of death everywhere, looking like musical notation against the sky. Music – that sound - if only - no, this was no place to think of that. The other part of his mind became ice-cold as he used every trick he knew to shake off the fighters and get to the bombers. This was it. No doubt about it. Jerry was hitting the airfields today ready for the big picture. The sky looked like a pinball machine. At West Forstling three Spits and two Hurricanes had been destroyed on the ground before the rest of the fighters got into the air, higgledy-piggledy, in no set formation, with clouds of black smoke obscuring vision. For once the Spits didn't need the advantage of height - *that's it*, position, a burst from the Brownings and a Stuka was spiralling in flames. His second. The dive-bombers were so unmanoeuvrable they were sitting ducks once you were in position, and especially vulnerable at the end of their dives. He peered out for the parachutes, and saw one opening - and one that didn't.

Christ, he couldn't see, John Gale realised. The sun was in his eyes. Attack out of the sun, that was the rule. He must gain altitude. She soared upwards; that's it, my lady. Up. Up. Was that a Spit going down? No time to see, only time to call a warning to Will, busy mixing it with two Messerschmitts, that there was another fighter behind. Good lad, Will.

Why the hell hadn't they had a warning? Thoughts raced through John's mind. What was this new radar thing they had at all these stations round the coast? Yet still they got through. So much for the secret weapon. Hundreds of the devils. And Dowding was putting up small pockets of fighters, little Davids against the Goliaths. Well, David won in the end, didn't he? Thank heavens for the Spit.

Whoa, my beauty. He heard the thud on the side of the machine, bullets, no harm done he hoped. Steady now. Junkers in his sights, press the gun button, a satisfactory blaze of smoke. Got the – no, the blighter was still coming on. And on. Plucky these Huns. Another burst from the Brownings. That was it. Gone. Dogfights they called these in the last war. It sounded so nice and clean, when his father talked about it. A duel in the sky between knights of the air. He didn't know what it was like in the last war, but it sure as blazes wasn't like that now. Smoke, fire, burned alive, chaps with their faces gone. No, mustn't think of that. Pick out a target, or were they picking *you* out?

He'd had that dream again last night. Everything was red . . . fire, blood? He'd always been scared of blood. It seemed ominous to him, even the prick of a rose thorn, a sign of mortality. And when he dreamed about it – he glanced at Will flying alongside. His thumb was up. So he'd got it then. One more for the squadron. One for him, too. His third now. Excitement began to return.

For some reason Jessica came to mind. He'd go and see her. He'd tell her – he wanted to talk for once. Odd, for him to want to talk to a girl. Odd girl she was, too. All fiery eyes, and bouncy curls. Too slim though. No curves, not like Vanessa's softness. All the same, she had quite a voice. He was glad she'd met with Art's approval. He was looking forward to seeing how the mess took to the revamped band. One in the eye for Gerry Rhodes and his dyed-in-the-wool aristocratic mob. He'd have to land now, his fuel was nearly exhausted. That's if there were anything to land on. He circled – yes, the landing field looked okay.

The airfield generally was chewed up pretty thoroughly though he noticed as he brought the Spit to a stop. The raid was over, at least for the moment, and the engineers and ground personnel were already out there, busy repairing the damage. The Luftwaffe wasn't going to make a mess of West Forstling and get away with it. The sky looked empty now. Impossible to believe the ugliness it had so recently contained.

He climbed out stiffly. Graham had already landed, Will was just lopsidedly coming in – trouble with the landing gear, John supposed, the tyre looked flat. Will would have to be careful. Hope someone had told him.

The adrenalin flowed out of him. He felt weary, drained, as routine took over. The ground crew rushed up to check damage and refuel. There was Spy, too. Spy was always there, eager for his statistics. Statistics could wait. He was looking at Will's landing.

A swoop of grey, the roar of a Merlin engine and another Spit was coming in fast, *too* fast, behind Will Donaldson's. Will's Spit, with its shredded tyre, forced to touch down sooner than its pilot planned, slewed to one side and ground looped across the grass. Then the wheel dug in and the Spitfire went up on to its nose and stood poised for perilous seconds, on the point of turning over. It steadied itself, and Will, his face pale, climbed out as ground crew rushed towards him. The second Spit came to a halt, and out climbed Gerry Rhodes.

'What,' said John, with deadly calm, 'the hell do you think you're doing, Rhodes? Couldn't you see he was in trouble?'

'Dear me, was he?' asked Gerry nonchalantly. 'I'm so sorry, old chap. Didn't notice.'

Will forced himself to sound controlled. 'Next time you want to play cowboys and Indians, Buster,' he said quietly, 'pick on someone else.'

Gerry's eyes narrowed. 'The American way of life. Get back to your corral, Yank.'

Only John's swift intervention, catching hold of Will's arm, saved Gerry from a straight right to the jaw. 'Cut it out,' he said angrily. 'Both of you.'

The guts had been blasted out of the cottage and the clapboarded front was missing. It was a giant dolls' house – the floors and possessions exposed for all to see, a teddy bear clinging to the very edge of the gaping hole. Yet the cottages either side were untouched; brown paper strips had even kept the window glass intact. What fate decreed that this one home should be bombed while its neighbours survived? Jessica wondered. It had stood for three hundred years and was gone in moments. One family homeless, and without a father. The rest of them had been in the stone shelter built in their garden, but Jamie Wilson had always been obstinate. No blasted German was going to drive him out of his bed! Until one did.

Cicely had been there of course, chivvying the WVS into looking after the widow, organising the salvage, soothing frayed nerves, serving tea, trying to comfort. She had wheedled Jessica into accompanying her. She couldn't refuse, for there might be something she could do to help.

Besides she must not yield to the temptation of avoiding her mother. The problem had to be faced. She could never return though to her old feeling of affection, if not love, not now she knew what her mother was capable of. Now Jessica saw her dispassionately - and came to an objective understanding of her mother that made seeing her bearable. The rest was easy. Cicely would never realise just what she had done, how she had torn the slender thread which had tied them together.

So this was war, thought Jessica tiredly, when they returned to the Manor. Not the drone of engines in the sky, the battle over their heads of Messerschmitt against Spitfire, but the terror in children's eyes, the disbelief on the widow's face, the dust-covered boots by the door that their owner would no longer need.

Still Kent seemed to be taking it phlegmatically. The local newspapers gave more coverage to the murder case at Addington, the lady who had knitted one hundred and forty garments for the war effort, to the appeal for all those called Dorothy to subscribe for a Spitfire - than to the battle itself. Yet she'd noticed an air of growing tension, for all it was unexpressed.

'Jessica!'

By the sugary note in her mother's voice, she knew she had someone with her, and reluctantly went downstairs.

'Darling, *look* who's here.'

John was lounging on the sofa. He stood up as she came in. She had given up all hope of seeing him today, with the constant activity in the air and continued raids. She was relieved he was safe yet hated seeing him in her mother's presence, knowing full well the calculations that were running through Cicely Gray's mind; half flirting with him herself, reluctant to pass him to her daughter, for all her plans.

He gave Jessica his warm, lazy smile, yet his eyes were

tired, she instantly noted, and the smile did not reach them.

'Really, Johnnie dear, I think if you could you'd have another portrait painted to give you more excuse for being here,' laughed Cicely.

'I'm surprised Michael can find time to paint us pilots at all,' he replied disarmingly, 'with you as his constant muse, Bubbles.' The charm sounded mechanical, even to his ears, but it came automatically.

But Cicely laughed, pleased with the compliment. For a crazy moment Jessica saw them as two of a kind, then instantly chided herself. John was of her world, not her mother's.

'Why don't you two get on?' he asked curiously, as they walked across the lawn, Jessica hurrying him away from the Manor as fast as she could.

She didn't want to discuss her mother with John. She wanted to be alone with him out on the hill or in her own home, not to talk about Bubbles. But John wouldn't leave it alone.

'Tell me. Just because she wants you to marry a fighter pilot?' He'd nearly said 'me', he realised to his surprise. It had seemed the natural thing.

'She doesn't like my singing.'

'Whyever not? Surely she'd encourage that?'

'No.'

'Jealous?'

She hesitated. 'Yes and no. I think it's because I sing in my own style, not hers. If I sang as she does, she might take some pride in it. But with me singing the way I do, I think she might feel undermined in some way.' Where had that thought come from? It was the first time it had occurred to her, and yet she was sure she was right.

'Why undermined? You're not thinking of heading for the fleshpots of the London stage, are you?'

'I wanted to,' she said. 'My mother stopped me. There – now you know.'

'Nobody could stop you if you wanted to enough,' he said absently, thinking of the vicarage and his battles to go to university.

There was no point in telling him of her mother's treachery. That was her own minefield to walk through.

'They bombed the airfield today,' he went on suddenly, needing to talk. 'And Detling – you heard about that? Massive raid. Lots of people killed. Women too. But everyone seems to think it'll be a big show tomorrow. Perhaps on second thoughts I'd better skip the dance tonight.'

'Shouldn't you be with your friends in the mess?' she asked worriedly. She had no idea what life on an operational station was like, but imagined a close group of pilots needing to talk tactics and equipment, as united off duty as they were on.

'No,' he said shortly. 'It's good to get away. And this is better than the pub.' He hadn't meant to say that – hardly the most tactful way of inviting a girl out, especially Jessica. It was true, though. With some girls you could relax. And then there were other types – like Vanessa – who simply took you over body and soul, almost carnivorously, until they'd had their fill. He was going to stay away from her. He must. He needed to concentrate in the air – on staying alive, not on women. But Jessica wasn't like either type of woman though. No wonder that fellow with a limp was keen on her. He felt sorry for the poor chap but all's fair in love and war. Love? What on earth made him think of that?

'Each day there are going to be more and more,' he said abruptly, thinking of the sky thick with bombers. 'We'll shoot them down and still they'll come.' Idly he poked a piece of bread through the mesh of Astaire's cage with his finger – then cried out and stared down at his hand, trembling slightly.

'He nipped me,' he said bemusedly.

'Oh, I'm sorry, I should have warned you.'

'It's bleeding.' His voice rose slightly.

'John, what's the matter?' She was alarmed by his expression.

'Blood,' he said. 'It's blood.' He forced a smile. 'Sorry, I have a thing about it. Pretty stupid in a fighter pilot, eh?' He looked at her, almost in appeal.

'No,' she said quickly. 'Not stupid. Let me look.' She took hold of his hand and examined it. 'I'll dab some antiseptic on it. It's not deep. Poor old Astaire just thought it was part of his supper.'

'Any other girl would have laughed,' he said slowly, taking hold of her hand as she turned away to fetch the antiseptic cream. The look on his face made her catch her breath. He pulled her towards him, and into his arms. 'Jessica,' he said wonderingly, and his lips found hers. He held her against him so tightly she felt moulded to his body, then as his lips fiercely demanded a response she relaxed and gave herself up to his embrace as her mouth flowered under his. She felt his hands moving up and down her body, straining her closely against him, and she came alive, not wanting to pull away now but press ever closer, until he gasped a muttered 'Jessica' and the lingering image of Vanessa sweeping back her long golden hair dissolved into the August afternoon.

Why on earth had she agreed to this second date at all? She'd said yes in a weak moment. Gerry was a dead loss in one respect and she'd seen hardly anything of John. In fact, she'd heard that he'd been seeing Jessica. She frowned. Must be Bubbles' persuasion. He'd come round eventually, though; Vanessa had seen that spark in a man's eye too often to be mistaken. So when Graham somewhat diffidently invited her out again, she'd said yes. His devotion was flattering; it would do her morale good and would get her away from the drudgery of squeezing one more supper out of rations for her mother and herself. She'd been going to go out with Seb Cartwright, but he'd called from West Forstling to say that he couldn't make it. Force landed at Manston or something like that. She had thought Graham was better than nothing, but now she was here, she was bored.

A walk, he'd said. She knew what that meant, or at least with anyone but Graham it would have. So she had insisted on the cinema, or if it had to be a walk then one with a decent pub at the end of it. She wanted to go to the White Stag at Doddingham where all the officers went, but he wasn't keen on that idea.

'I can't think why on earth you want to come trudging across these muddy fields,' said Vanessa crossly, wishing she'd put on her gumboots. 'I see enough of them during the day.'

'I'm sorry, Vanessa,' he said awkwardly. 'It's just that during the day we're so enclosed. It's good to be out in the air, to know that somewhere near there's streams and woods and fields, and some kind of ordinary day-to-day existence.'

'If you call mucking out a cow-shed a normal day-to-day existence,' she grumbled, stumbling over a bramble and cursing as it caught her bare leg. At least she'd had the sense not to put stockings on.

He caught her arm with wiry strength. 'I shouldn't have brought you here. We should have gone to the pictures, like you wanted.'

'It doesn't matter,' she said generously, glancing at him. 'Only, could we sit down for a while? My shoes—'

'Oh, I'm sorry,' he said contritely. 'Here. The ground will be damp.' He spread his raincoat for her, and she collapsed on to it, legs sprawling.

'Well, what do we do now?' she asked, smiling at him.

'It's nice just to sit with someone like you.'

She looked at him. Was he serious? she thought, astounded. Devotion was all very well, but there was no need for him to be so spaniel-like. She wasn't used to men like Graham. She gave a light laugh. 'You mean you're sick of the sound of my voice?'

'Never! It's like poetry. After you've been in the air - to hear a woman's voice - *your* voice—'

He was so intense. Vanessa didn't know how to react, except that she was going to get tired of sitting here with the dusk falling, and damp rising. 'If we hurry,' she said firmly, to thwart this outbreak of emotion, 'we can get to the White Stag by 9.30.'

The Luftwaffe fighter pilots and bomber crews settled down for the night; Britain had had a reprieve this Wednesday. Their cloudy skies had saved them. The

Germans had only been able to put up about eighty dive-bombers and one hundred and twenty Messerschmitts. But tomorrow was going to be different. The weather men checked the weather for the next day, Thursday August 15th, anxiously. Over in England the RAF ate, drank, and convinced themselves they were merry. For both sides, tomorrow would be the big day.

There was a little cloud over the Channel the next day, but not enough to deter Göring's bombers from making their way to bombard Britain into submission in the north and south. Nearly two thousand Stukas, Dorniers, Heinkels, Junkers 88 and Messerschmitts raided Britain relentlessly from eleven o'clock to sunset. But they had underestimated Dowding, C-in-C Fighter Command. The north was strongly defended. In the south they destroyed airfields, radar stations and factories – but at a heavy cost. By the end of the day, the wireless was announcing one hundred and eighty-two German aircraft had been shot down, and hardly any British. That evening the Luftwaffe licked its wounds; surprised but not yet defeated.

John Gale, one of the many Spitfire pilots in the air that day, shouted out in sheer exhilaration. Will Donaldson, listening over the Spitfire's radio, thought his flight commander had taken leave of his senses as he sang at the top of his voice: 'Run Junkers, run Junkers, run, run, run, Out of the way of my gun, gun, gun – Whoops there she goes . . .'

With his practised deadly calm, all Will's adrenalin went towards perfecting his dead-shot aim, to keeping himself in the air, to his precise organised flying. No exhilaration for him; it was just a job, a job he had set out to do and would carry on until he'd finished. Besides, he owed a life to Johnnie Gale.

The mess was full of excited chatter. Today the usual ban on line-shooting was by common unspoken assent suspended. There were no jeering choruses of 'There was I flying upside down . . .' when Seb, none the worse for his Manston experience, shouted: 'Three of the bastards. Coming at me from four directions, Tally-ho. I nailed the lot of them.'

'Popping them down like grouse, dear fellows,' Gerry was crowing. 'Bagged four,' his hand trembling only with excitement today.

'Did you see that, old chap?'

Overgraphic arm movements swept glasses from the bar as they described the downfall of yet another Dornier.

Confirmations, expostulations, clatter, flying gear discarded, men swarming into the mess for the evening meal. A time of undoubtedly exaggerated claims, but no word of losses. Not yet.

'Like the famous bird, dear boy. Ever decreasing circles and then flew up its own—'

'It's the VC for sure this time.'

Amused, Will Donaldson listened, feeling part of them and yet not *of* them. They had no doubt they were going to win. Nor did he, he supposed. But dispassionately he wondered just how, and how long it would take. There couldn't be more than a few hundred fighters in defence and heaven knows how many aircraft ranged against them. The British listened on the wireless to the German propagandist Lord Haw-Haw, but only to laugh at him not to tremble in fear. Yet Will couldn't help noticing the supposedly secret works sprouting up round Kent. The tank traps, the pill boxes, and even less ostentatious earthworks that seemed to serve no particular purpose. If Britain were occupied, she would need a Resistance, but these British would never openly admit to that now.

He didn't understand the Brits a lot of the time. The inhabitants of Massachusetts called themselves the Hub of the Universe; here in this small island they never doubted for a second that *they* were. The ignominy of the Boston Tea Party might never have happened. It was still 'Rule Britannia'. The British seemed to win through by giving no apparent thought to the possibility of failure. Though looking at the abrasive nerves, the sudden angry flare-ups from time to time, and the lines round eyes that belied the confident words that tumbled out of mouths, Will wondered whether this were true. Tempers were short, and once again he was the target. After the last incident John Gale had allotted Will a different room-mate, but it had only delayed the inevitable confrontation.

This time young Maxwell was the innocent cause as he burst out with the mess version of 'Deutschland über alles'. When lack of invention ground the chorus to a halt, Gerry struck up dramatically, one eye on Will:

'Oh say can you see by the dawn's early light,
The tart take her leave of her Yank of the night . . .'

Will listened in silence as Gerry gave his bawdy rendering, the mess watching to see what he would do. He heard it to the end, then walked out of the room. The mess watched him leave silently, and returned to its former occupations, obscurely disappointed. Not for long. After five minutes Will returned, carrying a clarinet. He climbed on the table and played, all eyes on him. Even Gerry's drunken cackles were silenced as the sounds of the 'Stars and Stripes' floated out solemnly and majestically, all dignity restored.

'Gee,' Seb whistled, 'that man can play. Can that man play?'

To give good measure, Will went on to play Gershwin. Eerily, hauntingly, the sound cast a hush over the mess, until at length he jumped off the table, laid down the clarinet and picked up his beer again.

'You've been keeping quiet about that,' said John to him later.

Will shrugged. 'I'm not here to play music. That belongs to life back home.'

'So what's your clarinet doing here?'

Will hesitated and then, grinned, stymied. 'I guess I just like to keep it around.'

'If a man can play like that, he's got a duty to play here. Not just look at the damn thing. Think about it, Will. Why don't you play with the band? Jessica's going to sing with it. There's many in the mess here won't like it, you playing with airmen, but what the hell? It would be fun to see their faces.'

'Barriers again,' said Will. 'I don't care for that. But there are reasons I can't play.'

'Such as?'

'Like I said, music's my life back home. Here, my job's different.' But it wasn't the real reason. The real reason was Jessica Gray.

'Think about it, Will.'

'Okay, okay. Now you think about this: Jessica Gray. You're seeing a mighty lot of her, John. Take care.'

John cocked an eyebrow at him, annoyed at this intrusion. 'I'm in no danger, Will,' he said easily, too easily.

'I wasn't thinking of you.'

There was a silence. 'War affects the way things are between men and women, Will,' John said slowly. 'These aren't normal times. You can't think logically, you can't act logically. Mere survival has to come first, because other men's lives depend on your thinking that way. It *has* to be war first, women second. Her cousin knows that. She plays the game right.' He stopped. He hadn't meant to mention Vanessa. He hadn't even been consciously thinking about her. He'd thought he was over her. It was easy enough to think so, when he was in the air or when he was with Jessica. The two seemed part and parcel of one another: survival in the air depended in some way on her. He passed a tired hand over his eyes. He was cracking up. He couldn't think straight any more. All he knew was that if he allowed himself to think of Vanessa, he would be lost. Even now, the memory of dancing with her – that hair, those shoulders, the very way she moved against him – he felt himself stiffen. But she was trouble, big trouble.

Saturday 24th August was sunny – fortunately for Frittingbourne cricket team which was playing Westling, a time-honoured duel fought over the years with gusto and intensity. Yet it might be the last time it was played, Jessica thought suddenly, instantly reproaching herself. They were still here, weren't they? The Germans hadn't invaded – yet. The Luftwaffe had left them no peace.

On the 16th they were back again in strength, and on the 18th, and on and on and on. The Saturday dance had been cancelled last week; no one had the strength for it and the will to believe that they would be stood down in time to get ready for it.

Winston Churchill's orotund voice urged them to keep calm, to keep on fighting: 'Never in the field of human conflict was so much owed by so many to so few,' he had said a few days ago. One of the Few was John, another that nice American, Will Donaldson, but still the Germans were coming over, though never so many as on the 15th August. At night now everyone huddled in Anderson shelters, or in their concrete bunkers built in gardens. By day civilians emerged to carry on with routine living, or as routine as they could make it. By day the fighter pilots battled overhead in their small closed world; were doing so even now.

Thousands of feet beneath them Jessica sat on the grass, her mind not on the match before her but concentrated on the dance this evening that would begin when darkness fell, and the day fighters were released. She'd be singing with the band for the first time in public; Art had pronounced himself satisfied with rehearsals. It was about to begin. She would see John. They'd dance together. She'd be in his arms, share again the special something there was between them. He came over when he could, tired, always tired. Up at three for dawn readiness, not stood down till dark fell, that was the pattern of their lives. Eyes bright, wild; seeing a world of which she knew nothing, seeking she did not know what. But he needed her, of that she was sure. John. Her feelings for him were beginning to overwhelm everything else, putting everything into the background, even the war. Not singing though. That was bound up with him. Now she had someone to sing for, to share her voice with. She seemed to be bathed in a glow of wonder that swept her through the days.

In front of her the white-clad figures batted and swerved and ran, their calls heard dimly through her thoughts, lost in the summer haze and the sun warm on her back. She glanced up at the black dots whirling above them; the rest of the spectators seemed oblivious that up there a battle for their own survival was going on. If the battle were lost, this cricket match would never be the same again; never the same lazy, summer grace, the confidence of centuries of Kentish independence.

'Howzat?' The sharp crack of leather on willow, the outflung arm, the triumphant shout.

'Howzat?' The sharp crack of the Brownings, the yellow-nosed, grey Messerschmitt mortally hit, out of control, spiralling down, down towards them, the pilot desperately seeking control. Too low to bale out, he was looking for a place to crash land.

The air filled with screams. Players and spectators scattered as the monster zoomed low, ploughing through tree-tops which slowed its fall, hitting the ground, bouncing and slithering and cartwheeling over on the Frittingbourne cricket field.

'Come away, darling,' Cicely screamed, seizing her.

'No, he may be alive,' and Jessica began to run towards the wreck.

'Don't be a fool, Jessica.' Tom Ackroyd raced after her, dragging her to a halt. 'It'll go up in flames when it catches.'

'No - he—'

'Then I'll go.' Pushing her violently to the ground to stop her, he ran on towards the heap of fractured metal, the smell of petrol increasingly strong. He and two other volunteers dragged the pilot out, and were twenty yards away when the wreck went up with a 'Whoomph!'.

The pilot lay on the ground, still, bloodied but alive. The crowd was strangely silent, then as if impelled by some unseen orchestrator, rushed forward with a concerted growl, menacingly, waving belts, anything they could lay their hands on.

Jessica threw herself towards Tom and his companions to form a defence line. 'Get back,' she shouted. 'Back!'

Before her vehemence the mob halted, uncertain, and the village policeman pushed his way through, followed by the newly named Home Guard, racing to the scene of the crash. The ugly moment passed.

Jessica knelt and bent over the pilot, listening for breath and heartbeat. For one moment a pair of bewildered blue eyes looked into hers, full of pain, then they dulled and his head slumped.

'He's a goner, Jessica,' said Tom unemotionally. 'Nothing for you to do here.'

She turned to him, unable to believe the gulf between their thoughts. 'It could have been one of ours,' she said slowly. It could have been John.

'What the devil's he doing?' The CO was hell-bent on getting another gong, that was obvious. John couldn't follow him, it was suicide. They'd all be goners then. The CO hadn't noticed the snappers coming out of the cloud above. So he went in alone and took on five Messerschmitts.

He had a duty to follow; he had a duty to stay. There was no real choice for there were two others in his section. 'Look out, Wagtail Leader!' John yelled over the radio. '109s behind you!' He was too busy after that to notice what happened.

He landed exhausted, face streaked, coming in with a damaged engine and a row of bullet-holes in the fuselage. Airmen busily filling in bomb craters scattered. As soon as he'd halted they resumed their task.

'Blood on you, sir,' said one of the ground crew, concerned.

He put his hand up to his forehead. A bullet splinter had grazed him and he hadn't even noticed.

'CO's bought it, sir. Flying Officer Rhodes saw him go.'

He'd expected it, but hoped against hope. He wanted to cry out, shout, weep, but did none of those things. He nodded coolly and said, 'Thanks, Bert. I'll tell the others.'

The dance was wild that night, the band louder, the voices more raucous. She'd dressed with extra care, wearing an old but glamorous evening dress of her mother's that had hung unregarded in her cupboard. Cicely, whom it did not flatter, had given it to Jessica. Its golden folds set off her slim figure, and twisting and turning in front of the mirror she knew she looked her best. The dress came with matching jacket to cover its low neckline but after a moment Jessica grinned and discarded it. In for a penny . . .

Standing waiting to be introduced by Art she was

nervous. Once out there, once the first notes rang out true and clear, she was not. Heads turned from the dance floor as they heard her voice singing the mess favourite, 'Smoke gets in your Eyes'. A nod from Art when she finished, and a roar of applause from the floor. Inside her, something was singing still.

At the back of the hall, Will Donaldson talked steadily to the girl next to him.

Jessica sang two more numbers as agreed, then, thanking the band, ran down the steps to join John. It was a celebration for him. That morning he'd had his promotion to flight lieutenant confirmed. Something to cheer about, wasn't it? He was also acting CO now the old man had gone. So had young Maxwell, and half a dozen others he could hardly put a name to. They had come and vanished so quickly over recent days.

Vanessa was in high spirits. Graham might have brought her, but she had no intention of staying with an NCO. She was on the dance floor continuously, a laughing, whirling figure in her scarlet lace dress. 'Jess, that was lovely,' she stopped to say, 'you are a clever old thing,' before pouncing on John herself and waltzing him off. By coming with Graham, she had reasoned, she would be able to dance with anyone she chose. Graham certainly had his uses.

Deflated, telling herself it was just Vanessa's way, Jessica watched them. She lived for the moments when, tired after the day's flying, he might arrive late, sit in the oasthouse room and talk endlessly. Or on the rare days he or the squadron were stood down, they would go out in the Lagonda and sit in pub or meadow. He would talk about the war now, as though by talking about it, he could erase it from his consciousness, not seeming to care whether or not she understood his talk of bandits, Immelmann turns, snappers and tactics. He did not want to hear her talk of village life, of the daily fear of bombs, of the misery and difficulty of coping with rationing, of the constant air alerts, the screeching sirens, the endless shortages and appeals for money.

'Dance, Jessica?' Will Donaldson, seeing what had happened, laid his hand on her arm and she turned to him, startled. She had been absorbed in watching John dance with Vanessa, holding her closely, the way he did Jessica. They were only dancing, yet something troubled her. She shrugged it off. After all these weeks she knew he was not interested in Vanessa. He behaved to every girl like that. It came naturally to him.

She went into Will's arms, and was surprised at the ease with which they moved together. She enjoyed it so much that she forgot to watch John and Vanessa, and lost track of what Will was saying.

'You're a shaman, I guess. That's why you're good for John.' He had followed the direction of her eyes.

'A what?' she asked, startled.

'It's what the Red Indians call the person who intercedes with the spirits on behalf of a sick person. Or more generally he was a peace-maker. I guess you have the power.'

'What are you talking about?' she laughed. 'You make me sound like Minnehaha.'

'You're half right. Hiawatha was a shaman among the Mohawks. And I guess we all have the war disease. Look at them.' He waved an arm at the frenetic scene around them. 'John's lucky. He's found you, and you have the cure. Ah, well. "Love's mysteries in souls do grow".'

' "But yet the body is his book",' she picked up the quotation unthinkingly, and felt him react. In surprise, she presumed, then was startled herself and looked at him in such astonishment, so clearly wondering how an American could know John Donne, that he laughed.

'My father's a professor at Amherst,' he said. 'That's what you were wondering, wasn't it?'

'It was rude of me.'

'No,' he grinned. 'I guess not.' And put his arms round her again.

'Have you heard this man play, Jessica?'

John appeared by her side, glanced from one to the other and took her arm possessively. 'Go on, Will. Get up there and play.'

'But—'

'That's an order, Will.'

Reluctantly he disappeared and returned five minutes later with his clarinet. With a few murmured words of apology to Art, he began to play Gershwin.

'You listen, Jessica. He's really something,' John promised.

He was more than that. Two minutes after he began to play, something indefinable happened to the band; it ceased to be a medley and became a harmonised whole. Sounds came from the clarinet that ran through Jessica like silk, that seemed to speak to her alone, made her want to join her voice to it and sing, each urging the other on to further and greater acts of creation. His figure, tall and slight, every muscle and breath concentrated upon the sound he was creating, mesmerised her. It was indelibly fixed in her mind forever as he effortlessly expressed in music what she was still striving to attain in song. Then he switched to sentimental popular dance music and the atmosphere changed. He became a good clarinet player, and that was all. Jessica strove to recapture the magic but it eluded her.

John tossed down yet another beer, a wild look in his eyes that she had never seen before. He didn't seem like John at all but a brash stranger who inhabited a world she did not understand.

'Tell me what's the matter,' she pleaded inadequately.

'Matter?' He turned on her belligerently. 'Nothing – I'm drunk, that's all. I've got a lot to get drunk about. I've got another Messie, I've been promoted. Oh and did I tell you the CO's bought it?' he added savagely. 'I'm a blurry flight commander and acting CO. Come on, let's celebrate, Vanny.'

He stretched out an arm and grabbed Vanessa again as she whirled past in Graham's arms.

She giggled and they started a dashing tango, locked close together.

Jessica watched numbly, trying to tell herself it meant nothing. At the end of the dance, John stayed holding or rather hanging on to Vanessa until the band began to play again and Will once more picked up his clarinet.

' "A Nightingale Sang in Berkeley Square", by God,' John roared, as he lurched past with Vanessa. 'Listen to that, Jessica. Will's playing our song. Go up and sing it with him. Go on,' he cried belligerently when she made no movement, 'I want to you to sing it.'

'I can't – Art hasn't asked me – I—'

'Can't, eh? Thought you were going to take London by storm. Scared you can't do it, are you?'

She gasped, giddy with anger and hurt. 'No,' she blazed. 'I'll have the whole of this hall quiet in two minutes.' She ran to the dais where Will stood in front of the band, oblivious to everything but the sound of his clarinet.

'A nightingale sang in Berkeley Square . . . I'll swear,' she joined in.

Taken by surprise, Will turned to her, seized by hope, excitement, overwhelming joy. He'd known what would happen, must happen, if Jessica sang with him ever since he first heard her sing that summer's day. The day he'd seen her look with adoration at John Gale, the man who'd saved his life. So he'd gone out of his way to avoid her company, tried to avoid playing the clarinet publicly. In vain. He'd done his best, and it had not been enough to stop the inevitable. The wonderful, glorious inevitable that he went forward triumphantly to meet. There wasn't a damn thing anyone could do about it now. Not even John Gale. His eyes lit up as Jessica's vibrant husky tones picked up and enhanced the sound of the clarinet. As with the dancing, so now with the music, she seemed to know instinctively when to let him take over, and he when to yield to her, so that voice and clarinet fused into melodious unity, each the richer for it. The dancers stopped to listen, hushed; then the band too, so that only those two pure sounds were to be heard dropping into the stillness. When the song came to an end, Will laid down the clarinet, and said so quietly only she could hear – or was it for himself alone? – 'Yes. Oh, yes.'

'Whooah!' A raucous cry rang through the hall. John was standing on his head on a table waving his legs in the air, Vanessa supporting him and giggling at his side.

On the stage, Jessica turned to Will spontaneously, jubilant, her eyes sparkling. It had worked. The song had come right. At last she could sing it, feel it. Thanks to one man.

From his upsidedown position, the room a haze, a sick feeling in his stomach, John Gale focussed on the sight of Will Donaldson, a blurry pilot officer, putting his arm round Jessica Gray.

'What the hell are you doing, Donaldson?' he roared, into the room's sudden silence. 'That's my girl. My girl Jessica. Jessica,' he roared, swung himself down – and was sick all over the table. 'Jessica, where are you?' he demanded thickly.

Quietly she detached herself from Will and walked over to him.

'I'm here, John.'

Chapter Five

'Jessica, really! Aren't you listening to anything I say?'

Cicely's impatient voice cut through Jessica's half-hearted attempts to interest herself in her mother's designs for shelter clothes. 'I've decided. Trousers, that's the thing. They could look quite fetching - not like those awful things the Land Girls are wearing. And a siren suit. Plain, of course, but well cut. And loose enough to fit over my nightie.'

'Don't forget you may need to dash to the lavatory while you're in the shelter,' Jessica pointed out mischievously.

'True.' Cicely considered the problem seriously, her brows knitted. 'Perhaps Maggie could . . .' She chattered on while Jessica busied herself folding the blankets quickly organised for Frittingbourne's effort to help the stricken town of Ramsgate after yesterday's devastating bombing raid; eleven thousand people were huddled in tunnels cut through the chalk cliffs, many having set up home there, having none other. Such had been the damage and death toll in the town that for once Cicely made no attempt to rush over and give relief, suddenly preferring to organise from the rear. She had been shocked into silence when they first heard of the raid, as if only just aware that the playground in the sky could reach out deadly tentacles to the ground below. Ramsgate was not far away. She turned her thoughts to happier subjects: clothes – and Jessica's possible marriage to John Gale.

'You're miles away,' she teased shrilly. 'That's why you're not listening. It's love, isn't it? Dear Johnnie – is he coming today?'

'Mother!' said Jessica forbiddingly. 'Look out there.' Surprised at the vehemence in her voice, Cicely looked up blankly into the cloudy sky, where the familiar pulsing sound of enemy engines indicated the Heinkels on their way to bomb Britain into submission. 'He has a job – there's a war on.' Her voice faltered at the impossibility of trying to reach her mother, lost in her own world.

'I know, darling,' said Cicely, surprised. 'Why do you think I'm spending all my time designing clothes for Mrs Thing to make up for me? Shelter clothes. I'm preparing, you see. I just thought that when he brought you home last night he might have said when he wanted to see you again,' she added, hurt.

When he brought her home . . . Jessica smiled wrily to herself. John hadn't been capable of taking anyone home. He had collapsed completely after his dramatic outburst, and been borne off to his quarters by four almost equally unsteady gentlemen. It had been left to Will to drive her home.

And that's when it had happened. He'd said nothing at first. A stiff, awkward silence stretched between them. To break it, she said inanely: 'I like your car. A Lincoln, isn't it?'

'Yup. Lincoln Zephyr. No self-respecting American is

without a car after he's twelve, and I guess I'm no different to the rest. I picked this jalopy up from a guy at OTU.' He didn't mention the guy concerned wouldn't be needing a car again, ever.

A further silence.

'What was that tune you played, right at the end? The solo. I didn't know it,' she asked, feeling instinctively she was taking a risk but not knowing why. The melody had been with her ever since and, as well as the melody, the memory of the haunting intricacy of the patterns the clarinet had woven with the rest of the band – unusual, evocative, and exciting.

'I guess you wouldn't. I wrote it,' he replied shortly.

'But it was wonderful.' She paused, vainly seeking for words.

'Wonderful' – what a stupid word for that elusive glory.

'Yup,' he said simply.

She laughed. 'It ought to have lyrics,' she said impulsively.

'It has.'

'Oh.' She realised she had reached a quicksand unawares; too late to pull back, uncertain of the way forward, an uncharted hazard. Or had she known it was there and subconsciously sought it?

'Interested?'

'Me?' she replied guardedly.

Will slammed on the brakes, and stopped the Lincoln so abruptly she was flung forward, gasping.

'Goddammit, Jessica,' he burst out, 'why are you holding out on me? You sing like that – a voice just crying out for the clarinet, for *my* clarinet, *my* music – and you clam up on me like a downtown school-marm. You're an artist and you know it. You must know it. Tonight, we made music, *music*. Not you, not *me*. *Us*. We got somewhere no one else has trod before. That's for real, Jessica. That's heaven-country.

'So what the hell are you doing fooling around in the country teaching school kids, when out there—' he gestured into the night – 'is a dark world crying out for the light you can give it. If anything's going to stop this war being a pushover for Hitler it's spirit, not muscle, that's going to count in the end. Folks have got to believe there's something other than rationing and air-raid shelters, something worth fighting for, and – goddammit, Jessica, you're *laughing*!' He banged his fist angrily on the wheel.

'No. Oh, no, Will. I'm sorry. It's just that—' he glared at her – 'there's a ladybird on your nose and—' Her voice fell away as she saw the look on his face, and caught her breath. She had the fleeting impression that it would take but the slightest movement from either of them and they would be in each other's arms, hearts and lips together as had been their music. She was aware of each freckle on his face, each wave of the light brown hair. His nose, his mouth, his firm chin, seemed as well known to her as her own. Something hovered intangibly, tantalisingly, close. Then John's image swept before her, strong, demanding, all-consuming, and the fantastic notion vanished. It had all been her imagination, must have been, for by her side sat Will, stony-faced with anger, demanding: 'Did you hear one word of what I've been saying?'

'Yes,' she retorted, more belligerently than she had

intended. 'And, if you want to know, I agree with you.'

He expelled his breath in a long sigh. 'Then what,' he said deliberately, 'are we hanging around for? Let's get moving right now - tonight if you like. There's a guy I know in London books bands, singers for night clubs, concerts, links with the wireless. He'd take you like a shot. I could maybe come up too some nights when the heat's off here. We could work out our own sound. Jessica,' he said quietly, but she could see the fire lighting his eyes, 'I'd write such music for you, your heart could not hold it. Jessica, we'll bathe the world in song, and fill the skies with music. Jessica—'

A whole world began to open, a world of music. Songs began to tumble around in her mind, falling over each other to soar into the starlit sky. Hopes, ambitions, dreams, all her glorious tomorrow now but one word away: yes.

'Oh, Will,' she cried, seizing his hands impulsively. But even as the answering light appeared in his eyes, she checked herself. How could she have forgotten John so quickly? She would be going just when he needed her. She dropped Will's hands, drew back aghast.

'I can't leave,' she cried in anguish. 'Not now.'

He slumped back in the seat, the tension draining from him, leaving him deflated. 'Why not now?' he asked warily. 'I tell you, there's a way. Why not now? Isn't music the most important thing in the world for you? Because if it isn't, there sure is something wrong somewhere.'

'Well—' Why should she feel wrong-footed with his clear eyes on her? 'John needs me,' she said defiantly. 'I'd have to ask him.' She could not look at Will. Then:

'I love him,' she blurted out. 'I realised tonight – when I sang "Berkeley Square" – I've never been able to put it across before. But tonight the song came right for me, so I knew then that I love John.'

There was a deadly silence, a sharp intake of breath, then: 'Okay, lady, that's the way it is then,' he said nonchalantly, starting the Lincoln.

She shivered involuntarily as she recalled the scene. Last night it had been so dumbfounding it had hardly registered. Today, she was torn between an excitement that beat at her heart, the promise of new worlds opening up, and mortification that Will so little appreciated her reason for rejecting him. She had the obscure feeling he thought the less of her for it. But could he not see how torn she was? How great a sacrifice she was making? John needed her. She'd ask him, but if he said no, she'd stay. Her place had to be with him now – no matter what the cost. Later, perhaps, after this horrific war was over . . .

Yet she tossed and turned all night. Why did that melody of Will's haunt her dreams, the song that sought a singer, leaving unanswered the sound it might have been, a fragile butterfly that eluded her grasp and floated unfinished, undefined, into an endless night?

'Brickie, are you listening?' Cicely broke into her thoughts. Why did everyone have to ask her that? thought Jessica savagely. Oblivious, her mother swept on: 'What do you think? Shall we be bravely defiant, have a party next Sunday, September the 1st? We'll call it a Spitfire Party. Everyone who comes must donate something. Wouldn't that be fun? I could sing – patriotic songs, of course.'

'What a splendid idea, Mother. I could sing with you,' replied Jessica gravely.

Her mother shot her a look, and changed the subject.

She waited in vain to see John on the Monday evening. The Germans had picked out West Forstling as a main target that day. More than seventy bombers came in to strafe and bomb the airfield; the sergeants' mess was obliterated, incendiaries fell through the roof of Kippen Manor and a follow-up raid in the afternoon undid all the work the maintenance men and ground crew were putting in on repairing the landing field. Packed like sardines in air-raid shelters, the civilians of East Kent listened to the roar and rumble overhead, the crump of bombs, and knitted or chatted determinedly on. When John flew from the forward landing ground on the cliffs back to West Forstling there was nowhere safe to land so the squadron was diverted to Biggin Hill. While Jessica waited, he drank heavily at the White Hart in nearby Brasted, boasting of the blonde beauties of Mid-Kent, and only after closing time did it occur to him he could have telephoned.

Tired, weary, drained of energy, he came to her on the Tuesday. He sat beside her on the downs, his thoughts obviously miles away, and stared into the blue distance of the evening as he idly plucked petals from a daisy. By his side lay his uniform jacket for the evening was still warm from the heat of the day. At last, he reached across and took Jessica's hand.

'Have you forgiven me for yesterday – and for Saturday. Not too pretty a picture, eh?'

'Nor's war,' she replied valiantly. 'But it happens.'

Should she tell him now about Will's offer, or wait? She'd wait. 'It's all part of it, I suppose.'

'No.' He rejected this almost violently. 'There's a seamy side, but some things have to be kept apart or there's nothing to come back to. *You* have to be apart. Do you see what I mean?'

'No,' she said simply, 'but I want to help.'

'You can't,' he said bitterly. 'No one can help once you're up there. Not really. When you've got Germans all around you, there's no one can help but yourself. It's like—'

'The Keystone Kops,' she supplied frivolously, then instantly regretted it.

He frowned, but luckily did not seem to be listening to her words. 'There are others around you, of course, a lot of the time, and yet you remain alone, master of your fate. Every nerve tensed, waiting for action, trying to think and act simultaneously, to keep cool but alert, ice-cold and red-hot at the same time. And down there, you can see the patchwork of fields, houses dotted around – and you know that's what you're fighting for. And that's how *you* can help – just by being here, and by being what you are.'

'But I thought things were getting better,' she said in horror. 'That not so many fighters were coming over?'

'But we're growing more tired – and the bombers are coming now in earnest. Every day it gets worse. More and more of the bastards. Hordes of them. You dream about them. God, the dreams . . .'

He was silent for a moment, then with an effort went on: 'It's not all bad. There're times when you feel exhilarated, so excited you want to laugh, shout for the sheer glory of skimming through the clouds. It makes every man a poet, being up there. You want to sing – like *you* sing.' He paused, then said, 'Saturday night, at the dance, you sounded pretty good – you and Will.' He glanced at her. 'He's a fine musician, isn't he? It must be good to have a gift like that – and like you've got,' he said carefully.

'Yes,' she said, her cheeks glowing. Now, now was the time. She sat up excitedly. 'Oh, John, he told me he'd got a friend who booked bands and singers, and that I should sing with one of his bands, and that he, Will, would play when he could. He wanted me to go to London right away,' she said. She was going to add: 'And he'll write songs for me', but didn't. That bit was between her and Will.

'What did you tell him?' John said apparently lazily, but she could see him tense.

'I, I – said I'd ask you what you thought.' Her face was expectant.

She saw him relax. 'Because of school?' he asked.

'No,' she joked. 'Because of the hop-picking, silly.'

He caught her in his arms and kissed her, then abruptly released her. 'That will teach you to make jokes at my expense. Suppose I said I couldn't wait for you to go?'

'Can't you?' she said uneasily.

'I'll show you how much I want you go to.' He drew her to him and kissed her again.

Her thoughts were a jumble. He hasn't answered me yet. Oh, I love him, love him, love him . . . Then: Will's right, there *is* something – I felt something take over when I sang with him, as if my voice had been waiting. It just seemed to dovetail naturally. It's the song. Because I love John. Nightingales singing . . .

Then all thought was blotted out as John bent over her and pushed her gently down on to the grass, his body half covering hers, and began to kiss her, his arms wrapped about her. She felt their warmth running along her side, through the thin cotton of her summer frock. As her lips parted under gentle pressure from his she felt him unbuttoning the front of her dress, feeling for her breasts, the touch of his fingers on her skin, then further unbuttoning and his hands moving down, down her slim body. Instinctively she stopped him, her hand holding his wrist, then wished she hadn't as he sat up and slightly unsteadily took out and lit a cigarette. What his thoughts were, she could not guess.

'Did you really mind?' he asked after a moment, not looking at her, his eyes scanning the evening sky with a sort of detached professionalism.

'No - yes,' she said, muddled. Had she minded? The touch of his hands sent a thrill within her she had never felt before; she wanted it to go on, but something had made her stop him.

He laughed. 'Make your mind up, madam. Which?'

'No, but—'

'Good, then we'll start again,' he said gently, tossing away the unsmoked cigarette. This time he went more slowly, and she lay in his arms gazing at the sky above his head and wondering how such beauty could ever hold menace. He was part now of her song of life - she owed everything to him. Their lips met again. She felt warm, heady as his hands gently caressed her.

'You don't want me inside you, do you?' he whispered

at last. She didn't understand at first, and when she did said no with such force that he laughed again. 'You're still a virgin, aren't you, sweetheart?'

For some reason this made her uneasy, drove a wedge between them, made it seem they were of different worlds. She pushed him away, though gently enough that he still lay beside her. She sat up, straightened her clothes, and clasping her knees, stared ahead, not looking at him.

'Come on,' he said, scrambling to his feet and pulling her up. 'Time for Astaire's supper – and mine.' Looking down at her averted face he took it between his cupped hands and kissed it so sweetly that her uneasiness was swept away. She returned his kiss fervently and heard him say in a husky voice: 'Jessica, don't go to London, will you? I don't want you to. Don't sing for anyone but me, will you? Ever? Promise?'

Ever? Promise? The words were far away and John was near. She raised her head, and thought she had never been so happy in her life. 'No, John, oh no, I won't.' And the sacrifice was to her the symbol of their love.

'Do come, Jessica. Graham's a dear, but such a bore! At least I persuaded him to go to the White Stag. It'll be livelier there.'

'Why, didn't he want to go there?' Jessica enquired curiously.

'No. Some nonsense about its being the officers' pub, but I told him that was rubbish. It's a village pub, open to everyone. And if you're there, at least he won't be staring soulfully into my eyes all evening. Anyway, Johnnie Gale might be there. We could cycle over together.'

Jessica glanced at her. 'As a matter of fact,' she said

reluctantly, 'John's picking me up to go there anyway.' Why did she get the feeling Vanessa knew this already?

'Oh, well, that's all right then,' said Vanessa carelessly. 'He won't mind giving me a lift.' She flashed a brilliant smile at Jessica.

But I mind, thought Jessica crossly. It wasn't that she wanted to be alone with John all the time, but so often Vanessa was an intrusive presence, an exotic orchid dominating her surroundings.

The air of the pub was thick with smoke, the bar full of blue uniforms; a few stalwart locals had secured the old bench seats in the beamed bar, determined not to be driven out either by Hitler or His Majesty's Air Force, but times had changed. Whereas a few weeks ago the locals would have resented the intrusion, of the laughing, joking crowd with their uniforms and unfamiliar accents, now they could not do enough for them, proud of them if bewildered by their presence. Pints were handed out with each new line-shoot; each one, watery though it was, finding an eager home.

The noise hit Jessica's ears like a tidal wave and John grasped her arm reassuringly. Unlike her, he seemed to come alive in the noise and the smoke. Like Vanessa. This was his world, a part of him, warm, welcoming. A life-raft in unknown seas.

Graham came to meet them and Vanessa greeted him with a charming smile while her eyes flashed quickly round to see who else was there.

They fought their way through to the corner where miraculously Graham had bagged a table, and Vanessa seated herself so that she could survey the crowd – and vice versa, Jessica thought sardonically.

'Well, look who's here.' John plonked down their glasses of beer on the table. 'Hey, Will, you old devil,' he called to the far end of the room.

Rather reluctantly, Jessica felt, Will came over, nodding coolly to her. She noticed somewhat to her surprise that he was with a girl, a small dark-haired Waaf with sparkling eyes, whom he introduced as Molly Payne. In order to avoid talking to him, she found herself engaged in animated conversation with Molly who slipped in beside her on the bench.

'Yes, I'm in the station ops room,' she replied to Jessica's query. 'I'm a plotter.'

'A what?'

Molly laughed when she saw Jessica's expression. 'Sounds posh, doesn't it? But it's not that complicated. Catch them choosing me if it was! We just shift blocks and arrows around on the map, according to what the controller tells us.'

'It must be fun,' said Jessica enviously.

Molly looked at her curiously. 'I heard you sing last Saturday,' she said. 'And you envy *me*?' Jessica flushed.

'Gosh, I'm sorry,' said Molly impulsively. 'I can see I've put my foot in it somehow. Take no notice. They call me the Brick at home.'

'Do they really?' said Jessica, laughing. 'That's what my mother calls me.'

'But isn't your mother—' Molly stopped. 'Here I go again,' she said resignedly.

'The famous Bubbles Gray,' finished Jessica for her. 'Yes.'

'I do see now why you envy me,' said Molly seriously. ' 'Nuff said. I—' But whatever she was going to say next was interrupted by the door of the pub bursting open and two uniformed figures lurching in. One of them was Gerald Rhodes.

'Christ,' said John disgustedly, 'he's drunk already.'

'Come and have a drink, my darling,' crowed Gerry, spotting Vanessa. After listening to Graham with ill-concealed boredom, she brightened and leapt up to join Gerry at the bar.

'Mac,' warned John, laying a hand on Graham's arm, but he threw it off impatiently. This was not the mess. He went over to the bar. 'Can I get you a drink, sir?' he asked Gerry quietly.

'Ah, the gallant flight sergeant,' said Gerry with an exaggerated start. 'Still here, are we?'

'I'll buy Vanessa and you a drink—'

'Do you hear what he says, darling? As though a lovely thing like you wants to put up with Sergeant Prune all the evening. It's too bad.' And he turned his back on Graham and leant over the bar.

Graham put out his hand and yanked Gerry round to face him. He was rewarded by a push that sent him staggering back. He recovered in an instant and came at Gerry with a roar. But by this time John and Will were there, John pulling him back with a 'Don't be a bloody fool. You'll be court-martialled'.

'This one's mine, fella,' came in Will quietly. He pulled Gerry close up to him by the lapels. 'You're jazzed out of your mind, Rhodes. You're out.' And spinning him round, he caught hold of his collar and frog-marched him from the pub. When his companion emerged, Gerry was being forcibly and ignominiously held under the cold water tap in the outside privy. With a contemptuous 'Here', Will pushed Gerry towards his friend. 'Get this lush home.'

Inside, Vanessa was pale, half-scared, half-pleased at being the cause of an incident. 'Take her home, Graham,' said John wearily.

He flushed.

'Graham doesn't have a car, Johnnie,' said Vanessa sweetly. An involuntary glance passed between them, so quick it was caught only by Will returning to the group.

'We'll take her home,' said Jessica resignedly.

'No,' said Will quickly. 'I guess it's on our way. No problem, is it, Molly?'

John couldn't get Jessica out of his mind. He told himself repeatedly this was no time to be serious about a woman. But more and more Jessica's lively intelligent face obliterated Vanessa's hold on his senses. He found himself thinking about her at odd moments – in the cockpit or in the mess, dreaming about her almost as if she were some kind of good luck talisman. Thrusting into the clouds, into the sun, facing up to the enemy, it seemed almost as though she were there by his side urging him on, protecting him. Stupid, but after all why not if it helped?

Jessica.

Old-fashioned sort of name. Like Jessica Matthews. 'Over my shoulder,' he hummed . . . and his Jessica could sing too. Boy, how she could sing! To hell with Will. He hadn't liked seeing them together, and he'd surprised himself by his vehement reaction to the idea of their singing together. Especially in London. Why? John wondered. It wasn't as if Jessica's feelings for him were in doubt. He was experienced enough to realise that. She'd made them ingenuously clear. Except that, he frowned, she was shying away from letting him make love to her fully. Natural enough, he supposed, in a virgin. But he'd never had much trouble before; gentle persuasion usually worked - anyway, it was probably for the best. She was a serious-minded girl. She'd expect marriage, and most certainly Bubbles would. And, God, he was so tired. War was no time to think about marriage. No, he'd better hold back on the sex front. Yet he wondered briefly what it would be like before dismissing the thought. Time enough for that. He needed Jessica for other things than sex.

Yet there were still times, with the adrenalin still racing through him after they were stood down, that Jessica's image would vanish altogether, and the other self take over, the self that required only physical satisfaction, nothing demanding, just the haven of a woman's arms. Any woman. Any available woman. But in particular one who tantalised him, and tempted him to his Nirvana.

Vanessa's picture adorned the walls of the mess. She had become the acknowledged squadron pin-up, though somehow recognised now as Gerry's property. Graham faded into the background. She was not unkind to him, he simply ceased to exist as far as she was concerned. An Earl's son, even a younger one, came well before an NCO in her engagement book.

Day after day Graham took up his Spitfire, grimly determined to get on with the job in hand, unostentatiously scoring his tenth victory. The new CO put him up for a bar to his DFM and an immediate commission.

Gerry's score went up too. As showy in the air as on the ground, he scored two victories on one sortie, was hit, baled out, returned to the mess and continued his interrupted drink; his eyes grew brighter the harder the going got, his behaviour more frenetic, and in all of this Vanessa was his willing partner.

Jessica tried to dismiss John from her mind during the day, lest she should dwell too much on the dangers he faced. She continued the routine of wartime life; collecting for victory, digging for victory, cooking for victory.

The endless dogfights in the sky were so frequent now that few even bothered to raise their heads and follow them. White contrails etched against the blue were beginning to be commonplace. Still the local press went on determinedly recording 'real life' events; weddings, births, garden shows; the war news was kept strictly relegated to the back page. It helped them survive, she realised now.

When would she see John again? She never knew. He didn't know himself. They were scrambled continuously by day; he was free in the evenings but tired, so tired, sometimes unable even to drive out to Frittingbourne Manor. If she cycled over to the pub then he seemed only vaguely pleased to see her. But he would come, that she knew, when and if he could. If he could . . . no, life could not be so cruel. She shut her mind resolutely to the thought that one of those dots above their heads was John, battling for his life. Each day the battle intensified, the Luftwaffe now gathering strength for the final onslaught. The right conditions for a sea invasion were fast approaching and would soon be gone. The weather perversely favoured the Luftwaffe. On Friday the 30th, a heavy raid caused carnage at Biggin Hill, and next day battle was resumed in strength again.

Eggs and bacon grew cold at West Forstling as the raids began at eight o'clock. Gerry Rhodes leaned over Will Donaldson as he gulped his so-called coffee. 'Some day, Yank, we'll play a return match,' he promised in a pleasant voice. 'See if you can fight someone when he's not pissed.'

Will drained his coffee, and put the cup down carefully. 'Time the fat lady sang, pal. Suits me fine.'

B Flight was scrambled first, led by Flight Lieutenant John Gale, DFC.

'Wagtail Red Leader: forty bandits south of you, Angels fifteen. Snappers above.'

John acknowledged.

Gerry Rhodes, leading Blue Section, was thinking about Vanessa. What a girl! Life could be fun with a girl like her. If only – well, perhaps everything would come right again when this damned war was over. He'd make her his permanently then. He checked his numbers two and three.

'Close up, Red Three.'

'I hear you, Blue Leader. Roger.'

Messerschmitt in front, so close he could see the injured pilot. Funny how rarely you thought of the pilots. 109s were just big black shapes in the sky that had to be shot down. You had to get the better of them, like women or . . . His mind wandered.

Careful! Where was that damned Yank? Red Two. Good pilot. But he thought of the coming showdown with some pleasure.

He switched his thoughts to the evening ahead. They saw things the same way, he and Vanessa. Life was an adventure, fun, if you approached it in the right way. Even the snappers coming at him now. Gun button to 'fire'. There goes the blighter. No, another burst – Christ, what was that? The whole aircraft jinked and shook with vibration, dull thuds registering – machine gun hits!

Bloody 109 on my tail. Blast the woman. Mind not on job. He weaved, climbed, twisted, turned, but couldn't throw the yellow-nosed devil off. Immelmann turn to get on the tail. No, the blighter was up to that one. Well, at least if I go, I'll take him with me. The smell of smoke filled his nostrils. Fire! It began to register through his concentration. Every pilot's nightmare. Bale out. Twisting, he saw the flames licking at his boots. He pulled the canopy open, unclipped his harness, ready to bale out. Too late – another burst of fire hit the perspex, throwing him back into his seat with the force of the Spit's reaction. Everything felt sticky. He couldn't see anything. The cockpit was full of smoke. Must get out, his hand pulled off his oxygen mask and flying helmet. Christ, now he was stuck. Stuck! One jerk now, concentrate, one hard pull. It worked and he felt no pain as the flames licked his hands and face, and burned away his clothing, felt nothing but the blast of air – clean air that beckoned him to freedom.

Will Donaldson watched in horror as the figure swung down in flames beneath its opened chute. He circled till he saw it ditch in the sea, and, certain he had noted the place, waggled his wings in encouragement.

Fighter Command lost forty-one aircraft that day.

One of them was Gerry's, but the current was strong and square searches failed to locate the pilot before darkness fell.

'I'll have to tell her, Will. She's supposed to be meeting him tonight. We can't just let her wait for him. I'll go.'

Will looked at his flight commander coolly. 'I guess I'd better.' Their eyes met and it was John's that fell away.

'No,' he said abruptly. '*I'm* the flight commander. My job.'

'Not too good an idea, Johnnie.'

'What the hell do you mean?' John reacted violently. Will had obviously noticed. Had anyone else? Had Gerry? Blast Will! He was wrong anyway. He had himself well under control.

'It doesn't take too much imagination when you see the way you look at her sometimes.'

'God damn you, Will, keep your nose out of it. There's nothing in it, nothing at all!' And he went out, banging the door.

John found Vanessa at home, preparing to go out for the evening. She was alone in the small cottage. When she opened the door, her expression changed to one of startled surprise, then triumphant pleasure, then sudden realisation when she saw the look on his face.

'Gerry?' she asked faintly.

'There's no confirmation yet. He's missing,' said John stiffly, twisting his cap in his hands.

'You'd better come in.'

'No, I—' But she was already leading the way into the small living room with its huge inglenook and oak beams. She sat down on a chintz-covered sofa, gazing at her hands, the flouncy frills of her dress incongruous in the tense atmosphere.

'He'll probably turn up,' John went on. 'He went in the drink and was still afloat when Will last saw him.' Vanessa made a dismissive gesture. He sat beside her and unthinkingly put his hands over hers. 'Gerry's a good sort.'

But he was not thinking of Gerry at all. He was thinking of the girl at his side, her warm sensuality intoxicating him. Presently she raised her head and looked at him.

He caught his breath.

Her blue eyes melted with tears. Involuntarily he moved towards her and the dam broke. 'Vanessa,' he cried hoarsely. Then her arms were round his neck; he was smothering her face and neck with kisses, muttering fierce, possessive words of passion, and was lost.

Gerry Rhodes lay in the Canterbury Hospital, only a slit in the gauze indicating the face beneath. The twenty per cent of his body with third-degree burns was covered in tannic acid, beneath the hard crust of which wounds were beginning to fester. He lived in a dark world of pain, the occasional bright flashes of consciousness shot through with only one image. He fixed his thoughts on it tenaciously; if he could make the picture constant, stop the flickering, he would remain alive. One image, one girl: Vanessa.

Jessica loved the smell of the hops as she pulled them off the bines, ignoring their rough scratching on the unprotected parts of her arms. The first week of September, the delayed beginning of the hop season this year, was hot, very hot, making war seem all the more incongruous.

The sun was warm on her back through the thin cotton frock she wore, working next to Molly, sharing a basket. It was all hands to the fore this year, now that so many regular hop-pickers were in the forces. The local troops had been roped in to help, and the hop-fields echoed to their rough banter and strange accents.

Molly had insisted on spending her forty-eight hour leave hop-picking.

'I miss it,' she said forthrightly. 'I've been coming every year since I was a kid, apart from last year when I joined up, and by golly I'm not going to miss it this year as well!'

She had arrived, round face already pink, uniform skirt covered with an enormous pinafore, and proved still to be a nimble picker. Then Will had turned up unexpectedly. Jessica glanced up to pick up a new bine and there he was. He grinned cheerfully as though nothing had happened between them.

'Molly here lassooed me in. I'm stood down for the day. I wanted to get to see how you folks made that booze you call beer in those quaint round houses with the funny roofs—'

'Quaint – oh, you mean the oasts,' said Molly, laughing. 'Like Jessica says she lives in, lucky thing. If you really want to do the tourist thing, Will, you can get Jessica to take you across and explain it all. I'm going to get some picking done and earn my keep.'

Unwillingly, Jessica lay aside her bine and they walked over towards the two oasthouses at the far side of the hop gardens, white cowls gleaming in the afternoon sunshine, leaping horse finials standing out against the blue sky. Jessica was tense lest he raise the subject of London again.

She couldn't bear it. She had to blot all thought of it from her mind. Will wrinkled his nose.

'What the blazes is that smell?'

'It's the sulphur they put in the furnace to keep the hops a good colour,' she replied in relief; he too was avoiding the subject. 'Once smelled you'll never forget it.'

'You can say that again,' he agreed. 'I—'

But what he was going to add was never said. The distant sound of engines became a thudding roar, the specks in the sky black harbingers of death as six German fighters roared in low over the fields. With a speed that amazed them both, Will propelled her towards the slit trench dug at the edges of the hop-garden, pushed her into it and leapt in after her, landing half on top of her as the lead plane roared over the field, strafing it.

'Bastards!' he breathed. 'They're heading for West Forstling again. Listen to that, will you, and hope they don't aim short.' The sound of falling bombs as the Dorniers followed their escort shook the garden. Then there was an eerie pause.

'Jessica?'

'Get your elbow out of my neck, can you, Will?' she panted.

'Sure. Anything to oblige.' He shifted his weight. In almost the same breath he went on: 'That song you were singing when I first met you – sing it now.'

'Now?' she said in disbelief.

'Can you think of a better time? You weren't planning on going anywhere for the next five minutes, were you?'

'Not at all. It's my idea of a nice summer afternoon, lying in a slit trench with a mouthful of RAF uniform.'

'Sing, sweetheart, sing.'

A trifle self-consciously she began. He listened intently as she sang the verses, joining in the chorus, either humming or whistling them with her.

'Pretty Betty, don't fail
For I'll carry your pail
Safe home to your cot as we go
You shall hear the fond tale of the sweet—'

Then another bomber swept over, drowning the sound.

'Sing,' he hissed in her ear. Obediently she continued:

'Pray let me alone
I have hands of my own
Along with you, Sir, I'll not go—'

Another Dornier swept low.

'Go on,' he insisted.

At last she reached the end.

'No more is she afraid
For to walk in the shade
Or to sit in the valley below . . .'

In the vacuum of silence after the bombers had receded into the distance, the song seemed to echo all around the garden. They caught each other's eye and the ridiculousness of the situation struck them at the same moment.

'Do you sing up in the sky in your Spitfire, Will?' she asked, when she could stop laughing.

'Only when I take my clarinet along,' he yelled over the noise of the next Dornier.

'I wonder the Germans haven't surrendered by now.'

An all too-near crump and they burrowed further down into the trench.

'I'd a darn sight sooner be up there,' he said, spitting out a mouthful of grass and dust, 'than crouching down here.'

'I'll date you somewhere else next time,' she shouted back unthinkingly.

He turned to her sharply, his face inches from hers. She saw a muscle twitch. If he asks me now to go to London, she thought to herself unbidden, I'll say yes. I'll go, I'll go *now*. But he said nothing. Then after a moment, abruptly: 'You left some words out of that song. What was the dame afraid of? Why was she afraid to walk in the shade? Why wouldn't she marry him at first? And what did nightingales have to do with it?'

'I've no idea. But those are all the words that have survived,' she said. Was she glad or sorry the moment had passed? 'Perhaps it's all there ever were. Perhaps that's part of its mystery. It's an old Cornish song, and they're a mysterious people.'

'Mystery.' He stared at the hop-garden. 'I guess that sums it up. It's got a haze round it, that song, like it was trying to tell you something. Listen—' And he whistled a few notes. 'It's got something about it. I could do something with it. Sing that chorus bit again,' he commanded. Obediently, she did so.

'Yeah,' he said thoughtfully. 'I could use that. Get to

its soul. You see, rhythm's got to an interesting point now. Jazz, blues, swing, boogie-woogie – doors are opening – who knows what'll come next. I guess I'm going to go through some of those closed doors and find out what's behind them. Now this nightingale song of yours is a pretty interesting door. People don't want folk songs at the moment, of course. They want ballads, love songs, simple and direct, but it'll do us till we get going. If you come in on the upbeat—'

'Will,' she said warningly.

He looked at her face, inches from his, and grinned. 'How'd it go now? "Pray let me alone." I guess Pretty Betty wasn't seeing things too clear so far as her man was concerned.'

'You're wrong,' she said, sharply. 'John and I are right for each other. We *are*!' She broke off disconcerted, realising she had walked into a trap. There was no need for him to say a thing. Pointless to tell her that need blinds you, war blinds you, that in the dark the nearest support may crumble with the coming of the light.

That was 3rd September. The war had begun exactly twelve months earlier. The early days of the month were fine and hot. While Kent was bathed in sunshine the Luftwaffe benefited. Each day the skies were filled with raiders, relentless streams of bombers. One sortie was only distinguishable from the next for the pilots by the nearness with which they came to death. Sometimes West Forstling, sometimes an advance landing ground, sometimes Manston – they all began to look the same.

Today, the 6th, it was Manston. John Gale hadn't

been to his own quarters - if they were still there - for three days. God, he was tired, incredibly tired; he seemed to be welded into his Spitfire now, just part of a machine that went on and on and on. By night you drank, then you slept, then you climbed into your Spit again and soared into the skies to fight. Always those armadas coming towards you, like bee swarms, more and more and more. And less of you, so it seemed, though they said not. There were constant replacements coming to the squadron, a haze of young faces eager to be part of history - and soon were. Only the regulars, the experienced, survived; the others never had time to learn. It was all right if you kept going, didn't think about it. But if you did—

Then suddenly: fear. What if he didn't pull through? What if that Messerschmitt in front of him pulled the trigger before he did? What if—? Fear. He mustn't let it get a grip or he was done for. Uncertainty killed. Fear downed. But there it was, paralysing his mind, insidiously taking control. Please God take this fear away. *Take it*! Jessica. Think about Jessica. Fix your thoughts quickly—

When they were stood down that evening he went in search of her. He was quite determined, completely and unquestioningly set on his course of action. He took her by the hand, and led her into her small garden. There with Astaire and Lind as witnesses he kissed her formally and said: 'Jessica, will you marry me? Now?'

Seeing her look of disbelief, he went on hurriedly: 'I know we haven't known each other long, but perhaps we haven't *got* long. I want you for my wife now. I want to marry you just as soon as ever we can. I want to know when I'm up there that somehow we're together—'

'But—'

'Don't you ever say anything but but?' he teased, with a choke in his voice.

'Sometimes I say yes, John. Yes, please.'

Chapter Six

'A spring wedding,' Cicely had declared excitedly. 'We'll have a marquee of course. White lace for your dress. I'll get hold of some somehow. And orange blossom.'

'No, Mother,' said Jessica quickly. 'John wants us to get married now.'

There was a dead silence. Then, plaintively: 'Now? But how can I prepare everything in—'

'As soon as we can,' Jessica cut in steadily. 'That will be in two to three weeks' time, as soon as the banns are called. Saturday the 28th, we thought.'

John had wanted them to get married even sooner, by special licence, but the new CO had refused permission. He needed every pilot he had at the moment. She was oddly relieved, selfishly wanting time to adjust, to think about what had happened. She was being swept along by events in a haze that pushed reality one step back. The only moments it came close enough to touch her were those she had alone with John. Without his presence, she could not believe that this had happened, that the blue bird of happiness she had reached out for so often was hers. She tried to think of their future together, but gave up the attempt. She could not think beyond their wedding and the consummation of their love. No holding back. Together. For always. Somehow the prospect did not seem real.

'I've managed to get masses of ivory satin, darling. That will be even better than white lace with your sallow skin.' Her mother erupted into the oasthouse on the Saturday morning before with this momentous news, just as Jessica was leaving for the hop-garden.

'Mother, what does it matter what I wear?' Jessica clutched her hair in despair.

'Don't do that, dear. It makes you look like Medusa or something. And what do you mean it doesn't matter? Brickie, this is your wedding day I'm talking about. Heaven knows you're not exactly cut out for grace and elegance, but you might try for once. Now, I've been to see the food people and we can get extra rations for a wedding. There'll have to be a cake. Goodness knows how but Mrs Thing will see to that - and sandwiches. Oh, and chickens, I've already seen that man Jones. How lucky drink isn't rationed.'

Her voice rambled on and Jessica tried to control herself. Did anything ever register with her mother? Did she even remember what had happened at the party she had given just two months ago? Now all these arrangements. All this fuss. She and John wanted to get married quietly, just the two of them, with Will and Vanessa for witnesses. But it wasn't going to be like that. Oh, no. Her mother was intent on asking everyone; it was going to be *her* day, war or no war, and what was worse, John seemed to be siding with her now.

Jessica had even felt resentful at how well the two of them got on, but then reproached herself. Soon she'd be free. Cicely produced lists of names that passed her by in a haze. But if John wanted it, that was fine. The only thing he hadn't seemed to like was the idea of Vanessa being a bridesmaid. Yet she couldn't not ask her, and her earlier jealousy of Vanessa was water under the bridge now. She hadn't told her the news yet, but Vanessa was coming to lunch tomorrow, Sunday, and she would tell her then.

But by then Vanessa knew.

'He's asking for you,' Will had said abruptly, when she opened the door early Saturday evening. She had expected to see John, or Graham perhaps. Certainly not Will, lounging on her doorstep. She sensed he had little time for her, he was one of the few men who had never responded to her signals.

'He's asking for you,' he repeated.

'You'd better come in,' she answered flatly after a moment. Then burst out: 'I can't, Will, I can't.'

'I tried to talk him out of it,' he said bluntly. 'It's no place for you. But his parents are there – and they'd sure be glad to see you.'

'The Earl?' Vanessa paused, then remembered her fears. 'But I'm not really his girl, Will. And I'm no use at sickbeds.' She looked at him pleadingly, as though he should understand that she was not made for this – that Gerry was amusing, prestigious as an escort, an eligible husband – of a sort – but shot down and burned . . . ? She shuddered.

'He's asking for you, Vanessa,' was all Will replied. 'I'll run you there.' He was rewarded by a look of gratitude. At least she wouldn't have to face the ordeal alone.

On the threshold of the room in the Kent and Canterbury Hospital, the nurse looked uncertainly from Will to Vanessa.

'Have you told—?'

Will nodded. He'd explained that all Vanessa would see would be white bandages and gauze. That underneath was a hard layer of tannic acid, which crusted black to protect the skin growing underneath. That Gerry wasn't really making much sense because he was so heavily drugged. That she need only stay a minute till he registered she was there. That he knew Vanessa was a real sweetie and wouldn't want to let Gerry think she'd deserted him. This was precisely what he did think, in fact, but Gerry's parents had pleaded with him to try.

'Vanessa', was all Gerry mumbled incessantly, and if she would see him just for a minute he would know that she hadn't deserted him.

Will took her by the arm quite firmly. 'Okay?' he asked.

She nodded but already he could feel her trembling.

The room was almost in darkness; in the corner a white figure, limbs suspended clear of the bed, only slits for nose and mouth – and not even the eyes uncovered. Will felt Vanessa flinch, heard a stifled gasp, and tightened his grip.

'Hi, fella,' he drawled casually. 'How's it going? I've brought Vanessa.'

The hole moved. Vanessa was shaking, pulling away. Only Will's arm restrained her. The lips, what there were of them, moved, but there was no sound. Will kicked her on the ankle, none too gently.

'Hallo, Gerry dear,' she managed in a whisper. 'You

look—' Then with a violent jerk she pulled herself free and ran out of the room. Will cursed silently.

'Vanessa,' came the hoarse reply.

'I guess we've got to go, Gerry,' said Will easily. 'That nurse is looking mighty threatening.'

'Vanessa,' whispered the voice again.

'Be seeing you right soon, Gerry.'

Outside a few strides and Will caught up with Vanessa, standing shuddering against the corridor wall, face towards it, shoulders heaving.

'What the hell kind of a woman are you?' he said quietly, swinging her round, none too gently.

She burst into loud sobs. 'I can't – you don't understand – God, I feel sick.' And she ran into the toilet, coming out looking pale and wan a few minutes later.

Will stood waiting for her, arms folded, eyes like steel. 'Hadn't you figured out that war isn't all boogie-woogie?'

'No,' she burst out, 'and why should I? I'm not married to him. We just had fun together a few times. It doesn't make me his nursemaid, does it? You don't understand – I'm no good at this kind of thing – why don't you get Jessica here? She's much better than me at it.'

'Because you're the one he wants, though God knows why,' said Will grimly. 'Anyway, Jessica's got enough to do at the moment, she and John.'

'What?' sniffed Vanessa. 'What about Jessica and John?'

'Their wedding. Three weeks today.'

'Their *what*?' Vanessa stared at him uncomprehendingly.

'Didn't you know? I guess I pulled a boner?' Had it

been accidental? Not really. He'd wanted to see Vanessa's reaction.

'Married? Jessica? To Johnnie?' Shriek after shriek of hysterical cries echoed through the corridors, till nurses came running to console her that Gerry would recover and Will was given the answer he feared.

That same day, 7th September, the Luftwaffe had changed tactics. Assuming that Fighter Command was on the way out, they made their big gamble, a throw of the dice to win them the war quickly. They began to bomb London. Nearly four hundred bombers escorted by over six hundred fighters relentlessly forged a path over the Kent coasts towards their target. Every squadron was scrambled that afternoon, but instead of going for the airfields yet again, the huge formations droned steadily towards the capital.

Jessica did not see John till seven o'clock when he was at last stood down through weariness. He was dulled by tiredness, barely able to talk as she led him into the small garden, flooded with the setting sun. Overhead the drone of bombers continued sporadically.

'Don't let's go anywhere,' he said. 'Let's just stay here.' He sank down on the wooden garden seat and put his arm round her shoulders. 'They're bombing London,' he went on jerkily. 'Will got one, though. So did Mac. That's something, eh?' He grinned, and fell silent, far away.

'You'll win in the end, won't you?'

'Do you know,' he said in surprise, 'I believe we will. I didn't, not at first. Now I do. Must be something to do with love and marriage and—'

'Oh, John.' Impulsively, passionately, she threw her arms round him, knocking him sideways and falling across him.

'Hey, careful. No wonder they call you Brickie. I thought you didn't want to – till we're married.'

'I don't. But I can display a little enthusiasm, can't I?'

'Not too much, Jessica my love, or I won't answer for the consequences.'

She sighed, sat up straight, and placed her hands meekly in her lap. 'Is that better?' she enquired.

'Why do you think it so important, Jess?' he asked seriously. 'It's only a matter of weeks after all.' He sounded hurt. He'd wanted to get married right away, was never so sure of anything than that his salvation lay in Jessica. Not Vanessa. No, he would not think of her, a good-time girl if ever there was one. But by marrying Jessica he could harness his good luck to him. So it seemed important to marry soon before his luck ran out in this battle for survival in the sky, day after day. Why didn't she want to make love with him now, though? No woman had ever resisted him for long before. And nor would Jessica, he was sure.

'Let's go indoors,' he murmured. 'Please. I promise I won't go too far if you don't want me too. *Please*.'

'We'll be married in three weeks, John. Let's wait.'

'Does a ring make so much difference?' he asked, trying to keep impatience out of his voice.

'It's not that, John – I can't explain.' Her words stumbled over one another. Why couldn't she explain? 'It's just I don't feel it's right, yet – we don't know each other. When it's time, something inside tells you – and it's not now.'

'Come inside for a little. Just come and lie down with me. We can just be close.' His lips met hers.

'Just for a moment. But—'

His lips stopped her words and thoughts, and he took her upstairs to the bedroom where the smell of the hops lingered still. Outside Lind began to sing as John's lips found hers.

She was swept away on a tide of sensation as his mouth wooed her, teased her, tantalised her, and she felt him removing her clothes, stilling her protests with kisses. Not that she minded the touch of his hands on her body. Or did she? She wanted him to stop, she wanted him to go on and on, until from somewhere she found the strength to stop him. She jerked her head sideways.

'John, no, not now. You said you wouldn't.'

'You'll like it, I won't hurt you.'

'I can't - John, *what's that*?'

The sound rang out clearly, all around them.

'Church bells.' He stared at her white face.

'Church bells,' she repeated fearfully. 'John. The invasion. *It's started*!'

'I must get back to the squadron.' He seized his shoes and put them on quickly. 'My God, what a time to start. Hell, where's my cap?' he muttered. Then, casting a quick look at her, he seized her in his arms and held her close. 'Don't go, don't leave me,' he said, and ran from the room. As she peered from the dormer window he was already sprinting towards the Lagonda parked in the roadway.

The ringing of the church bells proved to have been a false alarm. But the streams of bombers making their way throughout that night to London were not. The Blitz had begun, and by morning over four hundred people had died.

The old grey Norman church looked solidly secure, flanked by its green yews. It was hard to believe that its peace was under threat; that at any moment the air raid siren could blast once again through the air. How quiet it had seemed on Sundays throughout this summer with no church bells ringing to herald the services. Jessica shivered at the memory of last night. False alarm, but how terrible it had been. Now the congregation flooded in on this Day of National Prayer, to pray that the 'Few' might be successful in driving back the enemy, in delaying the invasion fleet that everyone knew was poised on the other side of the Channel. Tomorrow moon and tide would be right for invasion they said, and would be so for ten days. Yet to Jessica, sitting in the old oak pew with its ancient Jack in the Wood symbol carved at one end in propitiation to the old gods, it seemed impossible to imagine any other way of life.

The squadron had flown for seven days without a break and were in desperate need of a rest. Operational fatigue they called it: the unnaturally bright eyes that seemed fixed on far horizons, the frenetic wildness, the dancing, the nightly drinking. But when Jessica spoke to John, his attention was all on her and he would hold her, tightly, desperately, as though unable to let her go.

Michael sat on one side, Cicely on her other, Maggie proprietorily behind them, to hear the banns read. Her mother behaved as though she were the bride elect, not her daughter, so great was her triumph.

'Blessed are the pure in heart . . .' Jessica joined in the

hymn, her voice ringing out rich and confident above those around her as she glanced down at the small diamond ring on her finger. She was aware that she was drowning her mother's voice, that Cicely was tense with annoyance, but did not care. She wanted to sing. She would sing at her wedding. A small unease took hold of her. A fear . . . What if she could really sing no more? She was sure John did not really mean it; once they were married he would see things differently, want her to succeed, understand that she lived for singing as did he for – for what? She thought with a sudden surprise that she did not know. The war, flying, took up all his conversation. How much there would be to find out about each other. She tried hard to concentrate on what the Rector was saying as she shifted uncomfortably on the hard hassock. He was praying for the deliverance of the country, but even this did not penetrate Jessica's preoccupation with her own happiness. It seemed impossible that anything could prevent her wedding day.

Vanessa staggered away from Sunday lunch at Frittingbourne Manor feeling as though her artificial smile would be plastered on her face forever. Jessica and Johnnie? She knew he'd been seeing a lot of her – but marriage? It must be because of Frittingbourne Manor. He wanted to marry into Cicely's and Michael's circle. Yes, that was it. He couldn't really want Jessica, not after *her*. How could he prefer Jessica to her? And Gerry . . . she shivered at the recollection, then blotted it resolutely from her mind. She had no responsibility towards him, none at all. They'd had a few good times, but not as good as she'd thought they were going to be . . . He might be an Earl's son, but there were limits. And the last straw was she had to be a blasted bridesmaid to Jessica. *Brickie*. It was too much. And tonight she had to pull herself together for a date with Graham. Why on earth had she accepted? Then she remembered.

By the middle of the week London's death toll had risen to over six hundred. The city recovered from the first shock and its carefully laid plans in case of air raids were put in motion: Incidents room, shelter wardens, the incessant running to the Anderson or public shelters, became part of Londoners' routine lives. The Luftwaffe bombed by day and bombed by night. Now they used different tactics, to ensure the greatest number of bombers got through. Instead of separate raids, massive formations came over in successive waves, intended to swamp the fighter and AA defences. But at last they were beginning to leave the hard-pressed airfields alone; that was one blessing – and one that was to cost the Luftwaffe dear.

'Don't be late, Johnnie dear. Tell that silly old Hugh Dowding it's your engagement party tonight.' It might have been Cicely's own from the way she pouted so charmingly. John looked at her uncomprehendingly. He was hard put to it to raise a smile. Bubbles was beginning increasingly to grate on him, and he found himself shying away from her arch behaviour towards Jessica's cheerful strength.

'I'll have a word with Göring,' he managed to joke. Another day, another battle.

At dispersal he found Will and Graham and the rest of his flight, greeting them with a nod. No need for anything more. They were well used to the drill now. Readiness to scramble, to take on the first wave. Available fifteen minutes, ready to take on the second wave, and available thirty minutes as reinforcements. Today they were down for first wave. They were unusually silent. The gramophone was scratching out its mournful 'Smoke gets in your eyes', now accepted as the squadron song. Darts were being thrown with apparently nonchalant hands, the odd book was studiously perused. But all thoughts were on one thing: the telephone. Over in the ops room even now their fate was being plotted step by step on the table as the reports came in from Sector HQ and the local Observer Corps centre. They had to wait for another hour before they were scrambled, the hut a haze of cigarette smoke, with others stretched out on the grass or sitting in the sun.

Soon the air was full of the sound of roaring Merlins, throttles forward; then the roars changed to murmurs, as they lifted into the air. West Forstling lay behind them, and there was nothing but the rushing slipstream and an appointment with destiny.

'Wagtail Blue Leader, come in Blue Leader. Bandits south-east of you at Angels 20. Acknowledge.' This was a hell of a way to spend a Saturday afternoon. Should be at the stumps.

'Roger, Blue Leader. Call acknowledged. Keep climbing on 045. Fast as you can.'

Then they were there. Hell, they were above them, while they were still climbing. It had been better recently but why the hell could Group never get the height right? To be caught climbing . . . that's how Gerry had gone. No, don't think of Gerry. Don't think of Vanessa. Think of Jessica, Jessie, Jess – There my beauty, press the button and the Browning sang; the air full of smoke, one for you, Lord Haw Haw. Crow about that if you can. And one for Göring ahead. No, the devil had side slipped, turning. Where was his wingman? There. Good old Mac. Rely on him. God, what was that fool doing – that's a Hurri, not a 109.

Tonight he'd see Jessica. The engagement party. But most of all he'd see Jessica. Hang on to that . . . hang on . . . my beauty. He wondered whether knights of old on their chargers felt as he did. To hell with knights and chargers – there was work to be done.

She ran out of the house and down the steps and was in John's arms as soon as he had sprung out of the Lagonda. Will quietly slid an arm round Molly's shoulders as they sat in the back of the car. Jessica jumped into the front seat and John set off again for Whitewell Court Hotel where the dance was being held. Jessica had made an effort, this time without Vanessa's help, and gone on a shopping expedition to Maidstone to acquire a long primrose-coloured cotton skirt, evening blouse with cap sleeves and an ornately embroidered golden bolero. She felt for once fashionably and becomingly dressed – until they arrived and she saw her cousin.

Vanessa looked outrageously beautiful in an off-white dress, the scarlet poppies in her hair matching her lipstick in a blaze of colour. A mischievous smile crossed her face as she saw Will and Molly talking earnestly. She took Will by the arm, swinging him into the dance, leaving Molly standing alone.

'Hold on, honey,' Will called out to her. 'I'll just

shimmy with Jean Harlow here and be right back.'

'You're not very flattering, Will,' Vanessa pouted, nestling closer, both arms round his neck. 'Don't you want to dance with me?'

He grinned down at her. 'Sure, why not?' But she sensed his detachment.

'I can't get anywhere with you, Will, can I?'

'Do you want to?'

She laughed. 'I'm not used to being ignored.'

'Macintosh is a good guy,' Will said seriously. 'You ought not to play him around like you do. And Gerry—'

'Don't,' she said sharply, but he went on. 'He's being moved to East Grinstead, Vanessa, so that this guy McIndoe can take a look at him. He does wonders.'

'Don't,' she cried again, more firmly. 'I'm sorry for him, Will, but he's not for me.'

'Not like John, I guess,' he said softly.

She looked him straight in the eye. 'No,' she said coolly. 'Not like Johnnie.' Her arms slackened, and she took up a more conventional position.

'Jessica's your cousin, and she's over the rainbow at the moment. Don't do anything to upset that, Vanessa.' It cost him something to say it. Was Jessica happy? She believed she was, so there wasn't a damn thing he could do about it. And John? Was it what *he* wanted? John was getting tired. He was beginning to make mistakes. A certain look came into their eyes. Operational fatigue. The squadron must be sent north on rest soon, surely?

'Don't be silly, Will,' said Vanessa, giggling artificially. 'What *could* I do? This is their engagement party after all.'

* * *

'Tom?'

He was standing alone, gazing through the window over the gardens, and did not turn when he heard Jessica's voice. Jessica had tried several times to see him, to tell him her news, but he always seemed to be out. In the end, she had been forced to write to him.

'I'm sorry, Tom,' she said, not knowing quite how to reach him.

'Yes, I think you will be.'

She caught her breath. 'That's unfair.'

'Once we said we'd never lie to each other.'

'I'm not lying!' she countered angrily.

He turned to look at her then. 'Perhaps,' he said, almost to himself. Then: 'But where are your dreams now, Jessica? Where is your song?'

'Come true,' she said defiantly. But the song?

He smiled. 'I wish it so for you, I do indeed. But don't forget that song, will you, Jessica?'

'It's *my* life –'

Facing each other like angry duellists, they were interrupted by Will and Molly.

'. . . to congratulate you.' Molly's voice trailed off, as she glanced from one to the other, sizing up the situation. Then she slipped her arm through Tom's. 'We haven't met, but I need a partner for this dance. Will here's all feet; it's the American pioneer in him.' And she swept Tom away.

Jessica was left face to face with Will. 'Well,' she said belligerently, 'are you going to prophesy doom and disaster, too?'

'Should I?' he enquired politely.

'No, I'll make him happy.'

'Sure,' he agreed.

'And he me.'

'Sure.'

'You don't believe it, do you?' she burst out. 'But he's a wonderful man.'

'I owe my life to John Gale,' he cut in angrily. 'Do you reckon you need to tell *me* that? He's a great guy. Period.'

'Then why—?'

He eyed her thoughtfully and began to whistle softly. She started to say something, then broke off and listened, interested despite herself. 'That's the nightingale song, but you've done something to it – the tempo. Will, it works!'

'*That's* why. You had a choice. Music or marriage. You blew it. You took the easy road.' His voice held no condemnation, was matter-of-fact.

'Easy?' Jessica's voice rose high. 'What do you mean? I'm getting *married*. I can have *both*.'

'Don't sing for anyone but me, will you?' she heard the words ringing in her ears. 'Promise?' 'I'm *happy*,' she added pleadingly.

'Sure. So was Hans Andersen's nightingale when it flew into the emperor's cage. Now, I'm going to do my stint up there with the band – are you going to sing at your own engagement party?'

'No,' she flung back at him.

'Scared?'

'Scared?' she said slowly, staring at him. He was goading her, she knew that, but she was not going to let even Will think she was afraid of singing. It was her voice, and in any case, singing at her own engagement party was singing for John alone. In a way. She ran after him. 'What have you got organised?'

He stopped. 'Love songs. "You're Driving me Crazy", "Ain't Love Hell"—'

'I don't know those.'

'You will, sweetheart,' he murmured. 'No, I was kidding. How about "Yours", "Love is the Sweetest Thing", "A Nightingale Sang in Berkeley Square"?'

'That will do fine,' she said steadily.

John hardly registered Jessica was singing. He was listening automatically for the sound of bomber engines – and there was none. What the hell were they planning now? At least Bomber Command were doing a good job on the invasion barges over there. Between them, they'd—

'Johnnie, you haven't danced with me yet.'

He swallowed, then remembered. It was his engagement night. His face lit up with false enthusiasm, and he swept Vanessa on to the floor. He had little choice, but at least he was safe from her now. Even so, his body began to respond to the sway of hers within his arms. Damn her, she was clinging too close. What if Jessica – no, she wouldn't realise. She'd even had the damn fool idea of asking her to be a bridesmaid. Will had noticed something, that was for sure, but he would never say anything. He edged Vanessa gently away from him. But she was satisfied.

On Sunday 15th September, at Bentley Priory, Fighter Command HQ, Winston Churchill was standing on the ops room balcony overlooking the plotting table with the tote of squadron availability beyond. Waafs pushed their blocks and arrows further and further towards London with their magnetic rakes, according to the information they were fed through their headphones. The Prime Minister glanced at the tote, now completely full of twinkling lights.

'What are our reserves?' he growled.

'There are none,' was the reply.

No one knew it then, but that day was to prove the climax of the Battle of Britain. At West Forstling, however, it seemed just one more stage in the long drawn-out struggle. Their second scramble of the day was in the afternoon. Thirteen squadrons clashed with enemy bombers and fighters over Kent. Down below, people watched the black specks wheeling and darting, followed the white trails and counted the black ones falling earthwards. Charles Gardner had popularised wireless reporting with his blow by blow accounts and now people watched the battles as if they were cricket matches. Or seemed to. Only the foolish would believe, however, that the Kentish men and women were as blind to their peril as they appeared. Two days later Hitler postponed the invasion of Britain indefinitely.

Jessica could not bear to watch any longer. The garden offered no refuge. She walked up to the Manor in an effort to take her mind off what was happening in the sky and found her parents listening to the news bulletin on the wireless. One hundred and eighty-three aircraft had been shot down. How many British, though, and was John's one of them?

It wasn't. He was being debriefed from the last sortie of the day. Spy's was not an enviable job. The intelligence officer had to probe, querying claims, asking questions, when all you wanted to do was forget all about it, sink yourself in a beer. Or two.

Will had made a mistake up there today . . . unusual for him. He was up for the DFC after his last kill. John's own second gong was supposed to be coming through too. A bar to his DFC. Gongs – a piece of metal on a ribbon for making the correct split-second decision. If you hadn't, you'd have been dead. Will had nearly bought it this afternoon. The Spit might be a lady, but she didn't like diving, that was for sure; the enemy knew it, and took advantage of it. There was a limit to how much longer they could go on. The CO said they were to be sent north. Thank God! It couldn't be soon enough for him. Get out of this hell.

Jessica knew something was wrong when he arrived. Bright-eyed, irritable, he was barely polite to Bubbles and Jessica extricated him from the Manor and talk of wedding arrangements as soon as possible.

'Pub,' he said. 'Let's go to the pub.'

'I must feed Astaire and Lind first.'

'Feed the bloody birds,' he grunted. 'God, how boring.' She did not say anything and he seized her arm and pulled her towards him. 'I'm sorry,' he said penitently. 'It's been a rough day.'

'I know,' she said. 'I heard. But now it's not. Because you're here, and alive.'

Alive. Not like the CO who'd gone into the drink, or Phil who had simply blown up, not half dead like Gerry Rhodes, bound up like an Egyptian mummy at East Grinstead. Alive. Half the squadron seemed to be strangers now. How many of the originals were left God only knew; John hadn't even the energy to reckon it up.

The green bower of Jessica's garden enclosed them, Michaelmas daisies in full bloom, the air heavy with the scents of dusk. He saw her bending over to feed the two birds, watched the lines of her body under the thin dress, watched – and wanted.

'Jessica,' he said hoarsely.

She turned, surprised at the urgency in his voice, then gasped as he drew her into his arms and kissed her roughly. She was disconcerted by the look of his face, the narrowing of his eyes.

'Jessica, I want you – now.'

'No, John,' she said. 'Not now. Not like this. Please let's wait.'

'Wait?' he repeated disgustedly. 'Christ, it's summer, we're going to be married in two weeks. I might be dead tomorrow. Just tell me, what in God's name are we waiting for?'

'I don't know, I can't explain – and I shouldn't have to,' she cried, trying to free herself, but he caught her arm and pulled her back, his hands squeezing her breast through her dress, then travelling roughly down the curve of her body.

'John,' she panted, 'no, please. Not this way.'

'What way?' he grunted, forcing her down with him on to the grass. 'Listen, Jessica, please darling, I need you. *Now* . . .'

Whatever he needed her for it wasn't love. Not at that moment. He seemed a stranger. Panic took her over. If she gave way – and so it would be doing, for at this moment she felt no desire for him – it would ruin all she felt for him. She couldn't explain, she couldn't argue, she just knew this was so.

'Soon, John.' She was hardly aware of what she was saying. 'Soon. Another two weeks. That's all.'

Something was wrong, very wrong. Why couldn't she? Why wouldn't she? There must be something wrong with her.

Her arms were round him, trying to reassure, love . . . but he pushed her away and, half crying, said wildly, 'If I'm shot down, you'll wish you had. It'll be your fault.'

Chapter Seven

What the hell had made him say that? Now in the bright light of morning John was faintly ashamed of himself for taking it out on Jessica when heaven knew only she was keeping him going. But he needed a woman. Christ, how he needed one.

They'd been at readiness since dawn, just waiting . . . for it all to start again, for them to be flung into the mêlée once more. The day was damp and cheerless. The waiting was worse than the action. Conversation at dispersal dwindled to zero as they strained their ears for the alert, willing something to happen so that they could replace thought with action, have the blessed catharsis of running for their Spits, chocks away, and onwards and upwards into the air away from the depressing life below. He could go to see Jessica tonight. He could explain . . . she'd understand. But, hell, why couldn't she? It wasn't much. Or was it? Was she perhaps right? He loved her now, needed her with a fierce possessiveness that he'd never felt before. He was tired, he knew it. By the time they were married they'd have won; victory and a new life with Jessica. Hell, this waiting! Why didn't the bastards come? He ground a cigarette stub under his foot nervously.

Wherever his thoughts turned, they always came back to this: the heavy leaden weight that no amount of beer, no woman, could remove. Could he face it again, yet another battle, another yellow-nosed monster aiming right for you or creeping up behind? He'd had a long talk with the CO on tactics. Tackle the bombers as a priority, not the fighters. It smacked of avoiding conflict, but it made sense. The Spit squadrons were only to go up in pairs, two high, two low; no more letting them swan off on their own, Gale. Formation, discipline, to hell with derring-do. Try telling that to the Polish squadrons! It was like trying to fly in formation with a bunch of excitable puppies.

Formation was all very fine, but in the end it still came down to one thing for the poor devil in the cockpit: a 109 trying his damnedest to shoot you down. He wondered whether the others felt like this: Will with his calm detachment; Graham with single-minded intensity; Seb with his bull-dog tenacity. Raining now. Would they never come? The entire day passed and they did not. At Fighter Command Dowding could hardly believe it – they hadn't come. Was it a trick, or could it be victory?

The sudden euphoria at Fighter Command did not extend to West Forstling. At six o'clock they were stood down. Anticlimax hit them all. Unable to bear the mess, with its frenetic talk, John Gale thought about the evening. Irritable, depressed, he was in no mood to see Jessica. He'd go to the pictures. Alone. The Ritz was showing *Night Train to Munich*. No war films for him. He'd go to the Granada. *Pinocchio*. A kids' film. Why not go and 'Whistle a happy song', he thought ironically. It couldn't depress him more.

There weren't many people in the Granada that night, being a Monday. But sitting with a friend was a girl he recognised: Vanessa. He saw her shining blonde hair with a sense of doom. She turned and saw him. As their eyes met, he rose and with sinking heart went towards her unquestioningly, a man with no strength left to resist.

Thunder rumbled in the distance as Jessica lay awake. No word from John. Had he flown today? Surely not. The wireless said there had been little activity in the air, but suppose his squadron had been the one of the few chosen to fly today? Perhaps that was why there was no word. But why hadn't he come this evening?

She had thought and thought over what had happened, first bitterly regretting it, then reasoning that she was right. Yet reason didn't always comfort. She turned over and thumped the pillow. There was something in her that made her obstinately resist making love before their wedding. He needed her, yet she had stopped him. She'd try to explain when she saw him but, for the first time in her life, didn't understand herself. She was in love, she wanted nothing more than to belong to John completely. And yet . . . She listened to the sound of the rain beating against the window, but sleep would not come. There was still that unanswered question: why not?

Scramble!

Immediately there were men running over the grass, leaping out of deckchairs, running out of the hut, Mae Wests on, charged with adrenalin.

John Gale ran, as he ran in his dreams every night. Cockpit check, throttle forward, the wave of the hand to Bert, chocks away and into the air, leading his flight in close formation. Today the lift into the air failed to give him the usual spurt of excitement. It was a job, that was all. Perhaps that was how Will and Mac coped with it. Forget about the flying itself, they were there to knock out Germans. Raids hadn't stopped, but they'd changed. No longer the massive formations by day at any rate, but sporadic hit and run sorties on selected Kentish towns.

Fifty-plus bandits, control had said, heading for the Medway towns. Dorniers must be reproducing like rabbits; no matter how many they shot down, more always came. And the fighters came with them. Twenty thousand now and no sign of the bastards. Yes, there they were. Black devils, two thousand feet below.

'Red Leader, 109s above at four o'clock. Angels 24.'

It was Will's voice, calm, reassuring. Thank God for Will. The oldest trick of all, a second formation, up sun above them, waiting till they dived. He informed Ops they'd made contact, then suddenly exhilarated, he shouted: 'Red Section, climbing attack, tally ho.'

Taken by surprise the Messerschmitts were sitting ducks. Unable to control their dive, two of them went hurtling onwards, caught by the fire of the Brownings. Twelve joined the mêlée with the oncoming Spitfires. Now the first formation was coming up behind them. John Gale felt the crump of machine gun fire; he would turn *inside*. That would stop their game. Inwardly he was calm, a part of him watching from outside, detached. Why couldn't he turn in? Why not? *Why not*? The sky seemed full of parachutes, flame and smoke, black dots dancing in front of his eyes. The radio was dead. What the hell height was he at? The instruments were gone. Thank the Lord the Brownings were still in action. A hit . . . Another one for Jessica. He owed it to her. He hadn't had the courage to face her yet. Not after Monday night . . .

The whole aircraft banked and shuddered. What the hell was happening? He was losing height, the petrol gauge plummeting, a hit in the tank – not good. He could smell petrol but remained calm, still detached from it all. He'd have to land . . . but he wouldn't make it back to West Forstling. Manston? Forward landing ground. No hope now. Bale out? A quick look down. No, too low. Spiralling. 'Down, down, I come, like glistering Phaethon.' Who had said that? Did it matter? He might catch fire. Like Gerry. Gerry – Vanessa. No, he wouldn't think about that. Jessica – what was it he'd said to her? Crazy. He must have been mad. He'd tell her so. He'd have to crash-land. Find a field. That one!

The long grass came up quicker, and at a crazier angle than he would have believed possible. Please don't let it catch fire! he breathed in a maelstrom of emotions and fears. His father. His father wouldn't let this happen. He was down with a sickening crunch and a lurch and slither, earth, grass and stone being flung in all directions, tortured steel creaking. He was down, he was going to make it.

The petrol didn't explode, the aircraft didn't burn, but the anti-invasion barricades so neatly hidden in the long grass caught the careening, bucking Spitfire and flipped it over. He was dead when they cut him free.

* * *

On his way back from the flight hut, Will Donaldson ran into Graham Macintosh. One glance and there was no need to ask whether he'd heard. They nodded to each other, and carried on their separate ways. There was nothing to say.

The oasthouse looked warm and comforting in the fitful sunlight of the evening. Will paused before the door, cursing the CO. Wasn't it enough to cope with his own grief, without this? 'You know the girl, don't you, Donaldson? Splendid. I'll leave her to you, then. I'll write to the parents.'

'Sir, I—'

The CO looked at him. 'She'll take it better coming from you,' he said easily.

Damnfool thing to say, Will thought savagely. He couldn't blame the CO, though. It was happening all the time. He couldn't know this one was special. He lifted the old brass lion knocker, and let it fall; he heard her footsteps running. She'd be thinking it was John.

The door opened. He registered her pale intense face; the pulse at her throat; the small V of the neckline of her brown-patterned summer frock. Afterwards they remained imprinted on his memory. He saw the look on her face change from surprise to realisation as she took in instantly why he was there. He never forgot it.

Her mouth parted slightly, but she could not speak. He saw her swallow.

'This afternoon,' he said.

'Missing – he's missing, injured?' A wild note of hope.

'No, Jessica.'

She tried to speak, failed, tried again. 'I wanted to tell him but he didn't come – he didn't come.' She knew she wasn't making sense and stared at Will blindly.

'I'd better come in,' he said. It was the last thing he wanted to do.

She pushed a nervous hand through her hair. 'I was just going to feed the birds,' she said in a high voice. 'I'd better do it.'

He followed her through to the garden. 'Lind's been singing a lot today,' she said conversationally. 'Astaire hasn't been too good, it's getting more difficult to get – oh!'

He heard the intake of breath, the slight movement of her body, and in a stride he was with her, holding her arms then pulling her into his as she gasped and doubled up with agony. He held her to him closely, fiercely, as though by this means they could gain mutual strength. Then she gulped and visibly drew herself together: 'How – no, I don't want to know. It wasn't fire, was it? Was he—' she stopped '– bleeding?' 'Pretty, stupid in a fighter pilot, eh?' she heard John saying again.

'Neither.'

'What does it matter anyway, he's dead,' she said dully, defeated.

'I guess it does matter, Jessica. If not to him, to the rest of us. His second gong came through today, and he shot another one down. He won't be forgotten. He did something.'

'They're words. They don't mean anything.'

'Do you think I don't know that?' he retorted angrily.

'But there's got to be some way to reach you, Jessica. And at this moment, there's only words.'

She looked at him through a haze. 'If anyone could reach me, you could. But no one can, can they? We're all alone.'

He went straight to bed that night when he got back from Frittingbourne Manor. Jessica had asked one thing – that he tell her parents. Unwillingly he had done so, sat there through the sobs, the woe, the embraces, and behind all it Cicely's one obvious thought – that there wouldn't be a wedding. That was almost the worse of the two ordeals.

Will lay in bed unable to sleep, grief burning his eyes, and thought about John Gale. Thought of the talks they'd had about religion, politics, of the better world there'd be when this war was over. Of thought versus action. The virtues of intellect versus emotion. He thought of John's telling him about his father, about how he'd left home for Oxford repudiating his father's religion, intellectualising himself out of it, but how he'd begun to wonder these last few weeks whether he was right; begun by distrusting emotion that led to packed churches in times of crisis, but gradually that distrust was becoming suspended, a belief in the validity of emotion taking its place, leading to a kind of faith.

A better world? Would there be one? John had died hoping so. Died a hero, everyone would say. But he was just a guy, like all of them, bloody scared and wouldn't admit it. And it struck Will that that was the better epitaph.

* * *

'Let's go dancing, Graham,' pleaded Vanessa. 'We could go to the Corn Exchange.'

'I can't, Vanessa. Not tonight. Tonight's different.'

Perhaps he had been commissioned, thought Vanessa. Another decoration. People were always telling her how good Graham was, and there was no doubt his devotion to her was useful. He had been surprised and flattered when Vanessa had continued to see him when she could have had her pick of the pilots in the mess. He had stoutly defended her against murmurs of disapprobation when she failed to visit Gerry Rhodes after her first disastrous visit.

'I've – we've had some bad news,' he said awkwardly. 'Will's gone to see Jessica to tell her.'

Vanessa looked blank, then a look of horror came over her face, a sudden chill gripping her as Graham went on: 'John Gale's bought it.'

The china blue eyes opened wide and blank. 'John?' A shrill shriek. '*Johnnie*? Dead?'

Graham nodded, too overwhelmed by his own misery to wonder at this overreaction.

Vanessa burst into hysterical sobs, leaving Graham awkwardly comforting her. It was a shock, but these things happened, he managed to get out. With no outlet his own misery grew. John Gale dead. Part of his life was wrenched away and he must bear it alone.

Jessica closed up inside herself. She made no more contact with West Forstling. She continued hop-picking dry-eyed, calmly telling Cicely not to fuss, mechanically undoing all the wedding arrangements with Maggie's help. She refused to have a chat with the Rector, as her father awkwardly suggested. She refused all invitations. She attended the funeral, met John's parents there as she would have done at the wedding, shared their grief, talked of him and the life they would have had, and nothing touched her. She had determined that nothing would.

Will telephoned once to ask her to come to the airfield; she refused, and he did not try again.

Tom was her only ally. He was of Frittingbourne as she was, part of her roots. Not as John had been, swooping from the sky, scooping her up and then letting her fall. Tom asked quietly what plans she had. Plans? She had no plans. She was a schoolmistress. Term had started again, and whatever time she had to spare she spent in the garden. People declared it unnatural. She would have agreed with them, but to her there seemed no choice.

She talked to no one, for no one could help her. Inside lay guilt she buried deep for fear it would destroy her if she faced it. To her it was straightforward enough: John had said it would be her fault if he got shot down, for she had failed him in her love. And he *had* been shot down. Her oasthouse, once a refuge, became a prison, locking her in with her memories. Her only defence was to empty her mind of everything and everyone save the job in hand.

It took Vanessa four days to come to see Jessica. Wrapped up in herself, Jessica had not registered her absence.

'Hello, Jess.' Vanessa was paler, slightly less exuberant. 'Sorry not to have been before. How are you, darling?'

Jessica shrugged.

'Jess, I'm so sorry,' cried Vanessa, hugging her as in the days of old, genuinely sad for her. The strained atmosphere between them for the past few weeks vanished.

'There's nothing you can do, Vanessa,' said Jessica, trying to respond. 'Nothing anyone can do.'

'I was jealous when you got engaged, Jessica. Did you realise? I feel guilty now.'

'Jealous? Why?' asked Jessica, frowning.

Taken aback, Vanessa covered quickly. 'Well, there were you engaged and – happy. And there was me who'd always wanted to marry a fighter pilot, with Gerry shot down in hospital . . .' She managed a look of pain.

'Oh, Vanessa,' sighed Jessica, laughing to her own surprise. 'You could have every pilot on the station at your feet if you wanted. You've got most of them there already.'

But I didn't have that one, thought Vanessa bitterly. Not completely. When it came to the crunch he'd chosen Jessica. God knew why. It must have been the money. Fond though she was of her cousin, she could see Jessica wasn't exactly a pin-up. And John had wanted *her*, Vanessa. Goodness knows he'd wanted her! She remembered their last night together, after the film show, the touch of his hands and the way she'd had him moaning in her arms as she tantalised then satisfied him. A smile rose to her lips at the memory. Hastily she removed it. Was it only five days ago that he'd been alive and in her arms, loving her, passionately loving her? *Her*, not Jessica.

'I suppose I was lucky,' Jessica was saying. 'I had him all to myself. Someone like John. It always did seem too good to be true.'

Someone like Johnnie Gale! thought Vanessa bitterly.

Jessica didn't know the first thing about him. If only she could tell her . . . Perhaps she should. After all, Jessica shouldn't go on thinking Johnnie a whiter than white hero for the rest of her life. It wouldn't be good for her, for that way she'd never meet anyone else. She'd never look at Tom, for instance, if she held up Johnnie as a model for comparison. For a moment Vanessa wavered, then decided to bide her time. It would come. Perhaps inevitably, she thought, suddenly remembering her own plight, with panic sweeping over her once again.

'Oh, Graham, must you keep on? I'm sorry, I wasn't listening.'

'I said,' his voice raised slightly, 'we're being posted next week over to the Cotswolds. Apparently, they've just noticed that our squadron has been on operations continuously since the beginning of July, and now the day battle's slackening slightly they've decided they can do without us. We're going.'

He had Vanessa's full attention now. 'Going?'

'You won't be sorry, will you, Vanessa? I know I bore you.'

'No, no—' her voice trailed off. 'I'm sorry, Graham. I've a lot on my mind.' All sorts of alarm bells were ringing in her brain. She drew closer to him on the sofa. 'Graham, I'm so sorry. About your being posted. It means we won't be able to see so much of each other. Unless I moved too, found a job near you.'

Pure astonishment was in his voice. 'I thought you'd be glad to see me go.'

'How can you think that, Graham? You don't understand me at all, do you?' There she was right. 'Just because I like enjoying myself, having a good time, flirting a little, that doesn't mean I don't know what's important in life, what I really want.' She inched closer to him, until the smell of the rosemary rinse she used on her hair filled his nostrils and made his senses swim.

'Vanessa,' he said urgently.

Graham Macintosh was a skilled lover, both astonishing and delighting her. For all his ineptitude socially, when it came to basics he was confident and assured. Life might not be so bad, thought Vanessa dizzily some time later. Besides, he was commissioned now.

Graham Macintosh believed himself the happiest man in the world, and Vanessa vowed in gratitude that she would keep it that way.

News travelled fast. Will entered the mess and was greeted with it from all sides: 'Macintosh has snatched the fairy off the Christmas Tree.' Will looked puzzled. 'The blonde princess is to marry our favourite flight sergeant.'

'Macintosh and Vanessa Gray?' queried Will. He tossed down a couple of glasses of beer while he thought it over. He could never get used to this tepid watery concoction, but tonight he needed something to help him to think.

On Tuesday he went to the mess dance alone. He didn't want Molly there, for this time he had a purpose. Macintosh would be there with Vanessa, having achieved her heart's desire – he had been recommended for an immediate commission for gallantry. There were still a few rumblings about his admission to the officers' dance before confirmation had actually come through, but it was generally reckoned he was admissible now, and Vanessa would not hesitate to take full advantage of this at the first opportunity.

She arrived, blooming, on Graham's arm.

Will waited some time for her to be free, then spotting his opportunity coolly took her arm. 'My turn, I guess.'

'Why, Will, I didn't know you cared.' She flashed him a smile.

'Cut it out, sweetheart. I need to talk to you. Let's go out on the terrace.'

'You'd better make sure Graham doesn't see us,' she said lightly. 'He's the jealous type.'

'This won't take long. I want to know how Jessica's getting along,' he began carefully.

Something that might have been relief flooded her eyes. 'She's taking it frightfully well,' she replied brightly.

'She's not and you know it,' replied Will unemotionally.

'What do you mean?'

'You know her better than anyone, Vanessa. You've grown up with her. She was in love with John, and being Jessica, that means it's serious. What's she going to do?'

'Nothing, she says,' muttered Vanessa shortly.

'She ought to—' He broke off. He wasn't going to discuss that with Vanessa. Now to the point, 'What have you said to her about John, Vanessa?'

Her eyes danced. So she was right. But she must be careful. 'What should I say? What a hero he was, how he died for his country, how he died with her name on his lips—'

'You're a goddamned bitch, Vanessa,' Will informed her without heat.

She was taken aback. 'What do you expect me to say, Will?' she burst out. 'That he was a lying cheat? That he was sleeping with me while he was engaged to her? That he didn't want her at all, not the way he wanted me.'

'But you're not going to tell her that ever, are you?' Will said flatly.

'I don't know,' she said sullenly. 'I think she ought to know. She can't go through life believing in a lie.' She stole a glance at him.

'There are only two people she can find that out from,' said Will slowly. 'She'll never know from me, and I'm going to make pretty damn sure she doesn't from you. So we're going to get this straight now. The squadron's leaving next week, and you're coming with us as Macintosh's wife, I gather. You won't tell Jessica about John before you go.'

'If I do . . .'

'I'll find out,' said Will evenly.

'So?' she sneered.

'And I'll tell Graham you're carrying John's kid.'

She cried out, then laughed nervously as he watched her. He was right. It had been a logical guess, but a guess all the same.

'It might be Gerry's,' she flashed.

'No,' said Will. 'If it was you'd have been to East Grinstead to see him, see if you could stick being married to him. You haven't, and being pregnant's the only possible reason you're marrying Graham Macintosh – unless you've suddenly come to your senses and realised what a good guy he is. I think you've just found out and you're running scared, lady, running scared.'

'You can't prove it,' she hissed.

'I don't have to.'

'I'll make Graham a good wife,' she said defiantly.

'You can be darn sure of that. I'll keep tabs on you.'

'What's it to you, anyway?' she asked suspiciously.

Will paused. 'Let's just say I owe John Gale a life.'

'I hope you don't mind.' Molly was waiting outside the school gates in her uniform. 'Will asked me to come along. He's worried about you.'

'He has no need to be,' said Jessica shortly, then, ashamed of herself, apologised. 'But I'm all right, really I am.'

'You don't look all right,' said Molly bluntly. Jessica looked strained, dazed. 'Are you going to Vanessa's wedding?'

'I suppose so,' said Jessica. She managed a grin. 'I suppose that sounds churlish.'

'No,' said Molly. 'That's how we all feel about it. What a chump Graham is! Oh, I keep forgetting she's your cousin.'

Jessica laughed. 'I agree with you. But she's fond of him. I don't know why the special licence, though.'

'The squadron's being posted, that's why. Didn't you know?'

'No.' Jessica's thoughts whirled. Relief was part of it in a way; so was a strange kind of emptiness, as though a further prop were knocked from her life. If only it had happened earlier, before . . .

'Are you going too?' She summoned up a smile.

'No, I'm station staff. I'll still be around.'

'I'm glad.' Jessica said it spontaneously and realised how much she meant it. Molly looked pleased. 'Won't you miss Will?'

'I suppose I shall.' She shot a look at Jessica. 'But there's nothing like that between us. He's a good friend, but it's not going to be wedding bells. Not for yours truly.'

'Oh.'

'He's a long way from home and I'm a friendly face.'

'Does Will need that? He seems so self-sufficient.'

'I wouldn't say that,' said Molly, surprised. 'He's got some pretty thick armour plating up, though. He was training to be a professional musician back home, he says. It must have cost him a lot to throw it up and come over here.' She chattered on until they reached the oasthouse.

'Come in and have some tea,' Jessica invited.

'What wouldn't my mum give to see this?' Molly laughed, as she entered. 'We only knew oasthouses when they were full of hops, and old Bill the dryer putting our potatoes in the ashes. Scrumptious! Hey—' she broke off. 'You've got a visitor.'

Tom stood up and cleared his throat. 'Sorry, Jessica, the door was open so I thought I'd come in and wait. I've brought the books you asked for.' His eyes travelled to Molly.

'Hey there, partner,' said Molly cheerfully. Then, in mock disgust, 'He doesn't even recognise me, and there I was clasped in his arms but a mere two weeks ago.' Too late she remembered the occasion.

Seeing her face, Jessica said gently: 'It's all right,

Molly, the world hasn't stopped, you know.' But it had for her, trapped in a warp of her own making.

Tom put the books on the table, and came back to them.

'Of course I recognise you,' he said. 'Molly Payne. I've been living off that turnip salad you told me about ever since.'

'Splendid,' said Molly. 'I'll come and share it some day. With Jessica.' They exchanged worried glances.

Will sat down in the old chintz-covered chair, his long body awkwardly arranged, legs sprawling.

'This is one swell place here,' he said wistfully. 'I'm going to miss it – miss Kent, that is,' he amended. 'You've heard the news?'

'Molly told me you're being posted,' Jessica replied stiffly. She was used to the idea now, and betrayed no disappointment. She sat down opposite him, hands clasped round her knees. So much was happening; they were all leaving, Vanessa with them. Why didn't they just go? Why this need to say goodbye? She wanted to be on her own, yet dreaded it.

'Yup. I'm being posted, but not to the West Country. I'm headed north. Yorkshire, they tell me. They're forming an all-American squadron and they need flyers like me with combat experience to train the new boys. 71 Eagle Squadron, they're calling it.'

'I'll miss you,' she said sincerely.

'Come with me.'

'What?'

'You have to do something with your life, Jessica. Join up. Be a Waaf. Apply to Uxbridge as a musician. That's where RAF music is organised from. The CO of

71 Squadron needs me bad and I reckon I could get you on the station strength quick as a spit. Then we could make a start on the work. Get that sound going. You could sing.'

'No.' The word stretched between them, the silence razor-sharp.

'Okay. If that doesn't appeal,' he went on, carefully measuring his words, 'I'll introduce you to the fellow I know in London.'

'No.' The word was almost choking her.

He stood up quickly, fighting for control. 'Just what are you planning to do then?' he asked with deadly calm.

She stood up to face him, temper roused.

'I knew it,' she said. 'You came here to lecture me. Again. You came to tell me I've got to live, and all that nonsense. You're just like everyone else, Will. Well, you're wasting your time. That part of me, of my life, is over.'

'Goddammit, it never began. Are you telling me that you don't plan to sing any more?'

'Leave my voice out of it.'

'How the hell can I? How the hell can *you*?'

She faced him trembling. 'It's my voice. I decide what to do with it.'

'You can't. You've a God-given duty to do something with it, woman. He gave it to you, now give something back to Him.'

'By singing to the forces, I suppose. Entertaining the troops.' Her voice was scornful.

'Sure, and what the hell's wrong with that, Madame Melba? What's wrong with high and mighty you making them think there's a world here worth fighting for? Sing for victory, sing for a better world, sing for John Gale if you like.'

'No,' she moaned, clasping her hands over her ears.

'Jessica.' He came to her in alarm. 'What the hell have I said? Have I gone too far? What is it? Why look like that?' He was shaking her to get some response.

'You don't understand, Will,' she panted, 'you don't. I want to sing. I want to sing more than anything. I always have, I always will. But I can't, because I promised John I wouldn't.'

'Are you crazy?'

'No, I promised him I wouldn't sing for anyone but him. He asked it of me and I promised. So I can't.'

He let her go abruptly, and after a moment said quietly: 'He wouldn't have meant it, Jessica. He wasn't that sort of a guy. He was under strain, fatigued. If he made you promise that then he wasn't seeing things clearly at the time. Men say things when they're in love they don't mean seriously.'

'Maybe, but he's not here to ask, is he?' she said steadily. 'And I promised. I owe it to him—'

'Owe? Why owe?'

She was silent. She had said too much, allowed him to trespass on the private ground that was hers and John's. The reason for which she could never break her promise she could not tell him.

He came across to her and took her hand, drawing her down on the sofa. 'Listen, Jessica, I want to explain. You know I'm a clarinetist; I was all set to be a professional but the war came along. I started classical, but got interested in jazz and what Benny Goodman was doing with his clarinet to turn jazz into something different: swing. I was going to play with the Dorseys, then war came along. I haven't forgotten, maybe I'll get back to it, but I just like the clarinet doing everything and anything. The sound of it stirs something in me, takes me over – it's my life. I like messing around with the band here a lot, but it reminds me of unfinished business. Where do you go after swing? An unfinished sound in my head, if you like.

'But when you sang that night with us on stage, I knew what it was. It was like I'd known it all my life and never put it into form. There was a great clarinet player called Willman in England a couple of centuries back. They said he got sounds like liquid honey out of his clarinet, and that when he accompanied the singer Eliza Salmon there were passages you couldn't tell which was voice and which clarinet. Two of her uncles were clarinetists and she learned to sing to their accompaniment, so her voice grew rich and resonant. Like yours, Jessica, like yours.

'Any good player can blow an obligato to complement the voice, but getting the pianissimo right, getting the right tone into it, getting it right instinctively because the voice is with it, *that*'s what we can do. Only us. That's the sound I've been after all my life, and not just any voice. Your voice. Made for clarinet. Made for my sound. Melody and harmony. Voice taking over where the clarinet leaves off, then dovetailing, blending into one whole – and that's what I'm after. The whole. See here, I brought my music with me.'

He picked up his case and took out the clarinet,

putting it together with loving care, testing the reed. Jessica watched curiously, interested, wary. He held his breath, praying he'd get it right.

'Sing, Jessica,' he urged gently, 'you just have to sing . . .'

He began to play the nightingale folk song she'd sung to him; she listened for a moment, then got caught up unwillingly in that tempo, the new idea; the clarinet was demanding, insisting, and hesitantly she began to sing. How could it hurt, just one song? Her voice carolled the chorus, the clarinet first following her, then pausing, then picking up the melody of the verse when she halted, so perfectly blending in that one seemed a part of the other.

'As she sings in the valley below.'

The sound came to a stop and lingered in the air about them. He laid the clarinet down. 'You see,' he said, triumphant. 'It's possible. It's a start. It is there somewhere waiting for us. We'd find it.'

She was silent, torn, shaken, tempted by a passion she had not reckoned with.

He picked up the clarinet and began softly to play again. Another melody this time.

'That's your song, isn't it?' she said abruptly. 'The song without the singer. You're cheating, Will.'

'No,' he said. 'You're cheating. Cheating on life. Here are the words. Now I want the singer.'

She took the piece of paper and looked at it. Her eyes filled with tears as she glanced at them, heard herself singing them in her imagination, then gave it back. 'I can't, Will,' she said slowly. 'I can't. I promised. Find another song, another singer.'

Without a word he put the clarinet back in its case, and rose to his feet. He walked steadily through the doorway, quickening his pace along the path until he reached the parked Lincoln. As the sound of the engine died away in the distance, the silence closed around her once more, welcoming her back into its sterile embrace.

Part Two

Where the Primroses Grow

'Pray sit yourself down
With me on the ground
On this bank where the primroses grow'

– *The Sweet Nightingale*

Chapter Eight

'Assistant Section Officer Gray!'

Jessica halted as she walked away from the operations room. Molly was calling after her, conscious that now Waafs were under the same disciplinary code as the RAF, the correct formalities must be observed.

Biggin Hill was somewhat of a 'show' station this year, well known for its battle of Britain rôle and sufficiently near London for celebrities to call in all too frequently with the accompanying bull their visits engendered. Here too the Waafs held a somewhat privileged position. Last year, just over three months before Jessica arrived in early December, one of a relentless succession of raids had wiped out the Waafs' quarters, together with forty of the occupants. For the rest of the winter they shared the same discomforts as the men in an airfield whose buildings had been completely flattened (the last one by the station commander, who surmised that the Luftwaffe would not leave them alone while a single building stood). The winter turned the field into a nightmare; billets were miles away and the station buildings merely tented or temporary.

Now the station was rebuilt, but not unscathed. In April a raid destined for London had dropped a load of incendiaries on Biggin Hill, doing yet more damage. Biggin became the least popular posting in the country, with a corresponding upsurge of respect for the hitherto somewhat scorned Waafs who actually applied for posting here.

Molly caught up, grimacing at the need for public formality and lapsing into their usual friendliness. 'You've heard the news? Two missing today. A scrap over France, of course.'

Of course. The squadrons were still in action, though the night fighters were taking on blitz bomber formations. Rodeos, Roadsteads, Circuses and Rhubarbs had replaced the dogfights of the Battle of Britain.

Jessica did not comment, for there was nothing to say. The war went on with its endless slaughter, damage and heartbreak for civilian and serviceman alike.

'Target for tonight is Shepherd's,' went on Molly after a moment. 'Coming? There's a dozen of us going on a late pass.'

'Why not?' Jessica joked. 'Now what shall I wear – my pink satin or the real silk?'

'How about your charming little costume in blue?' Molly chimed in to the well-worn joke.

'Oh, you're right, just the thing, with regulation knickers underneath.'

'And a fashionable darn on each stocking ankle.'

One of the crowd, for another evening. But being with Molly was far better than being alone. Thank heavens for her. Jessica had volunteered for the Women's Auxiliary Air Force three weeks after John's death, much to Tom's disapprobation, just as soon as the school could find a replacement. It seemed to her that she might, by joining the WAAF be doing something in some small way for John, by helping his friends, his service. No amount of hysterics from her mother, of cajoling from her father, of patient reasoning from Tom, had swayed her. None in fact had reached her. On one level she went about daily life calm and dry-eyed; on another, deep inside herself, a vast emptiness shot through with searing flashes of pain concentrated her thoughts on this one path to the future. A path that would take her away from her mother and Frittingbourne. And, unacknowledged to herself, away from all temptation that she might yet succumb and follow Will's beckoning hand. In the WAAF music could not throw its spell around her.

'You're doing the wrong thing,' Tom had said lightly, as she packed her books at the school for the last time.

'Perhaps, but I shall do it all the same.'

And that was all. Routine, dull, gruelling training was just what she needed, for only physical weariness would make her sleep at night. After training was complete, and she had gone through officers' selection process in a daze, she had gone to Biggin in early December, three weeks after Molly. She had been promoted to section officer and suggested that Jessica joined her at Biggin. 'Mud and muck,' she said cheerfully, 'but you won't mind that, will you?'

Mind? Jessica minded nothing any more. After those gruelling weeks of training with fellow volunteer airwomen, she could endure everything; listening to the excited chatter about boyfriends and clothes, and forcing herself to join in whenever she could. The hardest to endure were hours of enforced inactivity in the operations room. If Molly were on duty, fine; otherwise it was hard to keep from thinking. So she welcomed the emergencies, the sudden sprints into activity. Her free time could be filled with visits to the pictures, to the White Hart at Brasted and other favoured pubs, and dances. It had been agony at first, especially the dances. To feel other men's arms around her and know there was no John coming, to force herself to be merry, not for her own sake but for theirs, and then gradually to find it becoming not easier, but automatic; that if she switched off inside, 'flung roses riotously, riotously with the throng', in the words of the poem, it became easier. When physically exhausted, there was no time to sit and ponder. Did it help in the end, though? Probably not.

Once at Biggin Hill, she had Molly's help. She said nothing, behaved as though all were normal, and Jessica was grateful. Now the WAAF had come into its own, Jessica was showered with invitations, much as the pilots disliked dating fellow servicewomen; she accepted some, rejected many, and few persisted. For all her popularity, the message got through. Good companion only. She was emotionally numb. It was a conscious decision on her part. Some day the reckoning would come, but not now, and that was all that mattered.

Will Donaldson's squadron was operational at last. The old Hurricane wasn't so bad, but he sure missed his Spit. That Ju88's rear gunner had nearly got him – thank the Lord for Klodarski! Something to be said for those individualist cowboy tactics after all. He grinned to think what John Gale would have said about the Eagles' radio discipline. Calling in clear, no codes for them, ceaseless chatter about 'back home' and dames, interspersed with 'Jeesus they're clobbering me, guys. Come down and get 'em'. They hadn't got any yet, though. So far the losses were all on the Eagles' side. Crashes mainly. But they'd come through, sure as hell they would, now they were further south and away from Yorkshire. Hell, how that wind blew on the moors. He was used to low winter temperatures back in Massachusetts where he'd been raised, and in Ithaca where he'd been to university, but Yorkshire was something else.

Jessica was wishing she hadn't come. She should be used to these mess dances at Southdown, the house taken over by the RAF as the temporary officers' mess. She could even study the band objectively without wishing she were up there, without wondering what would have happened had she – no. They were good for a local band. She ground her cigarette out. She was smoking too much, everyone was. That vocalist was terrible. There was no way she was going to stand and listen to her.

'Jack, do me a favour. Dance with me.'

'Wallflower, eh? Unusual for you, Jessica me darling. Only for you would I desert my beer.'

Not soon enough, she thought ruefully as he breathed over her during the fox-trot. It was a run of the mill evening dance but she found herself enjoying it, making the right responses automatically without effort.

'We're being posted next week – the gen is West Forstling. Do they have girls as beautiful and funny as you, Section Officer Gray?'

'They do indeed,' she said gravely, ignoring the lurch in her stomach. 'In fact—'

She stopped. That appalling vocalist was crooning 'Berkeley Square'. She was transported away from Southdown back to Kippen Hall, to a smoke-filled room and the man she loved, back to the oasthouse garden and John Gale bending over Astaire's cage. The pain grew and overwhelmed her. No, she wouldn't think of it; she couldn't let it affect her. Excusing herself, she broke away from her partner and pushed her way outside to the terrace into the twilight, fighting for control.

Her partner had followed her. 'Are you all right, Jess?' he asked anxiously.

'Sorry, Jack – old ghosts,' she said with an effort at a smile. Everyone, after all, knew her story. John Gale had been well known, a frequent visitor to Biggin.

He looked embarrassed. 'If you're sure you're all right,' he murmured, and quickly retreated.

Old ghosts were embarrassing. Once ghosts were allowed in, you were finished. Any pilot knew that. She sighed. Everyone had ghosts here, private ghosts of their own: friends, families, sweethearts. What right had she to inflict hers on others?

Molly was by her side, having observed her exit. 'You'll have to do something, Jessica, you know,' she said matter-of-factly. 'You're cracking up.'

'I'm not, I'm doing fine.' Her defiance sounded weak even to her own ears.

'Look, I've got a forty-eight hour pass this weekend – why don't you wangle one, too? I've got to see my parents. We could stay with them on Friday, then book into a hotel for Saturday night. What better for a May evening than a night out in London? We could go to a show. Shall we? Just the two of us?'

Anywhere, without 'Berkeley Square' ringing in her ears.

'For heaven's sake,' Vanessa flung herself irritably into a chair. 'Aren't we ever going to get away from this dead and alive place?'

'You were keen to come here,' Graham pointed out reasonably. 'You could have stayed in Kent.'

Reason held no sway with Vanessa. 'I didn't have much alternative.'

'You could have stayed with your mother.'

She did not answer this. 'I thought it would be fun down here in the Cotswolds.'

'So it will be once the baby's come. There'll be mess dances—'

'Oh, goody goody! Old Pork Face condescending to me.' The CO's wife was not a favourite of Vanessa's.

'You're just tired out because of the baby. Only just over a month to go.'

'It might be early, the hospital said,' reflected Vanessa idly, twiddling a teaspoon.

'Good, then you won't have so long to wait.'

She stood up. 'I'll be glad to get rid of this heap.' She looked down at her stomach with disgust.

'I think you're beautiful like that,' said Graham truthfully.

'You're a dear old thing, Graham,' she said idly. 'Oh, but it's so boring in the country. At least in Kent there was a bit of life. It's just deadly here. And everything getting dreary. One can't even get any lipstick now, and clothes rationing. You've no idea how *difficult* it all is.'

'You won't have to worry about clothes when the baby comes,' said Graham incautiously. 'You'll be too busy.'

Vanessa shot a look at him. 'Oh, yes,' she said. 'But you'd like to look after him sometimes, wouldn't you? Take some leave to give me a break. I could go up to London now and then and stay with Millicent.'

'Millicent?' asked Graham, frowning.

'That old school friend of mine. She moved away. Married and has a flat in Mayfair. She's invited me up any time I like.'

'Come in, love. Don't stand there all day waiting for a silver lining.'

Jessica laughed and entered the small hallway.

'You'll have to share with our Molly, but you won't mind that, will you?'

'Not unless you've got your famous bean soup for supper, Mum,' said Molly affectionately, kissing her.

'Get along with you.'

Mrs Payne was an older version of Molly, round, bright-eyed, and bustling. Molly's three younger sisters trailed in silently to inspect their big sister and her friend. 'We sent them away at the beginning, but they were so unhappy in the country, we brought them back. Just in time for this lot.' Mrs Payne grimaced. 'We never got round to sending them again. Better to go together, that's what I say.'

'Mum,' said Molly warningly, 'no alarm and despondency now.'

'Perish the thought, love. Our lips are as stiff round here as the smell in the shelters. It's under the stairs for us now. Hope Hitler leaves us alone tonight – he's been a bit subdued recently – but then you'd know all about that, wouldn't you, in your job?' She sounded faintly wistful as though Molly's job took her into enchanted realms that her mother would never know.

After a quick wash in the bedroom, since the house in common with the rest of the neighbourhood did not boast a bathroom, they sat down to tea in the dining room which was almost entirely taken up with table and chairs to seat the six of them.

'Of course, your mother's Bubbles Gray, isn't she?' Mrs Payne chattered on. 'Father and me went to see her in *Hearts and Diamonds*. Lovely she was. Beautiful voice. It must have been fun for you, being her daughter.'

Jessica started to speak, then realised she could not shatter her hostess's illusions. 'Yes,' she said quickly, 'yes, it was.'

Molly gave her a grateful look and changed the subject. 'Aren't we waiting supper for Dad, Mum?'

'He won't be back till the morning. On nights at the Post this week. He's a section warden now, you know,' she announced with pride. 'Got four blokes under him. So full of himself you could pop him with a pin. He'll be back before you go, though. His loss. He's missing his favourite Woolton Pie tonight.'

'What on earth is that?'

'If Lord Woolton says it's all right, then that's that, but sometimes I think he's not got round to tasting it yet. I put potatoes, turnip and a nice bit of spring greens in it. It does look funny, I grant you that, but don't taste too bad if you shut your eyes.'

'Yes, it does,' muttered Angela, the youngest child.

'You shut up and thank the good Lord you've anything in your tummy at all. And be thankful I spared you tin-helmet pudding.' She produced a tin of peaches with pride. 'I've been saving them specially. Otherwise it would have been pot luck. Ah well, better pot luck than humble pie, as the posters say.'

'We'll just pop in for a drink and a sandwich. There'll be lots of service people there. It's early enough.'

Early enough it might be, but this Saturday evening the Crackers Club, just near Piccadilly Circus, was already crowded. Jessica looked round. 'I feel we're here on inspection,' she said uneasily, 'to be picked up. That isn't what you had in mind, is it?' she asked suspiciously. 'You really do have tickets for the theatre?'

'Yes, I really do. What a mind you have! Here's the evidence. *The Cochrane Revue* at the Savoy. Now have a martini and stop fussing. Even if it is a bit of a pick-up place, we don't *have* to be picked up. We're independent women.'

These women didn't look as if they valued independence, thought Jessica, looking round. She'd been to too many of these places now to be under any illusion. Out to vamp, despite the make do and mend campaign, with every cheap adornment under the sun. There were precious few servicewomen in uniform like her and Molly, though blue and khaki male uniforms were crowding everywhere. Goodness knows what they'd do when the threatened clothes rationing came in.

'There's Will,' said Molly suddenly, rising from her seat.

'Molly, don't!' Jessica's instinctive protest died on her

lips. How could she stop Molly saying hello? But in a trice she was back at West Forstling, hearing a familiar laugh, seeing a familiar tall figure, deceptively casual in the way he was lounging in a group of RAF-uniformed men, his arms round a girl who was very definitely not in uniform. Molly rushed over to him.

'Molly, honey, well here's a piece of serendipity,' Jessica heard him say. Molly murmured something and Jessica braced herself. Will turned to look at her, then seeing that she made no move to join them, slowly detached himself from the girl, eased out of the group and strolled over to her.

'Jessica, how are you doing?'

He made no attempt to kiss her, merely shook hands; his eyes took in the WAAF uniform, but he made no comment.

'Very well,' she said awkwardly. This was ridiculous. This was Will, her friend. She knew the few freckles on his cheek, she knew the quiff of his hair that hung over his temple for all he pushed it back. She knew the lazy smile that crept over his mouth and then into his eyes, the long sensitive musician's fingers. But there was no smile today. John's shadow lay between them. 'How are things with you?'

He shrugged. 'Kind of fun now we're operational. They're a great bunch in 71. That's a few of the guys there, those with the Eagle flashes on the left shoulder. You staying around here?'

'At the St Ermin's, on a forty-eight hour pass. We're stationed at Biggin. Molly and I are off to the Savoy – theatre,' she added hastily. Her voice sounded stilted even to her own ears.

'We're taking in a show, too,' he said casually. 'The Windmill again, I guess.'

The Windmill. Nudes? That didn't sound like Will. Was there a faint look of mockery in those hazel eyes watching her so coolly?

'Your girlfriend will enjoy that,' she said sweetly. 'Or is she one of them?'

He looked at her and simply said, 'Be seeing you, Jessica.' He returned to the group, leaving her feeling annoyed at descending to such cattiness, and irrationally deflated. What had she expected after all?

It began with the up-and-down uneerie wailing of the air-raid siren. People were so used to it now they didn't even leave the theatre for the shelters when the announcement came. The singers and actors usually continued regardless of the sound of bombers sweeping over, even of the crump of explosions that shook the theatre. Tonight though it seemed to be a false alarm, although the all-clear had not gone.

The doorman shook his head. 'They'll be coming,' he said with gloomy relish.

Aldwych underground station had been entirely given over to shelters, the branch line closed down, but even so there was a knot of people still fighting to get in, so full was it of overnight sleepers. People had taken up permanent residence even on the stairs, there was precious little room for casual passers-by, and what there was had long since been filled. The smell hit them even at the entrance.

'Be blowed to this,' said Molly. 'Let's try somewhere else.'

'The public shelter,' said Jessica. 'We could try that.'

'Let's try to make it back to the hotel, even if we have to shelter-hop. See if we can beat Jerry to it. Are you game?'

'You bet.'

A few people scurried by, but mostly the noise was of passing vehicles. The two girls ran gingerly through the darkened streets, laughing as they bumped into passers-by or lamp posts. 'One to us, and hoots to Old Göring,' Molly cried as they panted up to the doors of the St Ermin's Hotel.

The basement, with its solid three-foot thick walls, the remains of an old monastery, made an excellent shelter. It was already full of women in an array of nightdresses with fur coats hastily pulled on over or trousers pulled over pyjamas, and servicemen looking ill at ease, powerless to do anything but sit and wait, joking uneasily. Some were playing cards, some already endeavouring to sleep, although the lights were not yet out. Someone had brought down a gramophone, and the Squadronnaires were providing music for the irrepressible to dance to in a small space at one end of the basement.

A pair of strong uniformed arms, seemingly disembodied from their owner in the crush, pulled Jessica through the throng. Molly scrambled after her, and they managed to squeeze into a corner.

'All right here, me darling.' Jessica managed to sit on the floor, her head against the soldier's knees. Just as she was beginning to doze fitfully, the armada arrived; the roaring overhead menacing, pulsating. The first wave arrived just after eleven. It was to prove the last and most terrible night of the Blitz and the bombers did not stop until dawn, by which time their incendiaries had set London ablaze from end to end.

* * *

Broken glass lay everywhere. Dust rose from the rubble, vying with the acrid smoke to fill their nostrils. Charred embers floated through the air. The sky was still a mass of red from blazing fires as, bleary-eyed, they tumbled out of the shelter. The all-clear had not sounded until half-past five and they had only managed a few hours' fitful sleep before getting up to face the chaos outside.

The Chamber of the House of Commons had been wrecked and lay in ruins. Many streets were blocked, there was no public transport running, and fires raged out of control as the fire engines ran out of water to cope.

'They say the water mains were hit,' a porter told them with lugubrious pleasure. 'Couldn't get the water to the engines to put out the fires. And Old Father Thames is right down, too. My, Jerry's let us have it all right! They had to choose, so they say, whether to save the old Westminster 'all or the 'ouse. So they chose the 'all. Guy Fawkes must be laughing his socks off.'

'How about south of the river? Bermondsey?' Molly asked anxiously.

'Everywhere's been hit, love,' said the commissionaire, hearing her question. 'Very bad there. They hit the emergency dam in the basement of the old Surrey Music Hall. Killed a lot of firemen and lost all the water, too. What with that and the river being so low—' He shrugged. 'Bad down there, it is.'

'Mum and Dad!' Molly turned to Jessica. 'I must find out if they're all right.' She came back from the telephone, white-faced. 'The operator says all the lines are down. There's been a lot of damage there.' Her voice broke. 'Jessica, I've got to go and find out.'

'I don't think we'll get through. It'll take forever with no transport. Let's try, though.'

'No,' said Molly sharply. 'Not you. We've only got a forty-eight hour. I can walk. It'll take you all your time to get back to Biggin.'

'I don't care, I'm coming.'

'I do,' said Molly. 'I've got a reason. You haven't. I don't care a monkey's if I lose my commission.'

'Do you think I care about that?' cried Jessica. 'I'm coming.'

Molly glanced at her. 'All right. Let's get our things, and leave them down here.'

Jessica collected her own bag and waited impatiently in the foyer, now swarming with people. She waited – but in vain. Molly had gone alone. The idiot! She'd need someone with her – just in case. Jessica would have to follow her, she couldn't leave her alone. Besides, as a WAAF officer, she might be able to help with rescue work. She turned to go and cannoned into Will who was tearing into the hotel lobby.

'Oh!'

Will pulled her into his arms, his face slack with relief. 'Jessica, thank the Lord you're okay! When I heard the news, I got straight down here. I didn't know if you'd have made it back. Honey, I—' He stopped and pulled her to him roughly, the distant cool Will of yesterday disappeared as if he had never been. For an instant she clung to him, then remembered.

'Molly's gone,' she cried, pulling out of his arms. 'She's trying to get through to Bermondsey to see if her parents are all right. I've got to catch up with her. We're due back at Biggin at five.'

Will swore. 'She'll never get through,' he said. 'It's chaos out there. Most roads are impassable, all the railway stations out of action. No buses. How the hell's she going to get there?'

'Walk,' said Jessica succinctly.

'Okay, let's get going,' said Will simply. 'I've got the Lincoln here. Most of the City roads are closed, but we might get some of the way and walk the rest. Westminster bridge is blocked, no use trying to cross here. We could go west and double back south of the river or risk going east.'

'East. Let's try. Let's hope.'

Outside the hotel, evidence of Hitler's blitz over the winter and spring was everywhere, from the ruins of Christchurch opposite to the damaged Westminster Abbey. The scene round the House of Commons was still chaotic, although the ruined Chamber itself lay within. Though they could not see it, the swarms of firemen still there and the smell of burning was testimony of the damage wrought. A year ago Churchill had spoken here for the first time as leader of the country, and now it lay in ruins. The Lincoln slowly nosed its way eastwards, until Will said impatiently: 'We'll cross the river here. I guess we'd be better off walking.'

'You know the way?'

'Sure,' he said, 'I used to walk this way with Molly. If the house is okay, she'll be there; we can pick her up and take her back. If it's not—' He left the thought unfinished.

They picked their way through roads covered in rubble, some to the point where they were unrecognisable as roads, forced to make countless detours to find a way through.

'Just here. It should be here. I recognise that tobacconist's.' Jessica clutched Will's arm. 'But where's the street?'

A gap of forty feet lay between them and the next standing dwelling. A sick feeling welled up inside Jessica's stomach. A mere gap? But she'd slept here only twenty-four hours ago, eaten with the family. Mrs Payne's words came back to her: 'It's under the stairs for us now. Better to go together . . .'

Will put his arm round her shoulders, seeing the emotions passing over her face. 'There's Molly,' he said quietly.

She looked up to see Molly coming towards them, her face blank, eyes staring, accepting their presence unquestioningly. 'I shouldn't go any further,' she said conversationally. 'There's nothing to see. It's all gone. Not enough left to have a decent funeral with. It was fire, you see. Fire. Oh, God!' She covered her face with her hands.

Jessica threw her arms round her friend, could feel her shaking before she pulled herself away and said with a funny smile, 'You know all about being strong, don't you, Jessica? You'll have to teach me.'

'No,' said Jessica. 'I know nothing about it. Strong is only a word people use to describe your outside, not your inside.'

Molly wasn't listening, wrapped in a world of her own. 'The fire was still going; I couldn't get near. I could see Angela's toy bear, though. I managed to rescue it, I thought she'd like that.'

'She's alive?'

'Staying with neighbours. My aunt will look after her, I suppose. The other two, and Mum and Dad—' She stopped, then burst out: 'You read in the papers what a marvellous job all the air raid shelter wardens are doing, but in the end there's nothing any of them *can* do. All so busy being jolly, keeping going, but what comes after? I didn't know where to go, what to do, then someone saw me, grabbed my arm and sent me off to the incident room. Some stuck-up woman behind a desk regaling me with useless information – questions, nothing but questions – and asked was I all right? Of course I was all right. My whole family wiped out – Dad went back to try and help and a chunk of concrete got him – what else could I be but all right? I came back then, thought I might find something, help other people, but you can't get near. It's too hot.'

But there was something they could do. A word to the warden, and they were directed to the nearest safe site for rescue work, near the Town Hall which had received a direct hit. For three hours they worked in the wake of a heavy rescue team, easing the passage of the wounded, clearing rubble, saving pathetic possessions till, covered in grime, hair streaked with cinders, they had to leave for Biggin Hill. Molly had to be almost dragged away as though just being here contributed to the easing of her pain.

Why had she said she would come out with him? Jessica thought wearily. Will had stayed on in the mess, to 'see about a few things' he had said, and now insisted on taking her out, the last thing Jessica felt like after yesterday. 'Molly's the one you should be with,' she pointed out, as the Lincoln twisted and turned round the lanes.

'It wouldn't help too much at the moment,' he said soberly. 'It's you I want to see.'

'Why?' she said bluntly.

'I guess I was kind of cool in the club.'

She relaxed. 'You had your hands full,' she replied lightly.

He dismissed this impatiently. 'It was a shock – seeing you so changed.'

'Changed?' she repeated, startled. 'I'm not changed.'

'Guess you are, Jessica. You've not been singing, have you?'

'Have you been checking up on me?' she asked sharply.

'Nope. But it shows in your eyes. They're not alive any more. You're stuck in the past.'

'You expect me to forget John in eight months?' she asked angrily.

'Don't be a knucklehead. You don't have to die inside to remember someone.' He paused. 'I guess I'm not doing too well here, am I?'

'No, Will, I'm not up to this. Not after yesterday. What does my singing matter beside that?'

'We're pawns in this war, Jessica. We can use only what we've got to fight it. And you're not. Now, how about tea?'

They drew up outside an enormous old roadhouse, obviously converted from an old barn, standing in the middle of the countryside.

'I'm coming round to the idea of tea. They don't go for it in Massachusetts. The Boston tea party still rankles. Have you been here before?'

'I've heard the men talking about this place,' she said with interest. 'I've never come, though. Now, Will, look – no more lecturing me about singing. All right?'

'Scouts' honour.'

'You don't have scouts,' she said suspiciously.

'We do at that. Right near where I come from on the old Mohawk Trail there's a scout camp where the Indians used to hold their war councils. Beat that, honey.'

'I surrender,' she said, laughing.

Inside the building was heavily beamed and surrounded by a musicians' gallery.

'A band could play up there, I guess,' he murmured innocently.

'What's the Eagle Squadron like?' asked Jessica meaningfully.

He grinned. 'Not too good while we were fooling around during the winter with nothing to do except train. Flying Hurricanes, too. I miss the Spit. Now we're in 11 Group we're seeing some of the action, and it's beginning to turn around. We've been doing a mighty lot of hip-shooting and now we're putting our guns where our mouths were. We're converting to the Hurricane IIa now – it's more manoeuvrable.' He went on to talk tactics. 'The news is we're going to North Weald. I'll be pretty near London.' He paused, but she did not comment.

I'll see more of him, was her first thought – the pleasure replaced immediately by fear. But Will had only seen the pleasure for he touched her hand lightly.

'Let's go for a walk, if you've finished up your whole year's ration of jam and cakes.'

'You don't do so bad yourself,' she observed, 'in the sweet tooth department.'

'Ah, well, you know how they define a Yankee from

our part of the world: one who eats apple pie for breakfast – with a knife.'

'Do you miss it, Will?' she asked curiously, as they paid the bill and left.

'Apple pie or the States?'

'The States, you idiot.'

'Oh, yes. There's times when I stand in these small fields and can smell so clearly the smell of the Berkshires, hear the rushing of the Deerfield River, and I feel all closed in. I look at your pretty clapboarded cottages that have stood since Queen Bess was around and see only the huge, handsome clapboarded inns and homes of Massachusetts; feel as if I could walk right into the Red Lion – that's the inn at Stockbridge where my folks are – and order ten of their blueberry muffins right off.'

'We have muffins, too. You do like England as well?' For some reason she was anxious he should say yes.

'Sure. I like its pubs and its folks, and I like the way your hair bounces red in the sunlight with those crazy curls, and I like your beer, and those cute little flowers.' He indicated some late primroses. 'The babies are cute, too – and the women.'

'Like the one you were with on Saturday?'

'That must be what I had in mind.'

He took her hand, and squeezed and kept it in his as they began to stroll down the lane. Then he stopped abruptly, gazing into the woods bordering the narrow road. 'What are these little blue fellows?'

'Early bluebells. Don't you have bluebell woods in Massachusetts?'

'We have bluebells, sure, but they're not like these. Not—'

She glanced at him. 'Like a magic carpet,' she finished.

He jumped over the stile and squatted down, studying them. 'When you look at each one, it's just a flower. But together – they're like that nightingale song of yours, Jessica. Got the same kind of feel. I could *play* these bluebells. Come on, Jessica, come on.' He seized her hand and pulled her over the stile into the wood.

'Steady, Will,' she half cried, half laughed. 'You can't go dashing over magic carpets. They have to be trodden on gently – like dreams.' Yet she found herself jumping down after him caught up in his excitement, not knowing why.

'Sure, but you have to run after dreams or they vanish. Come on, Jessica, run!' He looked behind for her, and grabbing her hand pulled her after him, stumbling over roots, hidden by the mass of blue.

'What on earth are we running for?' she panted.

'To get to the point where the magic is. After the flowers end.'

'But you can't find the end of a rainbow,' she cried, cursing a bramble which tore at her leg.

'Yes, you can. There's a crock of gold there.'

'There's no crock—' She gave up, and panted after him as he bounded through the carpeting bluebells.

They emerged through a thicket of trees into a clearing and stood staring in amazement. 'Well, I'll be darned!' he said, whistling. 'Look at that – and you said there was no crock of gold.'

'It's just an old bandstand, Will,' she said uncertainly, old memories battling with a sudden flame of hope.

He turned, seizing and pulling her in front of him, folding his arms round her so that she could not move. 'Just an old bandstand, Jessica?' he whispered into her hair. 'Look – can't you see the ghosts that trod those boards, hear the music coming out of it even now? Lost in a magic wood, timeless, the music playing on.'

'A bandstand, Will,' she cried, fearful to be dragged into something that part of her refused to recognise.

He paid no attention. Releasing her abruptly, he raced up the old steps on to the bandstand, transported, conducting, waving his arms around.

'Do you know what I'm playing?' he shouted down to her.

'The clarinet,' she shouted back, laughing.

'Right. I'm conducting – no, *playing* – Mozart's Clarinet Concerto.' He whistled to his own non-accompaniment.

'Will, you're an idiot.'

'Now what am I playing? Come up, Jessica, and listen hard.'

Caught up by his exhilaration, she ran up the steps, listening hard to silent notes.

'Can't you hear?' he cried. 'It's the melody, Jessica. My melody, the song without a singer.'

Hearing her intake of breath, he took her hands. 'Won't you sing again, Jessica? For John, for me, for yourself?'

She stifled a sob. 'I can't, Will, you know I can't.'

'Look at me, Jessica. I ask you once more, I won't again. Look at this and think of what you can do, think of what you could give people. That's the answer to yesterday. It's in yourself. Nobody else.'

'But I promised—' The anguish passed and a shutter came over her face as she ran down the steps, leaving him defeated on a deserted bandstand.

Molly came back from compassionate leave a week later, composed and quite determined.

'I'm going to apply for an overseas posting,' she told Jessica. 'They're taking WAAF officers for code and cipher work, the Middle East, Cairo. I'm off to see the Pyramids.'

'Oh, Molly, are you sure? I'll miss you.'

'Quite sure. Want to come?'

'I'll think about it.' For a moment she longed to make her own escape, then realised that this wasn't her road. There was an ordeal to be faced first.

'Odd the little things you think about,' Molly said abruptly. 'I keep thinking how I didn't turn round to wave again when we left the house. Usually I waved – waved – twice.' Her voice trailed off. 'Did you feel like this, Jessica? Stupid guilt, as though it were all your fault?'

A shiver ran through her. 'Yes.'

'And do you feel it still, or does it pass?'

The truth? Or should she say what would help Molly most. Inside her those words spoken so long ago now churned around over and over: 'It'll be your fault if I'm shot down.' 'It passes,' she said. 'Sometime, pray God.' But the last was only to herself.

'But the time to act,' said Molly, 'is before it passes. That's what I'm going to do now. Act.' She paused. 'Shouldn't you?'

Chapter Nine

She stepped down from the train, the only passenger to alight at Lenham.

'Section Officer Gray?'

The Waaf saluted and Jessica climbed into the station gharry behind the girl. She had barely enough time to realise she was back, to appreciate again the old lane she knew so well leading down to the village, the blackberry bushes sprawling by the sides, picked clean already for all it was so early in the season. Nature's free gifts were treasured in this autumn of 1941. Sloes, cobs, elderberries . . . anything edible would be harvested.

She had expected to feel an inner recoil, and was surprised to find something in her responding pleasurably to the familiar scenes. Lenham village, the winding road up through Doddingham, sweeping on past remote downlands with their fresh breezes and old mysteries hidden in their green fertility. The ordeal might not be so great.

'Shouldn't you?'

Her friend's words, spoken so apparently easily, Jessica had at first sloughed off, then when Molly had left in July, thought about again. Take action to change her life? But she was doing fine already. She had joined up, been commissioned, left Frittingbourne and all it meant to her, made a success of her job as a WAAF officer in the ops room, had taken part in the social life of Biggin Hill till her feet nearly dropped off with dancing, and her jaw was stiff with smiling.

What more? she had demanded of herself fiercely.

With her promotion to section officer had come realisation that this might mean posting away. She might go abroad to join Molly, go to New York or Washington, perhaps. No, that was too much like escape. She needed to be in the front line. Needed? Perhaps work, too, was an escape. Unwillingly, painfully, she had seen what Will and Molly had been trying to tell her. She was running when she should be standing still, turning around to face the pursuing enemy, even going back to meet him. She had to return to West Forstling and Frittingbourne, or she would never be free.

She requested a posting to West Forstling and got it. Not many volunteered for Kent, although the Battle of Britain was long past. She had not been here for nearly a year, not even for Christmas. Now, looking at the lanes, trees and bushes almost meeting in a triumphal arch of welcome over her head, her spirits began to rise. She could face anything, she felt. Let the ghosts come.

But the mood evaporated as the gharry entered the gates of West Forstling airfield; the sombre, quickly erected buildings brought back memories, stark and uncompromising. Kippen Hall she could have reckoned with, but this was different; an unfamiliar territory to her, it had been daily life for John. Here was his billet, this his dispersal, operations room, and office. She pulled herself together; was she going to collapse at the first hurdle?

The Waafs' headquarters and billets were well away from the men's, a separate enclave strictly guarded by WAAF hierarchy, a difficult task with so many young girls. For many of them it was the first time away from home, and even in the midst of war they arrived in expectation of a holiday atmosphere. It was quickly dispelled. They were guarded by dragons fiercer than any they met at home; worked so hard that what little time they shared with the airmen whose field they occupied, they hardly had the energy to enjoy.

The WAAF contingent at West Forstling had trebled in the last year, as with women's conscription in April Waafs took over more and more jobs hitherto done by airmen. Women mechanics, women storekeepers, women drivers, were becoming everyday sights.

The Queen Bee, the WAAF officer in charge, was clearly conscious of her status. She was a severe-looking woman who faced Jessica across the desk disapprovingly, having taken some time to acknowledgc her presence and salute.

'Section Officer Gray, I was against your posting here. I've seen your records. We're here to work, not to scrounge postings near our homes. I don't believe in weak links.'

Instead of being angry Jessica had a wild desire to laugh, but managed to keep a straight face. The woman in front of her had a huge flabby chin and broad forehead. An immediate image of Disney's Willie the Whale leapt into her mind, the whale who wanted to sing opera at the Met. Wonder what Queen Bee would look like as Madame Butterfly? She managed a 'Yes, ma'am', which seemed to be all that was required.

The frosty eyes relented a little.

'Welcome to West Forstling, Section Officer Gray.'

It was easier than she had imagined. This was a different West Forstling. The squadrons had changed, the Spitfires given way to a newer model, the whole field had a different air. No longer the frenetic atmosphere of the Battle of Britain, but a steady entrenched determination to get the job done. Jessica began to relax. The hustle and bustle of squadron life put flight to shadows. As at Biggin offence was the keynote. Take the flight to the enemy in France, sweeping in squadron or wing strength to pick off enemy fighters one by one, disrupt services, strafe airfields as a year ago they had strafed and bombed West Forstling and its sisters.

Jessica forced herself to face familiar sights without flinching. For a few days she stuck to WAAF quarters, then at the weekend she decided to take the bull by the horns and go to the mess dance at Kippen Hall. The WAAF officers, except those on duty, went as a body, which made it easier. Thanks to women's conscription, there were precious few village girls left to attend, and the Waafs' stock rose. No problems about what to wear. They wore their uniforms. Jessica applied what was left of her last irreplaceable lipstick with care, as though it would help in this, the greatest test of her strength.

The squadrons were released earlier than in Battle of Britain days, and the dance began at eight o'clock. She entered in a group with the rest of the officers, and made herself chatter so that she had no time to react to her surroundings.

'Still the same Jessica, eh? Don't they feed you at the

Bump?' A hand clasped her shoulder as she entered the mess.

'Art!'

The band was still the same, though the squadrons might have changed. So was Art, the same roly-poly, goodnatured broad-faced man she'd taken to so quickly last August. Was it only a year ago? It seemed another age. She summoned up a smile of pleasure.

'Are – are all the boys here?' she asked.

'We lost Eddie on the drums. Got a good replacement though. You'll like him. Jazz man. Gets a bit wild, but he's okay if we give him a solo once in a while. We'll ask him to go easy on you at first.'

Jessica heard the words in dread. 'Art – I can't.'

'Can't?' he queried, puzzled.

'I don't sing any more, Art,' she said bluntly. 'Not since John.'

'You mean you—' Art gave up. 'I suppose you know what you're doing, Jessica,' he said worriedly, 'but that seems plum crazy to me. What'll I tell the boys?'

'Just tell them what I've told you. Things are different now. I'm a Waaf – I—'

'You're telling me they're different – ma'am,' he said taking in her braid for the first time. 'Now I see.'

'No, Art, it's not like that – it's nothing to do with my being an officer.' She laid her hand on his arm, but he disregarded it and strolled off whistling – and deeply hurt.

'Hell's bells and buckets of blood,' muttered Jessica, using one of Molly's favourite expressions. What would she do now? So much for the new life.

* * *

Molly in Cairo was sharing her sentiments. The voyage out had been appalling – hot, humid, and the ship conditions all but intolerable. Stops at Freetown and Lagos had done nothing to impress her with the glamour of working overseas. Nor had arrival in Cairo. Stuck in a hotel with amenities less than those boasted by Bermondsey, she was on a course supposed to teach her about signals in the Cairo HQ.

The heat and proposed work made her long for Biggin. Her new comrades were fun but they weren't Jessica. And these four walls were not home. Properly home was part of the past, but the present seemed to offer no prospect of an alternative. The tears that she had never shed in Britain could not be held back here. She wept for a whole night, soundlessly, so as not to disturb her room-mate.

The next day she got up and smiled cheerfully, talking of a visit to the Pyramids. But inside a steady core of determination had been born that was only to grow over the coming months.

The ops room at West Forstling was much quieter than at Sector ops room, Biggin Hill, but the efficiency demanded was as great, if not greater. There were long periods with nothing to do but to enjoy the company of the other girls. Then Sector ops would be on the phone, the state board amended, squadrons scrambled, and the familiar routine would begin. Every so often the station commander would wander in: amiable, a First War veteran with an MC ribbon. Then the Wingco would dash in. He always seemed to dash everywhere. Wing Commander Geoffrey Swift did not believe in flying cautiously. He revelled in the thrill of active leadership, and when the squadron was stood down would frequently fly solo, unauthorised patrols. Every so often higher authority would discover and frown on such escapades. Wingcos such as Geoff Swift were too valuable to lose on exploits of derring-do. But he carried on all the same.

Nothing had changed. Anxious to get the ordeal over, Jessica walked up the stone-flagged path bordered by late nasturtiums to the front door of Frittingbourne Manor. She found her key, hesitated and put it away again. She didn't belong here now. She was a visitor. Perhaps they wouldn't be in. Almost hoping it would be so, she paused in front of the old wooden studded door, then pulled the bell handle, hearing the familiar clang dying away inside. Perhaps they wouldn't be in, perhaps, perhaps . . . But the door opened.

'Miss Jessica!'

'You're still here then, Maggie?'

'Too old for factory work, Miss Jessica. Mrs G, she'll be so glad to see you. They're having their dinner, miss.' Her face lit up.

Jessica walked into the quarry-tiled hall, the familiar smell of beeswax polish filling her nostrils. Nothing here to suggest undue deprivation. All looked as it had during her youth; only the gas masks hung carelessly in a corner, the two pairs of boots ready for the dash to the shelter, had changed. No sign of any other occupants, so Cicely had clearly managed to continue staving off requisition orders.

Even the smells of Sunday lunch were the same, though not even Cicely, surely, could wheedle the butcher into providing those enormous joints Jessica remembered so clearly. It would take their meat coupons for a year.

She stood uncertainly on the threshold of the dining room, looking at her parents as if they were suspended in a time warp. Then the illusion passed as they saw her.

'Brickie! Oh, Brickie darling.' Her mother looked genuinely pleased to see her, Jessica registered with surprise.

In a moment she was crushed to Cicely's bosom.

'Darling, you're thinner than ever. Don't they feed you at the awful place? Oh, darling, those shoes! What did I tell you?'

Then she was in her father's arms. 'Why didn't you come? You could have come. Darling, Jessica.'

'I'm stationed at West Forstling now,' she said steadily, to another scream from her mother.

'But we've rented out the oasthouse. You can't leave property unlived-in now,' Cicely said anxiously. 'They keep saying they need homes for bombed-out East Enders, and don't pay a penny. Imagine!'

'Of course.' Jessica hesitated. 'The piano. I—'

'In here, darling.'

Jessica relaxed, grateful to her mother for this rare sensitivity.

'We'll have such fun.' Cicely's clothes were beginning to show signs of age, Jessica noticed. Fun in that respect was over. Or was it? After all, now it was fashionable to make do and mend. 'The station commander at West Forstling is a poppet, an absolute poppet. I'm singing there next week for a station visit from royalty, or is it Churchill? I don't remember. Anyway, I'll have a word with Ferdy, make sure you're treated properly.'

'Don't you dare, Mother.'

There was a short silence. Then: 'Oh, well, still the same old Brickie.'

Still the same old Brickie. Why had she hoped it would be any different? Jessica wondered bitterly, as she walked down the drive, out into the lane that led to the village. People didn't change. It seemed strange to be back now, like being a visitor from another planet. She was no longer part of Frittingbourne, though here too there was a sense of resignation to the probability of a long struggle ahead.

Tom's face lit up with pleasure, as he opened the door of his cottage. 'Jessica! Come in.'

'I'm posted to West Forstling,' she explained, as she followed him into the cottage.

'Is that wise?'

'Yes.'

'Shall I see something of you?' he asked carefully, leading the way through to his large prized cottage garden, now almost entirely given over to vegetables.

'You can come up to the airfield.'

He grimaced. 'I'd feel somewhat out of place. We Home Guarders don't care to mix with the more active types. You must have some free time, we can go for some walks . . . Have you heard from Molly? Didn't you say she was in Cairo?' he asked.

'Not since she was on the ship. I had a card from Lagos. She wasn't taking to the heat too well.'

'You know, I have a feeling she'll be back, too. That Cairo won't be where she'll end up.'

'I hope so. I miss her.'

He smiled rather bitterly. 'I'm beginning to get used to

people coming and going, Jessica. While I just stay here. Waiting for an invasion that won't happen now.'

'It's a job someone has to do,' she said awkwardly. 'You told me yourself that someone has to teach the young. And someone has to organise Civil Defence.'

'You'll be launching into "Keep the Home Fires Burning" soon,' he said lightly. 'Who'd look after Astaire and Lind if I left, that's what really bothers you, I know.'

She laughed, as glad as he that the tension was relieved, and went to inspect her charges.

'They didn't take to the blitz at all,' Tom said. 'Lind stopped singing completely, but he's started again now.'

'Good.'

'And how about you, Jessica? Have you?'

Bubbles Gray was singing. The huge old drawing room of Kippen Hall, usually the dance floor now, was packed with airmen and officers alike. Tucked in somewhere at the back was Jessica. Strange faces, strange voices, and no John. Almost a year now since he was killed. No one here remembered. Even Art and the band would scarcely remember him, so many had come and gone since then, so many coffins buried, so many men flown away, never to return. Odd how hearing her mother's singing brought back the past more vividly than anything else.

Bubbles had difficulty projecting her voice over a band so was accompanied simply by a piano, to the disgust of Art Simmonds which he barely suppressed in Jessica's presence. Yet Bubbles put her songs over with a tinkling charm that was ageless. For the first time Jessica acknowledged how talented her mother was. Her style had lasted, not disappeared with the closing of the curtains on *Hearts and Diamonds*. She saw her father watching with pride, and shared in it. Cicely Gray's style was not part of this war, it belonged to an era that was gone forever, but her songs might survive it. A rush of pleasure that this should be so made Jessica the first to embrace Cicely when finally she came off the make-shift stage, gathering the folds of her blue satin dress carefully and gracefully in one hand.

'Why, Brickie darling—'

'Brickie? You dare call our formidable section officer Brickie?'

'Toots, darling, she's my daughter.' The station commander registered nothing but pleasure at being so addressed by Bubbles Gray. 'That's what we used to call her at home; she was always falling over her own feet.'

'She doesn't now, ma'am. Best dancer in the Waafery,' interposed Wing Commander Swift, winning Jessica's gratitude forever. 'Let's show them, Section Officer Gray.'

'Thank you, sir,' she said as they quickstepped, reasonably efficiently for Jessica, out of earshot.

'Don't mention it. We all have parents. Bad luck having them so close at hand. Brickie?' He laughed. 'Ridiculous. I'll call you Ginger, if you like.' He tweaked a curl. 'What's your real name?'

'Jessica, sir.'

'This is a dance, Jessica, no sirs. Just for the evening you're privileged to call me my lord. Or Geoff if you prefer.'

'My lord will do.'

'Astaire and Rogers are on in Maidstone this week. Will you come?'

Torn from the present, back into the past, back to John Gale and his '*Do you like Ginger Rogers*? . . . *Can you think of one good reason to refuse me*?' But later she had refused him something, refused the one thing that cost him his life. Caught unawares, a hot tide of confusion swept over her.

'Well, I—'

'Good. Saturday then.'

'Is it – I mean, is it – regulations?'

'Nothing in King's Regulations says officers can't date officers. Aren't many of them I'd want to, mind. That gorgon of a Queen Bee, for instance.'

'I hear from your mother – charming woman – you've something of a voice.' The station commander, Group Captain Cornwall, marched round the room as though still on the parade ground.

Jessica was dumbfounded. She'd had no idea why she'd been summoned for this unusual interview, but this was the last thing she had expected. All her old fury against her mother erupted. She'd thought she had escaped Bubbles' toils, but she had not. What was she up to now?

'We want more of that round here. Morale, that's the important thing.' The Group Captain did not seem to notice her lack of response.

'Yessir,' she supplied.

'Organise a concert, will you? You can sing. Give them a lead. Bit of this, bit of that. Few songs. Get them all singing. Few laughs. Two weeks' time.' He stopped abruptly.

'But, I—'

'Those ENSA people are a toss-up. One airfield gets Vera Lynn and Edith Evans, the next gets Mrs Bloggs who once sang in the school choir. So we'll start our own stuff. Better for the men. Organise it, get them involved, there's a good girl.'

'But—'

'And that's an order.' He wheeled round with a charming smile on his mild-looking face. 'And if you need it to come officially through Bossy Drawers, just say the word.'

'No, sir, but—'

'Good, good.'

'So I told him, darling.' Cicely was carefully polishing her nails with her homemade buffer. 'Why not have a concert and get Jessica to organise it? She could sing herself. She's a nice little voice.'

Michael looked at her despairingly. 'Do you want to drive her away again, Cicely?'

'Drive her away . . . what do you mean? I'm helping her. You always said I didn't encourage her enough. Now I am.' She genuinely meant it. Jessica had been away too long: she was not within Bubbles' control – though she did not acknowledge, even to herself, that this was the reason. Perhaps she'd stay at West Forstling if she was able to indulge her silly fantasy about her voice by singing in the band.

The hillside was bathed in the golden sunlight of autumn, rusts and yellows taking the place of green as the year tired. Jessica sniffed the season's scents, rich and mellow. She was sitting on an old tree-trunk overlooking the panorama beneath the lee of the downs, a spot where she and John used to sit. He'd died one year ago today. The wild cobnuts were ripe; she remembered how they'd been going to pick them, how they'd been going to gather the sloes to make sloe wine – or was it gin?

A year and the pain not yet lessened. It was suppressed but not alleviated. 'Have I kept faith, John?' she whispered, but only the sighing of the autumn breeze answered. What should she do? They could order her to organise the concert, but nobody could order her to sing; that was her choice. And no choice at all. Her own desire made her want to seize any excuse to sing again. She remembered the terrible tussle within her after Will had gone, the anguish that made her curse him for throwing the chance at her, forcing her to say no again. And for the last time. There was no going back to him. She had had no choice, but the battle within her was no less fierce for that. The guilt was still dormant in her, unassuaged. Suppose she and John had made love that night; he would have been less tense, happy, might not have died. Or would he? Was it not some kind of selfishness in her that made her think herself the sole pivot of his actions? Or was that argument too an escape route for herself? She argued it, this way and that, but was left with the same answer; she had promised not to sing, and that was an end to it.

'Jessica?'

She turned to see Geoff Swift striding towards her.

'I thought I saw you setting out along this path. Mind if I join you?' Taking her silence for assent, he sat down on the grass beside her. 'How's the concert going?'

'I've organised a few acts already. Art Simmonds is enthusiastic. They'll want to do some jazz numbers.'

'And you?'

'Me?' She dithered, taken aback.

He paused, chewing a piece of grass thoughtfully. 'I've been listening to the station gossip about you, Jessica. You were engaged to a pilot, weren't you? Just about to get married when he was killed. You were a first-class singer, used to sing with the band, until he died. You haven't sung since.'

'I don't sing any more.'

'Ah.'

'What does "ah" mean?' she asked defensively.

'It just means I understand now why you clammed up on me last night at the pictures. Warm, tender, but something missing.'

'What?' she asked belligerently.

'You were.' She turned to look at him, speechless. 'Now you may say that's pretty big-headed of me, that you just didn't take to me, but somehow I don't think that's it. I got the impression you were trying awfully hard.'

Jessica scrambled to her feet. 'Look, do you mind? I'm on duty soon, I must be getting back. I'm sorry if I disappointed you.'

'You didn't disappoint me.' He reached up and clasped her wrist. 'Sit down. That's an order from a superior officer. I'm going to tell you the story of my life.'

Unwillingly she sat down again.

'I had a wife when war broke out. I was posted to France in thirty-nine – stayed there in the thick of it till *blitzkrieg* broke out. Then I managed to get back to

England from Bordeaux, one of the few lucky ones. We called the winter of thirty-nine to forty, the "Bore" War. My wife must have found it so, for when I got back she'd gone off with someone else. I haven't seen her – or my kid – since. Common enough story, but it didn't feel very common to me. It still doesn't. I don't think I'll ever feel the same about anyone else. So it doesn't matter much to me whether you give me a handshake, a chaste kiss or leap on me and tear my clothes off at the end of the evening. But it will to you – eventually. You can get out of the habit of loving. Believe me – I know!'

'Vanessa, please don't go.'

'Graham darling, it's only for a weekend. And Johnnie will be all right. You can look after him, and Monica will lend a hand when you're on call. He'll be fine. I'll only be away three days. You don't begrudge me a bit of fun with Millicent, do you?'

He was silent. How could he stop her going to London for the weekend? Yet he felt it was the thin end of a very thick wedge. He bent over the baby's cradle: Johnnie. It was a sweet gesture of Vanessa's to think of naming the baby in John Gale's memory.

'Come along, old fellow, come along.'

Flying Officer Graham Macintosh was now with a Hurricane squadron, converted from day to night fighting. His keen eyes and sharp reactions were ideally suited and he'd been posted to Great Chingford in Essex. He liked it. His only problem was Vanessa. When she was good, she was very, very good, a wonderful wife who made him the envy of the mess. If they only knew what he had to face on the other occasions! He put it down to depression after the birth of the baby, but found himself doing all the chores, including most of those for the baby. Vanessa liked showing Johnnie off, but her patience with the less showy side of motherhood was limited in the extreme. He had to let her go to London for the weekend; perhaps it would do her good.

Somewhat to her astonishment, Jessica enjoyed organising the concert. It took her mind off other matters, and relieved the tedium of the ops room routine. There was a surprising amount of talent lurking on the station. One mechanic turned out to be a former actor with a gift for mime; a young sergeant pilot named Morton had a trained tenor voice; four airwomen sang 'Don't Sit Under the Apple Tree' in a passable imitation of the Andrews Sisters; the station commander's batman delivered 'When Father Papered the Parlour' with aplomb; the bill was almost full already.

Only one thing disturbed her: the band. Their numbers weren't right yet. It was all very well to say they'd do a jazz number, but it wasn't working. Nor were their swing numbers.

'There's two days yet, Jessica. Don't worry yourself. The show's not till Saturday.'

'You could play like this for a month and it won't sound right,' she said in despair. 'Do you think it's the new drummer?'

'Danny's all right,' said Art shortly. 'And I'll be the judge of whether we're good or not. I guess a vocalist would help. Yourself, for instance.'

Jessica turned pink at this unexpected attack. 'I told you—' she began heatedly.

'Christ, what's that?'

The airfield siren was sounding, the tannoys crackling, but over the sound of both came the blast of aircraft engines. Enemy engines. Almost as Art finished speaking, they came in.

'It's started again!' He dragged her to the floor of the hangar as the three planes roared in, shooting up the airfield till thick clouds of dust filled the air. Looking up, Jessica could see figures sprinting to their Spitfires, leaping in, mechanics pulling chocks away, the roar of Merlin engines; then the aircraft taking off higgledy-piggledy, no formation, just get into the air to pursue the bandits, get their machines away for a repeat run. Eight got off before the bomb-carrying Messerschmitt 109 came in, dive-bombing the scrambling Spitfires with deadly accuracy. The resultant explosion shook the Number Two hangar, the very ground beneath them. Choking in a mouthful of dust, Jessica looked up to see the destruction in front of them thirty yards away. The bomb had destroyed one Spit completely, overturned and torn the wing off a second. And in front of it, twenty yards from them, lay its pilot, still, on the ground.

'Jessica, no.' Art clutched in vain. 'It's coming back.' His voice was drowned by the roar.

But she was up and off, not thinking of anything save the danger to that pilot. She reached him, took hold of him, dragging him underneath the protecting wing of the damaged Spitfire, covering him with her own body while cannon fire churned up the ground where he had lain. She stayed there for several minutes, till it was clear the German aircraft had gone. Then figures came running from all directions, pulling her gently to her feet and out of the way, loading the unconscious pilot into an ambulance.

The Queen Bee looked almost human. 'I'm sorry to tell you, Section Officer Gray, that Sergeant Morton died during the night.'

Died? He couldn't have. She'd wanted to save him. A life for John Gale's.

'It was an isolated hit and run attack, so Intelligence tells us. Stragglers from the dive-bombing raid on Dover. It shouldn't happen again,' went on the Queen Bee carefully. 'I understand,' she coughed importantly, 'that you are being recommended for an award. The British Empire Medal. You're a credit to the service, Section Officer Gray.'

Jessica wanted to laugh again, wildly, hysterically. A medal? For failing to save a life? She managed to say, 'Thank you, ma'am.' Then added: 'He was going to sing in the concert on Saturday. Thank you, ma'am,' she repeated, then saluted, turned and hurried blindly out.

She sat in the Station chapel, just gazing at the small altar and the vase of flowers that adorned it. Michaelmas daisies. She remembered them in her own garden that last evening when John had come. 'If I'm shot down . . .' She heard his words again, and for the first time thought about them; thought about John the pilot, not the lover; thought about what he'd been through. Up at three every morning they were on call for dawn readiness; continuous scrambles, stopping only to refuel; not stood down till nine or ten o'clock sometimes, then coming to see her. Because he needed to. They weren't normal times. He'd made her promise unreasonably not to sing in public again. Not normal times, yet she had given that promise. And now because of another pilot she was going to break it - not completely, but partly. Sergeant Morton was dead, and she was going to take his place in the concert tomorrow night. She would sing for John Gale, sing for Sergeant Morton and for West Forstling, and any airmen anywhere who wanted to hear her. If she could do something, just a small something, to help them fight, then she must.

'Forgive me, John,' she whispered, 'but I'll sing only for them, pilots like you, and airmen. Never for myself.'

'What is life to me without you,
What is life if thou art dead . . .'

They listened in silence. Then as the sounds of Gluck's '*Che Faro*' died away, they cheered. On the makeshift stage set up in the hangar for the concert, Jessica took their applause, then held up her hand.

'That was for Sergeant Richard Morton,' she said gravely. 'Now I'm singing for you. Art?'

The band came on to the stage. 'Let's go, Jessica,' he said. 'Give it all you've got, girl.'

While the top brass froze at hearing an officer, albeit a female one, so addressed by an airman, the other ranks in the audience responded with whoops of delight.

She gave it. She gave them old favourites, blues and current hits, then made way for the next act. Off-stage, she glowed, an excitement in her that could not be stilled.

'Jessica, my darling!' Art rushed up to her, hugged her

and kissed her. 'You can't stop now. Hey, woman, we need you.'

As she climbed into bed much later that night, she heard his words again. 'You can't stop now.' But I can, John. Oh, I can, she whispered. I promised you.

And all memories were blotted out but one - that of John Gale, smiling through a Kentish summer that seemed forever sunshine.

Flight Lieutenant Will Donaldson circled Fowlmere airfield paying a last farewell to England as the squadron departed for Northern Ireland. That was it with operations for a while, the penalty he paid for joining this new 133 Eagle Squadron.

'Let us to the battle,' had said the CO, addressing his new squadron. Some chance! It was back to square one, non-operational flying, till they were fully trained. Still, it was either that or be rested. No way did he want that. He'd stick it out with this new batch of Yanks, brash and inexperienced though they were. Wouldn't the States ever come into the war? Now that Russia was in, they must be able to see the cookie for the currants. If Hitler went on the way he was, he'd be soon in Moscow. Once Russia was conquered, would Americans lose their complacency and see what was happening in the world, how it would affect them?

The squadron had only just got their Spits in time for this move. Old models, it was true, but still Spits. Flying seemed identified with the Spitfire for Will. Together they were a unit, capable of infinite worlds of possibility. What was that poem pinned to the mess wall, written by one of his countrymen, John Magee:

Oh, I have slipped the surly bonds of earth
And danced the skies on laughter-silvered wings . . .

Laughter-silvered. Or music-silvered? How about that? The sky was the wrong place to deal out death; it should be given over to contemplation, to music, to the infinite richness of life - not to death. That made the Spit merely an instrument of war. And she wasn't. She was a song in herself. A song fit for a clarinet. But she did her job well. Efficient, deadly - though they needed the improved model to cope with this new German fighter, the Focke-Wulf. He'd like to have a go at one - or two - but that wasn't on the cards. The Luftwaffe didn't come over Britain now, except for the odd hit and run raid. Like that one on his old base at West Forstling. Well over a year now since John Gale had been killed. Unbidden, that other thought - six months since he'd seen Jessica.

Resolutely he turned the Spitfire. Destination: Northern Ireland.

Chapter Ten

'Jessica, you're wasting yourself.' Geoff handed her a drink, apologising for it. 'Not up to Manhattans here in the White Stag, I'm afraid. Though they'll get round to it soon enough, I expect.'

'If you think the whole of the US Army could change the ways of Doddingham, you don't know the Men of Kent,' she laughed.

Pearl Harbor and the consequent entry of America into the war were hardly likely to affect this hidden-away part of Kent. All the US bases would probably be in Norfolk. Perhaps Will was there by now, she thought idly. She glanced round the pub, the scene of so many memories, and for an instant it looked, despite the throng of uniformed customers, dull. She roused herself to listen to what Geoff was saying.

'I don't know what your reasons are for depriving the world of your talents. Why won't you audition for the Forces Programme on the wireless? You know as well as I do how important entertainment is to morale. And how important morale is. I'd support you in getting permission from your Director.'

'I'm doing my bit here,' she replied, trying to keep it light.

'Dances and concerts, and very, very occasionally when I call out the heavy mob we shift you to another base for the same thing. Anyone would think you were trying to do a Garbo.'

'Then anyone would be wrong. I'm not tall enough. You have to be tall to be so dramatic,' she laughed, deepening her voice several tones.

'Jessica,' he said warningly, 'you're not going to throw me off course. I'm on automatic pilot here. It just seems a bloody waste to me,' he pressed on. 'It's your life, but believe me, I'd have no qualms about booting you in the backside if I thought it would propel you into seeing sense.'

Her life. She tried to put the thought out of her mind, but it came back with sickening clarity. If they won the war, *when* they won the war, what would she do then? The years would stretch emptily ahead, years without music. Could she stand it? Yet she would have to because of a promise she had given. John had been dead now for eighteen months but she felt he was with her still, enriching her past but leaving her future bleak. If she had slept with him, would it have been different? Would he be here now? Had she betrayed him even by singing with Art at West Forstling again? Was it to please herself only? No, she must believe Will. She wondered again where he was.

Number 133 Eagle Squadron touched down, the Spits coming in on the bumpy fields like birds, their narrow undercarriages less stable on ground than in flight. Many of the pilots took their first critical look at the famous Biggin Hill. Still the sharp end of fighter ops. They'd shot their mouths off often enough about wanting to play an active part in the war – now they had the chance. No more jack-assing about in the bogs of Northern Ireland or grim Kirton. They were in the south where it was still all happening in the spring of '42. They were eager to take on these new Focke-Wulfs. Have a shot at the crack Abbeville Geschwader. Outside dispersal, one first duty. 'Old Glory' was raised on the flagpole and saluted. The Yanks were here and now that the USA was in the war they weren't going to be pushed around any more. They were here for action. It was going to be one hell of a summer!

Will walked over to the Station HQ, now fully repaired after the Battle of Britain damage.

'Flight Lieutenant Donaldson, sir. I asked to see you.'

'I don't understand, Art. Surely Biggin have their own band? They could get anyone – the Squadronnaires, Bert Ambrose.'

He shrugged. 'But they want the Singing Waaf. You know that's what the chaps are calling you?'

'It makes me sound like a kettle,' she laughed. 'You're right though. We're different and we're good. Far be it from me to demur at an evening away from barracks – *and* in civvies.'

She glanced down at the midnight blue Molyneux evening dress, as usual inherited from Bubbles. She'd never worn it before, but since Art and the Band were in white jackets she supposed she had to do them justice. She'd had to fish around and try to revive her last pair of civilian panties; this dress wouldn't cling very beautifully to the WAAF regulation knicker line or uniform bra. In fact, she squinted uneasily down, the back-line – or lack of it – had demanded no bra at all. Perhaps it was as well the dance was away from home territory. She'd never dare wear it at West Forstling. Art approved her gown with a long whistle as she carefully squirmed into the MG.

'Where are the others?'

'Gone ahead. I was on duty, so I waited to take you. Official driver, get paid extra. All of a shilling, maybe. To think I used to make that just by lifting the trumpet to my lips – didn't have to blow a note. Ah, well, that's King's Regulations for you.'

The evening was warm for May and the lanes full of scents with the hawthorn and chestnuts in bloom. Another spring. Despite the war, lovers were celebrating it all over the country, but she was alone. Then she dispelled such ridiculous melancholy. She had Art and the band, didn't she? She had work. But friends? Those she had grown up with were scattered into the forces, or married and lost track of. She had not even heard from Molly for some while. Only a note to say she was applying for another post. Cairo didn't suit her, she'd been ill. Tom she saw once in a while, but they had grown apart, she in the service life, he more and more bound up with Civil Defence and the school. Will? She didn't want to think of him and began resolutely to talk of the programme to Art.

'What do you think about "Let's Do It" instead of "Smoke"?'

'Suits me. Don't go and forget the key this time.'

'Officers never forget the key,' she pointed out loftily.

'You ain't an officer now, missy. Not tonight, you ain't,' he mocked.

Absorbed in an animated discussion on breath control

for voice versus trumpet, she lost track of the way and was taken by surprise when he announced: 'Here.'

'Where?' she asked blankly. 'This isn't Biggin. This is the middle of the country.'

Even as she spoke she recognised where she was. The lane, the stile – the wood. *The* wood. 'What's going on, Art?' she asked suspiciously. 'What is all this?' She was swept back a year, to Will laughing and shouting among the bluebells.

It was May once again. The bluebells were carpeting the ground with colour once more, and for some inexplicable reason Art had brought her here.

'Art?' she said again, uncertainly, questioningly. He simply opened the car door for her and waited. Inside her was a spark of wild joy, an ember of life that sprang into flame.

'If you'll follow me, ma'am,' he said, grinning.

But she did not need Art to show her the way. She climbed over the stile, pulling her long evening dress up to her knees in her impatience, jumped down and walked carefully through the bluebells in order not to damage any portion of this magic carpet, disciplining herself not to run, for all her pounding heart.

Then she heard the music. *That* music, *that* song. She picked up her skirts and began to hurry, running through the bluebells towards the music. As she came through the trees, there in the clearing was the old bandstand of last year, the evening sunlight falling on it. But it was silent no longer. A white-jacketed band played there, a band she knew, and with them a clarinet player. Will Donaldson. Seeing her there, transported, he played a last trill, laid aside the clarinet and ran down the steps to greet her.

'Your number, ma'am. Let me escort you.'

'Will! Oh, you fool, you *fool.*' Half crying, half laughing, she hurled herself towards him and into his arms.

He held her close for a moment, then whispered: 'Sing for me, Jessica. Give my song a singer. Now, while the magic lives. Then give it to everyone. To the world.'

That enchanted wood was a rainbow bridge between a few careless words spoken so long ago and the golden sunlight of the future, a path where music beckoned and song was sweet. A path that Will had first set foot on, paused and waited till she join him. It had seemed so hard; but now it was easy. It needed only one word, and she spoke it.

'Yes. Oh, yes.'

'You're sure this time?'

'I'm sure.'

'I've got the words here.'

'I know them, Will. I never forgot them.'

He looked at her, then led her up the steps.

'Okay, fellas.' She grinned, throwing her arms wide to them. 'Let's make music.'

Art leapt into place, Will picked up the clarinet, his eyes fixed on Jessica. Their audience was a million bluebells as she began:

> 'I heard a nightingale sing one night
> His sweet sad song of love
> But you passed on without a sign
> You'd heard his song above
> And the song was mine.'

Her husky voice floated out into the May evening, the clarinet's mellow tones mixing with it, fulfilling it, the band swelling the melody, fixing it for her to pick up once again. She turned to look at them as the last notes died on the air:

'Ah, then I held you in my arms
And our song began.'

Crazy, it was crazy. A Molyneux-gowned woman, with a white-jacketed band, here in a bluebell wood in the middle of nowhere, with a war on. As the music ceased, she turned to Will, hardly daring to meet his eyes for fear of what she might see.

'If I close my eyes, will all this – will you – disappear?'

'Not a chance,' he said quietly. 'Not this time.'

'That's it, then,' said Art flatly. 'We go on, RAF willing.'

'You'll do it, Jessica?' asked Will. 'No harking back? Any path fortune offers?'

She did not hesitate, looking at them there: Art, Danny on the drums, Richard, Barney, Vic – and Will. Her friends.

'Try and stop me now. *Per ardua ad astra* – and that's where we'll stop. At the top.'

'Hey, that's not a bad name. The Astras. How about that?' said Art. 'The Astras and the Singing Waaf.'

The Lincoln was a large car, but the space between them seemed small, non-existent, as Will slammed his door shut. Intoxicated by the evening, the music pouring through her still, demanding release, she breathed, 'Shall there be more songs, Will?'

'As many as your heart desires.'

'Will the world soon be singing them?'

'If you do. Only if you do.'

'Why me?' She knew but on this evening had to hear it.

'Because they're written with the sound of your voice in my ears, vibrating through me. In each note of the clarinet I hear it beside me – just as you are now. Jessica, it's been a year.'

His voice broke and he turned to her quickly. Then she was in his arms and he was kissing her on her eyes, her forehead, her lips; one hand on her back under the wrap, warm against her skin, the other on her shoulder. Then, as her mouth instinctively responded to his, on her breast through the thin satin and pushing the material impatiently aside, on her bare flesh, caressing, demanding. She wanted him closer, closer, part of her, to bind to herself forever the magic of the evening, that spell that only he could cast.

'I guess I love you, Jessica.'

At the sound of his husky voice, she opened her eyes. The flame in her subsided as, once put into words, fear fought it, old memories and old guilt flooding back.

'Will – I can't! We can't.' She drew away, gripped by an emotion she did not understand. 'How could I? How could *you*?' she cried, saying the first thing that came into her head. 'John was your friend.'

Blank-faced, he slumped back in his seat.

'I guess I got the song confused with the singer,' he said lightly, after a while. 'Kind of unprofessional. It must be that dress.'

It hadn't been the dress that had made her respond, made her want to lie with him among the bluebells, to feel his arms around her, to hear him whisper to her the words of love he poured into his songs, to lose herself in love for him as she did in his music – until the shadow of John slipped silently between them.

'It's the music that's important, isn't it, Will?' she stumbled. 'That's what we share?' He must agree, he must!

'Sure. I'd better get you back to the airfield now, or you'll be before the CO, not a mike.'

They drove back to West Forstling in silence. He watched her for a moment as she went through the main gate, showing her pass and not looking back. 'And the song was mine,' he quoted to himself as he viciously slammed down the accelerator of the Lincoln, left with the fruits of victory, bitter to the taste.

Jessica lay awake most of that night, listening to the rhythmic breathing of her room-mate, unable to sleep, her thoughts confused. Just why had she pulled out of Will's arms? John – that was the reason she had given. But he was becoming increasingly shadowy to her. Perhaps from fear lest the same thing happen again to her? She tried to think things through but the effort was too great and instead she concentrated on John Gale, on thoughts of how she had rejected him, too, when it mattered. If she still felt guilt for her treatment of the one, how could she encourage the other? But all the same she could feel Will's lips on hers yet, the warmth surging through her now as it had then. No more, though. It wouldn't happen again.

* * *

'Posting refused, Section Officer Gray.'

'Ma'am, I—'

'Dismissed.'

'Yes, ma'am.'

Jessica retreated, hardly believing it. Refused? After all the euphoria, their hopes and plans, now she could not get a posting to Biggin Hill. Art's and the boys' had come through. Why not hers? Will had been so sure it would be easy. RAF music was run from Uxbridge HQ; he knew a guy there he said vaguely. 'You seem to know guys everywhere,' she'd laughed. But they wanted more bands apparently, and they'd heard of Jessica Gray, the Singing Waaf at West Forstling – it would be a cinch to get their postings to Biggin to work up their act. Then, if Uxbridge top brass approved, 'You could "Scramble for the stars",' he'd said succinctly.

'*You*?' she picked up, frowning.

'Us,' he amended quickly.

So what had gone wrong?

'What's up, Section Officer Gray?' Geoff asked that evening, receiving no answer to his offer of another drink.

'Sorry, Geoff, I'm poor company. Nothing much up – just the rest of my life. I've been politely reminded there's a war on, and there are more important things than to allow Waafs to do exactly what they like. That sitting in charge of a bevy of girls at a plotting table is much more important to the war effort than singing a few paltry songs for the airmen.'

'And having a BEM on the strength is more important to the Queen Bee's position here than having you fly the coop to Biggin Hill.'

She turned an amazed face to his. 'Do you know, I never thought of that, Geoff.'

'That's because you're a dear little feather head who never sees further than her own nose.'

She aimed a mock fist at him and he ducked.

'Geoff,' she said thoughtfully, 'you sweetly offered to boot me up the backside once. Does that offer extend to booting other backsides?'

A glint came into his eyes. 'I'm not too keen on seeing you disappear to Biggin Hill myself, so I wouldn't. But my own posting's come through - one squadron here's moving down to the West Country and I'm going with it to command the wing. Fancy coming?'

'Sounds lovely, but—'

'Your heart's here.' He paused. 'Who's this Eagle Squadron chap then?'

'He plays the clarinet. An old friend.'

'Ah.'

'It's not "Ah" at all, Geoff. We play well together. We—' She broke off, aware that he was grinning and that her voice had suddenly become defensive.

'Uh huh.'

'You're impossible, Geoff. You think everyone is only thinking of one thing. Just you wait . . .'

There was a very select party at Station HQ that evening, to which by special permission the top Waafs were invited. By popular request, Section Officer Jessica Gray sang. The Queen Bee agreed with Wing Commander Swift that she had an extraordinary talent; after another glass of the very special punch handed to her by the Wingco she agreed that it would be a pity were the RAF at large not inspired by her singing, though doubtless service regulations were service regulations. After a third glass, she found most unexpectedly that she was unable to support herself, and the offer of assistance to a nearby room where she might recover seemed an excellent plan.

When she awoke five hours later she was surprised to find herself in what appeared to be the Wingco's bedroom with the patently irate Wingco sitting on a chair, arms akimbo, demanding to know how much longer she intended to invade his room. When, appalled, she had pointed out she could hardly leave at four in the morning by the usual exit, thus running the gauntlet of smirking airmen on guard duty, she agreed gratefully to his offer to assist her out through the back entrance. On the way, she found herself agreeing fervently that Section Officer Gray should indeed be posted to Biggin Hill, and without undue delay!

Biggin seemed more like Jessica's home now than West Forstling. Frittingbourne was her past. They had not worked out what would happen if Will's squadron were posted; for the moment it was enough that they could work together. After an uncomfortable visit to Frittingbourne Manor, with Bubbles demanding tearfully to know the reason for her transfer – something she had no intention of divulging – Jessica made the move as soon as possible. Jessica had to travel separately from the band, who had already been here a week, and got out at Sevenoaks station after several changes. Instead of the official transport, she found Will waiting there. As he came forward to grasp her kit, she greeted him somewhat apprehensively, but if their last conversation were uppermost in his mind he gave no sign of it. Nor did he make a move to kiss her. He had reverted to the Will she'd always known.

'You don't look in the least like a WAAF corporal,' she teased.

He grinned. 'My legs are better, I guess. How about a salute, by the way?'

'You don't rank one. All the same, if it pleases you.' She drew herself up smartly and saluted.

He returned it gravely, eyes dancing. 'You know, your mother was right about some things, I guess, according to what you told me.' He ran his eye over her critically. 'Those *shoes*!'

The squadrons might have changed, but everything else was the same; Station HQ with the familiar cupola that countless enemy raids had not managed to obliterate; the Salt Box Café, which had found itself marooned when the camp built on two sides of the Bromley-Westerham road was enclosed, and now with its almost Martello Tower shape was a familiar landmark; the remains of the Gable Hangar still unrepaired. And the familiar endless walks to get anywhere, so dispersed were the buildings and billets.

'What plans have you made so far?' Jessica asked eagerly. 'We've got to get going. Can we start tonight?'

'Nope. There's a thrash in the mess. Two of the Canadian squadrons being posted.'

'Tomorrow then,' she said, disappointed.

'If I'm not on call. I still have ops to fly.'

'But we've got to get started right away,' she cried. 'I've been thinking, Will. No use pussy-footing around.

We must have a concert just as soon as we can. Start with a bang, to get really known. And invite everyone. See if they'll send someone from Uxbridge. And I thought perhaps I'd write to Don Field – he's a music publisher. He'd love your songs. We could get things going—'

'Hey, hold on, will you? I thought it was supposed to be us Yanks went charging into things like buffaloes. Now, look, we're already working on a few numbers. There's a concert booked in one of the hangars next Saturday, dance afterwards. And as for Don Field – it's a great idea, but any publisher would appreciate a bit of demand for the item. Sure, bring him down, but I've also got that great guy I told you about, coming. Dave, Dave Prince. Now, if he could fix a BBC audition, *if* you passed it, if you sang my songs—'

'What do you mean, *if* I passed it, Will?' she laughed, then said seriously. 'Why do you keep saying "you", Will, not "us"?'

'Because I'm on active service, Jessica,' he said quietly. 'You and the boys, that's different. A lot of people could do your jobs. Me, I joined the RAF to fly – and fight! We've had several dicey missions this month over France. The FW190s aren't like Messerschmitts, and the Abbeville boys are top performers. They're learning to jump us on the return flight. We need all the experienced pilots we have.'

'But—'

'There's no but, Jessica. Not in this war. I'll play for you, every minute I'm free. But no more.'

'I'll have your songs, though,' she said, biting back her disappointment. 'Okay, then,' forcing a grin, 'let's get down to some numbers now – after I've reported.'

'Suits me,' he said laconically.

Jessica sat restlessly in the ops room, trying to concentrate on the job on hand and not the concert that evening. But the music was running through her head endlessly. 'Let them ration violets, Put on points the sky above—' It was a lively, jerky little tune, it would catch on. Mentally, she sang it through to the end of the verse.

'But whatever they do,
Don't let them ration love.'

She couldn't wait to get started. What time would she get off duty? Time enough to change, she hoped, now that she'd won grudging permission to sing in evening dress, not uniform.

If only Will hadn't been on call! She looked at the state board in front of her. There it was. 133 Squadron available thirty minutes. Suppose he . . . ? No, she wouldn't think that way. She hummed – to herself, she thought – until she saw a corporal looking at her in surprise. She rehearsed the words again. Tricky, that new song of Will's. She ran through it again. That key change in the last line of the verse . . . risky. They would start with old favourites tonight to get people in the mood – and then it would be Will's music, Will's songs. This Dave had to take to them, with their haunting melodies or jazzy unforgettable tunes. Then the BBC, Don Field . . .

'Section Officer Gray!' The tone was sharp.

'I'm sorry, sir!' She adjusted her headphones to relay the message from Group. 'Biggin Hill . . . serial 21 . . . Wing sweep over St Omer . . . Angels 15, Sir . . . Form A.'

* * *

Will Donaldson, leading Yellow Section, felt the Spitfire soaring into the air without his usual thrill of elation. Another sweep over St Omer. He cursed having been on call today of all days, with the concert this evening. But he'd be back in plenty of time. Meanwhile, forget about it, forget about music, forget about Jessica. Above all, forget about Jessica. Switch to the numbers. Perfect rhythm, perfect harmony, clarinet, voice. That last beat . . . No, concentrate like hell. The section spread out beneath him in echelon starboard, as they crossed the Channel, the whole squadron together in formation. Up above were the Canadians and below the New Zealand Squadron. God, it was beautiful. Silver wings against a blue sky. Music in the hum of the engines.

Thank God his fellow Yanks had all picked up RAF discipline now, no longer haring off individually the minute a bogey came in sight. They knew to save it now. Attack as a squadron, support the Wing, then peel off; above all now, you had to stick together over France if you were all going to get back. That newcomer there – Don Blakeslee – he was a real flyer. He was going places was Blakeslee, a natural.

Over the Channel, France in sight. Crazy, seen from up here, that the enemy never succeeded in crossing this strip of water to conquer Britain; that those barges stacked up in the ports never managed to make it across. The Channel was so narrow it was hardly a river by US standards, yet the people either side – phew, how different! He recalled his days in France before the war, the hedonistic Paris society and the down to earth French countrymen. He hadn't been surprised to hear about the organised help many French civilians were giving to downed airmen. Pilots were given standard lectures in evasion now; they were expensive to train, were needed back just as soon as they could make it. The French were a grand people, most of them, but there was the other kind who would sell their grandmother for a nickel. He supposed all countries had them. There'd be a reckoning in France after the war – if the Allies won. Of course they'd win sooner or later now that the States were in, and Russia. Hitler had to be some kind of fool fighting on two fronts at once. Had to be. Yet things couldn't be worse than they looked in the short term. The whole of the Far East had fallen, the Army had retreated in Burma, Rommel was forging across the Western Desert again, Tobruk under threat . . . it was all bad news. His countrymen were beginning to come in to Britain, though. And their hardware. For the moment they were wild, all going to win the war by themselves, but once they'd learned the hard way it would be okay. Had to be. Meantime . . .

He concentrated his thoughts. They were crossing the coast now, into the flak. Anti-aircraft fire thrown up at them from all directions. 'Here we go, fellas,' he called. Over the radio, the Controller warned the Wing Leader of enemy aircraft rising to meet them. All eyes scanned the horizon.

Focke-Wulfs. Must be thirty of them. Well, this is what I came for. Sometimes the Germans reacted, sometimes not. One hell of a sight the 190s were, with their square wingtips, huge radial engines and deadly fire power. Okay, attacking as a squadron. The Canadians to cover us, while we support the New Zealanders. 'Here we go!'

Then it was all fire, flashes on engine and wingtips, screaming dives and spiralling aircraft. Miraculously he was still there, mixing it with them, up behind the 190 on 'Alamo' Travers' tail. Straight bursts, and 'Alamo' was free. Probably never knew it had been there, thought Will briefly, turning his attention to 'Tennessee' on his port wing. Jeez, where did that come from? He was hit on the wingtip. 'Hell, I'm a "gone coon",' he breathed. Only Davy Crockett wasn't messing about 8,000 feet up when he told that story. No, he was okay, flying steady, no change in engine beat, instruments okay – wait, the oil pressure gauge, dropping fast! Whistling thoughtfully, Will switched on the radio.

'Yellow Leader to Yellow Two – got to get out of here, Tennessee. Give my regards to Broadway.'

'One Three Three landing now.' Thank heavens, Jessica thought as she left, her shift over. Just time to change. She threw on the dress, another relic of pre-war days. No new evening dresses – even Utility ones – on a Waaf's pay. She peeled off the stockings. No way was she wearing these thick things and she'd no silk ones left. She'd just paint a line up her leg like everyone else did. Perhaps she'd ask Will to get her some of those nylons she'd heard the girls talk about. She tried to brush her hair into some kind of shape, as usual without success. Its curls remained firmly where they were. Eight-thirty, only half an hour to go.

'Where's Will, Art?' she panted, throwing herself into the makeshift dressing room at one end of the hangar. 'I want to run through "Rations" again.'

'I thought he was with you,' said Art absently, unpacking the trumpet with loving care.

She stared at his back, suddenly fearful. 'No. I haven't seen him. The squadron landed over thirty minutes ago.' Panic crossed her face.

Art leapt up and seized her shoulders. 'Now don't jump to conclusions. He's probably in debriefing still.'

But he was talking to the wind. 'Not again, please,' she was crying, as she ran to the debriefing room. No joy. The ground crew – if he wasn't back, they'd be watching, waiting . . .

She made a strange sight for an airfield, in a bright yellow evening dress, oblivious of the whistling ground crews. She recognised Johnnie Martin from Will's ground crew, waiting near the Flight Hut, and clutched at his arm. 'Where is he?'

'Lord love us, miss – er, ma'am. Don't take on. He may have landed elsewhere. Baled out. There's Pilot Officer Austin still to come too.'

'But they'll have to be down somewhere soon,' she cried, 'their fuel . . .'

'Strewth!' Johnnie grabbed her as his last word was almost drowned by the roar of a Merlin in trouble. Streaming black smoke, a Spitfire was lurching in over the boundary fence, with a rough-sounding engine and veering from side to wide, wheels only half out. The station tannoy was already blasting out, ambulance and fire-tenders racing on to the airfield as the engine died and the Spit dropped several feet, bouncing over the field and slithering to a stop miraculously just short of the perimeter ditch. Hardly conscious of what she was doing, only realising that Will was in danger, Jessica began to run towards it, only to be yanked back unceremoniously by Johnnie.

'Don't be a fool,' he said, white with shock and with scant regard for rank. 'There's not a damn thing you can do.'

'I must—' But he held on to her.

The fire-tenders were running towards the Spit and Tennessee's labrador bounding after them. Tennessee jumped from the running board, raced towards Will's smoking wreck. The cockpit was open and Will was clambering out. He jumped down and ran clear.

Jessica stood transfixed, watching from the front of the hangar, Martin still restraining her. As the fire engines smothered the smoking Spitfire, the two men came towards the clutch of people at the edge of the flying field. Jessica, heart pounding, heard Will say to Tennessee, 'You think that's something? You should have seen me do it with no wings.'

Then he spotted Jessica, and came up to her nonchalantly. 'Checking up on me, huh? Didn't think I'd make it?'

'No,' she said steadily. 'But I'm awfully glad you have.' And found her eyes stinging with tears of relief.

The hangar was crowded, more than usual for a concert. Previously unknown artists were apt to be a disappointment, the pub offering more certain entertainment. But a home-grown Singing Waaf – an officer, too – and a new band, albeit from a satellite station, promised something interesting. Even the mixture of officers and airmen in the audience was different. It wasn't too often officers mixed with the lower echelons on these social occasions, let alone for a mere band. But this one clearly had the approval of top brass, judging by the braid that filled the first few rows. And civilians, too. The Yankee pilots were supporting it in force, judging by the racket coming from behind the blackout material serving as a make-shift curtain.

'They're our first target,' Will had said. 'Get them with us, and we're okay.'

'Right,' said Jessica. 'Simple. We'll start with "Stars and Stripes", and finish with "God Save the King".'

'Any old rubbish in between and we're made.'

'Quite so,' said Jessica equably.

The 'rubbish' went down well. After a few popular current US numbers, he nodded. The rhythm abruptly changed to swing and Jessica launched into 'Rations'.

It had been written for instrumental solos as well as voice, and was a good choice to launch the Astras on their way to the stars.

> 'Let them ration bluebells,
> Take away our pots and dishes
> Let them ration raindrops
> But don't let them ration kisses.'

Already the beat was beginning to catch on. 'And Will, I give you Will,' she cried, stepping back to give clarinet pride of place. By the time the next solo started, their audience was stomping the beat, and when Danny on the drums had finished his solo it was humming along with the tune.

> 'Oh let them ration sunshine
> Donkeys, elephant stew,
> But whatever they do
> Don't let them ration you.'

Jessica finished the song, and it was clear from the stamping and cheering that the Astras had arrived.

Dave Prince, the guy Will knew, turned out to be one of the ugliest men she'd ever seen – until he grinned, when a huge smile stretched right across his face, lighting it up. He was also one of the most dynamic. It was no surprise to her that he spoke with an American accent. No Englishman could have had quite such piercing black eyes, or hair cut – or rather not cut – in such a mop. He wasted no time in preliminaries.

'Okay, I've seen you, I've heard you. The lot of you. I'll get an audition at the BBC. There's a guy I know . . . No promises, but Dave Prince don't believe in moseying around,' he glanced distastefully at his surroundings, but thought better of commenting on them.

'Jessica.' Someone tapped her on the shoulder.

'Mr Field,' she greeted him excitedly. Before the show she'd been worried about whether she'd been right to invite him. Now she knew she had been.

'I need to talk to the composer. And you. I'm not promising anything – but just make sure you get through that audition. Then we'll be in business.'

Dave Prince frowned. 'We'll all be in business, Don. I do the records side. Right?'

'Half right,' said Don Field amiably. 'We'll talk.'

Will was waiting for her in the mess, and got up eagerly as she bounced in, a few days later.

'We've got the BBC spot, Will. Small spot, bad time, but we've got it. Regularly, barring our doing something dreadful. Now for the big one.' She sank into a seat, grimacing. 'I've got to face the Director.' She hesitated.

'Are you sure you won't change your mind about broadcasting?'

'I can't, Jessica,' he said flatly. 'You ought to know that by now. I'm on operations. I stay on operations.'

'And what about all you told me about its being just as important to keep up morale? Both servicemen's and civilians'?'

'I stick by it. But I'm a serving, operational pilot with a war to fight. Even if I thought the RAF would release me to play music, I couldn't walk out on the squadron. I'm needed here, Jessica – and it's where I need to be. I told you before, music is for back home. It's there to come back to after this lot's over . . . Don't look like that, honey. I'll be with you every time I can, you know that. And I'll carry on writing songs.'

'The first one. The first broadcast. Please be there, Will, even if you don't make the others.'

'Honey, I'll put in for a day's leave. A tribe of Mohawks on the warpath couldn't keep me from it.'

' "And when it's over and you're home again . . ." No, it's no good, Art. It's still not working. We'd better wait for Will.'

Jessica ran her hands impatiently through her hair. Only a week to go before the all-important 8th July broadcast. The interview with the Director of the WAAF had been unexpectedly easy. No objection was raised to her performing publicly, or to her attachment to RAF Uxbridge as a full-time singer with the Astras. She was relieved of other WAAF duties. In only one respect was the Director firm. She could not officially sanction the soubriquet the Singing Waaf.

Jessica had almost danced along Whitehall in her relief at getting official blessing. One thing alone marred her pleasure. The move by the Astras and their singer to Uxbridge would mean isolating Will at Biggin Hill. For all he promised to play with the band when he could, it simply wouldn't be practicable – not while he was flying operationally.

They'd played at many concerts and dances since receiving that first ovation in the hangar. The Astras and their vocalist were beginning to be known as a group. For all the Director's veto, the name the Singing Waaf stuck, unofficially. The Astras' poster photograph adorned many messes, not least West Forstling which took great pride in its fledglings.

But a broadcast was different from concerts, and Jessica was nervous. It needed different phrasing, different rhythms, style – oh, *everything*. Where on earth was Will?

He arrived in the middle of the next number, and took up his clarinet quietly, Jessica's eyes upon him.

After the rehearsal he broke the news to her.

'I can't do it, Jessica, the broadcast. My leave's cancelled. We've been temporarily posted to Lympne. There's talk of a big show.'

'What? But they can't just cancel leave!'

'They can and they did.'

'You're not telling me the truth, are you?' she said accusingly. 'Your leave wasn't cancelled – you want to go.'

'What? Are you crazy?' he said. His face went white. 'Jessica, I just don't have a choice, goddamn it! Don't you think I'd rather be in London with you and the lads, in front of the mike instead of in front of some Hun pilot? Yes, okay, I volunteered, they didn't cancel my leave. But I've *got* to go, for God's sake. I'm not here just to please myself.'

'How can you say that to me, when you lectured me so often?'

'We've been through that; it was different,' he said quietly, restraining himself.

'The hell it was! You're running out on me, Will, when I really need you,' she blazed.

He turned round and walked away without a word, leaving her sobbing with inexplicable rage. Of course she could do it on her own; her and the band. But she wanted, needed, Will there. It wasn't fair. It was his triumph, too, his songs, his clarinet accompaniment that made that special sound. It wasn't fair! Why this passion to fly, fly, *fly*, like John . . . John. Suppose Will didn't come back, just like John? That was it, she realised, suddenly calm. Of course she understood his need to fly. It was her own fear she could not face. Dread that once again her world would crumble. That she'd lose Will; never see his laughing eyes and lazy smile again, never sit side by side with him at the piano, arguing about a phrase, a melody, a word. Never see him hunched over his clarinet, the look of love on his face as he picked it up and began to play, then turned to her to take over where his golden-voiced clarinet paused. How, oh how, to continue if Will were no longer there?

On the evening of 8th July the Singing Waaf made her debut. Her rich, melodic voice went out over the air to millions of listeners, sometimes singing with the band, sometimes without. The critical part of her mind was telling her she was in good voice, that it was going well. They kept the best till last.

And this one's for you, Will, she thought to herself. Wherever you are. Was it the big show tonight? 'I heard a nightingale sing one night . . .' She stilled her fears and began to sing Will's song, its eerie melody dependent on her voice alone without his clarinet. And yet as she sang, it seemed to be with her, guiding her, complementing her, inspiring her, as her voice soared into the second verse:

'And then one night you heard it too
His haunting sweet refrain
And as you passed I saw you pause
And reach for it in vain
And the song was yours.'

And *their* song had begun. The Astras were launched. The band emerged from Broadcasting House elated, singing and cheering into the blackout. Jessica, swinging through the doors after them, collided with Will about to enter, immaculately uniformed.

She threw her arms round him in delight. 'Will, you're *back*! Oh, thank heavens.'

'Never went. They released us – big show's postponed. I did my darnedest to get here, but just didn't make it in time. Go well, did it?' he asked, keeping an arm round her. Too late, she remembered their last meeting, but he showed no signs of remembering it either.

'Well?' She hesitated, smiling, before she replied! 'It

was super! Super-dooper! Super-dooper-ific!' she cried, catching hold of his arm and waltzing him along the street.

'Careful now, you'll be dancing with a lamp post in a minute.'

'I'll bring it along to the Café Royal.'

Michael Gray turned off the wireless and nerved himself to look at Cicely. Her face was quite blank. Inside she was raging, however. And to think she'd been the one to start all this by suggesting Jessica started singing in concerts at West Forstling. Yet, however unwillingly, she was forced to admit that Jessica's voice was distinctive. It wasn't what she would call singing; no art, no delicacy. it wouldn't last. The BBC would broadcast any old rubbish at the moment. Anything.

Somebody should make them realise that this sort of thing wasn't what people wanted to hear at the moment. Perhaps she herself should have a word . . .

The Café Royal Brasserie was packed with uniforms of all colours, American, Australian, Polish and Canadian outnumbering the British, and the noise that the seven of them made in toasting their success simply disappeared in the general hubbub. By the time they stumbled into the darkness again it was gone two, the night was black and Jessica had drunk quite a few more glasses of champagne than she had noticed. Piccadilly Circus was dark as they skirted it for the hotel, sad in the blackout, without its lights. Only a few figures hurried by arm in arm. Another bottle of champagne was emptied in the hotel bar before the band disappeared to their rooms, leaving

Will and Jessica in the bar, she clinging obstinately to the last remnants of her drink.

'I don't care, Will. I don't *want* to go to bed yet. This is the night it begins! The yellow brick road to Oz. I feel like Judy Garland, I *am* Judy Garland. And Oz is out there. We've got to reach as many people as posh – poshible, Will. Millions and millions and millions and millions. All your songs. Everyone's got to be singing them, humming them, whistling them all over the world, even in Germany, like "Lilli Marlene". The whole *world*!' She flung wide her arms, catching him a blow in the chest. 'Isn't that what we want?'

He grinned. 'I guess so. Though,' he paused, 'tell you the truth, Jessica, if there's anybody listening inside that daze of yours, I'm not too sure what I want. I think I just want music.'

'Same thing.'

'No.'

She frowned and tried to concentrate on what he was saying. 'You write songs, I sing them, you play them – that's music. You need an audience to urge you on properly, you need to create *for* someone, and the more shomeones, the merrier.' She hiccuped. 'That'sh better.'

'Come on, Melba, I'd better get you to your room.' He gripped her arm, and despite her protestations led her up the stairs under the politely uninterested gaze of the hall porter, then along the corridor to her room. Here she stopped.

'I don't think,' she said carefully, fishing for her key, 'that tonight should never end. It's the most wonderful night of my life.'

'Tomorrow has a habit of creeping up on us all, sweetheart, and you're going to have a mighty sore head when it comes.'

'Not with champagne,' she said carelessly. 'I can drink as much ash I like. Let's go down and have another one.' And she started back along the corridor, until he arrested her progress.

'All right, let's have one here.' She waved the key around the keyhole ineffectually till he took it from her and opened the door.

'In you go, heart's delight. Alone.'

'Why?' she said belligerently. She put her arms round him and her head on his shoulder. 'I want you to share tonight.'

Will couldn't be there when it happened tonight, so she wanted him to share her joy now. It was all thanks to him. She didn't want him to go. She wanted to be close to him, have him hold her in his arms, share this moment; she wanted him to stay, and stay, and stay. She drew him closer, felt him react, but almost before she had registered it, he drew away, swearing. He pushed her through the open door, pulling it shut after her.

'And the song was yours,' he muttered wrily as he walked back along the corridor to the room he was sharing with Art, kicking viciously at the leg of an unfortunate table standing innocently nearby.

The room spun round her, a kaleidoscope of emotions, until she fell into a fitful sleep, half-full of dreams, half of nightmares. When she woke in the morning she thought briefly of what had happened, wondered just what Will had thought, what she had intended, come to that, and uneasily decided to ignore the whole episode.

The next three weeks were a jumble of meetings: with Don Field to arrange song publication; with Dave Prince, holding animated discussions over future plans, recording sessions for two of the songs, and several concerts scattered round Britain, most of them apparently in the Hebrides or the Scilly Isles. Art moaned bitterly. He did not take kindly to travel, and in particular to the privations of wartime travel, albeit with priority passes. Sleeping on barrack-room floors was not his idea of comfort. Jessica revelled in it, however, treating each concert as a new opportunity, each station as a new experience, doubling up for the night with girls from Lancashire, Scotland, Wales, all of whom told of unknown towns and villages, unknown hardships of life, and nitty-gritty everyday living that whetted her zest for the next stop. And sex! She blinked at most of the stories, both fascinated and repelled, but they did not touch her for this had nothing to do with her love. Love was what she had felt for John, and which remained imprisoned and untouchable for ever.

Will managed to get to the next two of the broadcasts. The third, on 31st July, he missed, unaccountably arriving late and meeting Jessica in the Kit-Kat Club afterwards.

'Trouble, Will?' she asked gently.

'Yeah, trouble. Not for me. We lost three pilots, Jessica. Jumped by 190s as we did a bomber escort back from Abbeville. And two new pilots killed in training last week. God, that's five out of twenty! Twenty-five per cent. Jumping Aunt Hannah, I'm *tired.*' He buried his face in his hands.

'Will,' she put her arms round him and could feel him

shaking, 'you mustn't drive yourself so.'

He sat up abruptly, as if retreating from physical contact. 'Thanks,' he said coolly, equilibrium restored, and gave her a twisted grin. 'They're resting me, so you needn't worry. I told them politely to stuff their Operational Training Unit so now I'm all yours. You have you a permanent clarinetist, Uxbridge willing.'

Before she could react there was an interruption.

'Jessica!' A waft of perfume spread itself sensuously over them. 'And Will. *Darlings*!'

Jessica gaped. 'Vanessa. What on earth – ?' Silk dress, nylons, lipstick. Of course, Vanessa would be the only woman in England who could get lipstick! After a minute another shock ran through her as she recognised – only by the hair and eyes – a familiar figure. Only they seemed alive. The rest was white, expertly transplanted skin and livid scars. 'Gerry,' she said steadily, 'how nice to see you. Er, Vanessa, where's—?'

'Graham? Oh, darling, he's at home. I was just up for the weekend and bumped into Gerry here. What a coincidence, wasn't it?'

'Good to see you, Donaldson.' Will took Gerry's hand coolly, in the spirit in which he was sure it had been offered.

'But the baby?' asked Jessica bewildered. 'Your little boy.'

'Johnnie? Graham's looking after him, and my neighbour too. She's awfully good. I don't have a moment's worry.'

I bet you don't, thought Jessica.

'Are you staying in town? I'll dash round and see you tomorrow, darling.'

'No, I'm not,' said Jessica drily. 'I'm a working lady.'

'You're a famous singer now, I heard. I've been telling all my friends the Singing Waaf's my cousin. That's what they call you, I gather. Little Johnnie's most impressed.' She glanced at Will. 'Graham's a dear old thing. He insisted on calling the baby Johnnie – after John Gale, you know.'

'Drink, Vanessa,' said Will abruptly, as she plumped herself down, pulling out the chair next to her for Gerry. 'Rhodes?'

'I'll help you.'

Vanessa nestled closer to Jessica confidingly as Will and Gerry departed to buy the drinks.

'Looks different, doesn't he? I'm used to it now, but it took a while.' She gulped, remembering. 'He's a good friend—' she shot a look at Jessica – 'believe me?'

Jessica shrugged. She didn't. Or on second thoughts perhaps she did. Vanessa's repulsion after Gerry's accident couldn't have vanished as quickly as all that, and it would be exactly like Vanessa to make use of Gerry's services as escort in town, without bestowing other favours. She felt great distaste and brought the subject round to Graham again. Vanessa answered monosyllabically, then brightened.

'Guess what? Our new station commander comes from West Forstling, so he told me. Used to command the Spitfire Wing there.'

'Geoff Swift?' asked Jessica sharply.

'Yes, do you know him?' asked Vanessa carelessly. 'He's nice, isn't he?'

'Too nice to be played around by you, Vanessa,' she said bluntly.

'How unkind of you, Jessica.' Vanessa laughed. 'So you call him Geoff, do you? My, what a girl you are. Geoff Swift *and* Will Donaldson. I'm so pleased you got over Johnnie Gale. He wasn't—'

'Vanessa,' cried Jessica, 'shut up! Firstly, Geoff is just a friend of mine. Secondly, I work with Will and I haven't—'

'Fancy,' said Vanessa archly.

Later that night Jessica agonised into her pillow. Forget John? How could she forget John? The pit opened up again and she felt a wave of longing such as she had not experienced for nearly two years, made all the more intense because she was beginning to realise its main ingredient was guilt. Yet when she finally fell asleep it was not John's face in her dreams but Will's that leaned towards her in love.

Chapter Eleven

'It doesn't scan.'

'It does at that. I'd say it was your breath control.'

'I'd say that was nonsense. It's you. You thinking the clarinet can sing.'

'It does, baby, it does, inside my head.'

'I'm not inside your head.'

'Not like you to admit failure.'

She threw the music at him amiably.

'Yow!'

'Now be serious, Will. Listen.' She sang. ' "For we have our today." It's wrong. It doesn't flow. Do you hear now?'

'I guess so.' He frowned, concentrated, strummed a few notes on the old Bechstein that Uxbridge had reluctantly transported into the requisitioned house allotted to them for quarters and rehearsal. What the Uxbridge Queen Bee thought of one of her brood sharing a house off camp with six men was not recorded, though doubtless imprinted on the memories of Station HQ staff.

'Maybe you're right. How about this?' He played it again. 'Lose a note.'

'That's it,' she said excitedly. ' "For we had today."

That's all it needs. Oh, Will,' her eyes sparkled, 'I'm sure that's it.'

'If the fog blurs our tomorrow,
When you are far away,
The sun will shine upon us
For we had today.'

'That's better. Let's try it on the band.'

'Let's get it right between the two of us first. That's the key with this song, I guess. It's not like "Rations" or "Sweet Nightingale".'

He moistened the reed, adjusted it and began to play. She should know the tune well enough by now and the sound of his clarinet playing it, but still she was gripped by its familiar excitement. She shut her eyes and concentrated, letting the music flow all round her, breathing deeply, steadily, ready for the moment when the melody would lift her voice into song.

'And when I hold you in my arms
Once tomorrow's passed away.
Oh then we'll love, remembering
Our lovely day today . . .'

'Yes, that's *right*!' she sighed, satisfied. She opened her eyes to find Will laughing at her.

'It beats me the way you sing with your eyes shut.'

'Why not? All the better to hear you with. What do you think? Does it work?'

'Yup,' he said. 'It works.'

'Voluble, aren't you? Here we are – you've just

launched a wonderful new song, a song to go down in the annals of history, and all you can say is, "Yup, it works",' she teased.

He shrugged. 'What more do you need? This? Hold my wrist, Jessica. Go on,' seeing her hesitate. 'Grab it.' He took hold of her hand. 'Feel anything?'

It was trembling with tension – or something else that made her hand respond to his. She kept it there, and he looked at her in surprise.

'Jessica,' he began quickly, seeing the expression on her face, but stopped as the door opened and Dave Prince erupted into the room, breaking the contact between them. 'All set for tonight? Good.' Not pausing for an answer. 'Got the new songs? Great. How's our Singing Waaf today? Good. Ready for the Dorchester? Terrific. Giving them plenty of bosom tonight?'

'Me or Will?' she asked sweetly. He didn't hear her.

'Good, good. Well, I'm off to HQ to see the Director of Music. In for a good old tussle again,' he said cheerfully, dashing out of the door. Then he poked his head round it again. 'By the way, neither of you has run foul of Ken Peters, have you?'

'Peters?' Jessica turned round swiftly.

'Yes. He's been stirring up a bit of trouble, so Dave says. At the BBC and the Dorchester. Nothing definite, but he doesn't seem too keen on the Astras. Watch out for him, that's all.' He left, the dust it seemed whirling with the speed of his departure.

'You know him?' asked Will.

'Yes,' said Jessica slowly. 'He was the band leader who auditioned me when I was eighteen, and then changed his mind.' She still couldn't bear to mention her mother's rôle in the rejection. 'I don't see why he should bear me malice, though.' With a sickening thud of her heart, she thought unwillingly of her mother. Surely she must be wrong? Cicely would never do the same thing again. Why, it had been her who had persuaded West Forstling to ask her to sing in their concerts. No, Cicely could have nothing to do with this – could she?

'Come on,' she continued determinedly, 'where's the new song you promised? "When it's over"?'

'It'll be ready soon.'

'Soon!' she said. 'We're doing the number, tonight, Will.'

'It's got to be right,' he said defensively. 'Just as good as it can be. You want it that way, don't you?' He smiled disarmingly.

'Of course,' she said resignedly. 'I'd just like perfection a little sooner. Hurry up!'

Will was notoriously late with his songs, seeming almost reluctant to let them out of his hands, sometimes allowing only five minutes or so rehearsal with the band, ten with her maybe. Yet somehow these were the ones that worked straight off.

'It was a whole lot less tiring on ops,' he complained.

'Music, Will, *music*.'

'Yeah. But I tell you, lady, I haven't gotten half as far as I want to in music for you yet. There's got to be something more. Something better. Our song's only begun. Not finished.'

'Let's hope old Göring doesn't get any ideas in his head about a surprise raid tonight,' muttered Danny as he set up the drums.

'He'll keep well away if he knows you're playing,' offered Vic.

Art was supervising the platform, and the band settling into their places, for once feeling somewhat nervous in these plush surroundings. They'd had to come in a tradesmen's entrance, such was a band's ranking. RAF dance it might be, but there was a lot of top brass around. 'One false move, lads, and it's back to the cookhouse,' said Art grimly, surveying the braid.

'Heaven help us,' murmured Jessica.

'I'll have you know, Section Officer Gray, that my spuds are very highly thought of in the sergeants' mess.'

'I prefer your trumpet, if that cook-up we had at Uxbridge last night was anything to go by.'

'Jewels, dance dresses . . . who'd ever think there was a war on?' said Vic, overawed, looking at the colourful tables round the edge of the dance floor.

'I would,' declared Jessica. 'Pre-war, most of those dresses. Look at those slinky outlines.'

'I am, I am,' murmured Will from behind, putting his hands lightly on her hips, and breathing down her neck.

She put her own hands over his, then suddenly remembering the last time it happened, removed them. 'I'm nervous,' she declared, for the sake of something to say. It was true enough. The Dorchester was different to RAF Nowhere in Particular.

'You? Nervous? The original Iron Duchess?' He grinned at her, and she wondered why something in her turned over. Stage fright, they called it. She'd never had it before, though.

'Will,' she said suddenly, 'it'll be all right, won't it? It's a big step forward. Different audience.'

This was a society audience. She thought fleetingly of her mother. She was in a sense walking into enemy territory here.

'Sure,' he agreed. 'It'll be okay. You and me, that's what we agreed. Remember?'

'Yes,' she smiled at him gratefully. 'I remember.'

The Master of Ceremonies was already calling for the Astras and the Singing Waaf - for the name had refused to die - and the seven of them bounced on to the dais. Thanks to quick publishing and publicity, their theme song was already becoming identified with them, and Jessica began to sing, the words sweeping out almost as though it were the first time.

'We heard that nightingale sing tonight
His spell of magic charms
But when at dawn he ceased, as all dreams can
I held you in my arms
And our song began.'

She neared the end, listening, waiting, longing for the clarinet to come in, pick up her last notes in fulfilment as it blended with her voice, one whole, then fading away, now returning, now triumphantly finishing in harmony.

She hardly heard the applause. For her, tonight, the applause was inward, between her and Will and the band.

Just before half-past ten, the BBC arrived to broadcast the band. Mikes were tested, dancers banished to their tables, and Art stood nervously ready. 'Just testing.' The mikes were ready, and an announcer in a dinner jacket informed the world that this was the BBC broadcasting from the Dorchester at the RAF Charity Ball, and here were the Astras and the Singing Waaf. Jessica cringed, hoping the Director was not listening.

For broadcasting the band had to play much louder, nearly deafening Jessica. It almost threw her, but she picked up again and for the second time that evening sang their theme song.

'It's going well, isn't it? Both new songs.'

'That third line – I wonder whether we dare switch the whole thing to a different key? Or to the upper register, in my solo. There's something . . .'

'You're such a perfectionist,' she said, sipping her drink. 'It was good. We put them over. That's what matters. They worked.'

'I guess so.' He was silent.

'What's wrong, Will?' she asked quietly.

He hesitated. 'The razzle-dazzle, I guess. Photo-sessions, journalists, recordings. I dunno.'

'I'm not keen either, Will. But it's all part of it.'

'Part of what?'

'Part of what we set out to do.'

'Let's dance,' he said abruptly.

In a crowded common room somewhere in Hampshire, Molly Payne was listening with the other FANYs to the wireless, to the voice of Jessica Gray, and Will Donaldson's clarinet. Remembering Art Simmonds and his band and West Forstling. It all seemed a long, long time ago, another life. At least Jessica had what she needed; she was singing at last. Had she forgotten John Gale? And Will? Molly wondered about the two of them. War swept everything, everyone, apart: families, friends, colleagues. Millions of shifting grains of sand in a desert, blown hither and thither. You didn't write – you rarely knew where to write to, even if you had the energy. But now she was established in England again, she could contact Jessica again. She would know well enough not to ask too many questions about what Molly was doing there.

Cairo hadn't worked out. Too hot, too humid. She got dysentery. Pale still, ill and thin six weeks later, she had been repatriated to the UK. It hadn't been the answer, that was all. But this was. Working with the agents to be dropped into Occupied France, close to the action, and if she had anything to do with it, soon to be part of it. Molly intended to carry the war to the enemy.

Beaulieu was the training school for the secret sabotage organisation, Special Operations Executive, set up with Churchill's mandate in mind to 'set Europe ablaze'. She intended to do just that. One hint that they would consider dropping women into Occupied France and she'd be there. Her French had been good already. Now it was better, for she hadn't wasted her time in Cairo.

Maybe, if she came through this lot, she'd get married. She'd settle down, have lots of kids out in the fresh country air, not like Bermondsey's. A tear stung her eye as she listened to Jessica's voice:

> 'For we'll have tomorrow,
> As we had today.'

'Well, here we are again, darling. Come and join us.'

'Thanks, Vanessa, but we have to play again soon.'

Vanessa pulled a face. 'Gerry darling, you persuade her.'

'Me? Persuade Jessica into anything? You have to be joking, Vanny.'

He pulled a face at Jessica, whose heart smote her at the light-hearted attempt at a grimace. The muscles weren't there any longer, and only a lopsided sneer came out. For some reason this made her feel warmer towards Gerry than ever before.

'Miss Gray doesn't like me, Vanny. Section Officer Gray, I should say.'

'Oh pooh, that was a long time ago.' Vanessa wrinkled up her nose. 'How are you, Will?' She gave him a mocking glance.

Will nodded at Gerry. Unwillingly, he and Jessica sat down.

'Do you know, I don't think he approves of us, Gerry. Isn't that deliciously funny?'

Gerry, Will. A sudden pang of guilt for the past shot through Jessica. Here she was, riding high – and John, lying in a cold grave.

Will shot her a sharp glance.

'Deliriously, poppet,' drawled Gerry. There was an uncomfortable silence. 'Well, I never heard the fat lady sing, Donaldson,' he went on. 'Only our Jessica here.'

'Haven't changed, have you, Gerry.'

'Only facially, dear Jessica.'

It was her own fault, she had fallen into his trap. 'You've embarrassed her, Gerry,' giggled Vanessa.

'I guess we'll be on our way,' said Will firmly, standing up, but Vanessa's eyes were suddenly fixed beyond him.

'Oh my God!' Her face went white. 'Graham, what on earth – ?'

Not even acknowledging Jessica and Will's presence, Graham Macintosh strode up to his wife and yanked her unceremoniously by the arm.

'Careful, Macintosh,' pitched in Gerry.

'So this is Millicent. Are you coming now, or do you want a scene?' Graham demanded.

'Hold it, Graham,' warned Will. 'There's a lot of brass hats here. Settle it outside, not here.'

'There's nothing to settle,' drawled Gerry. 'I take Vanessa out - why not? Attractive woman. Don't want to keep her bottled up in Cornwall, all to yourself—'

Will caught Graham's arm.

'Would you believe me, old chap, if I told you there's nothing between Vanessa and myself other than a sweet loving friendship?' Gerry went on.

'No,' said Graham softly.

'I rather thought not. Pity.' Gerry drained his drink. 'Are you coming, Vanessa, or going with hubby here?'

'With you, Gerry,' Vanessa said mutinously. 'Graham wants to spoil my fun, that's all. I'll be back in the afternoon tomorrow, Graham. As arranged.' They swept out, leaving him staring impotently after them.

'Graham,' said Jessica anxiously, 'Don't be a fool. You'll lose your commission if you have a brawl, and that's what you're heading for.'

'Did you know about this?' he asked Jessica, acknowledging her for the first time.

'I've seen them together once,' she said honestly.

'And I'm left at home to look after the baby! I'm allowed to help the RAF out when Vanessa's got time for it in her appointments book,' he muttered.

'Where's home now?'

'Down in Cornwall,' he said disgustedly. 'I tell you, I'm pretty tired of it. Damn all to do for a night-fighter there. Not like Essex. If it wasn't for Vanessa and the kid, I'd volunteer for—' he paused then resumed '—something more exciting. I tell you, they're a different breed down there.'

'It was good of you to fix this, Will, I'm glad we haven't got to trundle back to Uxbridge. Luxury! I feel like King Zog of Albania. Doesn't he live here, or is that the Savoy?'

'You don't look like King Zog. Not much, anyway.'

'Thank you, Will. You're so complimentary.'

He laughed. 'When you're ready to have me tell you how beautiful you are, let me know.' He raised his glass. 'You look like you slid down a rainbow tonight.'

'No crock of gold to fall in though – what's the matter?' She broke off, as she saw his sudden abstraction.

'Sorry.' He grinned. 'Just gave me an idea for a song.' He whistled softly. 'Last line of the chorus – "When you slid down that rainbow and into my arms." What do you think?'

Her eyes lit up, dancing. 'It's a possibility,' deliberately dead-pan.

'It's a terrific idea, and you know it. Listen here.' The tune began to take shape.

'Will, it's wonderful.' Impulsively, she threw her arms round him in her enthusiasm, to the interest of the rest of the bar.

'You've come alive again, Jessica,' he said quietly, taking her hand when she sat down again. 'And I'm not sure about the "again".'

'Since the bluebell wood, when you gave me music.'

'And you brushed me off,' he said catastrophically.

Aghast, she pulled back from him as a gulf opened between them. How had she been so unprepared? All these months it had been her and Will? Or had it been just the music? No, surely not that. She stood on the brink of the chasm, her mind numbed with the suddenness of the crisis.

Will regarded her with apparent amusement. Inside, his heart was pounding; let her say I got it all wrong. When she didn't, he went on casually, 'Don't look so stricken. I've gotten over it. One of those little things, that's all.'

'But—' She stopped. She couldn't deny it. That's what she had done. Then why did she want to shout, 'You've got it wrong, all wrong, you don't understand?'

'. . . in a big way,' he was saying, and she realised she'd missed what he'd been talking about. 'So they're going to absorb the Eagle Squadrons with them.'

'What? Who?'

'The US Eighth Air Force. Pretty soon, I guess. They've been over here a while now to get organised. They've finally done it. Around the end of September, I guess. Another month—'

'But it won't affect you,' she said, aghast. 'You've been made non-operational.'

'I'm going back,' he said bluntly. 'They'll want us experienced pilots to train the newcomers. They'll need all the help they can get.'

'The same old story,' she said bitterly. 'Will, there are dozens of pilots. Only one musician like you.'

'No matter, I'm going. I'm leaving the RAF and transferring to the US Air Force. I have formally to become part of the 4th Fighter Group, at any rate. Swear allegiance and all that. 133 Squadron will be part of 4th Fighter Group along with the other two Eagle squadrons, and I'm going with them.'

'But why, Will?' she asked desperately. 'I know you've tried to explain, but where's the glory in dying?'

'There's sure as hell no glory in letting others die for you. Anyway,' he said lightly, 'you never know, I might survive.'

'Don't make a joke of it, Will. I can't bear it. Don't you enjoy what we're doing?'

'I told you,' he said, weary now, 'the razzle-dazzle is getting to me. I hadn't reckoned on it somehow. My fault. It just seems life is a lot simpler up there in the clouds. You can see things clearly.'

'Including the one that shoots you down,' she said bitterly.

He stood up abruptly and she saw she'd gone too far. 'I'm going to turn in.' She got up too, walking beside him in silence up the hotel staircase.

'Cheer up,' he continued, 'it's not as bad as all that. Here, I'll dance you back to your room. Tango or rumba?'

She managed a wan smile. 'Rumba. But we'll be thrown out for being drunk and disorderly. WAAF and RAF officers can't do that sort of thing.'

'Wanna put a nickel on it?'

He swept her into his arms and rumba-ed madly up the corridor.

'Will, please don't go back on ops,' she asked jerkily, when they stopped outside her room.

'I have to, Jessica,' he said gravely.

'Suppose you go – like John—'

His mouth twisted. 'Is it the music or the man you'd miss?'

The shade of John Gale hovered. She looked at Will, realising no compromise was allowed, unable to answer.

Seeing the differing emotions pass over her face, he said casually, 'Good night, Jessica,' and walked steadily away down the corridor towards his own room.

She stood as if rooted to the floor, held back by two years of self-delusion, forced now to think things through for she knew this was the moment of decision. Think? She didn't need to think. There'd been too much thinking. She watched the distance between them slowly widen as Will walked, emotionally at any rate, out of her life.

What on earth was she playing at? Was she crazy? She dropped her bag and coat on the floor, picked up her long skirts and ran.

He glanced round, hearing the footsteps, and saw her running full tilt towards him. He walked on, then stopped so suddenly she cannoned into him, throwing her arms around him. He did not move.

'Will,' she said softly. 'Will?' Looked at him, at the couple of inches parting their lips, brought his head to hers and put her lips on his, waiting till hesitantly they came to life under hers.

Was she disappointed or relieved when after a long, first tentative, then passionate kiss, he held her close for a moment then tore himself away?

'Will,' she called in a low voice, then ran after him and caught at his sleeve. 'Are we all right?'

He gave her his old, lazy, warm grin, and said simply: 'It's sure looking that way.'

Yet still a shadow lay between them, perhaps had always been there. She could not sleep, and lay awake till she heard the birds singing their dawn chorus in Park Lane. Will, her heart was repeating. And John. But what about John? Easy for people to say casually it was time she forgot him, time to love again, but it wasn't as easy as that. She'd promised him she'd never sing for anyone else, and she had. She'd let him die, when he needed her completely. Suppose she did the same to Will? Suppose she failed him, too? Was she capable of love? That feeling of guilt spread over her again, making her toss and turn, and the shadow over her sun did not shift.

'Actually Gerry was telling you the truth,' Vanessa said off-handedly, flinging her bag crossly into the chair. She almost succeeded in making Graham feel guilty.

'But why do you want to spend the weekend with him so often?'

'Because we have a good time, together, that's why,' she flared. 'He knows people, we go dancing. There's nothing to do down here. Nothing! No fun.'

She made her own, in fact, but no point in telling Graham that.

'And how do you think I feel when I see you in a cosy foursome with Jessica Gray and Will Donaldson? I'm merely the husband.'

'Oh, Graham, don't be stupid. I tell you, there's nothing in it.'

'How am I supposed to believe that?' He stopped, disbelieving. 'You're laughing, you bitch.'

She wiped the smile off her face. 'Don't you dare call me that. Gerry's worth ten of you. You know nothing about me, not really.'

'I reckon I do, Vanessa. I've even begun to do a bit of thinking. Unusual for old Graham, isn't it? But I've begun to wake up. How do I know Johnnie's my kid, eh? He was early, you said. And you went around with Gerry Rhodes – until his accident. Is that why you go and see him? Is that it?' he yelled wildly.

Panic set in. This wasn't part of Vanessa's plan. 'No,' she shouted. 'No, it wasn't. Of course Johnnie's yours.'

'Prove it.'

'Okay,' she said, dangerously quiet. 'Easy. Gerry's impotent, that's why.' She began to laugh hysterically. It was all too simple.

'Impotent?' he said, taken aback.

'Yes. Amazing, isn't it? You can ask him if you like – if you've the gall. He had some illness. I can't remember exactly.'

'There's no proof—'

'Oh, for heaven's sake, Graham! I tell you he can't get it up.'

'All right, I believe you. All the same, I don't see why you have to spend weekends with him—'

'Fun, Graham, fun. Remember what that is?'

He couldn't any longer. His every waking hour not taken up with flying or looking after Johnnie was a mish-mash of worry about Vanessa. Then he started to think. All right, if Gerry was impotent, then why wouldn't

Vanessa sleep with him, Graham, very often? She was eager for it when she did, but different somehow. He'd been so sure there'd been someone else. The thought came that perhaps there was – and not in London. He'd keep a careful watch. Surely she wouldn't be such a fool as to play around on the station though?

'We've had an invitation from Geoff Swift.' Jessica came flying into the rehearsal room.

'Who?' Art waited till the end of the number before replying.

'Swift. He was the Wingco at West Forstling. You remember, Art. Now he's station commander at—' she frowned '—RAF Tregeddra? Cornwall, isn't it? So presumably that's where Graham is stationed, Will?' She hadn't heard from Vanessa since their last meeting, but hadn't forgotten her mention of Geoff Swift. That all too casual mention.

'Macintosh?' A flicker of interest from Art. 'Okay, let's do it. Okay, by you, Will?'

'When?'

'Third week of September.'

'Suits me. I'm reliable up to the end of the month.'

'What's the matter, Will?' She came up to him and took his hand.

'Nothing much.' He hesitated then said, 'I missed the big picture, that's all. The Dieppe show. That was the one postponed from July. 133 was on it.'

'But that was terrible,' she said, aghast. 'Thousands were killed.'

'On the ground. In the air we did a pretty good job. I wish I'd made it,' he said rather wistfully.

You'll be there soon enough, was her silent thought, but she kept her silence.

Since that night a week ago, they'd stepped one pace back emotionally, delicately walking round the edges of love; something held her back, he sensed, and instead of pressuring her, poured everything into his songs.

'I dashed right in last time, Will,' she told him. 'I see now we were both blinded. You were right. John and I needed each other; we were in love, but didn't love each other. So this time I need to be sure.'

He'd said nothing; he took up the clarinet and began to play, not a love song but a boogie-woogie number that he repeated incessantly till the whole mess rebelled.

Shortly before they left for Cornwall, Bubbles Gray gave a party and asked the Astras to sing. For a very good cause, she explained – funds for the restoration of Canterbury after the terrible June raid which had caused so much damage. It was for charity, she pointed out righteously. It was also to see at first hand what this famous group was like – as well as to enhance Bubbles' own local standing, while they were so well known. Not that that would last long now – she smiled. It was all for Jessica's own good. She'd see that in time. She needed to be close to her daughter again. Mothers and daughters should be close. Especially at the particular time she'd chosen for the concert.

'I don't like it, Will,' said Jessica uneasily. 'Mother has something up her sleeve.'

'Perhaps it's an olive branch.'

'They don't grow in her garden,' she said shortly.

She hadn't seen her mother for a year now, though she

had met her father in London several times. They behaved almost like polite strangers with no point of contact. He told her her mother was proud of her. Jessica replied she doubted that, hoping he would vehemently prove her wrong. He said nothing, and the last hope dwindled.

'Darling, how lovely to see you. Such a success. I'm quite proud of my little Brickie. So nice of you to come to sing for us. All the old gang are here to listen to you.'

'Thank you, Mother.' She could laugh again now. It was all so ridiculous.

'I even ran out and bought a record,' Cicely chattered on. 'Your father's been playing it all day. Oh, so nice to see you again, Pilot Officer Donaldson.'

'Thank you, ma'am,' replied Will, mouth twitching.

'Flight Lieutenant, Mother. Soon to be Captain in the American Eighth Air Force.'

'I can never remember all these ranks. You're the clarinet player, aren't you? I hope you manage to keep up with this daughter of mine. She has her own ideas about things.'

'I manage, ma'am.'

'Oh, do call me Bubbles.' She flashed the famous Bubbles Gray smile. 'I think it's so brave of you both to come here, you know.'

'Why, Mother?' asked Jessica suspiciously.

'Well, today, dear.' Bubbles looked hurt. 'I nearly cancelled it when I realised. I should have thought you'd remember. Both of you,' she added carelessly.

Jessica stared at her mother, feeling all the old foreboding flooding back.

'It's the day dear Johnnie was shot down, isn't it?' explained Bubbles brightly.

Jessica cried alone where she thought Will would not find her. But he did. In front of John's grave in the churchyard. She shivered. How could she have forgotten? Will put his arms round her and held her to him, but it was no comfort. He could not reach her.

'She did it on purpose, Will,' she said at last, drying her eyes. 'On purpose. Can you imagine?'

'Why would she do something like that, Jessica? You're imagining it. It was just a mistake to come down here.'

'You don't know her, Will. She hates me for my success, I see that now. I actually thought she might be a little proud of me. Pathetic, wasn't it? And I suppose she hates you, too, because you're part of what makes us successful.'

'If you're right, she's crazy, and you shouldn't be upset.'

'Sometimes I think she *is* mad.' Jessica shivered, staring at the wording on the gravestone: *Per Ardua ad Astra.*

'But the worst thing of all, Will, is that she's right. We had forgotten.'

'Forgotten what?' he said angrily. 'That it was the 17th, sure. But forget John? The exact time has damn all to do with it. He's still around me.' He paused. 'And you, too, isn't he, Jessica?'

'I—' she stopped, taking care with her words. She needed to explain exactly. 'I know now I never really loved John. Everyone was right all along. I was *in* love

with him. Blinded I suppose. But John loved me, because he needed me. So how can I just forget him now? Especially when I—' She broke off.

Needed her? thought Will. Maybe that was true. John had needed Vanessa, too, just needing anything and anybody to take his mind off what has happening, each and every day. Cracking up, that's what they'd said in the mess. He'd got the twitch. Will himself had damn near gone down the same path this July, so he knew what John Gale had gone through.

His mind went to the kid who was John Gale's legacy from the hell of the Battle of Britain. Tomorrow they'd be leaving for Tregeddra. He didn't trust Vanessa any more. He was going to make quite sure Jessica didn't see too much of the Macintoshes. Especially the youngest.

Vanessa looked strained, thought Jessica, as she changed for the dance. It was going to be a difficult evening, she feared. If only Molly had been able to come. It was a wonderful coincidence when on the telephone Molly had mentioned she was coming on a week's course to Porthcurno. When tonight was ruled out, Jessica and Will promptly arranged to stay on longer to meet her again. Tomorrow she was coming to the hotel. But meanwhile there was tonight to get through. She sighed. Perhaps she was imagining things. Perhaps it wouldn't be so bad, after all. She was wrong.

Graham looked pretty grim. She'd enjoyed meeting the little boy who was toddling now and chattering non-stop. He'd inherited Graham's dark hair and Vanessa's blue eyes, a charming picture. Graham seemed to be drinking a lot, though. Things obviously weren't right

between them. It was a pretty remote station for someone like Vanessa. RAF Tregeddra must feel like the last outpost of civilisation for her.

Even Graham was chafing at the bit. Night-fighting was his metier, he said; hanging round Cornish village pubs was not. Flying was infrequent at the moment. He'd put in for a transfer only to find it surprisingly turned down, on grounds of his essential presence at Tregeddra. The only interesting thing had been bumping into that little Waaf from West Forstling, Molly something, when he was in Penzance. Nice girl. Down here for a four-day course at Porthcurno. Now if Vanessa were more like her . . .

Jessica watched them from the platform where she was singing, Graham sitting morosely while Vanessa danced with everyone before finally with her husband. They made a handsome couple, dark and fair heads close together. How deceptive appearances were! On the dance floor they looked a devoted man and wife. Then she saw Geoff Swift cut in, clearly pulling rank with all his old social ease. That didn't seem to be the way Graham was taking it, though. He took a drink, and another, emptying the glass quickly. As if in slow motion, Jessica saw what was going to happen. Impossible to warn Will or leave stage mid-number. Graham shot out of his seat and, seizing Geoff's collar, hauled him away from Vanessa.

'Leave it, Macintosh,' rapped Geoff, white-faced as he turned on Graham. 'Leave it till later, you fool.'

By the time Jessica got there it was too late. Graham was past waiting; he took one swing at Geoff, sending him staggering back, before a couple of pilots grabbed him, restraining him.

Vanessa was sobbing as Geoff picked himself up, Jessica helping, the rest of the assembly interested spectators.

'Let's get outside,' Geoff muttered. 'The fool! I don't want you all involved in this. I'm not particularly proud of myself,' he said outside, 'but why couldn't the idiot choose a less public place to take a swing at me? It'll be a court martial, I'm afraid.'

'What?' Vanessa looked terrified. 'Can't you refuse to prosecute or whatever it is you do?'

'This is the RAF,' he retorted grimly. 'Not a pub brawl.' Then he softened. 'It's not your fault, though, darling.'

'Of course not,' said Jessica wrily, 'it never is.' She was boiling with rage at Vanessa who looked back at her coldly.

'Always good little Jessica, isn't it? Always you with the breaks. Never me.' She ran off blindly.

'Geoff, is it serious with you?' Jessica couldn't believe it. Not sensible, easy-going Geoff.

He grimaced. 'I don't think there's much permanent harm, thanks. Except to Macintosh, poor chap. I can't forgive myself for that. She told me he didn't give a damn. I should have known better, I suppose. But with Vanessa, somehow you don't stop to think. There she was, making her desires quite plain. You know how it is . . . Or perhaps you don't.'

'Yes, I understand, Geoff.'

The hotel Geoff had booked them into was perched in isolated grandeur on the cliffs of the Lizard peninsula, overlooking Mount's Bay.

'Better than the floor of the WAAF quarters, I can assure you,' he said. 'And if you're staying down on two days' leave, you can reap the benefit. Not much of the war shows from up there.'

The next day Molly came to visit them, and as the weather was still warm for late September they sat in the gardens, listening to the sea crashing on the rocks beneath.

'I thought you'd know enough about signals by now,' said Jessica, 'without doing another course.'

'Sort of,' said Molly, twiddling her cup. 'But wireless, you know, is fascinating the further you get into it.'

'I don't associate you with it, that's all. I thought you wanted adventure, to get away from England.'

'It's adventure of a sort.'

'Oh,' Jessica realised the unspoken message Molly was trying to give her and laughed as Will kicked her. 'How stupid of me.'

'How about you two?' Molly glanced from one to the other. 'There is a you two, isn't there?' she asked bluntly.

'Yes,' said Will firmly. 'There's an us two, ' and reached for Jessica's hand, as a warm glow of happiness spread through her.

After Molly had left, and with the tide out, they walked through the hotel gardens, clambered down the stone-hewn steps and into the rocky cove below, investigating the rock pools with enthusiasm.

'Back home as a kid I used to go to Cape Cod with my parents. That's pretty much like it is here in Cornwall. In fact, I reckon if you stretched a line due west you'd pretty well hit Falmouth – even the names are the same.

Then there are the islands. Nantucket was the one we went for. Like it is here, I reckon – wild, primitive underneath all the modern jazz. You know, its name comes from an old Indian word meaning "the place that is far away". The smell here – that sharp smell of rocks and sea-water pools – it really takes me back.'

'Will you go back after the war?'

'Let's win it first,' he said abruptly. 'Here.' And he pulled her down beside him on to a flat rock.

'It seems hard to imagine there's a war on, just at the moment.'

'Wait till the Spits take off from Tregeddra.'

'Are you looking forward to going back on ops, Will?'

He was silent for a long time. 'You know, Jessica, that's one hell of a question. I was looking forward to the swearing in, I guess, and meeting General Spaatz, and seeing Old Glory hoisted over the 4th Fighter Group. But it's going to be tough, giving up the RAF. We're keeping our Eagle badges though, and our RAF wings.'

'You said *was* looking forward.'

'It's the squadron, Jessica. I heard this morning, but didn't want to spoil our last day.'

'What about it?'

'It – it's been wiped out, more or less. Twelve of them,' he blurted. 'The squadron flew a bomber escort to Morlaix, never met up with the bombers who were late, went off course, got caught by strong winds, ran out of fuel, and were either shot down, baled out or crash-landed. Only one came back.' He had recited the facts calmly; now he beat his fist on the rocks. 'And you know what hurts, Jessica? I wasn't *there*! I couldn't even say goodbye.'

'Oh, Will,' she said softly. 'I'm so sorry.' She put her arm round him, felt his body tense.

'I know I said it was important playing music. But, goddamit, it *hurts* to think I was playing when 133 was going through that yesterday! And the hell of it – did I want to play music, or did I want to stay with you?'

There was dead silence; he tossed a pebble into the waves, followed it with another.

He went on soberly: 'I'm tired of the razzle-dazzle, Jessica, whereas you thrive on it. I've seen how you come alive to an audience. You respond to it, it's your life. But I'm not like that. For me, it's the music only. Just the music – and you. I want to play, to compose the perfect song for you to sing. And when I've attained that – it's a reward in itself, that and to hear you singing it. Not for it to be sung the world over. Back in the States each year, I'd go to Tanglewood – you heard of that?'

She shook her head.

'It's the biggest open air concert in the world, I guess. Every summer the Boston Symphony Orchestra plays in the woods. There's a big shed seating thousands but it's more fun to take a blanket and sit on the grass and just listen. All around you are real music-lovers, and the magic kind of gets you, binds you together – old, young, students, academics. I tell you, my music was born right there in Tanglewood. We'll go some day. It's the best thing in the world. That and this cove.' He turned to her. 'Being here with you.'

She took his hand, half-laughing, half-serious, as she said: 'Will, you make me laugh, you make me mad, you make me cry. And, Will, I love you.'

A sharp intake of breath, a faint flush spreading

through his cheeks, a slight reaction in his hand, then he turned to her, his face full of hesitant joy.

'Would that just be for now?'

Then she knew, no laughing now, just the overwhelming truth.

'No, that would be forever.'

The moon was bright that night. A bomber's moon. But there were no bombers over Mullion as they stood together at the window, the blackout drawn back for they were in darkness, the room lit only by the moon.

He took her face between his hands, and pushing her curls back, kissed her very slowly and deliberately.

'You've got your eyes closed again,' he said lovingly.

'All the better to see you with, feel you with,' she whispered.

'Open them. I love your eyes. I want to see them look at me while I—'

'While you – ?'

'Kiss you,' he said. 'First. Like this.'

All the music in her life seemed concentrated in her body in one gigantic melody as he carried her to the bed and lay down with her.

'And our song began,' she said, smiling into his eyes.

'It began long ago and has no end.' And his hands were on her, caressing urgently, gently, a love-song in themselves. 'Keep your eyes open,' he said. 'Please.'

She wondered why he asked so urgently and if he might be afraid of ghosts. But there were no ghosts that night. They were banished by this flame of light, dazzling, obliterating all dark, then she could think of nothing else but the fulfilment of the song. The music was winding home, she thought confusedly. Home, the love she'd wanted and searched for as a child, the times she'd run up to the manor door waiting for the loving presence to open it, but waited in vain. Now the door lay open, and love waited to take her into its strong caress. She gasped with pleasure and love, then felt him check and wondered why. 'Open your eyes, darling. Look at me.'

She opened them and saw Will, saw love. But it hurt . . . no it didn't. Yes, no . . . And their song began.

Chapter Twelve

Liverpool Street was a swarming mass of uniforms. Will and Jessica were swallowed up in the heaving throng of people as they fought their way through to the LNER train for Audley End. Every one of these people here could be feeling just as I do, thought Jessica, each one of them parting from someone they love. Each one with that slightly sick feeling of so much to say, and no time to say it. So strip off the thousand unsaid things and reduce conversation to banalities.

'When will I see you again?' she blurted out.

'I'll call you, honey. The first moment I can get a pass, or leave.' He brushed his hand fleetingly over her cheek. 'I'll be with you every opportunity I get. Word of an injun.'

'Honest one, I trust,' she gulped, trying to laugh.

'Very honest.' He hesitated. 'The train's not leaving for half an hour. Do you want a coffee? It'll be better than standing here like a couple of totem-poles.'

'Yes.' She seized the chance gratefully. 'It'll mean another battle though.' She was only too right. The counter was like the Tower of Babel with its multitude of heavily accented voices, but Will was adept at worming his way to the counter.

'Here. So-called coffee!' He made a face. 'I'll be glad to get back to US cooking at Debden and do without NAAFI rations.'

'I didn't think the Americans cooked anything other than steaks or Mom's apple pie,' she said mechanically, stirring the coffee intently, conscious of the minutes ticking by.

'They do. I'll write you a song about it.' He stopped and looked at her. 'Look—' he laughed '—These heavy farewells. I'm beginning to feel like I'm starring in *Dangerous Moonlight*.'

'Dangerous?' she echoed wrily.

'That was a dumb thing to say, Jessica. Listen,' his voice deepened, 'I've got to ask you. It's beginning to burn me up. I've no right – and this is a hell of a place to ask it – but I've got to. You and Johnnie Gale – I thought—'

She set down her cup carefully. 'You thought we had been lovers. Like you and me,' she supplied.

'I assumed—'

'Wrongly.' Her voice was clipped. So it had come. She had known it would. Better spoken than unspoken. But he should tread gently, gently, for this was between her and John.

'Do you regret it? Is that why you still think of him all the time?'

'Are you crazy, Will?' She looked at him, startled. 'I love *you*.'

'There's something – just something there I can't get at, Jessica.'

'No one gives one hundred per cent,' she said defensively.

'No, but there's a few per cent missing I can't account for.'

There was silence until she said miserably, 'It's not in my control if there is. I do love you.' Should she tell him? No, she couldn't. Her guilt was something she had to conquer alone. Her love for Will could surely cure it, bury it.

He reached out and took her hand.

'It'll come, Will,' she said, her eyes bright in appeal.

'Yes.' He glanced at the clock. 'I'd best be moving.' Hand in hand they walked back to the train. By this time it was packed. He turned and kissed her, once gently, then again almost violently before jumping in. She saw him forcing his way through to the corridor, then walking along by the windows. Greedily, absorbing her last sight of him, she followed his progress past the compartments till he reached the reserved seat, throwing his kitbag up on top of the others already cluttering the luggage rack. Then he found his way to the square window, cursing because he could not get it open behind its bars, mouthing things she could not hear, straining her ears in vain for some last message.

How ridiculous, she thought, I'll be seeing him in maybe two weeks. Why feel so sick – as though this parting were somehow immensely significant? Was he right? Was she holding back? Had thoughts of a hillside long ago intruded into that moonlit room? As if by failing one, she could make amends to another would-be lover? She pushed the thought away.

Then the train drew out, and with it her last sight of Will's face flattened against the square window of the carriage. The brown paint of the train seemed a fitting colour for an autumn farewell. No, au revoir, she told herself firmly, and set her face towards the future.

' "Today" is the second most requested record after Vera Lynn's,' Dave Prince read out from his newspaper proudly. 'That's "Slightly Terrific", me darling, as the good song says. And "Rainbow" is ready to go. Where's the new one Will promised?'

'I gave it to Don Field this morning. He wants a look before we launch it.'

'So do I. What's it like?'

'One of the funnies.'

'Swing? Danceable?'

'Very much so. It's called "The Apple in my Crumble".' She sang a few lines, grinning at the thought of Will's letter.

'Oh me oh my, it's Mom's apple pie, here at Debden, honey.'

'You're the apple in my crumble
You're the lover in my lane
You're the pearl in oyster pudding
And you're home with me again.'

'Sounds good,' he said absently. 'You sing it, I'll do the plugs. Hey, you remember I asked you about Ken Peters?'

'Yes,' she said sharply. 'Why?'

'I was right. It was him or us at the Dorchester, I discovered. And there was an idea floating around the entertainment business that service bands should perform only in service premises, no matter what the occasion. An idea, so I gather, heartily endorsed by Ken

Peters. I saw it off this time, but we'll have to watch it. We don't get support from Uxbridge on this one, but it's important for your future – and Will's – that the idea doesn't catch on. After the war . . .'

After the war. Now it almost seemed possible to talk that way. A few nights ago the BBC had broken into its programmes to give the news of Rommel's retreat at El Alamein – and this morning came the news of the Allied landings on the North Coast of Africa. Excitement lit up the country like a match in a petrol tank. The first sign that the tide was on the turn. Now it was not *if* we win the war, but *when*. And Will's song was going to hit the mood of the moment exactly.

Good news was needed all right. The thought of another winter of austerity ahead was depressing in the extreme. Stricter rationing, ever longer queues, shortages of everything, making do and mending, utility clothes with pockets and pleats forbidden – and still bombing raids making shelter life an ever-present necessity – all combining to make a grim picture for the months to come. And the train journeys! Ever longer, ever slower, especially without Will's lively presence. Already Art was showing signs of rebellion and sharing the house at Uxbridge was no longer the fun it had been. Cast perpetually in each other's company, the band tended to get edgy. Although the compensations were many as their fame spread, and they could look forward to a secure future post-war, the fogs of November were closing in.

Jessica sat nervously in the bar. Will was late. It must be the train. It would happen, the day they were to launch the new song on the air. She hadn't seen him since he left at the end of September, and now it was November. They'd spoken on the phone, they'd written, but that was almost more frustrating than nothing at all. The Eagle Club in the Charing Cross Road had been started for Americans in the British forces, and was busily dishing out its hamburgers and coke. The accents surrounding Jessica made her feel a foreigner. The ebullient American servicemen and their outspoken comments on seeing a Waaf sitting alone, made her uncomfortable today, whereas normally she would have responded cheerfully. Why didn't Will come?

Then he was there, sliding into the seat opposite her, and the world came right.

'Captain Donaldson reporting for duty.'

'Section Officer Gray very glad to see him,' she said softly. 'Oh, Will, I've missed you.'

'Me, too, honey,' he said quietly. 'No night goes by without I dream a song for you.' He smiled. 'Do you ever hear them way back in star-country?'

She could not find words. She put out her hands to his, and they stared at each, just content to be with one another again. 'You look tired,' she said inadequately at last.

'They drive us pretty hard up there.'

Hard wasn't the word. Perhaps it was because he'd been off the strength in the summer. Perhaps because the CO was driving the new inexperienced Yankees in their own interests, and his flight commanders had to follow his example. Perhaps it was simply because the new pilots brought with them the whiff of the wide open spaces of their homeland and the optimistic unseasoned hopes of youth, that he, war-weary as he was, found the going tougher than he expected. Here servicemen and civilians alike were war-seasoned, determined but worn down by the seemingly endless path ahead. He remembered what his father had told him of the coming of the Yanks to Château Thierry in the First World War in 1918. How they'd bowled down the long French roads in their lorries bound for the Front, singing, 'Johnnie comes Marching Home' at the tops of their voices. How he'd seen the French peasants staring in astonishment at them as they'd passed. Singing? On the way to the Front? They'd endured nearly four years of war in France before the Yanks arrived. They knew what war was. But if it hadn't been for those lorry-loads of men like his father, with their brash optimism, that war might have been lost. It looked like a repeat match now. All the same, the men with whom he felt at home were those who'd shared the last two years, the men who wore miniature RAF wings over the right breast pockets of their new brown US uniforms, their American Wings now on the left.

'Beef it up on the high notes, Will,' said Art worriedly. 'It's not coming over.'

They had only held a ten-minute rehearsal of the new song before the red light indicated they were on the air.

'Okay, boss. Ready now.'

They struck up with their theme tune and another broadcast by the Astras was under way. The introduction of a new song was becoming routine now. Old favourites, new favourites – and one new song a week. New songs composed in snatched moments in the mess, during briefing, debriefing, dispersal – anywhere he could seize pen and paper, and shut himself off at least mentally from the racket around him. (No qualms about line-shooting here. The 336th Fighter Squadron of the 4th Fighter Group was the best and the world was going to know it.) This new song was a humdinger, Will knew. It was a band number principally; his clarinet was silent till the last verse, and he was able to listen to the sound he loved best; Jessica singing.

'You're my tea rose in the desert,
You're the Earl Grey in my tea . . .'

He took up the clarinet, began to play, and was lost in the world of music.

After the broadcast, Art burst his bombshell on them. 'I want out, folks. Sorry and all that, but I'm packing it in. I can't take the travelling any more, and the wife's decided to produce another young Simmonds. So all in all, it's back to the cookhouse door for me. Besides, it's not so much fun as it used to be. Too much like hard work now.'

Fun. Jessica thought about those dances at Kippen Hall. John Gale cavorting on tables; dancing with John, walking with John. Yes, they'd been fun. Or would have been if she hadn't been so desperately in love with him, which made the days mingled joy and anguish. *So* in love, and yet she'd failed him. Failed him then – and failed him now. It was retribution that Art was leaving.

'But, Art, must you?' Jessica cried in dismay. 'It won't be the same.'

He shrugged. 'You'll figure something out; the rest of the boys will stay. I'll hang on till the New Year.'

'What are we going to do without a trumpet, Will?' she asked despairingly afterwards when they were alone in her hotel bedroom.

'I'll think of something. Now come here.'

'I feel so – well – betrayed. I've been sharing a house with this man – and he's been plotting behind my back.'

'Queen of the melodrama! No plotting to it. Art's terrified of the fearsome Section Officer Gray. So are the others.'

'You're joking.'

'Nope. Not really. You *are* an officer, and that's the way things work round here. We'll go down to Uxbridge and discuss it. Now come here.'

'But—'

'Jessica, I've a forty-eight hour pass. Are you going to spend the whole night fussing about a trumpet?'

'No,' she laughed, coming to him arms outstretched, 'not when I can make love to a clarinet.'

The next morning, there was a surprise visitor. In fact, two. Directly to their hotel at Piccadilly Circus from the Uxbridge house, Graham, looking older and strained, appeared while Jessica was singing through a new song. He was clutching Johnnie, now a toddler, by one hand.

Jessica noticed immediately the absence of braid on Graham's uniform. He noticed the direction of her gaze and nodded.

'Back to Flight Sergeant. Look,' he said awkwardly, 'I'm sorry to interrupt you here – I could hear you rehearsing.'

'It's a pleasure, Macintosh,' Will told him easily as he strolled through from the adjoining room. 'I'm real sorry about the demotion.'

Graham shrugged. 'You don't get off lightly, socking a station commander in the middle of a dance floor.' He forced a grin. 'He's not a bad chap actually. I'm beginning to think he's as big a fool as I've been. Vanessa's pretty determined.'

'Where is she, Graham? In Cornwall?' Jessica felt conscience-stricken at not having kept in touch with Vanessa, for the baby's sake more than hers.

He shook his head and said bitterly: 'You can't expect Vanessa to live with an NCO, can you? And she could hardly move in with Swift, not that he wanted that, I gather. He's been posted, anyway. No, Vanessa's walked out and left Johnnie with me.'

'Left you with the baby?' Jessica was incredulous.

'What does this look like, a joke? I'm taking him to my parents, poor little sod. They'll make a fuss of him, but it doesn't make it up to him, does it?'

'And what about you, Graham?'

'I've put in for a posting.'

'Night-fighting again?'

'Not exactly.' He seemed disinclined to say more than, 'A station in Bedfordshire.'

Will looked at him sharply.

'Is that so?' he said quietly. 'You've got guts, Macintosh.'

'What I wanted to ask was, could you go and see Vanessa? She's left me Gerry Rhodes' address, but I somehow don't think she's living there.' Not if she was telling me the truth about Gerry being impotent, he thought bitterly. 'I'd like to know for sure, just in case I—' Then he said abstractedly: 'Do you know anything about eyes?'

'*Eyes*?'

'Yes. Someone told me something about brown eyes predominating over blue when it comes to—' He broke off as he saw Will looking at him, and changed the subject.

'I've got a lunch at the Ivy today. You can come too. It's about recording in the States.'

Will sighed. 'Can't you skip it? Tie up the knocker, say I'm sick, I'm dead?'

'What?'

'Favourite tag of Pop's. I don't want to go to any lunches. I want to spend time with you. Cancel it.'

'I can't do that.' She frowned. 'I promised.' Promised – she'd promised something else too, that had gone with the wind. Like John Gale. Was she to be of so little faith always? She was being stupid, she told herself. The present was the present, and she owed it to Will. 'Yes, I can. Of course I can.' She threw her arms round him. 'These things keep crowding in, Will,' she said ruefully.

'Only if you let them,' he said firmly. 'Anyway, you'd be a fool to go out in this.' He glanced at the fog closing in around the hotel. 'In fact,' he said thoughtfully, 'I'd say there was only one thing we *could* do.'

'Will?'

'Jessica?'

'Are you there?'

'Right here, lovely.'

She laid an arm over him sleepily. 'What are you thinking about?'

'I was thinking if I was Dickens lying in this bed, I'd be ordering tea and hot buttered crumpets on an afternoon like this. And a fire.'

'That's not very romantic.'

'On the contrary, I can't think of anything more romantic than tea and hot buttered crumpets in bed with the girl you love.'

'It would make an awful mess of the bed. I don't think Dickens would have liked that.'

'I guess I'm prepared to consider getting up and donning a heavy red plaid dressing robe.'

'You haven't got one.'

'An imaginary one.'

'That'll give the girl who brings the tea a shock,' she observed.

'That's a touch insulting. Don't you like my figure?'

'I adore it. In fact . . . I'd like some more.'

'Then I'll need those damn crumpets first.'

'I guess that was better than a lunch about pushing records in the States.'

Jessica pulled on her uniform skirt. 'Do you still miss the States, Will?'

Already dressed, he was lounging in an armchair, watching her.

'Sure. There're days when I just cry out for it. I've got to like it here in England, like the folks, but there's a part of me needs what's back there, at least to see it again. How big a part I don't know. I guess it's because you're all closed in here. I need to get back for a while. I long for the green endless rolling mountains, the clean rivers – not streams like you have here – and the sheer raw energy of the people. It's a different kind of confidence than folks have here. Here you stand confident in the past. There it's confidence in the future. I have to be part of that.'

Everything in Jessica cried out, 'What about me?' Surely he wanted her forever? Wanted to marry her? Take her with him? He hadn't said so. Just a vague promise to take her to Tanglewood. Hurt and pain made her burst out: 'I just serve to grace your measure, is that it? Is there a Chloe to go back to?'

'A what?' he said, startled. 'What the hell are you talking about?'

'Nothing. Just a poem John once quoted.'

'John.' He stood up abruptly. 'How many of us are in this room, Jessica?' he asked quietly. 'And in that bed? Two – or three? Seems to me you'd better make up your mind.' And seizing his greatcoat and bag, he walked out.

She stood stunned. How had that come about? Was it her fault? His? Did she know Will at all? Was he jealous of John? Did he have reason to be? her honesty compelled her to question. No, oh no. John was still with her, but it didn't affect Will or her love for him. Or did it? No. It was something between herself and her memory of John – something she must battle out alone. A terrible fear seized her. Suppose Will didn't come back. He'd taken his bag. They had another night before he had to return to Debden. But suppose he didn't. She'd go after him now. She ran out of the room, down the main stairs and out through the front entrance. A stultifying, choking thickness greeted her. Thick stifling fog was all around her. She could hardly see Piccadilly Circus for all it was so close and darkness hadn't yet fallen completely. Where would he have gone? The Eagle Club, of course. No, didn't he say something about a do at the Dorchester? Yes. He could only be twenty yards ahead if she'd chosen the right route.

She hurried along, cursing each obstacle, bumping into lamp posts and colliding with walkers, the fog clutching at her throat and nostrils. She put her scarf round her mouth to stop the choking. It was like a nightmare. First John, now Will. She must find him to put things right. Only this afternoon she'd been in his arms, he'd loved her. It couldn't vanish just like that.

She bumped into someone who went on with a muttered curse. Surely she must be catching Will up now. Wasn't that a garden? She must be in Berkeley Square. Of all the ironies. She was lost already, with no hope of catching him up, and she was in Berkeley Square of all places. Where our song began, she thought wildly. No, that was John. Yet it was the sound of the clarinet she heard now when she thought of that song. Will's clarinet. Another bump, this time into someone in uniform, and a quick squeeze. Choking with disgust, she kicked him sharply and ran, diving into a side turning; then, hearing his feet coming after her, turned again, walking on tip-toe so he did not hear footsteps and at last there was no sound of following feet.

She breathed deeply in relief and regretted it. The choking fog caught her again. She must get back; Will might come. But she was lost, where on earth was she? The fog had closed in even more, till it lay only a yard from her, a blanket she could not see through, not even to decipher the street names. She was ten minutes from safety and she didn't know where it was! She walked in the direction she thought was right, but it was hopeless. She sat down on a flight of steps and tried in vain to think. Cold and at her wits' end, she began to panic. 'Will,' she cried out ridiculously, 'Will!'

A face loomed above her. 'Jessica, for crying out loud. What are you shouting for?'

'Will! Oh, Will. I'm lost!' She clutched him desperately. 'Please don't go. Please come back. Take me back. Do you know the way?'

'Honey, easy. Look up there above you.'

He turned her round and two feet above her she saw the words 'Tradesmen's Entrance'.

'You've been sitting on your back doorstep. Lucky I came back. You might have had to wait for the milkman.' He paused, and said abruptly, 'Look, honey, I'm sorry I walked out like that. I got to thinking it was pretty stupid of me to be jealous of Johnnie Gale. He's part of your life, part of mine. I just don't want him too large a part, that's all. Forgive me?'

She began to laugh, holding on to him. 'Will, it's these leave periods, you know. They're too short. We get all on edge, then go and get lost in London Particulars.'

'In what?'

'That's what we call fogs like this.'

He shivered and drew his greatcoat round him. 'And you wonder I want to go back to the States!'

'What's that you're whistling?'

'New song. I got the idea, seeing you like that.' He

stretched out his hand and flicked aside the sheet.

'Sing it to me,' she said lazily.

He sang a couple of lines, and she giggled. 'Somehow I don't think the BBC is going to like that too much.'

'No matter. It'll be our song.'

She sighed. 'I'll have to get going if I'm to get to Gerry Rhodes' flat on time.' She'd reluctantly agreed to go to see Vanessa as Graham had asked. It sounded as if he were thinking about divorce. Surely Vanessa wouldn't want that? 'I'll hear the rest when I get back.'

'I'll come with you. There's time before I leave.'

'I can go alone.'

'Nope. I want to be there.'

Half an hour later they were at the Mayfair flat. The door was opened by Gerry. 'Ah, it's you, little Ice-Queen. Come to sing us a song?'

Vanessa got up from her chair, stubbing out a cigarette as she did so. 'I suppose Graham's been weeping all over you,' she said coolly.

Jessica ignored this. 'How could you leave John? You're his mother,' she swept straight in, ignoring Will's restraining arm.

Vanessa looked at her and smirked. 'Wait till you have a kid,' she said offhandedly. 'You'll find out how I can leave him.'

'Graham's been kind to you.'

'Don't lecture me, Jessica. Just because you've struck it good, doesn't give you the right to preach to me.'

'I want to help if I can.'

'You always were holier than thou. You just don't understand, Jessica, and you never have. I thought you'd have grown up a bit now you've been around.' She

glanced knowingly from her cousin to Will. 'Anyway, is what I'm doing so much worse than you two?'

'What on earth do you mean?' Jessica shouted.

'Ladies, ladies,' said Gerry plaintively.

'I haven't got a husband to consider.'

'No,' said Vanessa smugly. 'And if you knew rather more about men, you might not be so starry-eyed.'

'Vanessa,' cut in Will quietly, before Jessica could retort.

She laughed at him. 'Remember it doesn't matter very much now, Will.'

'What doesn't?' asked Jessica, bewildered. But no one answered her.

'I guess you're wrong at that,' said Will steadily. 'Just think it out. What if Graham decides to divorce you?'

'He'd never divorce me,' said Vanessa scornfully. 'You'll see. He adores me too much.'

'Good Lord!'

Molly's face lit up. 'Graham, what are you doing here? I thought you were stuck down in Cornwall. Are you flying Lysanders? Is Vanessa with you?'

'I've been posted here. About three weeks now. No, Vanessa's not here.'

'I'm here too – well, passing through.'

'On a cipher job?'

'No, I'm a parcel. Joes, you call us, don't you? I'm just here to get the smell of the place this time.'

Graham nearly dropped his drink. 'A Joe?'

'That's right. That's between you and me. So far as the world's concerned, I'm the little Waaf on the teleprinter at RAF Tempsford. But when the moon's right, in a month or two, when my turn comes, I'll book myself in on your flight, shall I? On the old Tin Lyssie?'

'But, are they dropping *women* now?'

'They seem to think it's a good idea,' she said brightly. 'We're not all dumb blondes, you know.'

'I don't like the idea of it.'

'You're too chivalrous, Graham. Do you put Vanessa on a pedestal too?'

His face changed and he said nothing.

'I'm sorry,' she said quietly. 'I didn't realise. Something's wrong, isn't it?'

'She's walked out,' he said, glaring at Molly as if it were her fault.

'I'm really sorry, Graham. I should have thought—'

'Why should you have thought?' he demanded thickly. 'Because I'm so dull no one could live with me?'

Molly set down her drink. 'Dull?' she echoed. 'Gosh, I hope not. It's Christmas tomorrow and I hate spending Christmas with dull folks.'

Debden now bore little resemblance to an RAF station. Uniformed Americans swarmed everywhere, talking, playing and full of vitality. There was discipline, but not the sort the RAF would have recognised. Each man was working out his own, it seemed. They were picking up formation flying fast, but still retaining their characteristic individualism.

Jessica had arrived with the band at Audley End, a station apparently in the middle of nowhere. They looked round in vain for transport, for there was no sign of an airfield. Half an hour later they were shunted into a small local train, and decanted shortly afterwards at

Saffron Walden, which was only marginally less rural. Here Will was waiting in a strange-looking vehicle – the station Jeep. He waved a hand at it. Jessica stifled her desire to dash into his arms, conscious of the onlookers' interest. She and the Astras were well-known faces now. She shivered and wished she'd taken up her mother's offer of a fur coat last autumn. She didn't like them but the warmth would have been welcome as they bowled along in the open vehicle.

Such food on the tables had not been glimpsed in Britain since before the war – and some of it not even then. Turkey, sweet potatoes, cranberry sauce, this was another world. A laughing crazy world, the mess resounding to names like Cowboy, Buck, the Kid, Alamo; but it was a world that meant business. Rather to her surprise she found she was accepted as Will's girl, though when she saw her photo adorning the mess, she realised why. She found herself flummoxed by the US army ranks.

'I can't get used to thinking of you as a Captain.'

'You don't have to call me Captain in bed if you don't want to.'

'Feel free to call me Section Officer Gray, darling,' she replied. Then, diffidently, 'Where am I staying?'

'Not with me, angel. Too dicey. The last chap who tried it got caught helping two Waafs out of his window after hours. We were still under the RAF then, and it caused a hell of a stink! In the end it was okay. Eighth Air Force took the view that for two he should have gotten promoted! And he was.'

She laughed uncertainly, and he said, 'I guess we'd best keep to the straight and narrow till I can get a pass for a booking in the New Year.'

She sighed. 'I hate all this,' she said finally.

'Do you think I find it fun? But there's not much doing here at the moment, so it should be a cinch to get a forty-eight hour next week. We're hanging around waiting for the new US fighters to come in.'

'What about the Spitfires?'

'The guys are all torn up over losing them, but they haven't got the range. They can't cover the bombers further than Paris, and sooner rather than later we're going to be taking the bombers right into Germany. They have to be defended then or we're going to lose a mighty lot of Fortresses. With our Thunderbolts fitted with droptanks as escort, we can get to the German border at least. So I reckon this is the last time you'll be seeing the Spits. Beauties, aren't they? I'll be real sorry to see them go. The end of an era for me.'

The end of an era. Jessica felt suddenly cast down. It was all happening so fast. Talk of bombing Germany with new heavy machines. Monty's army forging on in pursuit of Rommel. There was more than a hope now of victory; there was a relentless determination to drive towards it. And then what, for herself and for Will?

The hangar was packed out for the concert, every rank and Higher Command too perching on windowsills, boxes, anything, when the seating ran out. For the first time for ages Jessica found herself nervous about facing an audience. She had spent hours deciding what dress to wear, stripping off her uniform with relief and putting on these famous nylons that she'd heard so much about, twisting and turning to admire the result in the small mirror which was all that was permitted to pander to feminine vanity in the Waafs' quarters. It was almost like having no stockings at all, they were so sheer. How on earth would she stop them laddering? She dropped the red silk over her head, undecided. This was primarily an American audience. They were used to Hollywood glamour. Visions of Dorothy Lamour came to mind. Jessica's reflection did not resemble Dorothy Lamour in the slightest.

She peeled off the red and opted for the old blue backless dress. Yes, that was better. Glamorous she did not look, but at least she'd made an attempt. She produced the stub of lipstick she'd been saving for the occasion. She'd been too proud to ask Will for any. Especially after he'd produced, with a glint in his eyes, six pairs of silk panties from the States. One sight of the WAAF regulation knickers had been enough for him. He had fallen about laughing, somewhat to her indignation. She had nearly turned the gift down, but on second thoughts changed her mind.

The audience was different to an RAF one; the number of wolf-whistles for one thing. But they were appreciative and unselfconscious in showing their approval.

> 'You're my deckchair in November,
> My sunshade in the rain
> You're a spring song in September . . .'

She caught Will's eye and a thrill of happiness ran through her as he picked up the tune. Impossible to imagine they would part after the war. Impossible to imagine a life that did not include Will, a life other than a rainbow of music along which they would dance to a melody of love.

'And you're home with me again,' she finished as Art took the melody into a triumphant flourish.

Then the requests began, calls and shouts from the floor. After half an hour they were about to call it a day when there came one final request.

'How about "A Nightingale Sang in Berkeley Square"?'

She turned impulsively to Will. 'You don't mind, do you?'

'Go ahead,' he said impassively, but she sensed he did mind.

'You can't forget, can you?' she said sadly to him afterwards.

'It's not a question of forgetting, Jessica. He's still casting some kind of shadow over you. After all, like you said, the song first came right because of him.'

She looked at him sharply, hearing but not understanding the slight bitterness in his tone. 'I don't know . . . I thought so then but now I think it was you. I just don't know. And does it matter?'

'Only you can answer that.'

As they stared at each other, caught in an unexpected impasse, Art approached them, grinning all over his face. 'I found us a trumpeter, Will, for when I go.'

'How do, Captain Donaldson, sir. Miss Gray, ma'am.'

Steve Calston was a huge grinning black corporal. Jessica took one look and grinned back.

'How do you do?' she said.

'Listen here, ma'am,' said Steve grandly, 'this is how I do.' And he took Art's trumpet from him and played.

'Corporal,' said Will slowly when he'd finished, 'you just joined the Astras.'

* * *

'Jessica?'

'Hello, Dave.'

'Can you get over here right away?' He wouldn't say any more on the telephone, but when she reached his office in Wardour Street he was pacing up and down restlessly.

'Is Will around?'

'No, not till next week, but—'

'It's bad. You've just got a writ for plagiarism. You, Will, the BBC and Don Field.'

'What?' she said faintly.

' "The Apple in my Crumble".'

'But that's ridiculous. Words or music?'

'Words, but part of the protest is that the music is derivative too.'

'Nonsense! And anyway it would be impossible to prove.'

'That's why they're going for the words.'

'Just a moment, Dave. You sound as if you believe it.'

'When you've seen what they've got, you'll see why. Don's been chasing round all morning. He's instructed Bagins and Dewhurst.'

'I need to sit down.' Jessica collapsed into a chair. 'No I don't.' She leapt up again. 'It's just nonsense. Who's bringing the action?'

'No one I've heard of – Laetitia Gainsborough. Don says there was a lyricist called Sebastian Gainsborough – but he's never heard of Laetitia. He's doing some checking out.' He paused. 'Only one thing he did know about Gainsborough – he used to write for Ken Peters now and then.'

* * *

'Withdraw the song, then,' said Will later when he reached the hotel on his forty-eight hour pass. 'If that's all they're asking.'

'Don't you want to fight them?' said Jessica, amazed.

'We're in the middle of a war. Don't you feel there's enough to think about without fighting copyright actions? I can't get excited. There are other songs.'

'But the slur on you! I won't let it drop.'

'There's more to this than a song, but we don't have the time to figure out what.'

'Of course we do. It's important.'

'Important? Careful, Jessica. You're getting blinded by show biz. It was music we started out to explore.'

'I haven't forgotten that, Will, but I can't just stop. John always said—'

She heard his indrawn breath, then he took her in his arms, almost fiercely. 'Come to bed, Jessica, come to bed.' Already his hands were moving to unbutton her blouse, unfasten her skirt.

'Will, you're crazy. It's only six o'clock.'

'Then there's a long night ahead of us.' He kissed her passionately, possessively, as if to bind her to him by force, willing their differences to dissolve. She cried out as he bore her down to the bed, 'I love you, Will, I love you,' as if by so declaring she could bridge the gap.

'Jessica,' he murmured, his hands moving over her body, caressingly, lovingly, till she cried out again with pleasure. At the sound of her voice, he entered her with a muttered apology and the gulf between them was bridged.

But when at last she lay sleeping in his arms, he lay

awake, staring into the darkness, thinking back to the first time he had heard her voice, when the quest was but beginning and John Gale still lived. And now? The voice still sang, was still as pure in itself, but the quest, the dream itself, was vanishing under the harsh light of the day to day world. But it was still there, he sensed, if unseen. Still there, beckoning from a far horizon.

Jessica stirred and he kissed her cheek, drawing the blankets up around her till she slept again.

A week later, Dave Price rang again.

'Worse news, Jessica.'

'What?'

'The BBC are cancelling.'

'The song? But Will says he'll withdraw it.'

'Irrespective. They're pulling out. The merest hint of legal action and they get nervous.'

Something seemed to hammer inside her, sickening her, as though this heralded the collapse of her world. Then she braced herself. 'There's dirty work here, Dave, somewhere. And I'm going to find out whose it is.' She could not ever voice the fear still at the back of her mind; that the trail would lead back, sooner or later, to her mother.

It was March. The long harsh winter of 1942/3 was drawing to a close, the war seeming as far from won as ever with the Battle of the Atlantic raging at its height. But now the Eighth Air Force was beginning to get into its stride, Flying Fortresses making their long-range sorties over Europe, regardless of the RAF's warnings on the dangers of daylight flying. That was the American way. Put everything they'd got into giving the Germans the bum's rush.

The Astras' programme continued unabated, Steve Calston adding a new lustre to it, but without the BBC spot in the last two weeks, sales of records and sheet music slumped. Jessica had had no time in between concerts to track down the source of their problems, but worry gnawed at her incessantly. Ken Peters was obviously involved, however much on the sidelines, and Jessica made the connection with her mother. She curbed her natural instinct to rush down to confront her, however. She needed facts first.

Will managed to join her in London for an RAF charity ball and she talked incessantly about the problem until he rebelled.

'Jessica,' he cut in finally, 'will you be quiet?'

She stared at him.

'Look, I've had enough, my lovely. I don't want to hear any more about that damned song. *Or* the BBC.'

'You're right,' she said ruefully. 'I'm sorry. It's selfish of me. It's just that I can't forget what my mother did, and I'm terrified I'll find out it's all happening again, just the same way.' She hesitated, then told him the full story. 'The past can't die that easily.'

'No,' he said bleakly. 'It can't. And that's the trouble. I think *we've* come to an end.'

She stared at him, unbelievingly. She must have misunderstood. 'The end? You and me?' she cried. 'But why?'

'It's still there between us, whatever it is you hug to yourself.'

'Yes, but it has nothing to do—'

'Was it there last night?' His face was pinched and white.

'No. Oh, no, it wasn't,' she cried.

He came to her quickly, taking her in his arms. 'I love you, Jessica. You're my whole life. But I can't live with your ghosts any more, whether it's John Gale himself or something to do with your not making love to him. Even that damned promise you made not to sing! But whatever it is, the only way to get rid of ghosts is to turn round and say boo to them, I guess. And it's you that's got to do it. Not me. At the moment you're running right into this crazy razzle-dazzle life as some kind of answer. It isn't. Remember the song we started out with? The song about the sweet nightingale? "Afraid for to walk in the shade", that's you.'

It was like a physical blow, coming out of nowhere, felling her, rendering her incapable of saying anything but, 'No, you're wrong.'

He stopped her words fiercely with his kisses. 'I can't take it, Jessica. We're getting further and further apart. We don't even share our music any more. It's all business and records and lawsuits and agents. We've got the Thunderbolts arriving at Debden next week. I'm going to be there one hundred per cent, I need all the time I can get on them. I need to drive out the shadows.'

'You're leaving me for good?' she whispered unbelievingly.

He paused for an eternity, then smiled sadly. 'Let's do this Hollywood-style. I'll come back for you six months from today. You know what day that is?'

The 17th of September. 'The anniversary of John's death,' she said bleakly after a moment.

'Right. If you don't meet me, I'll know the ghosts have won out. If you come, let it be just and only for me.'

'And then?'

'Then I'll give you a heaven, Jessica, a heaven of music for you and me. When you're mine at last.'

As he tore himself away, she called out, numb with shock, 'Where – where shall we meet? What time?'

He paused. 'Like all meetings. Under the clock at Charing Cross. Seven o'clock.'

Chapter Thirteen

He would come back. After all, it was only six months. He must come back. Impossible that he would stay away forever. Optimism struggled to assert itself before the doubts began. He'd never said anything about their future together – perhaps there was none. Perhaps John Gale's shadow still hung over them, real or imagined. And wrestling with herself, she knew it was real. The promise she had made and broken, the faith she had never kept, the demand she had never answered. And now she was doing the same to Will. He didn't want her just for the duration, but forever surely? But he hadn't said so. The thought drummed ceaselessly around in her head.

Will and she were different. It wasn't just a passing affair. Or was it simply music that had drawn them together, the grand ideal that hadn't worked out because she wanted one thing, he another? No, that wasn't it. She loved Will. Was it true that she was holding back, even in their most precious intimate moments, when his arms were round her? Did he really think she was dreaming of John? She wasn't, but she knew that her choice then was casting its shadow even yet.

All her conscious heart was fixed on Will. If any of her

subconscious thoughts remained on John, how was she to know, and how to forget them?

What could she do?

She thought back to that fateful time when she last saw John, and had refused to let him make love to her; she had been so sure there would always be a tomorrow. And there hadn't been. Now Will, too, she was driving away. Perhaps she was incapable of giving herself fully, either physically or emotionally. No, she couldn't believe that, she wanted Will too much. It was *right*.

Then she began to realise. *It seemed so right*. When she had sung 'Berkeley Square' that first time for John, it had all seemed right. She had known it without doubt and for all time. And she had been wrong. This was what she was stumbling over. Not guilt at all, for that had been laid to rest. Now – was she wrong about Will? She had said to him 'forever'. Suppose she were wrong and she betrayed him also? That's if he returned, she thought with a sickening realisation, it might already be too late.

In her waking moments she believed Will would come to her again. And yet as night fell she wondered – suppose he didn't?

'Dave, look, I'm going to get to the bottom of this complaint about the song.' She had to throw herself into action of some sort. 'Who is this woman?'

'I haven't been able to gather much. Except that she's the widow of Sebastian Gainsborough. She swore a deposition that he wrote the song, has the manuscript, and Ken Peters swore that he had it in his hands five years ago.'

'You know what I think, Dave? I don't think the song was the root of it at all. I think it was a lever to get the BBC spot dropped.'

'Maybe, but it worked. And that accomplished, she's now offered to withdraw the charge if we withdraw the song.'

'No.'

Dave sighed. 'It's the easiest way out.'

'I won't drop Will's song,' she said obstinately. 'I'll go and see her myself.'

'Not advisable.'

'Why not?'

'Because you're a hot-head, Jessica,' he said bluntly. 'And we don't need more trouble – we've enough already. And more.'

'More?'

'Yes.'

'Go on,' she said resignedly. 'I can take it. I've taken enough already.'

'It's Steve. He's quitting.'

'*Quitting*? He's only just joined. Can he do that?'

'Unfortunately, yes, he's only on loan to the RAF. He's backing out now the BBC have pulled out. Wants a posting to a US band.'

'He didn't even have the guts to tell me face to face,' she said grimly. 'What about the others?'

'They're still with you. But we need a trumpet even if Vic becomes leader. I'll see what Uxbridge can suggest.'

'Dave,' she said, pounding her fist on the table, 'I won't be second-rate. I won't play on a diminishing circuit. No BBC, the big hotels won't book us. Pretty soon it'll be no Don Field, and no recordings. No, Dave, we stop.'

'Stop! You're crazy. You can't stop now.'

'No, I'm not crazy. We need to reorganise. We're not beaten, we're just changing tack, that's all.'

The train chugged on endlessly, stopping and starting, jerkily advancing only to halt again interminably. Squashed up against a throng of people in the corridor, Jessica fidgeted as they progressed through the Kent countryside. Choc-a-bloc with tank traps, army camps, RAF personnel, it still managed to look as a Kentish spring should. The hint of green in the trees, the lambs in the meadows, the primroses on the embankments. Sooner or later, when the Second Front began, even more people would flood into this corner of Kent; once again it would become a battleground, with luck this time the rear and not the front. Nowadays the war was developing into a triumph of muscle, no longer the David and Goliath days of the Battle of Britain. Slowly but surely Kent's green spring would be obliterated by a mass of brown uniforms.

But her thoughts only fleetingly went to the Second Front before she concentrated again on her own mission. Yesterday, Dave had rung with more information: 'This Mrs Gainsborough, it seems she was in musical comedy before she married. *Hearts and Diamonds* was her last. Her stage name was Peggy Milton. Had a good role in it – thanks, get this, Jessica – to your mother.'

She had been right. The clock had been rolled back nearly three years to Don Field and that fateful party at Frittingbourne Manor. She got out of the train at Lenham and was met by the same WAAF driver as when she returned to West Forstling in 1941.

'Welcome back, Section Officer Gray.'

'Thank you,' said Jessica.

Welcome to what? This time, however, at least she came to West Forstling as the fêted queen. She was greeted by the Queen Bee as an honoured colleague. But in HQ she missed the cheerful companionship of the WAAF officers' billets; the conversation and atmosphere at HQ she found stultifying. She was looking forward to the concert tonight, and to seeing Art again. After she'd carried out the purpose of her mission.

She received grudging permission for the use of the station car and driver again. The familiar lanes gave her confidence to face what lay ahead. The celandines, violets and early primroses in the hedgerows, even the sparrows chirping in the hedges, were signs of normality that raised her spirits. How she wished Will were here. Resolutely she dragged her thoughts away. She was back where John had ruled her heart and life. This was the stile they had clambered over, this the lane where they'd stopped coming back from Maidstone with Vanessa and Gerry. She grinned at the memory. What an idiot she'd been then! So excited at the thought of singing with the station band, so obstinate about dating fighter pilots. All those early struggles bound up with John.

Her mother was sitting in the drawing room, discussing a WVS committee meeting on the telephone. Her father came to meet her with genuine pleasure. He was greyer, still a shadow beside her ebullient mother, whose personality seemed if anything to have grown. Bubbles Gray put down the phone and came to Jessica with outstretched arms.

'Darling, how wonderful to see you,' she said, with every appearance of being genuine.

'Not really, Mother,' Jessica managed to say coolly. 'It's a matter of business.'

'Darling, how solemn you sound.'

'I want you to get that ridiculous plagiarism charge withdrawn unconditionally. The BBC have dropped me because of it and the mud is sticking. And more than sticking, Mother, thanks to someone - Ken Peters? Bill Rolands? - it's being *thrown*!'

'Oh, darling, what on earth can I do to help? I don't see—'

Cicely was already prepared. She had known Jessica would come, that was obvious.

'Don't make me go all through it again, Mother,' said Jessica wearily. 'It's degrading. Mrs Gainsborough is your protégée from *Hearts and Diamonds*.'

'Who? I don't quite see—' Hurt, bewildered, a multitude of expressions crossed Bubbles' face. Expressions, not emotions.

'Jessica, what is all this?' said Michael plaintively, glancing from one to the other, obviously longing to escape.

'Father, this is between me and Mother,' said Jessica. Michael seized the opportunity and vanished. 'I'm not going to argue, Mother. I simply ask you to contact her.'

'Even if I knew this lady, why should I?' enquired Bubbles sweetly.

'No reason, Mother, no reason at all. Except that I'm your daughter. Please, please, remember that. You won't ever have another daughter or I a mother. Can't we salvage something from the last few years? I used to be so proud of you, up on the stage, dancing and singing. The day didn't start till you had smiled at me. It could be so again, Mother. Don't you think it's worth a try at least? If there's any hope for us, it lies in your hands.'

'So there it is, Art,' Jessica said, as she watched him set up for the concert. 'No trumpeter – it's good of you to stand in tonight – no BBC, and we're disbanding the Astras, temporarily at any rate.'

'That's too bad.' He looked genuinely concerned.

'Listen, Art, is there any hope you'd come back in? If we forget all the razzle dazzle, as Will calls it. No recordings, broadcasts, hotel work. Make it what we set out to have, a band for the servicemen.' Seeing she had his attention, she went on, 'I've had an idea.'

'When haven't you, me darling?' he murmured drily.

'These Wings for Victory weeks they're holding all over the country – how do you feel about coming back in for the summer, now the baby's here. The Astras travelling round to play for dances and concerts to raise money for the RAF?'

'It's an idea,' he admitted grudgingly. 'I'll think about it, talk to the wife. Listen, me darling, no more trains. See if you can wangle road transport. Even get round Transport Command if you can. But no trains!'

She was singing, here at West Forstling where it had all begun, happy once more now that one small blow had been struck towards getting the Astras on the road again. Jessica's happiness lasted until, inevitably, someone requested 'Berkeley Square'. But why not? Will wasn't here. Of course she'd sing it. Prove to herself that he was wrong, that no thought of John clouded her love for him. She began to sing. Everything was the same as it had been that first time, except two things: John was not there - and neither was Will's clarinet. There was no magic in the song tonight. The listeners would not detect the difference, but she knew. John wasn't here. So she would sing it for him. She closed her eyes as the song went on and thought of John, of the passionate embraces, the frenetic happiness they'd shared. With a mounting sense of shock, then pure joy, she realised *it didn't work*. With a sigh of recognition, she greeted the fact that the song didn't sound right because Will wasn't there. All that time she'd put the song's coming right down to John's inspiration. It was that which had led her finally to his embrace.

Now she knew without question that she had been wrong. It had been Will all along, giving the words to her melody of life. The shadows of two and a half years rolled away and she saw John Gale for what he had been. Not only a hero, asking a love she had denied, but a frightened man, clinging desperately to something stable while his world was in chaos. And she had clung to him as an escape from her own problems. They had needed each other and imagined it love. The song ended and Jessica came down to earth with a sigh. No need to fear now that her love for Will was built on shifting sand, as had been her love for John. She was set free at last. Free to wait for Will. She'd ring him, tell him, act now. Why wait six months? But no, she owed him that time. The 8th Air Force was heavily involved; he'd turned to them, she had no right to distract him so soon. She must follow her own path until he came. But what if he was killed before that? She stilled the question; it was her punishment now to have to endure the months of waiting.

* * *

'He died, Jessica, last month. I was going to write and tell you, but I thought I'd wait till I saw you.'

'Poor old Astaire,' she said softly.

'Not so poor. He was chirping right up to the last.'

'Rather like me,' she said wrily.

'You won't give up, either,' Tom said. 'I suppose I see now why we could never have married. You'd plough through a field of concrete if what you wanted was on the other side.'

She laughed. 'No wonder my parents call me Brickie.'

'That's your third, Graham.'

'Can you blame me?' he asked. 'Anyone would think it was tonight.'

'You've done the run lots of times before. You know it backwards.'

'It's not me, you know that,' he said angrily. 'It's you.'

'If you can't take it, Graham,' Molly replied forthrightly, 'you should ask someone else.'

'Of course I'll do it. I've got to know the best is dropping you,' he said vehemently. 'And that's me.'

'It's only a short mission this time,' she pointed out. 'I'll be back in a month.'

'A month is a long time.'

'We shouldn't have let it get this far, I suppose.'

He reached for her. 'God, I'm glad we did.'

'Me too,' she said simply. 'I love you, Graham.'

'Come back, Molly. For Pete's sake, come back.'

Will recalled his first arrival at West Forstling, and finding John Gale upside down on the table – it seemed small beer compared with Debden dispersal. They were a wild bunch; he was so caught up with them now, a tight-knit group of go-getters, that he was managing to distance himself completely from Jessica. At nights he was tired after lugging the heavy P-47 Thunderbolt across the Channel and back, simply trying to control it, let alone fight with the thing. It was like a buffalo after the greyhound of the Spitfire. Too tired for dreaming. Up in the air when dreams came he dispelled them, called over the radio to one of the others, anything to concentrate. To think of women up there was the first step to going nuts - or to death. And Will intended to be very much alive in four months' time. He ticked off each day on a calendar. Rumour had it that before September they'd be flying into Germany itself. They'd need drop-tanks fitted on, of course, for the extra fuel. Germany. That was going to be one hell of a dicey do. But he'd be back. Nothing would stop him.

'Hello.'

Vanessa was as jaunty as ever as she plumped herself down opposite Jessica at the restaurant table, and made a face at the menu in front of them.

'I'll be glad when it's over and we get decent food again. At least the Americans eat—' She broke off, looked at Jessica and laughed. 'There,' she said disarmingly, 'I've given myself away.'

'Oh, Vanessa,' said Jessica wearily, 'you haven't really left Gerry, have you?'

'I come and go,' replied Vanessa airily. 'He doesn't mind. He knows the score.'

'Who is it this time?'

'There aren't that many,' she replied, hurt. 'This one's a real poppet. He's a bigwig up at a Bomber Group somewhere in Norfolk – I forget where.'

You would, thought Jessica.

'I've been there once or twice, but I prefer it down here. More going on.'

'Don't you ever think of Graham?' said Jessica, amazed. 'Or Johnnie?'

'Sometimes,' said Vanessa coolly, narrowing her eyes. 'I'm not the only one, you know. Lots of rushed marriages don't work out.'

'Not many mothers leave their children behind,' said Jessica bluntly. 'How can you abandon him to be brought up by grandparents?'

'He's out of the way of the bombing. You always did spout your mouth off about things you don't understand. Look, I didn't come here to quarrel with you, Jessica.'

'I'm sorry.' Penitently she reached a hand across the table.

'Where's Will?'

'Flying. We're taking a break.' Trying to sound casual. She hadn't meant to say that much.

'A break?' Vanessa paused. 'Not because of John Gale, is it?' It was a shot in the dark.

'Something like that,' said Jessica unwillingly.

'You had stars in your eyes about that man,' Vanessa said worriedly, fondness for her cousin sweeping over her again.

'Perhaps I still have.'

'He wasn't a patch on Will.'

'I love Will, but that doesn't detract from my feelings for John – he was a wonderful, exceptional man.'

'Jessica, you don't know you're born! Pilot maybe, not man. He wasn't a hero on the ground.'

Jessica paled, suddenly fearful at what Vanessa might say. 'I don't want to hear.'

'You're going to hear,' said Vanessa matter-of-factly. 'Will bullied me into not telling you. Blackmailed me, in fact, but I'm going to, if only for *his* sake. John was sleeping with me all the time he was engaged to you. Why do you think I married Graham so quickly?'

'Don't, Vanessa!' cried Jessica sharply.

'Because Johnnie's his kid, that's why. I'd just realised, when he got shot down. Now do you see why I was so jealous of you? Jessica, please,' Vanessa was alarmed by the look on her face, 'I haven't told you out of spite. I want you to see things as they are.'

Jessica stared at her unseeing, her thoughts a jumble. Then, slowly, she put out her hand and took Vanessa's. 'It doesn't matter, Vanessa. Not any more.'

Jessica stood by the telephone, her hand itching to pick up the receiver. It was easier to resist writing. But the telephone! All she had to do was ask for the number . . . it became a magnet. No, she owed it to Will not to do it. Only two months now. She was making a success of the Wings for Victory tour. She would complete it to show him what she could achieve in music for its own sake, and have something to offer other than apologies when he returned. She forced herself to leave the hotel telephone and go to the old Victorian theatre, where the concert was being given. It was packed with supporters of the Wings for Victory week. But the desire to pick up that receiver did not leave her. Will's face floated before her as they finished their programme with their theme song:

> 'But when at dawn he fled as all dreams can
> I held you in my arms
> And our song began.'

'Have you seen a telephone around here?' She hardly paused after the concert. She could wait no longer.

'Stage door, Jess.'

She waited impatiently for the operator and gave the number. No stopping this time.

'Debden Mess.'

'Can I speak to Captain Donaldson, please?'

'One moment, please.'

Endless seconds, then he'd be on the line, she'd hear his voice.

'I'm sorry, ma'am. Captain Donaldson's on leave at the moment. Will anyone else . . . ?' But Jessica did not hear. Deflated, she put down the receiver. On leave? Where? Who with? Where was he staying? Was he alone? She remembered how he'd found a refuge in Molly in the old days . . . Surely not! He would come for her on 17th September. She'd ring again. No, it was too painful. She would wait and cling to hope. Only two months now.

Will Donaldson tore out of the Eagle Club and began to run to the Underground. He'd made up his mind. Hell, to be so near! It was damn stupid, but he had to see her. Just hearing her voice on the records they played non-stop in the mess was beginning to get to him.

On that late June night he was an odd figure, running in uniform to the Uxbridge house. He hammered on the door. It was in darkness. No, that was the blackout up. Or maybe she was out. She'd be back later perhaps. But the house had a deserted look. A woman peered out from the house next door.

'They're away,' she said. 'Blooming good job too. All that racket all day long.'

Will walked back towards the Underground. Even in double summertime twilight was falling now. The time for lovers, and he was alone. His capitulation hadn't been fair on Jessica anyway. He'd said he'd give her six months and it wasn't too long to go now.

Graham's Lysander circled in the moonlight. The small circle of subdued flares on the ground was visible now. No trouble on the way over. The three Joes made themselves ready for the landing.

'You okay, Molly?'

No names, just Joes, that was the rule. To hell with rules! This was his Molly who had brought life to him again.

'Never felt better.'

He came in to land. It had to be quick: unload, pick up, and off again. Now they were down with a bump.

'Who the hell chose this field?' he muttered. Quickly the shapes of the three Joes dissolved into the bushes; he watched her small round figure in its peasant's clothes as long as he could before climbing back into the plane, the three agents to be picked up scrambling after him. Another month before he could return for her. Anything could happen in that time. There were tales of French collaborationists, of torture by the Gestapo. Let nothing happen to Molly, *please.*

'Visitors, Jess my darling,' Art yelled, and went back to their rehearsal room.

Visitors? Jessica came flying downstairs from her room. Will, it must be Will! It wasn't. She stopped dead. Her mother? Standing here in the Uxbridge house, cool as a cucumber? Only she didn't look cool. Rather uncertain, in fact, lost in the large gloomy Victorian hallway.

'Darling, could you spare me some tea?'

'Of course, Mother. You'd better come upstairs to my room. Art and the boys are in full spate.'

Bubbles chattered away inconsequentially despite the noise emanating from below. Jessica made some tea on the small electric ring in the corner, produced two mugs and wondered what the visit portended.

'I thought you'd like to know, Jessica,' said Bubbles casually at last, wincing at the milk bottle placed before her. 'I had a chat with an old friend, I ran into. Peggy Milton as was.'

Jessica looked up.

'She tells me that silly nonsense about the song was just a mistake. There were similarities, but basically they were nothing serious when she looked at it again.'

Jessica set down the teapot. She could hardly believe it. Was this another trick? She looked at her mother suspiciously.

'I thought it would be nice if we could go to a matinée together some time. Like we used to,' Bubbles said carelessly. 'We used to have such fun, didn't we?'

'Yes, we did,' said Jessica slowly.

'Do you think we could again?' Bubbles asked gaily.

'Do you really want to?' Jessica asked evenly. Her mother should make all the running.

'I think we could if we both wanted to.'

Jessica opened her mouth to ask further questions, then shut it again. She might genuinely mean it, she might have another plan. But she had no other mother and Bubbles was Bubbles. Pin her down and she'd flap her butterfly wings in horror. You took her on her own terms. That was how Michael remained so devoted to her. And that was what Jessica would do also, with care.

The day was approaching. Not long now before Will would come. Jessica was in a fever of excitement, throwing herself into work so that she should not dwell too much on thoughts of him.

She must think only about the Astras, and singing. But when Will came, what would happen? She supposed he would still want to fly missions now that the end was in sight. It couldn't be long now before they invaded Europe once more. Already, her mother had told her on the telephone, things were happening in Kent. For weeks civilians had had to have permits to enter a large part of their own countryside and many weren't allowed in at all. It had been an exercise, not the real thing, but it just showed that very soon now the Pas de Calais would be invaded in earnest by the Allied troops. Now that Sicily had been conquered, and the Allies had landed in Southern Italy, France would be next. It was just a question of time, surely. But how long? Another winter, another year? Even longer? The Germans would never compromise. Jessica shivered. Another winter of gloom and austerity. But at least by then she would be with Will.

'Great news, Jessica,' Dave called. 'The BBC want you all back.'

What would have been a great victory a few months ago, left her cold now.

'I'll think about it. What about Art and the boys?'

'Think about it? You have to start work. If Art won't come, find someone else. Or sing solo. Hey, a new formula. "The Singing Waaf sings for the boys in blue". You could sing American songs as well as British, and get both audiences.'

A tinge of excitement brushed her. Perhaps everything *was* coming right. Will returning, her singing to US troops over the wireless . . .

'We could get Radio America too.' Will could join in from Debden. Oh, if only these last two weeks would fly past!

'Hey, Will, you old devil!'

'Well, I'll be darned, Pete Bronski.' His old room-mate from Ithaca was the last person he had expected to hear on the telephone. He was prospecting in Alaska when he'd last heard of him. 'Where are you?'

'Some god-damned place called Wilburton. Just flown in. Say, Will, you doing anything special right now?'

Will hesitated. Tomorrow he was going on leave. The day after tomorrow was 17th September. Sure, he was doing something special. In fact there was something pretty special going on all round, come to that. The last few weeks they'd been testing these new long-range droptanks which had brought up a few problems at first. There'd been a bad show last month and Command was laying off raids till they'd gotten the problem on these new babies licked. Now they'd done it, they reckoned. That meant, here comes the Eighth Air Force, Germany. And *that* meant, not just the Reich, but the whole lot of it – the Big City, Berlin included.

What's more, Don Blakeslee had said something to him privately about the new fighter coming in for assessment. If he played his cards right the Group CO might let him take her up. That's if he was back from leave by then. Yet Pete Bronski, with whom he'd roomed at Ithaca, rated more than a casual brush-off.

'I'm going on leave, Pete. What's up?'

'Terrific! You can get your ass right over here. We've just about started ops and we're about to do some small penetration sweeps over the other side. Just diversion stuff at this stage. Our CO reckons we could do with a couple of experienced guys to go along with us. Stop us heading up shit-creek.'

'I've a date in London on the 17th.' Dammit, he couldn't turn Pete down, not just for a diversion sweep. The new groups needed all the help they could get with the invasion coming up. He'd be able to get himself back to London tomorrow night, easy.

Only a day now and he'd see her again. Will began to sing, battling with the seven-ton Thunderbolt, even heavier now with the added fuel – but these guys sure needed the practice. 'You're my tea rose in the desert . . .' He wondered idly what had happened over that damnfool claim Jessica had been so upset about. 'You're the—'

'Hey, Bing, cut it out, will you? Can't hear myself pray.'

Will grinned under his oxygen mask. Pete was okay. It was good to see him again and he was glad now he'd come along. The English coast slipped beneath them. They would have to keep radio silence now anyway.

He'd done what he could. At Pete's request he'd obediently given the squadron a few tips, as they dressed in the flight hut.

'Okay, it's like this, guys. There I was upside down, nothing on the clock—' A roar of laughter had greeted the old chestnut, which made it easier to slip in the meat. 'Stick together, stay in position, keep a good look out behind *and* in the sun. There's a pretty good chance we'll not even see a German but you never know. The name of the game's teamwork. Individual heroes are dead ones. Get caught on your own and some Jerry will pick you off like it's a turkey shoot. If we get into a fight, never fly straight and level for more than a few seconds, and keep that neck twisting. Remember you're up against old hands now.' Some seemed to be taking it on board, a couple looked as if they thought they knew it all already. Well, they'd learn.

Pete's squadron was keen, but like a bunch of wild steers compared to the disciplined, experienced men of the 4th. At the last minute, Will had heard that the 4th had been detailed on a mission themselves today, which made him uneasy about coming over to the 355th. His CO might take a dim view of him using his leave to fly with another group when the 4th was in the air. It seemed a good idea to cover his tracks, so Pete had put him down under some false name or other, he said, but these things had a way of catching up with you.

Over the coast of France now – some initiation for Pete's squadron, he thought. Flak exploded way beneath them, but it was hardly worth the effort. He sure as hell hoped the Abbeville boys would be asleep at the switch today. But they weren't. The Controller's voice began warning them of bandits to the south. Then they spotted them, like a swarm of killer bees. Will checked out the other two squadrons of the group. One high, one low. How was young Dean on his wing doing? Fine, there he was. Droptanks began to be jettisoned. Will released his and saw Dean's begin to fall away.

The Group Commander, flying with the high squadron, gave some orders; then a voice cut in, yelling, 'Yippee'. It might have been Pete, or just about any of this happy-go-lucky, go-get 'em lot, for most of the squadron was winging over and down on to some 190s below.

'Red Leader, watch those 190s above!' yelled Will, but Pete and his section were already diving like mad.

'Two 190s below, Blue Leader, I'll nail them.' Dean's P-47 wing was rising and he was going over and down. Hell, swore Will to himself.

'Blue two, reform, goddammit.' But it was no use, the P-47 was going full pelt for two 190s that were even now splitting up and turning. Will knew what would happen. Dean would chase one while the other would turn behind him.

'Blue Two, break left!' Will checked above him. There were several 190s way above – the original lot, just waiting for more of the American fighters to dive. Luckily the Group's high squadron was keeping their height; let's hope they'll keep that lot off my back, he thought grimly as he half rolled and dived after his wingman.

'Blue Two, break, break now.' Dean responded and began to pull round, while the second 190, spotting Will's diving P-47, rapidly half rolled and dived out and away.

Something was going on below too, but it was impossible to see any more what was happening to the squadrons down there; impossible to see who had peeled off, who was still in the midst of that dogfight to end all dogfights. Will headed for them, for one thing was for sure – there were certainly more 190s than Thunderbolts. Then he was through them, having snapped off a quick burst at a fleeting target. He saw one FW190, wing locked inextricably into its prey, tumbling with it in its last fall; he saw another 190 falling in flames and mentally gave a thumbs-up for American grit when the odds were against them.

The sky began to clear and he saw Pete's Thunderbolt, easily distinguishable by its overlarge representation of a busty Mae West on the cowling. He was doing okay was Pete. Dead behind a Focke-Wulf, lining up now. Come on, Pete, baby, fire! he willed him. Then Will saw the one diving from above. Diving straight towards Pete. Hell, he couldn't get there in time! Yes he could, no, yes . . .

'Red Leader,' yelled Will, 'break right, break!' He was in range. He checked behind, willing Dean to be there, but he wasn't, of course. With deadly precision he raked the 190's fuselage, seeing flashes along its length as his .50s slammed into the German fighter, then the flashes turned to flame and the 190 slowly rolled over on to its back and went down out of control.

Pete was okay, but Will was not. He had no wingman, but the German had. The second 190 had Will squarely in his sights. Too late Will saw him. Banking and weaving, he manoeuvred the big Thunderbolt into the clouds but not before he heard the thud of strikes on the aircraft. The engine was hit. Desperately fighting for control, Will felt the aircraft shudder, then the engine paused, coughed and stopped. As it finally died, the Thunderbolt began to lose height, then plunged in an inexorable dive towards the earth.

Jessica ran out of Broadcasting House into the September evening. She was glad in a way she'd had to record this programme – it took her mind off things. She struggled to get on a bus. There were no taxis around. No, she'd walk, or rather run. But it seemed no effort. Seven under the clock, she repeated endlessly as she skipped along. Only minutes and she'd see him again. Only minutes and she could tell him that the future was theirs, that never again would the shadow of John Gale come between them.

It was still light fortunately, at least she didn't have blackout to contend with. She pounded across the road past Eleanor's Cross, up into the station forecourt. And there was the clock, scene of so many rendezvous and partings, hanging impartially above them all. Many others had had the same idea obviously, for quite a crowd gathered there. Her heart beat at the sight of a blue uniform, then, disappointed, she remembered he'd be in olive-brown.

After a few minutes she began to feel she knew her fellow waiters; the girl with the brown coat despite the warm evening, the man in the long raincoat, the old tired-looking woman with the shopping bag. The clock struck seven. She looked about. He must have been held up, she told herself, stilling the ache in her stomach. The trains . . . She concentrated on the group again. The girl looked pregnant, ill. The man annoyed. Then he was claimed by an even crosser-looking woman. *Five past*. The girl shifted from foot to foot. *Ten past*. The woman's tired face lit up as a young man walked towards her. Now it was just her and the girl; others had come to join them but they weren't part of this intimate group that knew each other now through and through. *Fifteen minutes past*. A young man hurried up to greet the girl. All worry disappeared from her face, and Jessica rejoiced for her. But she was left alone. He was delayed, his train was late. *Half-past*. Curious glances now from porters. *Eight o'clock*. He wasn't coming. The train was cancelled. The pass. He would have left a message at Uxbridge. Of course, how *stupid* of her. She had to get home quickly.

She fought to get on to the Underground. Couldn't they see how desperately she needed to get home? The train crawled to Uxbridge, then trying not to panic, not even to think, she ran to the house she shared with the Astras. She pounded up the path, her key missing the lock through nervousness. He'd have phoned, left a message . . .

'No, Jess,' said Art curiously. 'No one rang. Only Dave.'

'Dave?' He might have news. Trembling, she asked for his number.

'Dave?'

'Great news, Jessica.'

'Will?'

'No.' He sounded puzzled. 'I rang to say the Dorchester want to book you again.'

So he hadn't come. He no longer loved her. He'd met someone else, thinking she would never be free of John Gale. It was her own fault.

No, she couldn't believe that. Will always kept his word. Even if it was bad news, he'd have come to tell her. Suppose he couldn't? Suppose he was dead, or lying in hospital? Fool that she was, that must be it! She'd ring Debden. But when she got through, she was told simply that Captain Donaldson was not there. There'd been a mission yesterday, and one today.

She put the phone down, fear creeping over her. A mission. He might be dead. She would go there tonight. No, she'd never get there. Tomorrow then, and refuse to leave till she got the information she needed.

The journey seemed endless. Alone at Audley End she waited for her local train. At Saffron Walden she managed to find a taxi, until at last she was before the orderly room clerk. Debden was a large station. He dealt with names. And this was just one more Waaf, albeit an officer, and one whose face was vaguely familiar. He ran his finger down the day roster lists. 'Not flying today, ma'am.'

'Yesterday?' she demanded. She could hardly bring herself to ask: 'Is he in the casualty lists?'

He looked again. 'No, ma'am. Say, aren't you the Singing Waaf?' He became almost animated.

'Yes. Please, is Captain Donaldson on leave then?'

Interested now, he looked at the leave roster. 'Why yes, ma'am, he sure is. I'm real glad.'

'And not posted?'

'No, ma'am. Still on the Squadron strength.'

At RAF Tempsford, Graham Macintosh was asleep. Peacefully, for the first time for months. Last night he'd picked up three Joes, one of them Molly, and they had a week's leave ahead of them.

Jessica stumbled back to the taxi.

'Are you all right, ma'am?' The driver looked concerned.

'I'm fine,' she managed to say. He wasn't dead. In her relief the truth had registered late. He was on leave – and he hadn't come.

'Bad news, I reckon,' he said to himself. She wasn't the usual kind of Debden doll. In fact, she reminded him of someone. Hadn't he seen her pictures in the paper? The Singing Waaf, that's who she was. Everybody's pin-up.

Alone on Audley End Station, Jessica stared down the line at the blue haze in the distance. From where would come the train carrying her back to – what? To nothing. To a life without Will. The fruits of success, so bitter-sweet in her hand, had turned to leprechaun's gold.

Chapter Fourteen

Thoughts jumbled chaotically in her head, night and day. I must work. Sing. Far away. Far away from that clock at Charing Cross Station with its minutes ticking away into eternity. Far away from Debden with its impersonal lists and statistics, with its roar of fighter planes and Yankee voices carelessly raised in laughter. Americans shouting and cheering – not Will lovingly calling to her over the green Kentish downs; Will's voice raised in excitement in rehearsal; Will's whisper as they lay side by side after making love.

'I don't care,' she said in the Director's office in Whitehall. 'Just give me permission to go wherever Uxbridge will send me. Except East Anglia.' Nowhere where there was a US base. She would not risk meeting Will as a stranger. The strained hello, the awkward goodbye. She must blot him out or she could not go on.

'Overseas,' she said firmly. 'I must go overseas.'

The Wing Officer pursed her lips. 'Are you sure you're up to it?' she'd asked, looking at Jessica's pale set face and clouded eyes.

'The Director wouldn't sanction overseas,' continued the Wing Officer firmly. 'Unless you fancy Newfoundland.' Her tone was sardonic as though she realised

Jessica's motives had little to do with music.

'No. Front-line. Italy, now that—'

'Out of the question, until things are calmer.'

'It's my work,' Jessica had said in a tone inviting no response.

'You *are* a serving officer,' the Waaf reminded her a trifle icily. Albeit a privileged one, she might have added, but the thought lay unspoken between them. 'You can't dictate where you're sent.'

'No one can force me to sing,' Jessica pointed out simply.

The Wing Officer opened her mouth to dispute this, took another look at Jessica's face and softened her tone. 'There are plenty of places in Britain to visit, Flight Officer Gray. Just as far off as Italy.'

'Can I see the Director – appeal to her?'

'The Director's not here. She's resigned and her successor hasn't taken over yet.'

And with that Jessica had to be content.

It was two days now since she'd returned from Essex, choked with disbelief. I'll meet you in six months, he'd said. But he hadn't. And even worse he'd gone on leave, obviously to avoid her, to let her wait in humiliation. No, Will couldn't be deliberately cruel. Perhaps he wanted to avoid hurting her, thinking she would never recover from John Gale's death, and deliberately forced himself to forget. Or worse – perhaps he only loved her as he loved music. They were bound up together. Apart from war. He had laid music aside and her with it for a new kind of life. He had no time for a woman with only half a heart, as he thought. How could he know how much she'd changed? How could she reach out to him? She'd written, and written again to the camp. He'd get the letters when he returned from leave. Yet in her heart she knew it was no use. Those letters would arrive at a vast emptiness that did not hold Will; he would be enshrined in her past as surely as John, unless she could reach him to explain.

She lay awake, tossing, half asleep, half awake, dreams and nightmares colliding in chaotic dance. Will swooping down from a deep blue sky, smiling, and as she reached out her arms imploringly, disappearing, walking away, dancing, running, down a long, long road, deaf to her cries, her shrieks, leaving her alone in a parched desert, blinded at every turn by dust and sun.

After five days, even her fighting spirit had to accept he was not coming. She would have to wait till he received her letter after returning from leave. Till then, she would blot it out. Another week to wait. Meanwhile there was work. And work she would.

Uxbridge, somewhat bemused, had fixed a schedule that suited her requirements, from the Naval base at Sullom Voe, Northumberland, and back through Wales.

In her impetuosity, wrapped up in her own misery, she had forgotten one thing. Back in the Uxbridge house she was speedily reminded when Art burst in through the door of their rehearsal room.

'Jessica? I just got the new schedule. What are you playing at, for Pete's sake? Is Uxbridge up the pole, round the bend, or is it you? Sullom Voe, Northumberland, then Wales. In a week? Starting Thursday?'

'Yes.' Her voice was clipped.

Art sighed in pure disbelief. 'Jessica, I know

something's wrong, but for Pete's sake think of us. You can't drag me and the boys round on a trip like this, without so much as asking us.'

She started at him aghast. 'Art, I'm sorry – I just hadn't thought. I needed to get away.' She looked so conscience-stricken that he laughed. She hesitated, then blurted out: 'It's Will. He's not coming back.'

'To the band? Well, you know how he feels about active service—'

'He's not coming back to the band. Or to me.'

Art said, 'Now you've got me, Jessica. You've had a bust-up? That's crazy. You must've got the wrong end of the stick.'

'From where I stand both ends look the same,' she said wrily. 'He couldn't have made it plainer.'

'In that case, Jessica,' Art said awkwardly, 'we'd better get this over too. Agreement was Wings for Victory, right? That's finished now, and you want to do the circuit again. So this is where we bow out again, me and the boys. Or rather, they can go if they want to, but my feeling is enough enough's for them too.' He paused, seeing her face. 'Look, Jess, when this crazy war's over, we'll all meet up again – talk things over. Right?'

'Right, Art.' She tried to smile. It was only temporary, she tried to tell herself, and there were other bands. Other accompanists. So why did she feel yet another part of her life was being torn from her? Don't think of the past, don't think of the future – a future wide open, bleak and grey without Will. Think of now. A now she could fill with one concert after another, singing till she dropped in an effort to cheer others – and to obliterate the past.

* * *

Will blinked and opened his eyes. For the first time he managed to concentrate on his surroundings, and see them clearly without that feverish mist. Immediately he struggled to swing his feet to the ground, gasping with the effort. His head swam and he lay back again on the coarse straw pallet that was serving him as a bed, trying to think. He was lying in some sort of wooden barn – or stable, from the smell – piled high with fodder. The top floor of a stable. It was dilapidated and the wind was whistling through the cracks. When he felt strong enough he'd peer out. Meanwhile he pulled the rough blanket over him again and concentrated.

How had he got here? Where was he? Not in the hands of the Germans, that was for sure. Think back to the beginning of that last flight . . . He remembered fighting the controls in vain, first one then the other engine conking out. He remembered baling out: the final desperate tug that released his parachute harness from entanglement, and the blessed cooling air that hit him, the jerk of the ripcord that released the canopy – and the awkward landing that winded him. Then the discovery that he had hurt his ankle in falling, and his dragging himself painfully to the bushes. They would be looking for him. He didn't have long. If only his darned ankle would stop hurting.

He had lain back against a tree trunk and tried to think against waves of pain. He took out his escape pack from his front pocket and examined it ruefully. Not much to survive on in Occupied France, even for the two days it was supposed to last, but it was something. He recalled the escape and evasion lectures they'd sat through, both in the RAF and now the USAAF. 'It's your duty to try to evade', the RAF had pressed home. The USAAF went further. Occupied territory was another war theatre – only in this one you fought on your own, under orders to get your ass back to base the soonest you could. Water, chocolate, benzedrine, a hook for fishing – some chance! A razor and a tiny compass. He took out the map and tried to study it, then looked at the compass. That way lay the Channel. That way lay Jessica.

With a stab of agony he remembered: tomorrow he had to meet Jessica. *Tomorrow he had to meet Jessica*! Why the hell had he agreed to fly that practice sweep? Some practice! He forced his thoughts away. If he was to get out of this mess, he mustn't think about tomorrow. Tomorrow was England, Jessica, a hundred forbidden thoughts. The next five minutes were his chief worry, for they were going to be important. They'd find the crashed aircraft and circle the area, move in, hunting him down like a cornered rat. He needed shelter. What did they advise? Scout a place out, watch it carefully for several hours. Then move in. He seemed to be in open country with few barns and miles of flat fields and woods. He couldn't be far from the coast. He recalled seeing a huge twin-towered church on the way down. No, too large for a village. Probably Abbeville. Solid, reassuring, but still in enemy territory.

He shivered. Never had he felt so alone as when he lay in the silence. He watched a beetle pick its way carefully round his legs; the damp air of autumn filled his nostrils. He faced the fact that he was alone in a French wood in Occupied France, with no earthly chance of getting back to Jessica tomorrow – if at all. He forced himself out of despair. He took a piece of chocolate from his escape pack, and nibbled it carefully. After that he felt better, and took a sip of water from the rubber bottle. Then he clambered unsteadily to his feet, found a fallen branch to act as a stick and cautiously hobbled off. At least his ankle wasn't broken. After a few hundred yards he stopped short, his ears picking up the sound of traffic. There was a road just ahead, and he dived under a bush. Two motorcycles, their riders in grey uniforms, roared by. A patrol on its way to the aircraft – and to him. His parachute would not exactly have been invisible as he descended. His heart thumped loudly in his ears. So that was the Enemy. Now that he had seen them, they were reduced to human proportions. Better the foe you see than the one you fear.

He lay under his bush for a time, then stiffened as he heard the sound of feet walking on the road. A group of four men, he could see by the boots which was all his view allowed. They were calling: '*Amis*', friends. Looking for him. But how could he be sure they were friendly? He dozed fitfully when they'd passed and the night fell. He was cold, damp and hungry. Tomorrow morning he'd search for shelter . . .

He'd found a barn and collapsed into the hay, only to be woken by a sharp jab. A middle-aged farmer was standing there with a pitchfork, wary, hostile. They stared at each other. Should he make a dash for it? He was too weak. '*Pilote américain*,' he tried, pointing to his battledress and the wings.

There was no response. 'Wings,' he tried again. '*Pilote*.'

This time he had a response. 'RAF?' grunted the man.

At Will's nod – it seemed simplest – he dropped the pitchfork and advanced with outstretched arms, breathing garlic. '*Restez ici.*'

Half an hour later a hunk of bread and some rough wine had been brought out to him by the farmer's terrified wife. Four hours later two other men appeared. Further embraces – and, more practically, a cart, and some peasant clothes for him to put on. A beret and blue overalls over his battledress trousers. He vaguely remembered being lifted up gently and put into the cart, being told to play deaf and dumb, '*un idiot*', of being lifted out, then the picture faded in a series of memories of different faces peering over him, a round motherly woman and a tall grey-haired man with glasses.

Suddenly he was wide awake. They were there again. 'Jessica,' he said quite clearly. 'I must get back.'

'*Pauvre enfant*,' he heard the woman say.

'*Je suis malade*?' he asked in puzzlement.

Their faces broke into smiles. '*Il parle français. Oui, mon fils*, ill for five days. *La grippe*.'

Five days. Then four days ago Jessica would have gone to the clock at Charing Cross; would have waited, and not found him there. Then what? Would she have assumed he had forgotten her? No, she would find out that he had been shot down. Wouldn't she? Too weak to wrestle with the problem further, he lay back, and in his weakness involuntary tears pricked at his eyes.

Three hundred miles away Jessica sang to her audience, not for them, not for herself, but for a kind of oblivion to life. It was her fourth concert in three days. From bleak Sullom Voe, she'd gone to Newcastle, Wales, and now RAF Banbury. Always folk songs, popular songs, requests – she even forced herself to sing Will's songs.

One thing was special about Banbury: Geoff Swift was station commander.

'Where's Will?' he asked bluntly over supper before the concert, looking in concern at her pale face and listless eyes.

'So far as I know he's on leave at the moment,' she said shortly.

'No more clarinet then?'

'No. He decided to go for flying ops, not music, while the war's on.'

'And no more Singing Waaf?'

'That's not fair, Geoff. But no, since you ask.'

'It's pretty obvious, Jessica. But why? I thought you two were Abelard and Heloise?'

'Well, we're not,' she said stiffly. 'Time for my convent, I suppose.' She forced herself to laugh.

'What happened? Were you still "desolate and sick of an old passion"?'

She stared at him. 'No,' she said at last, surprised at what an odd idea it seemed now. 'He may think so, but it's not true. Anyway, after the war he'll be going back to the States.' She tried to smile. 'Now how about you?'

'Haven't heard sight nor sound of Vanessa, I'm glad to say,' he said without rancour. 'For me, the old love for Jean is still all important, Jessica. I told you that would never alter.'

'But don't you care about Vanessa?'

He gave it his consideration. 'No, I don't think I do. Do you think she cares about me? I passed the time for her, that was all.'

'No – more than that. She's basically warmhearted, she liked you.'

'Warm something, anyway,' he muttered. 'Strange to think she's your cousin. As a matter of fact,' he said as if ashamed to admit it, 'I did find out if she was all right. She's doing the rounds of the GI show over in East Anglia somewhere. Strictly officer class. No more painting stocking seams on her legs for Vanessa. A new pair of nylons for every day of the week.'

So Vanessa was still engaged in her madcap existence. Hardly a surprise, but it simply added to Jessica's depression. Her world was desolate around her. 'Cry for louder music and for stronger wine' – she remembered saying that to John. The tables were turned now, she thought wrily as she waited in the makeshift curtained wings for Geoff to finish his introduction, her mouth dry. She felt hot all over, her skin burning, the words she spoke seeming to have no connection with her. She must be tired. Perhaps she'd take some leave. The signature tune was her worst hurdle. Will's special song for them. Hopeless now to try to drop it. It wasn't fair on her audience. She managed to stumble through it. The sounds that emerged were pure Jessica Gray, soaring straight to her listeners' hearts, but the effort behind them was prodigious, and even as she sang she marvelled that it could sound so smooth when every note seemed to be dragged forcibly from her aching heart.

But the strain told. Halfway through 'We'll meet again' – a song that meant so much to her audience – she coughed over a line, steadied herself and continued. Then it happened again, a stumble, hardly discernible to her audience but terrifying for her. I must go on, *on* she told herself. One phrase at a time. If I can get that out, I can get the next. Thus concentrating, straining every nerve, she managed to reach the end of the scheduled programme. With a sense of foreboding she knew she must ask for requests. And inevitably it came.

'How about, "You're the Apple in my Crumble"?'

It went all right until the last line of the first verse: 'So come back to me'.

The words tore through her nerves, echoing at her from all directions, blaring in her ears, mocking her. Monstrous faces seemed to close in, laughing at her. She swung her arms in front of her face to blot the horrible picture out, choked, tried again. Nothing. No sound at all. She forced it, she tried, she willed herself to sing – and nothing happened. She was aware of the audience shifting uneasily, then their faces swirled round her, closing in . . . in . . . She felt an arm round her, leading her somewhere – where? She didn't know . . . Then, oblivion.

The next few days were a haze of sleep and nightmare, longing for sleep, dreading it. A nurse bending over her. Injections. Then more faces. Words that seemed to have little to do with her. Collapse, overwork, fever . . . It took her a week to throw off the high temperature, but compared to what had happened to her that night, her illness was of little consequence. She could no longer sing. Every time she tried a garbled monotone would emerge, or no sound at all, until shock sent her back into a merciful blackness.

Lucette and Antoine were their names, but Will called them, as they seemed to call each other, Maman and Papa. There were three children, he gathered, but he only saw the teenage son Philippe who came to gaze excitedly at the curiosity in their stable. Will learned that he was sleeping in the stable of their small hotel-restaurant, the Auberge du Pont. The old Norman house, showing signs of the bomb damage the whole village suffered in the Battle for France, stood by a small stream which he could hear trickling in the stillness of night from his bed in the hay loft over the old stable. The Auberge du Pont was a Relais de Diligence, Papa told him. No stage coaches now, of course, but on market days the yards were full of tethered animals on their way to market: hens, goats, cattle. Other visitors to the Auberge were more dangerous, for German soldiers might call in at any time. Will was not therefore allowed outside at all, and only during the night could he exercise up and down the hay loft.

His ankle was improving daily, and impatiently he chafed at his imprisonment. But when he spoke of moving on, Maman and Papa simply shook their heads and invited him to drink another *calva*. The fiery liquid burned his throat but eased his fears. They gave him two books left behind – whether by one English traveller with catholic tastes or two different ones he could not guess – *Pride and Prejudice* and *The Green Hat*. Neither did much to take his thoughts off what was happening across the Channel. Jessica must be making enquiries at Debden. She *must* be. They'd tell her he was missing. It wouldn't be like her to give up. No, things would be all right there surely? Then fear seized him. He hadn't been flying from Debden. They'd assume he was on leave as planned. But Wilburton would have sent details through, wouldn't they? He tossed around restlessly on the narrow bed.

Peering out between the cracks in the wooden building, he could see the back entrance to the auberge across the narrow yard; a waiter was disappearing into one of the outhouses. Papa was carrying fish to his smoke house. Two German officers were strolling in the yard while deliveries were being made. The whole industry of the auberge world was moving round beneath his feet – and he a mere spectator. From the other side of the barn, the view was of meadows and bomb-damaged houses, a desolate scene he quickly turned from.

'All Londinières was ruined in 1940,' Maman said sadly. 'The villagers have no money to build it again, but one day it will be reborn. After the war . . . when we are free again.' A look of longing crossed her face. Only a year now and Philippe would be old enough to be sent to Germany as forced labour.

Papa spat on the floor. 'So you get back soon, *mon fils*, and fight, yes?'

'When?' asked Will bluntly.

'Patience, *mon fils*, patience.'

Not much patience was required after all, for that evening after rabbit stew and *patisserie* – no rationing here! – two men arrived, one wearing peasant clothes and with a thick accent, the other dressed nondescriptly but obviously educated. He spoke good English and the other deferred to him.

'We will begin preparations to get you home, Captain Donaldson. Once we are sure, of course.'

'Sure?'

'That you are who you say you are.'

Will sighed. 'How do you do that? I have my identity disc. Isn't that enough?'

The man smiled deprecatingly. 'They can be forged. The Germans are clever. There have been spies. You must understand, we have to be careful. Too many have been shot. For you if you are caught, it is POW camp. For us it is death or concentration camp. On every building there are German posters to remind us of this fact. Not that we will forget it when we all know someone who has suffered.'

They questioned him endlessly on camps, uniforms, even the colour of his mother's eyes. At last: '*Bien*, Captain Donaldson. And now we check with London.'

'And when my bona fides is okayed?'

'Then the line will get you out of France over the Pyrenees, back home so you can shoot down some more Germans, please,' he said simply.

'Okay by me,' said Will grimly. 'What line, though?'

The man said seriously, 'It is better you do not know. Jacques, our leader, will tell you perhaps. Now you will need identity papers, good ones. You cannot move in France without them. The Germans are skilled at recognising forgeries. But first we wait to hear from London, eh?'

'Just suppose they don't confirm my story?' Will asked curiously. 'What do you do then?'

The man turned as he was about to go down the ladder. He said nothing, merely drew his finger across his throat.

Of course. What else could they do? Will knew enough from lectures of just what the penalties were, the likelihood of betrayal of the lines, the set-up whereby no one knew more than a couple of names of associates. He was curious to meet Jacques. He must be some guy. All the same, the Pyrenees sounded a heck of a long way away.

He had a look at his small French map. There he was up round Dieppe. There were the Pyrenees. All that lonely long coastline. All the boats there must be – and all the German soldiers. Whichever way you looked at it, it was going to be a long way back to Jessica. Hang in there, lady, I'm still here. Still kicking, he told the silent night.

The Adjutant at Group HQ Wilburton stared at the request coming from MIS-X. This was the second chaser on this Captain Will Donaldson, whoever he was. He consulted the lists again for any strangers who might have flown with the group on the 16th. There were several that day; that was the mission for which the CO had called for volunteers from other groups, including one poor devil saddled with the name of Captain Ham Burger. No Donaldson though. He frowned. He was a careful man, and that Ham Burger was some damnfool name all right. He went to check round the officers' mess. There'd been a lot of missions since then, a lot of losses, a lot of new faces, but a couple of them remembered that the 16th was the mission where Pete Bronski went into the drink after staggering back to the Channel with a crippled P-47. Strangers? Hell, a lot had happened. No Will Donaldson that they could recall. Pete Bronski had some visitor flying as wingman. But his name?

'Hey, I got it,' someone yelled. 'Byng, that was his name. Byng.'

Even in the dying of the year Kent was lovely, despite its trappings of war. Jessica sat in Tom's garden, face held up to snatch the last of the autumn sunlight. Now the Allies were pushing ahead in Italy, surely it could only be weeks before Kent once again became a battlefield – this time a preparation zone only, God willing, as troops foregathered as they had in August. This time for a real invasion of France, the longed for Second Front. Only weeks . . .

She was tired, oh so tired. Illness had left her physically defeated. Shock at losing her voice had brought on a complete collapse. Her voice would come back, the doctor had said comfortingly. How did he know? He was only saying it. There was no physical reason for her loss of voice, the doctor had said; it had simply happened. When she was stronger . . . He let her go on thinking that rest would cure it. She knew better. She began to come to terms with her loss for she no longer wanted to sing without Will. Could no longer sing without him. Without the sound they had created together, there was no point in her striving any more. His disappearance was an abrogation of their whole union, physical and musical. He had turned his back on their music and love, and whether she wished it or not her voice was doing the same.

'A psychological block,' Tom muttered. 'I've heard of it before.'

'Will it cure itself?' she asked.

'I don't know, Jessica,' he'd said honestly, gently. 'I don't think anyone could tell you.'

Only one person knew the answer – she herself. And it seemed to be no.

What if Will came back? What if he returned, telling her it was all a mistake? Would all be well? She closed her eyes. Perhaps. Perhaps not. For it was not just his absence – it was the betrayal, not just of herself but of what she had believed to be truth. Truth of love, truth of music. Will's truth. And if that were so, would she want him back? The effort of thinking was too much, and she gave it up. She only knew she could not sing; not to an audience, not to herself.

The trees were changing colour now the harvest was in. Late Michaelmas daisies and chrysanthemums bloomed in Tom's garden; damp fruitful smells of autumn filled the air. The year was dying, and winter lay ahead. She looked at the large spider's web in the lilac bush, dew still clinging to it where the sun had not touched it today, and remembered the old tale about Robert the Bruce that she used to tell the children at school. There was a moral in that somewhere. It was time to put her web together again. There must be some new direction she could take, something to fill the aching void.

Tom came out into the garden, back from school early, to see how she was. Despite her improved relations with her mother, Frittingbourne Manor, with its memories of John and Will, stifled her and when Tom had diffidently suggested that she should come to stay with him she had gratefully accepted, despite the disapproval of the village. Still, Jessica was the Singing Waaf and could do no wrong, and gradually the tongues stilled.

'What's for supper? Since you were so keen to earn your keep here.'

'Stuffed herrings and apple bombes.'

'Very patriotic.'

'Tom, I think I've decided.'

'What?'

'I need to get out of England, go overseas – even if I

can't sing I can do cipher work. In Italy perhaps if I could get a posting.'

'You mean you want to escape.'

'If you like,' she said angrily. 'Anything wrong with that?'

The effort of anger made her tired again and she lay back in the chair. Tom came across in concern. 'I'm sorry, Jessica. I just feel you're not up to that kind of thing yet. It's not even two weeks yet.'

'In my mind I'm quite clear. I shall meet Molly and talk to her. I'm sure she's on a hush-hush job of some sort.'

'Very likely,' he said drily. 'She's as crazy as you are.'

'Do you mind, Tom?' she asked softly. 'About not being in the services?'

'Yes,' he said. 'I mind very much, but there's nothing on earth I can do about it.'

'Poor Tom.' Her hand closed over his. 'We none of us get what we want, do we?'

'Some people would think me lucky, headmaster of a school, not on the front line, living in this cottage.' He waved a hand towards the old beamed building with its quaint dormer window. 'All I can think is that winter draws nigh and even a cottage is too large for one. A hearthside needs two.'

'When this war is over—'

'Sometimes I think it's just going to stretch on and on and on like elastic,' he said bitterly. 'I think, now that Astaire's gone, Lind is just hanging on to see the end.'

'At least he's still singing,' she said absently. Then a pang hit her. Still singing. Only she, Jessica, had lost her reason for living. Which way to go? She stood at a crossroads, and they had removed the sign.

* * *

As soon as the two men came in Will sensed something was wrong. He'd had a feeling Maman was keeping out of his way. Papa was bringing his meals, but hurried away without staying to talk. His questions had only elicited the information that Pierre and Maurice would be coming this evening. And Jacques too, perhaps. An hour before curfew Pierre and Maurice arrived alone, climbing quickly up the ladder – remaining between him and the exit, he noted. They were apparently friendly but there was tension in the air. Then Papa joined them, sitting by the ladder. A tiny pulse of anxiety began to beat in Will's cheek. Then, out of the blue, Maurice's tones changed abruptly.

'You say you are Captain William Donaldson of the United States Eighth Air Force.'

'Yes'.

If he were Gestapo Maurice could not have looked more menacing. 'Of 336 Squadron based at Debden in Essex.'

'Yes. Look, what is all this? Have you contacted London?'

'*Oui*. And it is clear that whoever you are, you are not Captain William Donaldson of 336 Squadron. Who are you?'

'What? But, hell, I am—'

'*Non*. Captain Will Donaldson is alive and well and on two weeks' leave, monsieur. Now tell us who you really are.' The voice was silky, deadly.

'For Christ's sake, they must have sorted that mission out by now.' His mind whirled. 'I was supposed to be on leave but I flew with another squadron – I told you.'

Debden had had ten days to get the record straight. 'Of all the bloody muddles,' he said disbelievingly. 'Look,' he added desperately, searching for the French, so all three of them should understand, 'I did a mission with a friend at Wilburton at the last moment when I was supposed to be on leave. I flew under a phoney name.' And he didn't even know what it was. What a damn-fool idea that had been! 'I don't know why they haven't sorted it out by now, but that's what happened.' Fear began to seize him as he saw their blank, unresponsive faces. A fear they noted and ascribed to the wrong reason. Maurice's hand emerged from a pocket, holding a gun.

'Try harder, monsieur,' he invited politely.

'But that's it!' Will cried. 'That's the whole damn stupid truth! You think I couldn't make up a better story than that if I was a phoney? I was supposed to go on leave for two weeks from the 16th but I flew a mission at Wilburton instead of going on leave right away. For some darnfool reason, they didn't get the gen at Debden.' He stopped. 'You don't believe me, do you?' he said flatly.

'*Non,* monsieur. You volunteer to fly a dangerous mission when you don't have to. Unlikely.'

'But it happens all the time. And it was only a diversion sweep, for Christ's sake. It was bad luck we were jumped – you've got to believe me.' He got to his feet, facing his accusers straight on.

'*Non*, monsieur, you have to make *us* believe *you*.'

'But I've explained.'

'*Heraus*!' a voice barked right in his ear.

'Hell, what's that?' he cried, spinning round, thoughts of the Gestapo racing through his mind.

It wasn't the Gestapo. Her face was largely hidden by the scarf she wore round it, but it was young, attractive, authoritative. She must have shinned up the outside posts and in through the hay loft door to come behind him.

'*Ça va*!' she said carelessly to the man. There was a visible lessening of tension and the gun was replaced in the pocket.

'Would someone mind telling me what gives?' Will enquired, limp with relief.

They were all laughing now, shaking hands, kissing. The girl explained in excellent English – to his surprise with an American accent.

'Forgive us, Captain Donaldson. It is a trap when we are in doubt. If you had been German, you would have reacted in German to that shouted command. You did not. You reacted in your own language. Now please will you tell us your story slowly? Then again. Then again.'

After that they fired questions at him for an hour, sometimes in French, sometimes in English, until he was so tired he was answering mechanically. She noticed this. 'I am sorry, Captain Donaldson, but we must be sure. And we are not yet quite convinced.' She embarked on another series of questions about America, then England, till at last she nodded.

'Okay, now let me ask a few questions of my own,' said Will deliberately. 'First, how come you don't have an English accent?'

'I learn it in America,' the girl said simply. 'Before the war naturally.'

'And secondly, forgive me, but who the hell are you?'

It was Maurice who answered: 'I am sorry, Captain

Donaldson. We should have made it clear. This is our leader. This is Jacques.'

Autumn hung heavy in the air now, still, as if waiting like the war itself. Another winter ahead and now there was bad news with the Army only slowly forcing a way up the leg of Italy. November lay ahead, with its fogs and grey hopelessness. No Second Front this year. Restlessly, Jessica turned the leaves of a book. Nearly three weeks now since Charing Cross; two since her voice had gone. She'd been to see yet another doctor and her old music tutors, but the answer was the same. There was no physical reason why she could not sing. And yet when she opened her mouth no sound came out, no desire except to retch, an overpowering sickness that threatened to engulf and choke her.

Wait patiently, they said.

Patiently! Another day of waiting for the post, to see if there were a letter from Will, of calling Art at Uxbridge to see if there were news, until she was too proud to do so any more. More nights of restlessly turning, tormented by memories of Will's arms around her, longing to hear the words of love he'd whispered so passionately and which now it seemed she'd accepted so casually.

Art was about to leave. The rest of the band had been given another trumpeter and were going to soldier on as best they could without her, with another singer. The thought of returning to the world of music acted as both a magnet and a source of terror. She could conduct, she could train, advise – but not sing. So she would stay away. She dragged her thoughts firmly into the present as Molly arrived.

She looked little different, thinner perhaps, more strained, but her smile was as warm as ever, as she sat down beside Jessica in the summer-house Tom had built at the bottom of the garden when his conservatory had been smashed to smithereens three years before.

'Where's Tom?' she asked. 'I'd like to see him again.'

'At school.'

'Just as well. Time he found himself a lady.' Molly looked curiously at the cottage.

'He says he's cut out to be the perfect bachelor,' said Jessica.

'Nonsense! He's the slippers and pipe type. I thought I was, too – I mean, apron and kiddies. But war – and its tragedies – bring out different aspects of people. I seem to be a whole new person since – that day. Not nicer, not better, just different. Now I can't think beyond the next day, and—' she glanced at her friend '—the next mission.'

Jessica swallowed. 'Look,' she said quickly, 'I can't ask what you do, Molly, you can't tell me, but I can make a good guess. And I want to do the same. I've got to get away. I just can't bear knowing Will's in England, in danger, could be killed any day, and I wouldn't even hear about it. That I can't even see him, that he doesn't want to hear from me. I can't understand it and now I don't want to. I just want to throw myself into action somewhere as far away as possible.'

Molly was silent for a moment, then said slowly: 'For what I do you need fluent French.'

'Oh.' Jessica was deflated. 'I guessed as much. What about Italy? Do you think your people are doing anything there – I speak Italian well.'

'I don't know,' said Molly firmly. 'But what I do

know is that it wouldn't be right for you. Not at the moment at least. You can't go just to escape your problems with Will.'

'You did,' said Jessica gently. 'After the raid, I mean.'

'No,' said Molly. 'I went because I wanted to give as good as I got. That's why Cairo didn't work – too sedentary. I've calmed down now, and thought it out – and I know this is right for me. But what you want is an answer.'

'There's another reason I want to go to the front line,' said Jessica reluctantly. 'It isn't all escape. Let me tell you. I'm haunted by the way everyone thinks me so brave for getting the BEM – I *wasn't* brave. I just did it on the spur of the moment. Now I've got a permanent reminder of how I'm supposed to be, and I want to prove it to myself. I want to earn what I've already been given.'

'Braver to stay here and sing – do what you do best.'

'That's the problem,' said Jessica quietly. 'That's what I haven't told you. I can't sing any more. The doctors tell me it's a psychological block or something; every time I open my mouth it feels as though a huge stone is rolling across my throat blocking it, choking me.'

'Oh, Jessica.' Molly took her hand. 'I'm so sorry.'

'Bless you for not saying it will pass,' she said fervently.

'It's because of Will?'

Jessica shivered suddenly, despite the warm sun.

'Shouldn't you see him?' said Molly worriedly. 'Just to talk about it? He can't just blot out all you had together. Especially if you've this voice problem.'

'No,' replied Jessica. 'He's made his choice.'

Will had left her the shadow of a life. He'd left her

suspended in a grey world while he sped on dancing feet to new horizons. Perhaps after the war he'd write music for others, play for others, love— No, she must not think of it.

'Then you must find something else while the war's on,' said Molly. 'Plan for after the war, and meanwhile do what you can, the best you can.' She paused. 'Like Graham and me.'

'There is a Graham and you? Really and truly?'

'Yes, really and truly. He's like no man before or ever again. Only Graham. I've been so lucky. Odd to think we'd met but never really noticed each other, until the war brought us together again. And now we'll never part.'

Will peered out through the crack in the door, trying to inure himself to the smell of his travel mates. A smile had crossed even dour Pierre's face when he saw Will's expression as he was bundled unceremoniously into the covered wagon with a load of pigs.

'*Et voilà*, little pig, to market.' His broad face cracked into a grin.

It had taken a week to get Will the necessary papers, to kit him out in workmen's clothes – blue overalls, beret, and some form of passable footwear – and to din into him his cover story. A week in which he forced himself into patience, into trying not to panic. If Debden still had not sorted out the mess, what the hell had Jessica been told? What was she doing? What was she thinking?

'You do not look like a Frenchman,' laughed Maman. 'Too tall, too fair-skinned. We give you a Belgian mother. And you are dumb since birth. Your French is good, but not that good.'

Will glanced at the papers, a faint bubble of fear swelling inside him. That strange face that peered back at him under beret and stubble - was that really Will Donaldson, Captain in the US Air Force?

'There must be something,' Maurice explained, 'to explain why you are not in Germany, working in the factories. They take all our young men.'

Now that the moment had come, confidence drained from him. It was so desperately important to him to return to Jessica as soon as possible. She would have been told he was simply on leave; would assume he had tired of her, had given up hope of supplanting John Gale in her affections. He tried to convince himself that she would go on asking, that someone would tell her, she'd find out somehow, but the chance was there . . . Dear God, how had all this happened? What a fool he'd been ever to leave her, let alone take that fateful mission. But despair wasn't going to get him home. He took hold of himself and listened carefully to what Jacques told him.

He still hadn't accustomed himself to calling this girl Jacques, or got over the shock of finding the leader of the St Jacques Line was a woman. Most escape lines, he gathered, were routed through Paris, and used the major rail lines. The St Jacques Line used local lines through the countryside on the basis that there were less checks that way, though strangers were more noticeable.

'Provided we keep to the busy times, when workers arrive in the towns for work, it is easy,' Jacques explained. 'The passengers rush together through the gates; they are waved through. But strangers are noted on the trains, so we change often, and you keep away from Pierre, *hein*?' Pierre was to be his companion on the train after delivery of the pigs.

Will took an affectionate farewell of Maman and Papa before he got into the van in the yard, away from curious eyes. He knew every detail of this yard by heart, and the river bubbling by. Now he had his first sight of the bombed village of Londinières, the wide street with its shabby, damaged homes, waiting to be rebuilt once some end to the conflict came. The French were practical. What point in rebuilding when soon the English would come again, and more bombs, Maman had pointed out. Even the church was damaged. Bombs were no respecters of places.

He compared this village with his own native Stockbridge. It had the same broad highway, but where Stockbridge had solid, clapboarded, well-kept houses, every habitation here showed signs of deprivation and the soullessness of a country under enemy occupation. This was what he was supposed to be fighting for – even if it did mean pigs. He grimaced. He could see through his peephole crack in the door that they were driving along a country road with fields and woods on either side, and the occasional scattered hamlet. With its small hills and streams it should have been like Kent, but it was not. There was no lushness here, no variety, though it had a bleak beauty of its own. He tried to imagine how the Berkshires in his native Massachusetts would be looking now with their brilliant sweep of fall colour, and told himself that this flat, rather dull countryside was but the first step towards his seeing them again. They seemed a mighty long way away, but nothing could quench his optimism today, cautious though it was.

For about twenty minutes they were bumping over the cobbled streets of a small town, and he huddled down among the squealing pigs lest he be seen. The wagon drew to an abrupt halt and Pierre's face appeared at the door, motioning him to be still as the pigs jostled for freedom, then beckoning him out. A brief nod to another man who took over the van and they were walking into the railway station. 'Forges les Eaux,' Pierre grunted, thrusting a ticket into his hand.

Then Will was part of a swirling mob pushing through the gate for the train: workmen, peasant women with baskets, young office workers. It seemed as if every eye must be on him as he presented his ticket, expecting at any moment to see the whole of the German Army bearing down on him. He tried to resist the temptation of glancing around, and watched carefully where Pierre went, jumping aboard after him and pushing his way into a carriage with what seemed to be a score of other people. Don't sit in the same compartment as Pierre, he'd been instructed. No fear of that anyway. He found himself back in the corridor, seatless, and grinned when he realised his close proximity to the pigs was perhaps to blame.

Once somebody addressed him. In panic he could not translate it, then remembered he was supposed to be dumb. The man repeated it impatiently and Will pointed to his mouth. The man shrugged and turned to his neighbour. There was no control on this local train, but at Forges les Eaux they changed trains for Rouen, a main line. This time he was sitting in a compartment, huddled in a corner, when he heard the words '*Kontrolle. Papieren*', bellowed along the corridor. He centred his thoughts on Jessica to try to calm himself. He had to get back. He *had* to . . . Then they were there in front of him. Four soldiers of the Wehrmacht. The enemy. Good thing he was supposed to be dumb – he doubted if his dry mouth could have produced a word. They snatched his papers, scrutinised them carefully, muttered amongst themselves and were about to say something when the peasant woman opposite dropped her basket, and its contents – six pigeons – made the most of their liberty. In the ensuing fracas, the woman shouting, the soldiers angrily brushing off the pigeons, they forgot about Will, thrusting his papers back to him and departing rapidly. Will could have sworn the woman winked at him.

'I'm afraid it's my fish pie again, Tom,' said Jessica ruefully. 'I took the last of the spuds from the garden.'

'Better than I could do. I seem to live on swedes most of the time. You deserve a medal for getting fish.'

'You haven't seen it. It's not the sort I'd boast about. It's the sort even the cat thinks twice about.'

'Looks good to me. I'll keep you on as cook if you like.'

'But I'm in for the duration, remember? And,' she hesitated, looking at Tom's familiar face, 'I'll have to get back to work. I'm as better as I'll ever be, thanks to you. I've got to report to Whitehall the day after tomorrow.'

'What are you planning to do?' asked Tom curiously.

'I'm not sure yet,' she said. 'Anyway they'll tell me, I expect.' But she had some ideas which had been formulated while talking to Geoff Swift on the telephone.

'Don't forget me again, will you, Jessica?' Tom asked quietly. 'I've enjoyed having you here.'

She smiled at him, suddenly at home with him again, all the old warmth flooding back as though the last three years had never been. She looked round the room. Cosy hearth, blackout drawn tightly, meal on the table, Tom's old leather-bound books on the shelves, the huge wireless in the corner, the tinny gramophone – all etched on her mind. A refuge to come home to, if need be.

'Pilchard!'

Molly gasped out the code-name as the man unceremoniously yanked her off into the undergrowth. The Lysander quickly embarked its returning passengers and took off again, all in four minutes flat.

'Whoever picks these damn stupid names?' she panted, when they stopped for breath.

'Baker Street,' he said, matter-of-factly and dampeningly.

Molly sighed. She knew HQ chose them. Just her luck to get a literal-minded public school type. Their base was some way from the landing area for obvious reasons, and they had a night in a barn before travelling on to base the next day. She was used to it now, it was part of the job, this enforced intimacy, the interdependence.

'This is it,' said Pilchard, throwing open the door of the old house. It was so dilapidated the push nearly brought it off its hinges. 'Upstairs is us.' The house was a shambles, two straw pallets on the floor obviously being their bedding. An ancient stove in one corner, wood-fed, with a dirty saucepan. Two cracked cups, and a tin-opener.

Pilchard saw nothing wrong. 'Wireless,' he said, striding into the next room. It was badly concealed in an old bread oven by the chimney.

'Tell me more,' said Molly resignedly.

'Object: attack railway lines to Bordeaux. We need supplies from London, and to link up with Botany Bay.'

'What?'

'Code-name for missions outside Bordeaux.'

'First, though,' interrupted Molly drily, 'I think this place could do with a woman's magic touch. Mine.'

The train was chugging into Le Mans now. The approaches to a major town were obvious, and the cathedral's familiar silhouette confirmed it. The rest of the journey had passed without incident, with changing trains and waiting. This was the danger point. There was bound to be a check at the gate, and although it was lunch-time, the train was not very crowded. Still, his papers had passed muster once, more or less, Will tried to reassure himself.

The carriage emptied as it came alongside the low platform. Will made sure he was out first, so that he was not trapped in the crowd before he wanted to be. There was Pierre ahead of him; outside the gate they were to meet his next courier who would take him to a safe house for a few days. Outside lay safety. But he still had to reach it. Keeping Pierre in view, he manoeuvred into the middle of a group – and then saw what Pierre could see. This was no routine control. There must be ten of them, plus some plainclothes men who were definitely not French. It was too late for Pierre to turn, but instinct made Will drop to the rear of the group again, then further back, till he could dodge to one side of the platform out of sight of the gate. Where now? he thought feverishly. He saw Pierre being stopped, taken on one side. Quickly, he looked round the platform. Somewhere to hide . . . Nowhere. No other gate. No other train he could leap aboard. He could not cross the tracks in full view. Then his eye fell on a urinal at one end of the platform. A French carousel urinal, open and chest-high, and right by the wall next to the road side. Hardly believing his good fortune, he strolled in. He had only one companion, but it was no effort at that moment to busy himself – gee, he needed it. Then, heart beating, he hauled himself up and out into the street, strolling round idly to the front of the station in time to see Pierre, gesticulating wildly, being frog-marched towards a van. Pierre glanced at him with no sign of recognition, then the doors were slammed shut and the van drove off.

He was on his own. But he was still free – and still with a chance of returning safe to Jessica.

'It's just an office job,' Jessica said to Tom with a gleam in her eye.

'I suppose that means you can't tell me,' he said with resignation. 'Just like Molly couldn't tell us she's being dropped into France. It stuck out like a sore thumb. And now you. Promise me you won't suddenly jump a convoy ship to Russia, or take on the Luftwaffe single-handed.'

'I promise,' she grinned.

'Will you be near enough to come to see me?'

'Oh yes. On a forty-eight-hour pass I could. Or we could meet in London.'

'So you're based in London.'

'No, but I can get there easily enough. Now no more guesses. There might be a spy lurking up in the fir tree.'

She'd miss Tom's companionship. It would be nice to

meet in London. He meant home, in a way that her mother, try as she might now, could not. Tom was Kent, putting it grandly. And Beaconsfield wasn't that far from London. Sometimes, she gathered, she would have to travel to London in her job. She'd never heard of MI9 before though she knew there must be some organisation dealing with escapers from POW camps and returning shot-down pilots. Her rôle was to work on the reports given by returning airmen and correlate the facts with existing dossiers. Sometimes she would go to MI9's interviewing premises at Marylebone and sit in on the interviews. It wasn't singing, but it was interesting.

The new Director in Whitehall had been sympathetic to her other plan too, but had firmly scotched it, temporarily at least. The new idea, the Waaf Songsters, would have to wait.

need in London. He meant [illegible] was [illegible] another, [illegible] he might [illegible], and not. Tom was Kent, buying a [illegible]. And [illegible] wasn't that far from London. Sometimes, she gathered, he would have to travel to London in his job. She'd never heard of MI9 before, though [illegible] organisation dealing with escapes from POW camps and [illegible] shot-down pilots. Her role was to work on the reports given by returning escapers and to update the lists of [illegible]. Sometimes she would go to MI9's [illegible] premises at [illegible] and [illegible] on the [illegible]. It wasn't thrilling, but it was interesting.

The new [illegible] in Whitehall had been [illegible] with [illegible] other [illegible], but had [illegible] at least. [illegible], the [illegible], would have to wait.

Chapter Fifteen

In Kent in a few more days the old elms and oaks on the downs would have reached their full glory in a blaze of autumn reds, golds and browns. There were beech woods here at Beaconsfield, beautiful, majestic trees, yet the sight did not move Jessica as did Kent. She had been at Wilton Park for three days now; the old country house and park were magnificent surroundings in which to work, but she had to force herself not to see them as a prison. She made herself join in with the social life, which was lively since as well as M19, its American counterpart MIS-X operated here. The hutted accommodation in the park that had sprouted as the staff grew too large for the old country house itself, coupled with the secrecy of their work, meant Wilton Park became a closed, self-sufficient group, into which willy-nilly she was drawn.

But at nights no one could keep away the agony. Without singing, without Will, what lay ahead? Restless dreams filled her sleep; she tossed and turned, trying not to disturb her room-mate. She dreamed that Will would take her by the hand, then would be drawn away, her own hand gradually slipping from his grasp as he vanished over the horizon. Nightmares in which she sang, sang,

sang . . . and then would wake and realise that was the past. She could sing no longer and the agony would begin again. What was Will doing? Who was he with? Did he lie with someone else, making up silly songs about her breasts; whispering loving words into her hair?

Beaconsfield was the centre of the escape and evasion organisation, both for the British and Americans, though interrogations of returned personnel and the actual control of evasion lines were operated from London. To one department came streams of information gathered from German POWs, to her own the information from escaped British POWs and evaders. Here too the escape kits were designed, and lectures organised for all aircrew on the best ways of evading capture. If any office job could take her mind off singing, this was it. The debriefing reports would make fascinating reading – if she had not met some of the men involved and known of the human emotions and torments that lay behind these laconic pared-down notes of evasions: 'Then I took the road to Calais. A patrol passed me so I leapt in the ditch.' Lying, covered in mud, cold, in mid-winter, nerves taut, expecting that any moment the sound of the motorcycles would stop, boots would march towards him, guns be pointed . . .

'Then Madame Lepin hid me in her attic.' Despite the notices plastered everywhere threatening death for civilians who sheltered evading airmen – and not just threatened. Stories of treachery and betrayal reached them frequently – 1943 had been a catastrophic year for MI9, they told Jessica. The two biggest evasion lines had lost their leaders: Pat O'Leary betrayed by a Frenchman in March, Andrée de Jongh of the Comète Line arrested in

January; her father, who continued his work on the line, arrested and shot a few months later. Yet the lines had carried on. New leaders took over and both still operated. One line, however, a smaller organisation, had so far remained immune to betrayal. The St Jacques Line was named after the great saint who brought Christianity to Spain, St Jacques of Compostela; the pilgrims to his shrine created a chain of abbeys en route to Santiago. The namesake line used routes across the Pyrenees, well inland from the coastal routes used by Comète and its Basque guide Florentino.

Today Jessica was bound for the Grand Central hotel at Marylebone, for a debriefing session. The airman was the latest to come back via Gibraltar, carrying a message from Donald Darling, MI9's agent there, that 'this one could be interesting'. He was the latest 'parcel', as they were called, to be sent over the Pyrenees by the St Jacques Line.

Someone in the carriage was whistling. Her heart lurched. The tune was 'Today'. 'For we had today . . .' She turned her head away, just in case she should be recognised, and listened to the sound almost objectively. It was good. Could all that just vanish? Apparently so, for not even Dave had heard from Will, or Don. It was the final sign that he was turning his back on music. The sound of the clarinet took over in her imagination and she was still wrapped in melody as the train drew in, belching triumphantly, to disgorge its passengers into the reality of a November day.

The commissionaire at the hotel eyed her inquisitively. Involuntarily she flushed. She was becoming paranoid about being recognised. He nodded and she went on up to the second floor bedrooms now converted into temporary offices.

'Section Officer Gray,' she reported at reception.

'Thank you, ma'am. I'll just—' But whatever the Waaf was just about to do went by the board as an adjoining door opened, and a braided RAF officer appeared, an ironic expression in his eyes.

'Dearest Jessica, how lovely.'

'Gerry,' she said flatly. 'Gerry Rhodes.'

Don't run, force yourself to stroll casually. Stroll casually! With the Gestapo right there – for the men in plainclothes could be no other. When your only chance of getting out of this mess had been arrested in front of your eyes; your only chance of getting back to Jessica – *No*. Think what to do. Church, make for a church, the lectures had said. The priests were generally friendly, if not actively helpful, although there had been cases to the contrary. He would make for the cathedral he'd seen as he came in, that was it. He felt a momentary relief at a decision made. The sweat was running down his face, though the day was not hot. He fancied the people he passed were looking at him suspiciously. It must be his imagination. Yet he forced himself to slow down and began to breathe more easily.

After about half a mile he came upon an open space on his right, with a church. Should he continue on to the cathedral or take his chance with a smaller church? Better the smaller one, he decided. He went inside. It was clearly dedicated to Joan of Arc. She'd have her work cut out at the moment, he thought grimly as he knelt down to pray. And pray he did, half for cover, half in reality. The air was heavy with incense – half a dozen black-clothed women were genuflecting and lighting candles. Joan of Arc – Jacques was her modern-day counterpart, he supposed. He was cut adrift from the line now. He'd never see her again. What had happened? Had the line been betrayed? Jacques herself arrested? And Jessica – no, his best way of ensuring what he most desired was not to think of her, not to think of music, that other life, but to concentrate all his thoughts on getting out of this mess.

He opened his eyes cautiously. In the aisle only a few paces from him, two men were standing apparently engaged in discussion. But he could hear his heart beating as he stared unconcernedly ahead. He was sure they had noticed him. If they were friendly they would approach him. If not . . . when he glanced round again, they had gone. It could be nothing. He'd go to find the priest. No, he wouldn't. He was going to run like hell.

Instinct had him on his feet, leaving by a side door. He had been right. The two men had a gendarme with them, and were walking back towards the front entrance from the road. So much for churches being safe. They were clearly watched.

Which way to go? How? Then his eye lit on a bicycle, a blessed, blessed bicycle, obviously sent by St Joan. Pausing more to offer a prayer of thanks to God rather than an apology to the bicycle's owner, he jumped on and cycled off, cutting through narrow streets downhill. Downhill led to water, and once he was at the large river flowing through the city, he would know where he was. This looked hopeful – Rue du Port. Yes, the river was ahead. So far so good. But where the hell was he going?

Towards the Pyrenees, he supposed. A few evaders had come back from Brittany, but most seemed to reckon the Pyrenees were the safer route, over into Spain. If Jacques chose to go that way, there must be good reason.

Soon he was leaving Le Mans behind. He felt safer now though logically he knew he was more vulnerable in the countryside where strangers would stick out a mile and there would be no evading any patrols. And if Pierre had talked they'd be looking for him. The road began to make him nervous: long, straight, exposed, tree-lined. His early relief at being free gave way to depression. It was well into the afternoon and hunger overcame him. He wouldn't find anything in the fields at this time of year but raw vegetables. And returning evaders had all too graphically and crudely described the effects of resorting to them. What then?

He stopped, pulling off the road into a small valley dipping away on the left where he would be hidden from sight. It was then he offered a second prayer of gratitude – the cycle owner's wife had left her man's lunch in the saddle bag: rough country bread, pâté, and a curious sausage that he had seen in the shops, strong, fatty, heartening. An apple too. Regretfully he did without the wine. He needed his wits about him. Prudently he saved the last bit of bread. If he was going to cycle all the way to the Pyrenees, he'd need it. He was crazy. He'd never do it alone. All the same he was going to have a darn good try. He'd get to the Loire tonight. He still had the silk map, although he'd had to leave behind the escape kit except for the fishing line. Good trout fishing in France, so he'd heard, but that line did not look promising. Maybe he'd tickle a trout or two, as he used to back home.

Wonderful things, these French roads. Long, straight, paths to the future. He felt like one of the early settlers taking the Mohawk Trail to the west, seeking new lands to make their own. He began to whistle a phrase or two of a new tune, whistled it again then put words to it: 'Going west, going blest, riding proud upon the Mohawk Trail.' What was it Jessica had said? Something about Minnehaha? Her laughing face was suddenly before him again spurring him on, as he pedalled furiously along the road.

He had been cycling for four hours when he saw the patrol ahead, fortunately in a village street and busy with a lorry. Several German troop lorries had passed him going the other way, too many for his peace of mind, though he was getting to have a false sense of invulnerability. Quickly he dismounted, and after a moment casually walked a hundred yards back in the direction he'd come and took a turning to the right.

He must be nearly at the Loire now. How to cross it was the question. This road, if it led to the river eventually, might not be important enough to continue across it by a bridge. Well, he'd take his chance. An hour or two later, he arrived at the Loire – and swore. There had been a bridge. It had been blown to bits. Straight ahead, on the other side, he could see a steep wooded hill with church spires at the top. He could hide there – but how to cross?

Ah, well, he was a good swimmer. But he'd have to say farewell to his bucking bronco. He patted it gratefully and pushed it into the bushes, then worked his way along the river bank till he was well off the road. It was a wide river and the night was cold.

Shivering, he drew himself out at the other side. Who was it swam the Hellespont to get to his girl the other side? Leander, wasn't it? Only difference between them was Jessica wasn't there waiting with a hot toddy.

He needed to get dry and to sleep. He stumbled across a field, guided by the lights of the village. Where there were houses, there were barns and sheds, he reasoned. He came to a large house built in château-style; but he could find no way in, and ran behind the old rambling house next door, hiding by the gate, till he could make out his whereabouts. He heard a horse whinnying nearby and realised he was hiding by a stable with over it another hayloft. He was about to move when the back door opened and a young girl came down the steps to a garbage can. From her attire she was clearly a waitress. So he'd come to another auberge. All sorts of delights might be thrown carelessly into that garbage can, he thought hungrily. He'd been lucky in the Auberge du Pont at Londinières, so perhaps he would be here. Cautiously he approached the ladder leading to the loft, climbed it and peered in. Hay, blessed hay. The garbage cans could wait.

Taking out the last of the bread, removing his wet clothes, and this time allowing himself the wine, he covered himself in the hay, happier than had seemed possible only nine hours ago. A seventeenth-century song haunted his thoughts, 'Oh, have you seen my lady?' Its melody caressed him into sleep.

'This isn't really my kind of place,' said Tom apologetically, looking round the packed Kit-Kat Club.

'No. It was a bad choice for today,' Jessica said.

Noisy, frenetic – all the things that reminded her of the life she wanted to leave behind. A bad choice for Tom too, with its reminder that he was not in the services.

'Let's walk over to Jules's instead,' he said. 'After the play I feel I need some fresh air. This—' he gestured at the throng '—demands Noël Coward, not Turgenev.'

'That wasn't the best of all possible choices either,' said Jessica. '*A Month in the Country* isn't exactly easy Saturday night entertainment. I just wanted to see it before it came off, and I'm glad we did.'

'I'm not sure,' steering her through the doorway of the bar, 'that your premise is right. Isn't it more of an escape to see a play that stays with you, rather than one you forget as soon as you're through the door? Just a debating point, you understand.'

Dear Tom, so anxious to pin everything down and examine it. She smiled at him. 'I'll put that to the Brains Trust, Professor Joad. Anyway, I enjoyed it,' she said firmly. 'And I enjoyed that frightful meal we had before. And I enjoyed—'

'Jessica,' Tom cut in, 'you don't have to go on like this.'

'Like what?' Her voice was suddenly low.

'Forever forcing yourself onwards. I know how you must be thinking about Will all the time you're with me. I can accept that. I'm tired of living alone, for all I thought I was the bachelor type. We'll help each other.'

She looked at him questioningly.

'What I mean is,' he said gently, 'we could marry, just as we always intended.'

'Marry?' she repeated blankly. The word made no sense.

He laughed. 'Don't look quite so astonished. It's hardly flattering.'

She pulled herself together. 'I'm sorry, Tom, but it's hard to take it seriously. Oh, that sounds dreadful! I mean – how can we, when you know I love someone else?'

'Who's left you and won't come back,' he pointed out.

She went white. 'Will might return,' she muttered.

'People don't return. Or if they do, it doesn't miraculously come right.'

'Even if that's true,' she said slowly, staring into her glass, 'there's no reason to marry someone else, just as an escape route.'

'You can look at it that way,' agreed Tom. 'Or you can look at it positively. Before Will, before John Gale, there was a reasonable chance you'd have married me, wasn't there?'

Jessica tried to think back, to understand what he was saying. She remembered all those walks, the talks, the amiable arguments. Yes, she might have married Tom – but that was before singing had taken over her life. Then it hit her. There was no longer song in her life. Not *her* song. Even if she achieved her plan of training a WAAF quartet, she could no longer sing herself. She would never sing again without Will, and he had gone.

'Yes,' she said quietly. 'Once there was that probability.'

'Well then?'

'I don't know, Tom – I can't think. I'm a different person now.'

'Consider it a standing offer?'

'I'll do that.'

* * *

It seemed Jessica was destined to keep on bumping into Gerry Rhodes, who acted in a liaison capacity between Whitehall and MI9. Like her, he was called in on the 'special cases'. She was surprised to realise she disliked him just as much as she had three years earlier. The disfigurement and handicaps that prevented his flying again had done little to sweeten his nature. So she was taken aback when after the day's work was finished – it had lasted well into the evening – he asked, 'You're booked in for the night here, aren't you? Who are you dining with – the gallant captain?'

'Myself. My preferred company.' No way would she let on what had happened between herself and Will.

'Dear sweet Jessica,' he murmured. 'I hardly imagined I myself could be so fortunate as to win your charming company for the evening. I thought you might care to meet your cousin again. The dear lady is proving rather a handful. I'm actually worried about her. Isn't that quaint of me?'

'Vanessa? What's wrong with her?' she retorted sharply. 'There must be something or you wouldn't want me to join you.'

He gave the twisted leer that was the nearest he could now get to a smile. 'Believe it or not, it's from my sheer good-natured concern for others.'

Vanessa, accompanied by a US officer – top brass, Jessica deduced from his braid – was already at the Café Royal when they arrived. She was paler and thinner than Jessica remembered, her mouth an even more defiantly scarlet gash.

'Darling, this is Barney. Sorry, Colonel Barney

Heyerman. He's a bomber boy. A bomb – bomb – bomber-boy. Aren't you, darling? My cousin Jessica Gray, the Singing Waaf.'

The formerly glum-looking Colonel seemed interested. 'Say, really? Perhaps you'd get to come and sing for us?'

'I'm no longer singing, I'm afraid,' said Jessica stiffly, 'I've been told to rest my voice.'

'That's a real pity, ma'am. The boys would sure love to hear you.'

'Gerry told me you're ill or something,' said Vanessa vaguely, but did not notice when Jessica avoided answering.

Bright and chattering, Vanessa drank a lot as the evening went on, and the Colonel got quieter. 'Let's have another bottle,' she cried, holding the Dom Pérignon bottle upside down.

'I reckon you've had enough, honey.'

'I'll tell you when I've had enough. *Darling*.'

She flashed him a bright smile, which he did not return. Instead he began talking to Jessica. He seemed a nice chap though out of his depth, she thought. Safe enough to talk about bomber missions. No connection with Will. He wouldn't know him. Vanessa pulled at his arm demanding more champagne and on his refusal, thought of a new ploy: 'You think that Jessica can sing, but I can. I'll show you.' And before they could stop her, she was clambering on to the table.

'I'll sing for my supper,' she shouted.

'That's enough, Vanny.' Barney hauled her off the table with an arm round her waist, lifting her as easily as a kitten. 'Reckon it's time we went.'

'You go,' said Vanessa. 'I want to talk to darling Gerry. Gerry loves me, don't you, darling?'

'Don't be too sure of that, precious.' Light enough, but with a slight undercurrent that Jessica didn't understand.

'How's my kid, Jessica – Johnnie's kid? Remember Johnnie Gale, darling?' Then she burst into tears. 'I'm not as bad as all that, am I, Gerry? I only want to be loved.'

Will woke stiffly and slowly unfolded himself from his foetal position. He was shivering. He felt his clothes. Still damp but wearable. Now what to do? There was a door in the loft overlooking the yard and he peered out cautiously. He was hungry, God he was hungry, and the smell emerging from the kitchen at the back of the inn was almost making him sick.

A delivery cart came into the yard, the driver unloading baguettes and storing them in a basket by the kitchen door, at the top of a flight of steps leading to the hotel. He could see now the building was badly damaged, one half of it seemed to have been blasted away. 1940 again, he supposed, in the defence of the village against the advancing Germans. Still, this was sure no time for a history lesson, he told himself; he needed food, and quickly. Perhaps he could pretend to be a deaf mute and beg? No, too much of a risk. Too many people about for one of them to take a risk. Still, it was a reserve plan.

He went downstairs cautiously and sped up the steps, keeping to the bushes on one side. Nearly there. Perhaps he'd ask for the patron. *Je suis aviateur américain. There.* His hand was on a baguette when the door opened. Whoever it was, it wasn't the patron. A cook probably. Past him he could see uniformed figures in the lobby. German soldiers looking for something, some*one*, him perhaps? No, coincidence. His mouth went dry. Pointing to his mouth, and grunting, he retained the baguette in his hand.

A look flashed over the cook's face – fear had been written in Will's expression too plainly. A quick glance over his shoulder and a jerk of the thumb. Get out, was the plain meaning. Clutching the baguette, Will ran blindly out of the gate down the road away from the hotel, and into the fields near the river. Breathless, he stopped for a bite of the baguette, considering his next move. Water. He would go into the village again and search for drinking water. Somewhere there would be a fountain and the Germans couldn't be everywhere. Cautiously he circled back into the village, and found out it was called Gennes. Like Londinières its buildings were decimated by bomb damage. He must steal another bicycle. He shivered. Bicycle! To the Pyrenees. Who was he kidding?

This was where his damned Massachusetts Puritan ethic had landed him. Do your duty. See the new boys are okay. Why the hell hadn't Pete put the record straight with Debden? What was Jessica thinking? That was his damned Puritanism too – this insistence on a perfect world. Why hadn't he grabbed hold of happiness with both hands when he had it? What the hell did it matter if she still thought of John Gale? John Gale was dead, poor devil. Why did he demand perfection? Who the hell did he think he was – God?

He stopped at a fountain then, over his shoulder, saw a patrol coming up the street. Immediately the past was engulfed in fear of the present. The fountain was by an open space on which the village men were embarked on a game of *boules*. Will did not stop to think. He marched into the game and took up a *boule*; a French oath, until the men saw the approaching soldiers. Suddenly Will became one of them, his shoulder seized in fraternal greeting. Now it was his turn to play – awkwardly he rolled the *boule*, hoping the Germans knew as little about the game as he did. A chorus of approving shouts, even though the *boule* had gone miles away from its target. Once the patrol had safely passed, he nodded his thanks and turned to walk swiftly away. But one of his benefactors was talking to a solid, short French girl, and they now stood barring his way. No Jacques this, but a bulky peasant farm girl with a thick almost bovine face, watching him fixedly. He went to move past her but she grasped his arm, and, urged on by his benefactors, steered him with surprising strength to a cart on the roadside, where a man, obviously her father, sat holding the reins.

A stream of patois left him bewildered, but it was clear they wanted him to get in the cart. Too tired and weak to protest, he climbed in behind their stolid backs. Their route took them along a country road, past fields and woods and hillside covered in dead bracken. Once they passed a large château on the left, but nothing to tell him where he was or where he was going. A tumbril, he thought crazily, a tumbril to the guillotine, and this fat country girl who stared at him with unblinking eyes his executioner.

'And then what happened?' Jessica asked, interested.

Air Gunner Peter Murphy had just returned to the UK

from Gibraltar after being shot down near Beauvais. It was hard on evaders having to come to Marylebone for debriefing when all they wanted to do was to see their families and sweethearts, thought Jessica compassionately, but MI9 had to get the information while it was fresh in their minds in order to help other evaders.

Painstakingly, with the help of detailed maps, routes were traced and the helpers were named, strictly for MI9 use. Often only code-names were known to the evaders. Some cropped up again and again: Francoise, Tante Go, Florentino, Jacques, Maurice, Nemo . . . they were like old friends to Jessica.

'Well, it must have been a couple of days later, this woman comes back – "Jacques" her name is – and tells us to get ready. We're leaving tonight. There'd been a spot of bother back down the line, and two of their agents had been arrested. They had to get us over the mountains as quickly as possible, then get back to sort out the mess. There was a traitor somewhere, they reckoned, a stool pigeon planted by the Germans, and they were going to have to wipe him out. She's quite something, that one. Cool as a cucumber. Then this great Basque chap comes along – Joseph, she called him, to take us over . . .'

He went on giving details, graphically describing his adventures which a day later Jessica would see on her desk at Beaconsfield, reduced to dry reporting terms. 'They were going to have to wipe him out.' Just a laconic sentence. How many of these incidents there must be, Jessica thought, going unregarded, unrecorded. What of their families? What if there were a mistake? War had no time for niceties. They were all cogs in this machine which rolled on regardless of individual tragedies and passions. Just cogs: she one, and Will another. Wherever he might be.

Will swung his feet to the floor, fully aware of his surroundings for the first time. When the cart stopped, he had been hustled down steps and into this odd room before he had a chance to look around. A meal was plonked in front of him, some sort of stew – he suspected horsemeat – and a pitcher of rough red country wine which ensured that he fell asleep for several hours, realising that whoever his saviours – captors? – might be, they were not the enemy and seemed to have the right ideas about his needs. The meal had hardly been up to the Red Lion standards – he thought longingly of the comfortable clapboarded inn in his home town of Stockbridge, with its abundant and splendid fare fit for the Presidents it entertained – then pulled himself back to the present. Watching him in a chair, her gaze as impassive and fixed as ever, was the French girl.

'Where am I?' he asked abruptly.

He was in some kind of room hewn into solid rock. He could see through the window that similar caves seemed to surround a small central yard. In the centre of one wall was a huge rough fireplace, with a cooking pot suspended over the grate and trivet holding a kettle. Someone, the girl presumably, had lit a small fire. The simple bed was pushed into an alcove at one side. There was a window in the front wall and a little one covered in paper above the door. The ceiling and walls were simply rough-hewn rock. A few bits and pieces of shabby furniture furnished the room, and a candle sputtered on the mantelshelf. All this he took in before repeating his question slowly: 'Where am I? *Chez vous*?'

The girl grinned inanely and went off into a steam of patois, in which he could only make out the word 'troglodytique'. Troglodyte? What the hell was she on about? He swung off the bed and made for the door. Immediately she got up, and with another inane grin barred his passage.

'*Je veux sortir*.'

Nothing happened.

'*Il faut que je sors – je cherche une toilette*.'

Nothing. In desperation he made it abundantly clear pantomime-style.

Unbelievably she shook her head, grinning and pointing to a bucket in the corner.

'To hell with this,' he muttered, putting his hand on her arm to push her aside. One huge hand brushed him away and pushed him back, with no more difficulty than if he'd been a puppy. Desperate, he was forced to make use of the bucket, cursing silently. When he'd finished, her eyes were still on him. His watch was showing five o'clock and the light was beginning to go. What the hell was the idea? Fatigue sent grotesque nightmares chasing round his mind.

None of his questions produced any response, and finally he gave up the attempt. What had he gotten into? The girl sat at her post stolidly, arms folded, just staring at him. Had her father gone to fetch the Germans? Fear gripped him. No, that didn't make sense . . . why bring him here, if so?

A few minutes later, the father reappeared, blackened stumps of teeth showing as he grinned at Will, dumping a pile of vegetables and a skinned rabbit on the table. His intelligence level seemed a bit higher than his daughter's, together with his command of standard French, and Will managed to glean that he was in an underground village comprised entirely of caves hewn out of the rock; that this room belonged to one of the small farms operated from similar caves; he could see its courtyard from the window, but the farm was now deserted for it was no longer economic to run. No, they lived some kilometres away, but they knew people here. The people of Rochemenier were loyal Frenchmen. He need not fear. When could he go? Ah, monsieur, a deprecating nod . . .

The girl was grinning again. How old was she? Impossible to tell – any age from fifteen to thirty. He fought panic. Was he to be kept prisoner here? Some kind of plaything to a mad girl? Then, to his relief, there was reference to '*mon frère*'. '*Mon frère*' would take Will on to Bordeaux. There he knew a man who had a ship to take him to England.

'Bordeaux?' Will queried. But that was the most heavily guarded port in France, wasn't it?

The man shrugged. It was clear his responsibility would be ended when '*mon frère*' arrived.

And why couldn't he go out? demanded Will. The man grinned again, and jerked a thumb. 'She likes you.'

He began to feel like something in an old Fu Manchu movie – or was it Boris Karloff – as the man departed, and the girl took up her vigil again with unwinking gaze. Frankenstein's monster, that was that dame. Hell, his imagination was working overtime. It must be. He lay back on the bed, praying he wouldn't have to use that damned bucket again. She must eat and sleep sometime, surely?

After a few minutes she got up and began to prepare a rabbit stew, putting it in the pot above the fire. He averted his eyes from the preparations, feeling his stomach heave in revulsion at the sight of her pudgy fingers tearing at the meat. While it was cooking, she absented herself, whether through delicacy to attend to her own bodily needs or to get water from the well he did not know. He leapt up hopefully, but the door was wedged from the outside and he succeeded in forcing it open only to find himself face to face with her again. He sank back on the bed, head in his hands in despair.

The stew was surprisingly good. What the hell happens now? Will wondered uneasily. Is she going to sit there all night? The bucket ritual repeated, he lay on the bed, his back to her. Then dread as he sensed her rise, heard her heavy footsteps. One, two, three, and she was looming over him. Christ, not sex! Please God, not sex! Unable to bear the tension he turned and stared up at her in blind apprehension. A rough concern came into her eyes, and she stroked his head as she would a wounded animal. Then she blew out the candle and lay down beside him, her gross figure oddly comforting in the dark and lonely night.

It was her mother's birthday. Jessica could hardly not go, as her mother had specially asked to see her. This time she'd have to tell her.

A pilot was leaving as she arrived at the Manor. He had obviously just come from a sitting with Michael. How young he looked. Had so much changed in three years that Flying Officers at West Forstling now seemed mere youths to her?

The mellow golden sunlight of autumn gave glory to the red brick of the Manor, making of her visit a home-coming and not the ordeal she feared. Even her mother seemed mellow as she rushed out on to the steps to greet her daughter.

'Darling!'

The pilot looked round in surprise, grinned at his mis-take and hurried on.

It was not until tea had been served and drunk that Cicely burst forth with what she was longing to ask and with rare delicacy had refrained from till now. 'Darling, why aren't you singing any more?'

Jessica hesitated. So far she had kept up the fiction that she had had flu, with no mention of her voice. See-ing her mother looked genuinely concerned, however, she replied flatly: 'I can't, Mother.'

'Can't? You mean they've stopped you?'

'No, I've lost my voice. Permanently. *Really* lost it.'

'Lost it?' Cicely's voice was shrill. 'How?'

'I had a shock and it seems to have affected my voice.'

'Shock?' Her mother's voice sharpened. 'To do with that American, Will Donaldson?'

'Yes. He's given up music,' Jessica said steadily 'I – I haven't heard from him for ages. It looks like he's opted out for good. From music – and me.' Her voice wavered. She hadn't meant to say so much.

'It's just typical of American GIs! But your voice will come back, darling. You must be run down.'

'No. It's not possible, unless Will—' she almost choked on his name, discussing him with her mother – 'decides to take up music again.' And *me*, and me, and *me*, her heart was hammering.

'Nothing's impossible.'

'This is,' said Jessica bluntly.

'Why don't you ring him up, darling, and talk about it? Does he know?'

As she jogged back in the train to London, Jessica laughed at her mother's naivety. Just ring him up, as simply as that? What on earth was she going to do? Tom was gently pressing her to marry him, but she felt numb inside. Not as she had after John died; this was different. Without song, she had to change her life, not just during the rest of the war but forever. Tom was the path to that. With him she could have a different sort of life. They'd teach singing perhaps. She could fulfil herself through having pupils. Perhaps they'd have children. That brought her to the stumbling block. Could she go to bed with Tom? Make love with him as she had with Will? Stupid question. Of course she couldn't. Yet surely they could adapt to each other in that way too; they had so much in common that they could be loving and gentle in their partnership.

The remembrance of her passionate nights with Will almost made her cry out with pain, as though some emotional anaesthetic had abruptly worn off, leaving the nerves exposed to agony. No, she couldn't believe it. There *must* be something wrong. Will wouldn't just go without a word. Six weeks now. He hadn't replied to her letters. Nothing, not a word. Her mother was right. She should telephone. He was only a short telephone call away.

Full of sudden excitement, she hurried to a public telephone as soon as the train arrived in London. Her heart was dancing, pounding, at the thought of hearing his voice. Almost trembling, she asked the operator for the well-known number of Debden.

It rang and rang. Would no one reply? Then a strange voice answered. 'Orderly room.'

'Can I speak to Captain Donaldson, please?'

Silence. Then, 'Sorry, no one here of that name.'

'But there must be. 336 Squadron.'

'I'll put you through to the Adjutant.'

The Adjutant was out. His assistant answered, 'No Captain Donaldson here, ma'am.'

'But he can't have been posted out of 4th Group—'

'Not on the squadron strength, ma'am.'

She replaced the receiver slowly, adrenalin draining out of her. He'd gone. Been posted, without a word to her. Or perhaps he'd been killed. No, she'd have heard. She'd watched casualty lists received at MI9 and MIS-X carefully every day since he'd been back from leave. He had gone, perhaps overseas. That would make sense. He'd cut himself off completely from the old life. From her.

Demain. Always demain. Tomorrow *mon frère* would come to take him to Bordeaux. How long was it now? Two weeks? No, nearly three. The days were getting cold though he was warm in the cave.

The girl pampered him, fed him with stews and soups and rough wine, but still she sat there, a silent eunuch guarding a nightmarish harem. At nights she slept beside him – not, to his relief, for sex, but as she would lie beside a sick calf to give it warmth and encouragement. With no means of communication, he was forced to discipline his thoughts, and pin them on a far from certain chance that one day '*mon frère*' would come and release him from this torture. He tried to fill his mind with other things. He filled it with Jessica, trying to convince himself that somehow the news would have reached her by now. He filled his waking hours with music, with songs. He had no paper to write on. Instead he concentrated all his thoughts on Jessica. Listen, he told her invisible presence. Listen, I'm *here. Here. Listen.*

He set to music in his head a mediaeval love lyric, 'Oh Western Wind when wilt thou blow. The small rain down to rain'. He went on to create lyric after lyric of his own, pouring forth all his frustration and love into words that ran round and round in his head and then dominated his sleep.

'Jessica, *hear* me,' he would mutter, his forehead damp with sweat. In the nightmare that surrounded him, in this ghoulish existence, thoughts of her kept him sane. Nightly he dreaded that his guard would no longer be content with watching him, that her gross body would seek his more intimately, her hands reach for him, and though they did not, the fear was as bad as the reality might have been. Only by retreating into music was he free.

When he finally protested at his physical imprisonment, shouting abuse at his saviours, the man took him on a walk round the deserted farms, but not near the still occupied dwellings. There was the old cider press, dusty and still, and the walnut oil press. Fifty years ago this would have been the season for the walnuts, the man explained, knocked down from trees in the autumn for the shelling to begin over the long winter evenings, all the family taking part. They would provide oil for lamps and oil for salad dressings. There was a wine cellar too, where grapes were pressed and made into wine. The man even became quite human, as he described how the farm operated. Will eyed the steps leading to the road wistfully. I must be the only damn prisoner in the world that's got more to gain from staying than running, he thought grimly, here he at least stood a chance of meeting with the Resistance.

Even so he was tempted. Perhaps sensing it, the girl took to padlocking the door and pocketing the key, so that not only would he have to fight his way past her, but overpower her as well. She was built like an ox. He'd always counted himself as pretty strong, but she was something else.

At last, *mon frère* arrived, a tidier version of *mon père*. He was a shifty-eyed individual, and Will found himself relieved when told in guttural French that *mon frère* was not accompanying him to Bordeaux - too far (and too dangerous, was the clear implication) - but to Poitiers where he would be given a ticket for Bordeaux. Once there he would be given instructions on where to meet his next contact.

His papers were suitably dog-eared now; they would have to pass muster for no new ones had been volunteered. Despite his doubts - was not Bordeaux a heavily guarded and restricted city? - Will's spirits rose victoriously. He would be free at last. He was suddenly ashamed of his previous revulsion against the girl, who had done her best to help him. How damn stupid his groundless terrors seemed by daylight. Penitently he kissed her on the cheek, and hugged her, and was rewarded by the sight of large tears rolling unchecked down her face. His euphoria stayed with him to Bordeaux, only encountering one ticket inspection and a casual check of papers.

Now for the café in the Rue Malbec. He sat down at a table and waited for a man with a blue coat with a flower in his buttonhole. None came. He ordered a coffee – a *marc* would have tasted better – but he dared not risk it. Keep a clear mind – and stomach. He waited for half an hour, then an hour, and ordered another coffee when he felt he was attracting attention from the café owner.

A girl sat down at his table. 'Monsieur requires accommodation?' she enquired somewhat oddly.

The café owner plonked down another coffee.

'For you it is free, monsieur.'

Startled, Will thanked him, then gave his attention to the girl. Was she sent by the man in the blue coat? His daughter perhaps. She looked about thirty, with long fair hair and a face innocent of make-up. Convent-bred obviously.

'You're not Paul, are you?' he asked doubtfully.

'I not know Paul, but I take you home with me, yes?'

He got up and followed her somewhat uneasily. He had nothing to lose, and Paul obviously wasn't coming. He could always run like hell if she seemed to be taking him straight to the police. But she looked too innocent to double-cross him. They went through a maze of streets, getting uncomfortably near the port. Didn't he need a special permit for this? Suppose he got stopped? Finally she halted in front of an old house with shabby green shutters, four storeys tall.

'My room is in here. But first you meet Madame.'

She took him to a ground-floor room where a grey-haired, beautifully dressed woman looked up as they entered.

'This is your mother?' he ventured.

The girl laughed. '*Non, chérie.*'

The woman cackled. 'Put him right, Lillette. *Mother*!'

'This is a *maison de plaisance.*'

'*Maison de* – you mean a whore-house? You don't mean – For Pete's sake, you're not a . . . ?'

'*Une pute? Mais oui, pourquoi pas*?'

He could think of nothing that would not sound insulting so he grinned and shrugged. And he'd thought her so innocent-looking!

Madame cackled again, got up, patted him approvingly on the behind and said: 'You think we cannot work for *la belle France* too? You are perfectly safe here. But you stay in your room, *hein*? My clients are mostly German now. German sailors, you understand.'

'*German*? But—'

'We work for France, *mon ami*, and sailors talk. Now, no more. Lillette will look after you. You stay here, and we plan how to get you out. But patience, *mon ami, hein*?'

Lillette chattered as she took him to the room allotted to him. It smelled of cheap scent.

'It is sensible, yes,' said Lillette, 'to hide here? The one place the Germans will not raid. You see this one, it is for officers.'

That was to reassure him! He prowled round his new prison when she left him alone. Large bed, mirrors on the ceilings and walls. A bidet. Ah, well, it was one up on the troglodyte cave, and Lillette was more than one up on 'the girl'. If ever I get back to the States, I'm going to have one helluva story to tell my grandchildren, he thought to himself. But that brought him back to reality. His grandchildren? He had a sudden vision of his old age with Jessica by his side, and then it faded. Did she still believe he had deserted her? No, Maurice must have got a message through from Londinières that they were satisfied he was Will Donaldson. And Debden would have checked it once he didn't return from leave. Jessica would know now what had happened, that was for sure. They'd have told her. Wouldn't they?

> 'O Western Wind when wilt thou blow
> The small rain down to rain . . .'

Jessica, *listen*, he demanded, with all his heart's energy.

> 'Christ that my love were in my arms
> And I in my bed again.'

In my bed again . . . Jessica tossed and turned, trying to get back to sleep, but could not get those haunting words out of her mind. Where had they come from? It was an old mediaeval love song, wasn't it? She must have been thinking of Will. No, she wouldn't remember their nights together. It was too painful for they must have been built upon a lie. Not hers, as she had at first feared, but his. Oh, how she loved and longed for him still, yet his love was based on shifting sand, not rock. Rock was here in Frittingbourne where Tom lived.

Lind was singing, despite its being late November.

Soon it would be Christmas, the Christmas she should have shared with Will. The Christmas, she told herself firmly, that she would spend with Tom. She was looking forward to it now that the conflict within her was resolved.

'That was a wonderful apple pie, Tom, I'll come again,' she joked.

'You can have the pleasure of my cooking every day.'

'That sounds like an offer I can't refuse.'

'It wasn't a joke, Jessica. I'm asking you for your answer.'

She was poised on the brink. Wasn't the decision already made? Made when she knew Will was gone beyond recall; when she put down the receiver after that telephone call, the last hope extinguished. Will had decided to make a new life for himself. Now Tom was offering *her* the chance of a new life. They could make each other happy. The avenue of love, the only one for her that made sense, was inexplicably closed. Tom knew that, and could accept it.

Was it enough? It was more than many people had.

'Yes, Tom,' she said quietly. 'I'll marry you.'

Chapter Sixteen

Jessica stood outside the old Virginia creeper covered building. This was the village school at which she'd been educated till she was seven, when her mother had insisted on her attending a private school. But it was here she had come back to teach, and here she would return when the war was over, as it surely must be soon. Although the Allies' advance in Italy was slow, they were at least firmly established there. The Germans had been checked at Stalingrad on the Russian Front and now bombers were flying deep into Germany; the RAF at night, and the massive onslaught of the USAAF beginning to make itself felt in daylight hours. Next year surely would come the Second Front. Then victory – and peace. A time for rebuilding of lives. Meanwhile she had to be content with short forty-eight-hour passes to Kent.

The sound of sixty infant voices floated through the walls, uplifted in the morning hymn.

'So here hath been dawning,
Another blue day . . .'

Another blue day in the middle of December. Yet these chirpy voices sang like blackbirds, while devastation reigned all over Europe. What would have happened if the Germans had invaded? When victory came, these children would grow up in a free world, their confidence not misplaced. Sing unfettered. A choir for the future. And she could do that. She could train a choir even if she could no longer sing herself. The music would still move her even if it had to be vicariously. A sudden excitement gripped her. It was time to think of that WAAF Quartet again. She'd ask to see the Director. Beg, cajole, wheedle her into agreeing this time. It wasn't completely over. Music was music even if it was given birth by others.

'No more is she afraid
For to walk in the shade . . .'

Now why had that come into her head? She couldn't cope with thinking of Will yet. Still full of her idea, she ran into Tom's office. He looked up in some surprise as she burst in through the door. 'Tom, I've had an idea.'

'I'm sure you have. What is it this time? How to prepare Molotov cocktails in ten easy stages?'

'No,' she laughed. 'And don't get me off the track.'

Her eyes were sparkling. 'After the war we could train a children's choir. What do you think, Tom? You do the business side and me train the children. We could tour, do hospitals and bases, just the same as I used to. It could be wonderful. The Frittingbourne Children's Choir.'

'There could be problems,' he said doubtfully.

'You mean, children touring and so forth? Oh, we'd overcome them. Don't worry, there'd be a way. And we wouldn't just stick to choral singing – people might get bored with that. How about solos? There's young

Hodgkins. People like boys singing. We could even do comic songs – the hospitals would enjoy that – and concerts for children's causes. Even opera. You'd like that, wouldn't you?'

'Hang on a minute, Jessica,' he told her patiently. 'There's the small matter of my job, and suppose your voice comes back?'

'It won't – and don't make difficulties.'

'But I like teaching,' he said simply. 'I'm a teacher, not a business manager.'

Her face fell. 'Well, I could do it,' she said, not defeated. 'I'm sure Dave Prince would manage it for me.'

It hurt her to say the name, for he was part of her old existence. She had not seen him since informing him of her illness.

He was silent for a moment. 'Yes, of course you could,' he said at last, quietly. 'That would be wonderful for you. I can't expect to keep you here all the time.'

'Oh, Tom.' She ran to him and threw her arms round his neck. 'Don't be an old silly. If you're thinking you'd never see me, it wouldn't be true. If I'm going to be your wife, I'll look after you, be here, teach with you. Just have the choir sometimes,' she said wistfully. 'After all, the training would be done here. The children *live* here.'

'Yes, of course.'

'When shall we get married?' she asked brightly, to please him.

He smiled at her. 'After winter's over.'

'In the summer,' she said. 'June. I've always wanted to be a June bride.' A few words to please Tom, that cost her dear today.

Yes, a June bride, but her dreams had been of Will. Perhaps she wasn't doing the right thing. Then she reasoned it out again. Will had not been the man she thought, or he could not have left her. Tom would not let her down in that way. He was Tom, solid as Kentish ragstone. As would be their love. Would be? She questioned her own thought. When they slept together – for by unspoken agreement, their lovemaking had not yet extended beyond deep kisses more of gratitude than love – it would come. Then it would be real, not built on shifting sand.

The smell of scent was beginning to nauseate him as much as had the cave. But someone would be coming today to see him, he'd been told. He'd been here two weeks now, cosseted by the girls, all of whom slipped in to view *le beau pilote américain*, rather to his alarm. But Madame reassured him stiffly: 'We are all good patriots, monsieur.'

It had been made clear to him that he was invited to enjoy all the amenities of the establishment, including the girls, and most repeated the invitation themselves. He gracefully declined – lest, he said, by accepting one he offended the others. They giggled, and did not persist. But Lillette was different. He still marvelled that this bright-eyed, fresh-faced girl was a prostitute, not a novice nun, and moreover appeared to enjoy her work. 'Except *les Boches*,' she spat in disgust. 'But I do my duty, *hein*?' Her looks reminded him slightly of Jessica's, and when one night she slipped in beside him, he made no demur.

'How did you guess,' he said lazily afterwards, putting

out a hand to stop her from leaving, 'I was on the run?'

'On the run?' she queried, to his amusement blushing slightly that he wished her to stay with him.

'*Evadé.*'

'I knew you were English.'

'American.'

She shrugged. 'They are the same. I walk up and down many times. A Frenchman he look at my behind, a German he look at my breasts. Only an Englishman – American,' she corrected, 'look first at my face.' He laughed.

'And moreover,' she added practically, 'André, the café owner, pointed you out!'

Despite its attractions, the brothel became more and more claustrophobic, as he tried not to rebel against being out of control of his own life. But tomorrow, Lillette assured him, someone was coming.

'*Bonjour*, Captain Donaldson.'

It was Jacques. Her tall lithe figure had slipped into the room unnoticed. He stared at her in complete bewilderment.

'So, Captain Donaldson, you are returned to the Ligne St Jacques. That is good. You were lucky that Lillette found you.' Her tones were business-like and peremptory. '*Eh bien*, we go. Here are your new papers. You are an immigrant worker from Denmark.'

'I don't speak Danish,' he retorted, irritated at her brusque orders.

'Nor do the Germans,' she replied curtly. 'Come, Captain Donaldson.'

'Just hold on,' he said, annoyed. 'Don't I get to say thank you to Madame and the others?'

'I have done this for you. Come.'

'No,' he said, glaring at her. 'I've been here two weeks. It's not going to hurt the line if I'm another two minutes.'

She bit her lip, obviously angered. 'Very well,' she said slowly. 'But I come with you.'

Forced to agree, he went down the corridor to Lillette's room next door. It was clear from the noises within that she was working. Will flushed as Jacques laughed scornfully. 'Your hooker won't miss you. You Americans are such romantics.' Her tone made it obvious this was not a compliment.

Will restrained his anger with difficulty. 'Better that than—'

'Than what, Captain Donaldson?'

'Nothing. Let's go,' he said dully.

She might be a cold fish, caught up in her Joan of Arc kick, but she was competent. The train journey to Bergerac passed without a hitch. He followed her instructions implicitly, and at the journey's end climbed up into a lorry awaiting them.

'Just a few kilometres,' she explained, glancing at the driver. 'Then we meet our next contact.'

It was an odd place to find a new contact, in the middle of a huge vineyard, on flat land dominated by a large château. The Château Monbazillac, she explained carelessly as he raised an eyebrow. She seemed suddenly to be making an effort to be friendly.

'I used to see that on wine labels,' he joked, following her as she pushed through the vines. 'I never reckoned to—'

'Then I am afraid you have drunk your last bottle, Captain Donaldson.'

'What the heck—?'

She had spun round and was pointing a gun at him.

'This is the end of your journey, Captain Donaldson. Now what is your real name? Tell me before you die, so I can pass it on to Lillette,' she added scornfully.

He gazed at her uncomprehendingly, unable to believe this was for real.

'I do not like being taken for a fool. You fooled me, you convinced me you were American as you said. But you are German, are you not?'

Keep calm, keep calm. 'Would you mind telling me what the hell this is about – before you murder me, of course?' he said as coolly as he could.

'Pierre was arrested, his contact in Le Mans was arrested, Maman and Papa too. You walked free. The network has gone. The person who betrayed them was you, Captain Donaldson. The only one who could have done so.'

'You're wrong.'

'There is me, there is Maurice. No one else knew about the Le Mans contact.'

'How could *I* have told them about the Le Mans contact? You didn't tell me what was going to happen in Le Mans.'

For the first time a shadow of doubt came into her eyes. Then she dismissed it impatiently. 'Maman or Papa must have told you. Or Pierre.'

'For heaven's sake, if I've done my job what do you think I was doing waiting in the middle of a Bordeaux brothel? Do you imagine I'd have risked Lillette contacting you again? You think I'm crazy?' he said reasonably, trying not to let his voice tremble. 'Listen, let me tell you again – *Kapitän*!' he yelled deafeningly to somewhere beyond her shoulder.

In the split second her eyes were averted, he jumped on her, knocking her to the ground and forcing the gun away, wiry and strong though she was. She bit his hand, almost forcing him to drop it again, but with a curse he pushed her down and got to his feet. Then he pointed it at her, as she coolly got up herself, and said to her steadily, 'Now, listen, Jacques – or whatever your name is – and listen *good*. Is there any damn reason in the world, if I'm a German stool pigeon, I shouldn't just shoot you now?'

'*Non*,' she said unwillingly.

'Okay. So if I give this gun back to you . . . will you accept I'm Captain Will Donaldson, United States Eighth Air Force?'

A wary look. 'You could be bluffing me.'

'Sure I could. But why?'

'The rest of the line . . .'

He gave an impatient 'tch'. 'You'll have warned them from here to the Pyrenees about me. I'm not that dumb. I'm taking one helluva risk coming with you, but you seem pretty competent – I'm prepared to trust *you*. Will you keep your word?'

She glared. 'If the St Jacques Line says it will get you over the Pyrenees to return you to the fight for France, then it will do so.'

'Then say it.'

'I say I will get you home, Captain Donaldson. Now give me the gun. I take you, but I stick to you like glue. Day or night we are together. Yes?'

Will shrugged. He was getting used to lack of privacy, and wondered amusedly how far this would extend in her case. He couldn't see this ice-cold madam descending from her pedestal to watch his bodily functions, much less sharing hers. Though what the hell did it matter in the long run? He just wanted home – or the home that was England – and quickly.

'Here.' He handed the gun back. For a moment she looked at it, then tossed it casually into the woods.

'It would not look good to carry a gun if we are stopped.'

'You can say that again.'

'*Alors*, Captain Donaldson.' A smile lit her face for the first time since he'd known her. '*Aux Pyrénées*.'

Forty miles away from them in the small village of Casseneuil, Molly Payne stirred uncomfortably in the ramshackle house she shared with SOE agents Peter Allbright and John Seymour. The three of them formed a team. The house hung over one of the three rivers that met in the village. In case of a surprise search by the Germans, the wireless could be jettisoned from the window, and them after it. SOE life wasn't all it was cracked up to be at the training centre at Beaulieu. Was this really war? Lying here, day after day, coding messages to London, decoding replies, planning, constantly planning, for an operation that never seemed to happen. Waiting for supplies from London for the Maquis that never arrived, trying with their limited resources to carry out London's requests.

Easy enough in Baker Street to issue orders: cut the Bordeaux rail links, hit them time after time, to cut off supplies to this vital port; gather information on the defences at Royan, at the head of the Gironde estuary; ditto on the submarine pens at Bordeaux. But it wasn't so easy in a coastal area. The Germans were careful who they let in. You needed special passes. Peter had chosen this small village eighty miles from the city because of its position on the three rivers, one the Lot, which flowed to join the Garonne. And the Garonne led to Bordeaux. Traffic on the rivers, provided it was by small local boat which every household possessed, went relatively unhindered compared with by rail and road.

Now at last there was going to be action. The railway line would be blown tomorrow and then they'd move on nearer their objective: Bordeaux.

Clinging to the thought of her children's choir after the war, Jessica returned to Wilton Park happier than she would have believed possible a few days ago. Now she would start persuading the Director to allow her to train a quartet, the WAAF answer to the Andrews Sisters, she thought, grinning at the idea. And meanwhile they could get up a concert at Wilton Park. She mustn't think about that now, though. She was supposed to be correlating intelligence on the St Jacques Line to pass to the small Whitehall office that ran the lines – or at least funded them, for usually the leaders objected to overtight control from London.

Leader Jeanette de Pinet, known as Jacques, aged twenty-five. Confirmed number of 'parcels' over the Pyrenees, eighty. In operation since mid-1941. Northern network in disarray owing to treachery. Traitor being disposed of by leader of line. Jessica frowned. MIS-X wasn't going to like this news. Traitor thought to be German posing as American serviceman. All very well, but suppose the line made a mistake? Suppose he were a genuine serviceman? No, they'd have checked it out with Beaconsfield first. She passed on to the next item. Plans for re-establishment of Northern link in progress under Comte de Valois, Jeanette's cousin. It was inspiring to see how someone always came forward to fill the gaps left by arrests. When Dédée de Jongh had been arrested early in the year, they had thought it would be the end of the Comète line, but it was not. Someone had stepped forward to take her place.

She wondered what kind of courage it took to run an evasion line, what Jeanette de Pinet was like. The risks were great. Jessica remembered her BEM and was shaken again by a sense of her own inadequacy. She supposed that courage like love came in all shapes and sizes, but could never be convinced that hers was one of them.

Like love . . . John, Will, Tom. Her love for John had been one sort of love, first love, built on self; her love for Tom, another, comforting and durable. Her love for Will – she hid her head in her hands in sudden agony. Who was she trying to fool? There was only one sort of true love – that she'd shared with Will. Or thought she had. But he couldn't have cared. Or perhaps he really thought she would never come to terms with her guilt over John. No, he'd said he would come – and he hadn't. Her whole body was stiff with wanting him. Hopeless to think she could replace him.

She stared at the typewritten sheets in front of her and slowly they became blurred. Softly she tried them again:

> 'I heard a nightingale sing that night,
> His sweet sad song of love . . .
> And the song was mine.'

Nothing came out but a croak. She tried to cast her mind back to the ecstasies of song, to her voice that once soared effortlessly into the heavens. Had it all been for nothing? No, she told herself fiercely. She would learn by it. Force her energies into other channels of music. Throw herself into her work here. She began again, reading the list of 'parcels' successfully passed to Spain; glancing at the list copied to her from M1S-X of American evaders. So the line was still running. Good. They needed people like Jeanette de Pinet.

One journey merged into another. Will and Jacques took the cross-country route to the Western Pyrenees. He lost count of the times they changed trains, always coinciding with their being at their most crowded. Mamande was the one name he recalled; they had to get to Mamande, for they could not risk Bordeaux again. Then, unfit as he was and tiring easily, he simply obeyed instructions, which train to get, where to alight. Sometimes they travelled apart, sometimes together as sweethearts. It felt odd putting his arm round this stiff, unresponsive, totem pole of a girl, yet once, when a patrol passed nearby, she turned to him laughing, giggling, blushing in her role of country sweetheart, and he caught a swift glimpse of another Jacques. Stations came and went: Aire sur l'Adour, Tarbes, then by road to Pau, then Orthez, Salies de Béarn, Guinarthe.

And there they halted, walking over a bridge to a spectacular small town overlooking the river. She marched him up a series of steps leading up to the old ramparts. The houses were different now, white with red-painted beams and shutters, and orange-tiled roofs. He began to sense the South in the atmosphere. They came to a small garden at the back of a rambling old hotel next to a ruined château, the Hostellerie de la Château. An old man came out to meet them, and Jacques ran forward embracing him.

'*Bonjour, Georges.*'

Judging by the cries of delight, they were long-lost relations, Will thought sourly, dog-tired and longing only for sleep. Without a glance at him, still chatting, they moved into the old hotel. Jacques glanced back. 'You come.' She waved imperiously as if suddenly recalling her charge.

Wearily Will followed them up an old staircase to the upper regions. The old man threw open a door and ushered them in, beaming.

'The standard of accommodation is going up,' said Will when they were alone.

She made no reply except: 'You sleep there,' pointing to a small bed in one corner. 'I sleep here,' to make it absolutely clear.

Will exploded. 'Look here, lady. When I got near you last night in the barn, it was for warmth. It was damned cold. I'm not after your body. I'd sooner make love to an ice-box. *Comprends*?' Too late he remembered he'd used the intimate form of address.

'*Oui, je comprends.*' She seemed loftily amused. 'You prefer whores. But you sleep there, for all your fine words.'

'No problem,' he said through gritted teeth.

There was a hostile silence as they ate the simple meal brought by the old man. Will broke it first. 'Do we go on like this?'

She deliberately misunderstood him, and replied coolly: 'Tomorrow, perhaps the next day, we reach the Pyrenees. There you stay.'

'How long?'

'It depends. We need more than one parcel to take across, you understand. It is not safe to go at some times. It depends on the weather. It could be months.'

'Months?' His voice rose in alarm. Months of this? Months before he saw Jessica, made sure everything was all right. He had a vision of her slight figure stalwartly singing on - alone. Without his songs. It seemed almost a betrayal, a kind of faithlessness.

'Can't you get me back quicker than that? The invasion will be next year. I've *got* to get back. If not, I'll take my own chances over the Pyrenees.'

'You will wait. This is a command. If you are arrested—' the scorn in her voice was apparent '—you could betray us all.'

Useless to deny it. No one knew what they might do under torture. Unwillingly, he conceded her logic.

'How come you got into all this?' he asked after a pause.

She hesitated, obviously weighing up any damage that might ensue from a disclosure. Then said, 'My father, he was a Légionnaire d'Honneur from the last war. And my husband, he is *mort pour la France*.' She was clearly nervous that she'd said too much and that her real name could be traced.

'I'm not a traitor, you know,' said Will gently. 'I'm an American.'

'Of German origin, perhaps,' she flashed.

'English actually. If it matters. We're all Americans.'

'We have to be careful.' It was the nearest she had come to an apology. 'There are other lines – many have been betrayed. Pat O'Leary in Marseille – it is now run by an old lady. The Comète line, too, run from Belgium over the Pyrenees near here on the coast. It still continues but many leaders were arrested. New ones come along. Many others have been betrayed also.'

'You must trust me if these are real names,' he pointed out.

She flushed. 'One must be careful,' she muttered again.

'What happens if you're caught? Is it really death?'

She shrugged. 'The men are shot. The women sent to camps – after the Gestapo has finished. Then shot, perhaps. There are tales.'

Will looked from the window at the fairytale village around them. Impossible to imagine it as the scene of violence. Yet the Pyrenees had constantly been the scene of massacres and battles; at the hands of Hannibal, Charlemagne, Roland and Oliver, and in Languedoc, the religious massacre of Montségur in the Albigensian Crusades. No more fairytale place than that, and yet the whole population of the castle had been slaughtered in the name of religion. He remembered visiting it on a trip round Europe before the war. The smell of death had hung heavy round it still. Perhaps after this war was over, there'd be similar stories. Like these rumours of concentration camps that kept filtering through. Thousands being wiped out, so the stories went – anyone who didn't fit Hitler's idea of the Master Race. Will shivered. He had to get back for that invasion. Even his small contribution might help. If that meant going along with the Iceberg's orders, so be it. This was simply another combat area and Jacques, he steeled himself to acknowledge, was his CO.

'There is a *toilette* on the ground floor,' she answered his unspoken question.

'Do you come in with me?' he enquired ironically. 'Or am I allowed to go alone?'

A reluctant smile crossed her face. 'You are on parole, Captain Donaldson.'

When he returned she was already in bed. 'There is water there.' She pointed and it was clear that she did not travel with nightwear. The night before they had slept in their clothes. 'And you sleep there,' she emphasised yet again.

'Don't worry,' he muttered as he blew out the candle. 'I can do without frost-bite, lady.'

'Well, that about wraps it up,' Jessica said, smiling at the flight lieutenant. 'My questions are over. Enjoy your leave.'

The officer fairly zipped out of the door and Jessica replaced her notes in her briefcase. Where was it he lived – Wiltshire? He'd be back home with his fiancée in four hours if he was lucky. He was one of the few who had made it back to England safely from POW camp. It was hard on them having to be grilled here too. She rose to go.

'Jessica?' Gerry Rhodes had appeared in the doorway. 'Can you come back with me now? To my flat?'

'You haven't developed a sudden passion for me, have you, Gerry?' she enquired sweetly.

'I thought you might come to take your cousin away.'

'Away, this time? What's wrong with her? Away where?'

'Nothing that a good doctor – of the right sort – can't cure. And anywhere away from me.'

Jessica went white with alarm. 'What do you mean?'

'Come and see for yourself, darling.'

He hailed a taxi – no buses for Gerry – and she was forced to contain her anxiety until they reached his Curzon Street flat. Vanessa was sitting on the sofa, tense, drawn and chain-smoking from the look of the ashtray. She burst into tears when she saw them.

Jessica ran over to her, bent down and put her arms round her. 'What's wrong? What on earth's all this about?'

'Everything. I'm pregnant, Gerry doesn't want me, and I've nowhere to goooo—' The last word ended on a wail.

'Whose baby is it?' asked Jessica bluntly, looking at Gerry.

'Not guilty, on my honour, me lud,' Gerry said lightly.

'No, it's Barney's. He doesn't want me – or it. He's been posted back to the States anyway.'

'I told her I'd fix for her to get it seen to, but Madam's decided to have it. I've told her she's crazy.'

'By your standards, maybe,' said Jessica quickly.

His eyes narrowed. 'So she's got to go. Obviously. Hardly my responsibility to look after another man's bastard.'

'You didn't object to my living here when you needed an escort and hostess,' sniffed Vanessa.

'As you say,' he agreed, charmingly. 'But look what a mess you've made of that arrangement. If you're pregnant and living with me, the pater will demand I marry you. And be damned if I'll keep another man's kid.'

'It's your only chance of getting one,' she snapped back, 'with your little problem.' There was a horrified silence. Jessica glanced, puzzled, at the two of them. Vanessa, realising she'd gone too far, plunged on recklessly. 'If you'd been up to it, there'd have been no need. You ought to be pleased to have any kid you can pass off as your own.'

More by the look on Gerry's face than the words, Jessica realised what Vanessa was implying. She was about to say something – anything – to fill the breach when Gerry broke the silence.

'Out,' he said calmly. 'And you, Miss Ice Queen, get out with her.' He shot her an inimical look. He wouldn't forget she knew his sexual problems, Jessica realised, with sinking heart. She could do without his overt enmity.

'Gerry, I'm sorry.' Vanessa clutched at him. 'Please don't make me go. You shouldn't have been so nasty. Don't you care about me at all?'

'Frankly, my dear, as Clark Gable once said, I don't give a damn.'

Jessica went cold at the tone of his voice.

'Oh, well.' Vanessa tried to put a brave face on it. Jessica helped her pack, as she chattered incessantly. At the door she said nonchalantly: 'Thanks for everything, Gerry.'

'The funny thing is,' said Vanessa, throwing the last bag into a taxi, 'I love Gerry more than I've ever loved anyone else. If only he wasn't impotent . . . I've even got used to his face now.' There was a pause and Jessica could see tears trickling down her face. 'Where are we going?' she asked in a choked voice.

'There's only one place you can go,' said Jessica quietly. 'Home to Kent.'

'Most routes go over the mountains near the coast, but the St Jacques Line routes go inland. This one is higher than some, and there are many guards. But there are many ways of crossing, if you know them. Often we take the way through the Brèche de Roland.' She smiled. 'We show you the sights on the St Jacques route, do we not? But you have to be fit. We go cross-country now to a village near the frontier – and there you will wait. Now, your feet. How are they?' Jacques looked at Will's shoes and grimaced. 'I have not seen such shoes since Hector was a pup.' She broke off. 'Why are you laughing?' she demanding, glaring.

'That old Yankee expression sounds real strange out here.'

'My English is excellent,' she said stiffly.

'Of course.' He took the smile off his face.

She glared at him suspiciously, then continued: 'First we go a short train ride, then we cross the hills to Ossès because the border town near here, St Jean Pied de Port, is very heavily guarded. Then another short train ride and you can rest. We will have no trouble I think on this small local train.'

Her optimism was misplaced. They came through the gate at the small town of St Palais with merely a wave from the ticket collector – straight into a patrol of two Germans. Even then they would have had no problems had Will not made the fatal mistake of turning back.

'*Kommen Sie mit*!' barked the soldier. '*Papieren*.' Will cursed himself for his stupidity. To have thrown everything away when he was so close! They examined his papers carefully, talking amongst themselves. He had no difficulty in pretending he did not understand German, and managed – sure they could hear his beating heart – to produce a smattering of Hungarian he had learned from a neighbour in the States, which appeared to pass reasonably well for Danish. But it wasn't enough. '*Kommen Sie mit*,' they said again, moving towards the patrol car, he sensed more for something to do than from any real suspicion.

He had kept his eyes from Jacques. Where was she? What was she doing? If you're going to escape do it as soon as possible, he remembered being told. How the hell could he? He had seconds to act.

But Jacques acted first. A scream as she appeared to stumble and fall, her skirts caught up, displaying all of her long slender legs. Both Germans rushed to assist. In the few seconds' distraction Will managed to plunge into an alleyway between two houses, and scoot along behind them. Five minutes later, Jacques caught him up.

'*Alors*,' she said, 'we go. Through the country now. Quickly. They have your papers. Questions will be asked.'

'At least you don't think I'm a traitor any more,' he said, relieved.

She took the smile off her face. 'You would have pointed me out if you were. Unless you are very clever,' she added. 'Come, it is time to leave.'

Exasperated, he followed her into the low foothill

country. During the summer it must be beautiful. Now it looked bleak and unwelcoming, especially in his unfit state. 'There is the path,' she pointed. 'We follow that - it is not high. And, if we meet anyone, you put your arm round me like we were sweethearts, yes?'

'Sweethearts it is.' A vision of Jessica came to mind. He nodded. 'Sweethearts.'

'Okay, American, let us go.'

The road might not have been high, but it was long. Fifteen-hundred-foot-high hills surrounding them, they passed remote villages where they attracted local attention. Will left Jacques to buy bread and pâté, and walked on, fearing to give himself away. By the time they reached Ossès it was evening, and he was exhausted.

'This is good,' she said approvingly. 'Just another kilometre and we get a train.'

It was a freight train this time, not a passenger train. With an effort he pulled himself up into the open grain carriage, and gave Jacques a hand.

'When the train stops, we are there. St Etienne is the end of the line, and it is only a few kilometres.'

The train drew up at a small French railway station, and Jacques pointed to a long, low building by the side of the track outside the station. 'There is your new home, Captain Donaldson. It is an old smoke house. Just a few steps. You can make it. But wait. We must be sure *le chef de station* is not here.' She peered out cautiously and nodded.

They jumped out on the far side of the train and under its cover ran for the smoke house. It resembled the stable he had sheltered in earlier, but reeked of smoked meats and fish. At least it was warm. He looked longingly at the hay stored in one corner.

'Good,' she said. 'Here we are only eight kilometres from Spain.'

'Five miles to freedom,' thought Will. He'd write a song one day about all this – and that's what he'd call it. Soon now he'd be home. Excitement began to grip him. Nothing could go wrong now. Nothing.

'Is there any way of getting another message back to London?'

'It is possible, yes, when I return to the north. I have to leave you for a while to collect others. I will try to let London know you are still safe.'

This time the Director was amenable to the idea of a WAAF quartet, and the necessary permission was given. Overjoyed, Jessica threw herself into organising a concert for Christmas. 'A kind of audition,' she explained to Uxbridge. Quite how she was to find and train four singers into a group in time for Christmas she didn't know, but with the enthusiastic help of Uxbridge, she did. A concert at Beaconsfield was arranged, and, on Jessica's promise that they would be ready in time, a broadcast. Every spare moment away from her work was spent drilling the four girls into as near perfection as could be managed. At times she was in despair. The girls came to dread the sight of her fingers going up to clutch her copper curls in rage and frustration. At other times, she glowed with a sense of achievement. It hadn't been so hard as she'd feared, training others to make the sounds she no longer could.

'The Bluebirds is what we've decided to call the group,' she told Tom. 'After the Vera Lynn song.'

'Good choice,' he observed.

'They can sing at our wedding,' she told him happily.

'And when that's going to be?' he asked. 'Can't we make it earlier than June?'

She hesitated. 'Do you really want to bring it forward, Tom?'

'Yes.'

'Very well, let's make it Easter. I can get leave then.'

Down at Beaconsfield for a day, Gerry Rhodes was checking the list of names known to be shot down and missing, fate still unknown, in enemy-occupied France. He glanced quickly through the list of American personnel provided by MIS-X. He paused as he came to a name he knew: Captain Will Donaldson.

Hadn't Jessica mentioned Donaldson was still on active operations, that he'd given up music? Hadn't Vanessa told him Will had walked out on Jessica? That she'd been devastated? Curious, he rang through to discover exactly when Donaldson was shot down, and did some swift calculations. Will Donaldson was not yet confirmed dead. And Jessica was going to marry someone else.

A smile crossed his lips as he replaced the list in his file. No need to let anyone else see it.

'Seems to me the fat lady's sung for you, dear boy,' he said to himself. He hadn't forgotten coming off second best all those years ago. Second best to a Yank!

It was a hell of a way to spend Christmas, alone in an old cottage – though that description glorified it – halfway up a mountain, thought Will. The smoke house near the tracks had been too frequented to stay more than a night.

The next day Jacques had taken him across the tracks into the hills above the village and over to this disused stone shepherd's hut. The animals used to have one side of it, the shepherd the other. The accommodation was stark, though he was allowed to light small fires to keep warm. Not too large, for that would attract notice in the village, and being so close to the border German troops were stationed there. His food was brought to him by an old shepherd with square Basque face and jaw, who seemed to have no inclination to communicate other than by the occasional grunt when he put down or collected dishes.

Will could stand the loneliness. It was impatience that was harder to cope with. So near to freedom, and yet cooped up here. To stop himself from dwelling on it, he composed songs, scribbling melodies and words on scraps of paper supplied by Jacques. Yet that was almost more frustrating, because it made him think of Jessica, wonder if she had received his message yet, how long it would be before he was free to find her again.

The landscape here was different from the eastern Pyrenees which he'd visited before the war – greener, more equable, with characteristics of its own. The Pays Basque was a land of individuals, he'd discovered on his short journey through it. Sturdy square independent figures, with a unique language and customs. Each day he would collect wood for the fire, wary of chance walkers in the hills. There was a cave near the cottage to use as a refuge should he need it, but so far he remained undisturbed in his eyrie.

Jacques was away for three weeks and it was well into January before she returned. By then Will's morale was low. The songs he wrote seemed to mock him, with the fear that without Jessica they were pointless. Yet even if he got back and found her, there was no guarantee the situation would have changed – she could still be mourning John Gale. Only now it didn't matter, he realised. He didn't care. The only important thing was to be with her. He'd been every sort of a fool. He began to long for Jacques' return, for company as much as in hope of the long awaited Pyrenees crossing.

Then she was there. Quite suddenly. Coming through the door unnoticed, and standing behind him as he huddled over the fire.

'*Salut*, American.'

He jumped, then breathed in relief when he saw her.

'Am I glad to see you! When do we go?'

'Patience, *mon ami*. We have more of the party here. We prepare, and then we go. Perhaps others come too.'

Through the door came four men, all in various stages of exhaustion. After a huge goat stew brought in by the shepherd, they revived a little and Will found out one newcomer was a Pole, two English and one Scottish.

Will lay awake for a long while that night, listening to the snores, groans and restless stirrings of the newcomers. Jacques, curled up in her blanket, was the only one to sleep soundly. Will could not for thinking of Jessica. Those last eight kilometres seemed an insurmountable barrier. He'd had several lucky escapes, what if his luck ran out now? Night fears loomed large. What if Jessica had found someone else? Nearly a year now without a word. He imagined her singing on the wireless, singing his songs; he thought of the Astras and that whole world that went on while he lay here inactive, just waiting. And Jacques said casually, 'have patience'. He almost cried out in frustration. He rolled over and buried his head in the rough pillow that felt as if it were stuffed with wood. Jessica – he concentrated all his mental force on her – Jessica, *hear* me, *hear* me . . . Wait, wait, I'm coming back, coming back . . .

'Happy?' Tom kissed her gently, then drew away. 'No, I suppose that's a silly question to ask. Content?'

'Yes, content.' Was it true? She had to live on the plane where it *was* true.

'Good.' He kissed her again, gently, while she pushed the thought of Will out of her mind. No stirrings of her body with Tom, but a living refuge. Was anything wrong with that?

By unspoken mutual agreement, they had left love-making till they were married. Time enough, Tom had said. 'Let's get used to each other again first.'

Now 1944 had begun it was getting much nearer. It would be almost a relief not to have to worry if she were doing the right thing. To know she was secure as Tom's wife.

Vanessa's pregnancy was obvious now; she was exempt from war work, though she did some light helping out in her mother's dairy and seemed almost to relish Frittingbourne's quietness.

She often spent evenings with them. Tom and she had got over their former dislike; she now seemed to animate him and he to enjoy it. Almost as if she were trying to vamp Tom, thought Jessica, amused. Good old Vanessa. She'd never change. Though this time it seemed a less perfunctory and very genuine liking.

'What will you do after the baby's born?' she asked.

Vanessa shrugged. 'Stay in the dairy. Help Mother. Don't worry, Jessica,' she said forthrightly, 'I've had my fill of London life.'

'What about Graham?'

Her face hardened. 'I'm not going back to him. I've brought enough unhappiness to him – and anyway I don't know where he is. And the kid's better off without me.'

Jessica was restless that night, trying in vain to get to sleep. A week ago she'd seen the New Year in, the year of her marriage to Tom. She had thought her life ordered at last – and yet when she did sleep, she dreamed of Will.

She dreamed of tall mountains, of snow and a man struggling to reach her, trying to say something she could not quite hear then being swept away out of her reach. It was Will. He was trying again and fighting his way towards her, love on his face, confident that he would reach her, but as their hands touched, his slipped away and she saw him no more. What was he trying to say? It seemed important she should hear the words, but the roaring of the wind carried them from her.

She woke up in the morning, tired and on edge. Will – mountains – how strange. Was he really thinking of her? She'd heard of such things. No, it was those last reports she'd read of the evaders crossing the mountains. Her dreams had mixed them up with Will. Despondently, she packed her bag for the return to Beaconsfield.

"What will you do after the baby's born?" she asked.
[illegible] shrugged. "Stay in the [illegible] for a while
[illegible] work, I guess. [illegible]
[illegible] London for?"

"What about Graham?"

Her face [illegible]. "I'm not going back to him. I've brought enough unhappiness to him. And anyway I don't know where he is. And he's better off without me."

[illegible] was restless that night, trying in vain to get to sleep. A week ago she [illegible] the New Year [illegible] the [illegible] to [illegible]. She had [illegible] [illegible] and [illegible] the [illegible]. She dreamed of Will. She dreamed of tall mountains of snow and a [illegible] [illegible] trying to say something [illegible] [illegible] then [illegible] was Will. He was [illegible] again [illegible] his way [illegible] on his feet. [illegible] he would reach her, but at the [illegible], he slipped away and she saw him no more. What was he trying to say? It [illegible] that she should hear the words, but the [illegible] the wind carried them [illegible].

[illegible] in the morning, [illegible] the [illegible]. Will – mountains – [illegible]. She had always [illegible] of herself [illegible] of such things. [illegible] [illegible] the [illegible] in the mountains. Her [illegible] with Will. [illegible] she [illegible] the [illegible].

Chapter Seventeen

'Tom, I can't decide *what* I want to do,' Jessica said in despair. 'I want to carry on at Beaconsfield, I want to train the Bluebirds full-time, take them round the country, I want to start on the children's choir – and I want to be here with you when we're married.'

Now that 1944 was here, Easter was getting close, and Jessica's mother was beginning to get into her stride over wedding preparations, none too pleased that the date had been brought forward from June. 'Easter, darling,' she had cried in dismay, 'but what shall I wear? Such a difficult season.'

Tom laughed at her. 'Why not compromise?' he suggested. 'Stay at Beaconsfield till after the Second Front, train the Bluebirds for concerts within reach of Beaconsfield and London; then after the Second Front, apply for a posting down here – you'll stand a better chance once we're married.'

'You know, Tom, that's what I like about you. You always look on the practical side – what *can* be achieved. Whereas I—' she spread her hands ruefully – 'am always clutching at things just out of reach.'

'Everyone needs an angel around, when they're

reaching for the stars,' Tom said mock-pompously. 'If only in the theatrical sense.'

'It's going to be difficult living with an angel.'

'Not at all. I don't mind descending to your level once in a while.' He paused. 'We'd better make a decision, hadn't we? We can't hold back your mother any longer. Our wedding, I mean. Big or small?'

'Small as possible,' said Jessica firmly, conscious she'd been dragging her feet. 'I don't want Fleet Street rushing in. No headlines: "Singing Waaf opts for Marriage Instead". Just you and me, Tom, and our parents. Please.'

'Your mother won't like it.'

She pulled a face. 'It's our wedding.'

'People have said that throughout the centuries,' he remarked. 'Normally just before they give in and invite all the world and his wife and kids. There's Vanessa, anyway,' he added, 'she'll have to come – if she's still here.'

'Why do you say that?' Jessica asked curiously. 'Of course she'll be here. The baby isn't due till July.'

'She was in the middle of a furious row with old Mrs Tibbs yesterday when I called at the dairy. Could be she's getting restless.'

'Oh, I don't think it's quite that. I don't think she knows what she wants, that's all. Anyway, I imagine it's no fun being pregnant – no wonder she gets irritable.'

Tom said nothing, and when he spoke again it was on an entirely different subject. 'The children want to sing something for our wedding. How about that song you used to like so much – "The Sweet Nightingale"?'

'No,' was her abrupt answer. She flushed as Tom

looked at her in amazement. How could he have known after all? Perhaps she should force herself to listen to it. It might help to grasp the nettle firmly. She made herself smile: 'Yes,' she forced herself to say, 'that's a lovely idea. I can't think why I said no.'

But later, as she travelled back to London, the song came back, the melody possessing her, going endlessly round in her head. Why did it seem some kind of betrayal to have it sung at her wedding? 'The couple agreed to be married with speed . . .' But the couple were she and Tom. It made no sense, and the song closed in on her, mocking her, its cadences coming from all directions, until the train drew in to Charing Cross, and she was released into the swarming impersonality of the station.

Will clambered up the hillside after Jacques, mentally swearing at his unfitness. He had seemingly been appointed leader of the party, for it was he she imperiously summoned when there were odd jobs to be done. Jacques had already made a further journey back, and another two had joined their party. Before they could move off, yet another four were expected from another courier. Then, she said, though it was becoming increasingly unreal to Will, Joseph would come, the Basque guide who would take them over the mountains. Only eight kilometres to the border and he was stuck here, trying to control his mounting frustration.

Food and all other provisions, such as they were, had to be carried from the shepherd's hut lower down the hillside, to their own stone hut. The weather was increasingly cold, and fires had to be kept going continuously for warmth – the previous winter had been very severe and men had died of exposure during the crossing.

Jacques was apparently determined therefore they should all be in the best of health, and seemed worried by the condition of one Belgian agent, in his fifties, a civilian. The good of the party came first, she told Will firmly, when he became impatient.

From outright hostility, Jacques had reverted to a kind of armed neutrality towards Will, and since she needed his help seemed grudgingly to accept his company.

Now she picked up a pair of panniers and talked quickly to the dour-faced Basque shepherd and his wife. Will could only understand the odd word, and realised that they were talking in the Basque language which Jacques appeared to understand. She glanced at him speculatively from time to time, to his annoyance.

He tried to take the panniers from her, but she brushed him off. 'You gather firewood in this bag on the way back,' she said. It was an order. They set off again through the woods, only the fir trees green, the others stark and leafless on the mountainside.

'What were you saying back there?' he asked abruptly.

She glanced over her shoulder. 'We spoke in *L'euskara*, Basque, so you do not understand, Captain,' she said coolly.

'Listen, lady,' he said angrily, putting down the firewood he had gathered and grasping her shoulder so she was forced to stop. 'Okay, I have to take orders from you, but I'm getting mighty tired of being treated like a kid to gratify some latter-day Joan of Arc.'

She started to say something, but he swept on: 'I want answers, and now. How much longer before we can get over these damned mountains?' He nodded towards the louring grey peaks that soared upwards across the valley.

Her eyes flashed dangerously as she brushed away his restraining hand. 'You - who are *you*? You are a stranger in this land. You understand nothing, *nothing*, ignorant American. What is wrong with being Joan of Arc, *hein*? I am proud you think me so. *La France—*'

'When do we go?' he cut in quietly.

She did not give an inch. 'Come here, American.'

She led him through the wood to the edge of the hillside. Down below, the village straggled out along the road, its white Basque houses with their dark red-painted shutters and beams, making it look like a village of dolls' houses. Sometimes he could see the *pelote* games in the *fronton*, hear the shouts of the participants as the ball racketed round the walls. Sometimes the sounds of Basque songs, strange and primitive, would float up on the winter air, and he would wonder of what they sang. He could watch the German troops driving through the village, the police from the Gendarmerie driving off along the precipitous road to the border. Up here in the mountains he felt Olympian, remote from danger, from the life below in the valley.

All that was real was the thought of those eight kilometres burning away inside him.

'You see the château there?' Jacques pointed to the foothills of the mountains the other side of the valley, where the towers of a château poked above the trees. 'That is the Château of Bigorri. Our path lies near there. To get there is dangerous, yes?'

'Yes,' Will agreed bluntly. The château with its turrets

and towers looked like an illustration from a fairytale and just about as attainable.

'Tomorrow night,' said Jacques matter-of-factly, 'we go. The other four men join us tonight. You rest during the day tomorrow and at night we go.' Her eyes were suddenly alight, her rancour gone.

'You enjoy this, don't you?' asked Will curiously.

Immediately she rounded on him. 'Enjoy? What is there to *enjoy*? You are a fool, American.'

'Wait a minute,' Will said firmly. 'I've had just about enough of you. I say enjoy because it's written over your face. There's nothing wrong with enjoying danger – I guess it's the same feeling I get when I'm up in a Spitfire, or Thunderbolt.' The Mustang might be coming in right now, he thought with a sudden pang, a momentary vision of Debden overwhelming him.

Jacques looked at him suspiciously, then gave a half-hearted grin. 'You are right, American. I apologise.'

'You *apologise*?' Will whistled mockingly, then laughed as she began to get angry again. 'Come on,' he said gently, 'don't take life so seriously, though I guess that's a dumb thing to say to someone in your position. But lighten up on me a little. You've got to relax when you can.'

'I am the leader,' she replied stiffly. 'I cannot, as you say, lighten up. They would not respect me.'

'I think,' said Will, 'that anyone would have to be pretty much of a damn fool not to respect you.'

She flushed unexpectedly, then said awkwardly: 'Thank you, Captain Donaldson. But then there is my sex. It would be difficult—'

She looked almost human, Will thought, just an

attractive girl in her twenties, for once uncertain of herself. 'Tell me more of how you got into this game,' he asked curiously.

'Game, Captain Donaldson? It is no game,' she instantly flashed back at him.

'My name's Will. What's yours? I can't go on calling you Jacques. It doesn't make sense.'

'It makes much sense when there are many young men and me, all night long.' She hesitated, then said, 'My name is Jeanette.'

'That's pretty.'

'And I got into this game, as you call it, because my husband was in it. He was betrayed, arrested by the Gestapo. They tortured him. People heard the screams outside the prison,' she said, as if relating a story that no longer had the power to hurt. 'He died. They delivered the body back to me. They are very correct, the Gestapo. So you see I am already, as you say, suspect. I have several sets of papers.' She smiled. 'And none of them say I am Jeanette de—' She stopped. 'And you, Captain Donaldson, now I trust you with my life story, what of yours? You have a wife, children?'

'No,' he said shortly, then went on slowly: 'I have – had – a fiancée.' Wasn't she his fiancée? For the first time he wondered what Jessica had thought their future would be. Had they spoken of it? Perhaps not, for such was war.

'Had?'

'We'd parted for a time and I was supposed to meet her. I was shot down instead.'

'I think she will wait, Captain Donaldson.'

Wait . . . He stared at the grey January sky. He

thought of Jessica in England, singing on, though he was not there; others listening to her. He tried to recall her voice and could not. Perhaps it had all been a dream, one that could not last. Today was the only reality. A bleak mountain in Occupied France; a group of tired, frightened men trying to reach home, a girl who should have been rearing children daily risking her life in Resistance work, peasants carrying on their everyday pursuits. Wait? Perhaps, but who could hold back life? He took the girl's hands. 'Perhaps,' he said. 'Thank you, Jeanette.'

'And now, Captain Donaldson, *chez nous*.' She whipped off the cloth cover to reveal some pigeons. 'Tonight we have a banquet, a Basque speciality: *Salmis de palombe*. You know how they catch these pigeons? Every autumn the birds fly south to Spain, and the Basque men hunt them. They sling nets between the trees, low down, climb up into the trees with white sheets, and cry out to startle the birds. The poor birds, they are frightened, they fly low – skim along the ground – and are caught by the nets. *Et voilà*, into the pan.' Her expression grew serious. 'Like the Germans, *hein*? They lay the traps, and *pouf* the little *evadés* fall into them.'

But not tomorrow, please God, thought Will. Not tomorrow.

'Thanks for coming up, Tom. Guess what?' Jessica's eyes were shining as she slid into the seat beside him at the Kit-Kat Club. No fear of meeting Will here now, he wouldn't risk coming to their old haunts, she thought ruefully. It was an exercise in self-discipline, though, for her to come here.

'What can't I guess?'

'I've been posted to Marylebone, sort of part-time, so that I can train the Bluebirds officially. The Director intervened personally. You should have seen the Queen Bee's face as she was forced to tell me. They said I was too valuable to lose from MI9 but agreed I could combine it with training the quartet. Of course I won't be able to go on all the concerts with them.' She looked a little wistful. 'But I'll have the satisfaction of knowing I'm part of it. We've only got a month to get it going properly. I'll have to look out for a soloist, though. Helen is leaving anyway. She's applied for a post near her husband. Still, she wasn't that strong. Nice voice, but no animation somehow. And you have to have animation to sing in these uniforms – oh, and by the way, I've been promoted,' she said, laughing. 'You're not saying much,' she added, seeing him quietly sipping his beer.

'I'm listening a lot instead,' he pointed out. 'Congratulations.'

'I'm sorry, Tom,' she said contritely. 'It's just that it's so exciting.'

Exciting? She was surprised to hear herself use the word but it was. Exciting on one level at least for it helped to paper over the void beneath.

'If we get them to a good enough standard, we could all go on overseas tours. Italy, perhaps even further. The Far East, Burma . . . We could—'

'We?'

'Well, they,' she amended hastily, then saw he was laughing.

'I'm sorry – I'm just teasing. Of course you should go. After all, we can't expect to lead a normal married life till the war's over.'

A normal married life. The words echoed inside her head till she pushed them impatiently away. A normal married life, as the village headmaster's wife. That was what she wanted, wasn't it? Peace. Security. A man she could love quietly and calmly. Who would always be there. There was a sudden lurch in her stomach.

'No.' She smiled at him gratefully. 'Now, Tom, about this wedding.' Forget that sudden jab.

'You're not going to ask me again about the colour of the curtains, are you?'

'I've never asked you about any curtains and well you know it,' she replied firmly. 'Yours are fine by me. No, it's my mother – she's already started organising. She's invited half the county already. I think she's making quite sure I'll be there this time. She's already hoarded stuff to get a cake made. Several cakes.'

'Let her,' said Tom. 'It doesn't make any difference to you and me if we have a big wedding, does it?'

'No,' said Jessica, surprised. 'No, I suppose it doesn't really. Dear Tom, how wise you are.' She got up from her chair and planted a kiss on his cheek.

'What's that for?'

'First prize for common sense.'

'I'm not so sure you're qualified to be judge of that,' he commented.

'We leave at midnight,' Jeanette announced, looking round the expectant faces. 'Joseph,' she addressed the stolid Basque guide, 'you check their shoes, *s'il te plaît*, and give them the food.'

Now that they were actually leaving, Will cast a quick glance round the stone-walled refuge to imprint it in his memory. Here he'd lain alone night after night, sometimes listening to the sounds of the band floating up from the village, the trumpet blaring out its Basque music of concealed defiance. How he'd longed for the clarinet then, itched to join its sound to the music. How many times he'd composed in his head words of love that formed themselves into song, songs for Jessica, as if by wishing hard enough he could will them through the air to her as she lay sleeping.

Jeanette issued to each of them a packet of sandwiches and a small flask of water. 'This is for two days,' she pointed out grimly, 'though you will get a meal halfway across as well. *Eh bien*, Joseph, *tu es prêt*?'

The Basque nodded, took a swig from his hip flask, and went out through the door.

First step for home, Will told himself, excitement mounting as they emerged into the cool air, the moon palely lighting their way. Joseph led the group along the hillside parallel with the village, then down and across a small winding road, and then down further through meadows and rough ground. They crossed the main road leading to the village three at a time. It was not likely there would be patrols at night, but it was possible, Jeanette told them.

Once safely across they struck up with relief into the hills the other side. To his left Will could see the turrets of the château above the trees, but they turned away, up higher into the hills, slipping and stumbling in the mud, negotiating a way round boulders and trees until they reached a rough track.

'Be careful,' whispered Jeanette. 'Here we pass a house. We go in twos.'

Will breathed easier once they were off the track and climbing up a steep path with bleating sheep on either side. Now the general unfitness of the party began to become evident as the men's panting could plainly be heard. Jeanette at the rear urged them on, while Joseph ploughed grimly ahead. No talking was the order, and in any case Will had no breath to waste on words. They emerged on to a ridge and by moonlight he could see the outlines of mountains stretching far into the distance in all directions. Ahead tall peaks loured over them. Above the treeline Will felt exposed, as though they might yet be seen from the village, and was glad when they turned a corner on to an old track sheltered by the lee of a hill. The wind was sweeping down the track, freezing him to the marrow, and he wondered how the older man was faring. The wind blew too strong to turn to find out. It was all he could do to keep his balance.

'We rest during the day,' Jeanette called encouragingly. 'We walk another hour perhaps.'

In silence they stumbled on in the cold, each man following the feet of the one in front. Will could not guess whether some were having difficulty keeping up, for he needed all his energy to keep plodding on, the stones making themselves felt painfully through his thin soles. The track petered out into a narrow footpath; negotiating it involved clambering round stones and rocks, scrambling on all fours. Progress was slow, each man taking his own route past the piled-up scree. Half an hour later, Jeanette called a stop and did a head count, looking worried.

'We are one short,' she said simply. 'The Belgian. I will go back. You go on.'

Joseph simply started off again; it had evidently happened before.

Will stood torn between the horrors of turning back on to that treacherous footpath and knowing with sinking heart that he had no option. 'You can't go back alone.'

'You go on, Captain Donaldson. That is an order,' Jeanette rapped. Unwillingly he continued as she turned back to hunt for the straggler. He walked on for a few minutes, increasingly worried, then decided to turn back, whatever his orders. Crazy perhaps, but he was damn well going to do it.

In the dim moonlight he picked his way back carefully along the path, slipping once on the rocks but recovering his balance. He called out softly. The sound wasn't going to carry back to St Etienne, he reasoned, and anyone who heard him up here in this desolation would have reasons of their own for taking no notice.

He strained his ears – could he hear an answering cry? He listened again, every sense alive. Nothing. Yes, again a sound. He peered down into the darkness beneath him, moonlight making rock and scrub one.

'Jeanette,' he called again.

'Here, American,' came the answer. 'Below you. Be careful. I've hurt my foot. I try to come up to you. You take hold of me. Don't come down. It is an order,' she cracked out painfully.

To hell with orders. He began to edge slowly down. She was painfully crawling on hands and knees, pulling herself up by what handholds she could find. He wedged himself by a rock and reached out to pull her up. She collapsed, panting, beside him.

'Did you find—?' He stopped as he felt her shudder.

'Dead,' she said. 'He must have fallen.' Only the trembling of her body betrayed emotion. 'The Aintziaga, they call this mountain. It demands its sacrifices from those who dare to climb it.' Then, as if ashamed of this notion, she reverted to the practical: 'Joseph will take the body on the way back. But now, my foot. I think my ankle is twisted.' She tried to rise, but it would not bear her weight.

'We'll have to get you back to the village,' Will said with concern.

'No!' she reacted immediately. 'Now we rest in a hut till nightfall. Then tomorrow we will catch up with the others. I never go back.'

'In that case,' he stooped and picked her up with difficulty, 'I'll carry you to the hut.'

'Now we *both* fall,' she said resignedly. 'I am too heavy for you, Captain Donaldson.'

'You have a point there,' he agreed, panting, his mouth in her hair. 'But we'll make it.'

The hut was only fifty yards back, but it seemed like fifty miles at the slow pace he could go.

'More sheep than shepherd,' he said, grimacing at the smell when they got there.

'The others up there have a stew,' she said wistfully, when they had settled down as best they could. 'And a fire. Do you have matches?' she asked.

He shook his head. 'I've got a fishing line.'

She managed to laugh.

'And two bars of chocolate left over from my escape kit,' he went on, producing them with pride. Four months he'd been hoarding them, longing to eat them but holding back. 'I guess this seems the right time. If we eat our sandwiches now we don't have them for later on. And tonight,' Will went on firmly, trying to find some clean straw in the darkness, 'we sleep together. Be damned if I'm going to nestle up to a sheep for warmth.'

She said nothing, but lay down with her back to him fitting into the curve of his body.

'And tomorrow if you're not better, we go back,' threatened Will in her ear. 'Or I go on alone and you go back.'

'No,' she said scornfully. 'You would lose your way, and die. No, Captain Donaldson, the St Jacques Line will get you back to your *petite amie*, do not fear.'

His arms folded round her.

Molly Payne lay still, allowing waves of pain to roll round her on the hard board in the pitch-black cell. It was quite easy, she told herself, to withstand pain if she simply followed her resolve. Every time they asked her something, every time the pain followed, she simply cried out, 'Graham, Graham, Graham', incessantly as though it were the only word she knew. If she could get it into her subconscious mind also, even under more torture she would not reveal anything, even if by doing so it became a meaningless chant: 'Graham, Graham, Graham . . .'

What had gone wrong? The plan had been good, the explosion had completely cut the railway line. But they had been arrested as they entered Bordeaux. There was only one answer. They had been betrayed. Whether it was by one of themselves under torture, whether by one of the French Resistance or by a German plant, she would probably never know. She had to concentrate all her energies on not betraying the others. She had little doubt as to what her fate would be; her only doubts were of the limits of her endurance.

Life in England, when happiness had seemed possible with Graham, had receded to a blurred recollection of paradise she dared not dwell on. The only life was this cell, the loaf of bread thrown through the door every day and a mug of water. Nothing else until the call came in the middle of the night and she was dragged forth for yet another session. Her hands were roughly bandaged, where her fingernails had been the second target of attention. At least they had given her a smock of some sort now. For the first two interrogations they had stripped her – garment by garment for each unanswerable question, with inevitable consequences. 'You should be grateful,' the interrogator had pointed out as he left her. 'It might have been my men.'

She fell into a tormented sleep; Graham was there, warm, and loving and she was safe.

'I don't want to come.'

'Why on earth not, Vanessa?'

'Just what I say. I don't want to come to your wedding because I'll be seven or eight months by then, and I couldn't face all the old biddies. They're already beginning to whisper. When did I last see my husband? Mrs Wilson wanted to know. Jealous old biddy! I told her November, but it was clear she didn't believe me, the old cat. I tell you, Jessica, I won't be able to stand it. I almost wish I'd got rid of it. I could still, I suppose.' She shot a look at Jessica.

'No, you couldn't. Don't be silly, Vanessa.'

All the same she was worried. 'I don't think she's going to stick it out,' she said to Tom later.

'But what else can she do? She's married, she's pregnant, there shouldn't be much difficulty with the official register if she moves. How about my old aunt in Rye? She could do with some help in her tobacconist's shop and tea room. Vanessa could help here. I wonder if that's the answer?'

'Would you, Tom? Would she? Vanessa can be so difficult, you know.'

'My aunt would be more than a match for her. No promises, but I'll try.'

Whatever arguments he used, they were successful. He took Vanessa to Rye, settled her in, then reported back to Jessica.

'Even my aunt blinked at Vanessa first of all, but I think they'll get on all right. In fact they'll be good for each other. Whatever you say about Vanessa, she's good company, isn't she?' There was a note of reluctant admiration in his voice.

'Oh, yes,' said Jessica wrily. 'As many men have discovered.'

'It isn't like you to be catty, Jessica,' he said, almost in reproof. 'She's been through a rough time.'

Jessica stared at him. 'Look, Tom,' she said, 'I was brought up with Vanessa, I love her, but no one, *no one*, is going to convince me she's hard done by.'

'Whatever she's been in the past,' Tom said seriously, 'I think she's turned over a new leaf now. She wants a quiet life in the country. Like you and me.'

Jessica looked at him. 'Is that so?' she said quietly.

'Tom, you'd see good in Mata Hari.'

'Well, there is a school of thought which thinks she has been maligned by history,' he said thoughtfully.

Jessica laughed.

'Let's elope and get married just by ourselves, shall we? Now?' he asked suddenly.

'Are you going to take on my mother, or shall I?' she enquired ironically.

'You're right. I'd forgotten the thousand and one invitations.' He paused. 'Look, Vanessa asked me to tell Graham somehow about the baby. She refuses to write to him or tell him herself, and says if we're so sure he should be told, then we can do it. I think we should, don't you?'

Graham looked preoccupied, standing at the bar, oddly alone in the middle of a sea of uniforms.

Jessica promptly forgot her reason for being there. 'What's wrong?' she asked after greeting him.

He took her to a quiet corner. 'It's Molly,' he said bluntly. 'Her network's gone off the air. You know what that means.' His expression was desperate.

Jessica sat still, stunned.

'I shouldn't be telling you this, but I don't give a damn!' he said fiercely. 'I don't care about anything but Molly. I can't even think about the kid.'

'You're sure it means bad news rather than a faulty wireless?'

He shrugged. 'There's a lot of treachery going on at the moment. Networks collapsing everywhere. Baker Street never quite knows. The wirelesses go on transmitting, but whether our agents are behind them or not i their job to know. Several networks have gone, that's for sure. And there's a traitor operating in the Bordeaux area – that's where she was, and that's for sure too. It could be the wireless has packed up, but if that were the case she'd have got a message to us somehow. She's pretty resourceful. No, I think the whole *réseau* has gone and they managed to destroy or hide the wireless set before the Germans got to it.'

'And if she's been arrested?'

'If she's been arrested, it'll mean prison or more likely concentration camp.'

'Concentration camp? You mean the camps where they're sending the Jews till the war's over?'

He hesitated. 'No one knows for sure, but the rumours are it's more than that. Death camps, they're calling them, and not just for Jews. For any enemy caught in civilian clothes, spies like Molly – after the Gestapo has finished with them.'

Jessica was very still. Molly, gone. Molly, alone in prison, suffering, perhaps dead already. Surely it couldn't be true? 'Perhaps she's gone to ground?' she suggested, willing him to agree it was possible.

'Perhaps,' said Graham. 'That doesn't tend to be the case, though.' His face was a mask of agony.

'You'll let me know if you hear anything?'

He shrugged. 'If we hear, it will be good news. Somehow, I don't think we will. Anyway, what did you want to see me about?'

'It seems trivial now.'

'Tell me. Anything would help to take my mind off things.'

'It's Vanessa.'

'Vanessa?' he queried, as though she were someone he'd known casually years ago. 'What about her?'

'She's having a baby, and I don't think—'

'It's mine,' he finished for her. 'You're right, it's not.' He was silent. 'You know, Jessica, I suppose I should feel something: anger, loss, jealousy. But all I can think is that it's just one more damn complication. We're not divorced so I suppose legally that makes it my kid. Who is the father, incidentally?' he added, returning without much interest to Vanessa.

'An American colonel.'

'Poor devil. Did he suffer too?'

'No, he went home.'

'Sensible chap.' He drank off his beer and set the glass on the table carefully. 'It's not as though she's bad, Jessica. She just floats through life without an anchor. I suppose I'm lucky to have got out of it so lightly. Lucky to have met Molly, to know what love *really* is, like you and Will.' He spoke absently, then saw her face.

'There is no me and Will, Graham. He decided to do without me.'

'You're crazy,' he said forthrightly. 'Will would never do that. He loved you from the word go.'

'I thought so too,' she said miserably. 'But there was a hitch in the shape of John Gale.' Memories flooded back. 'If I hadn't been in love with John when I met Will, it might have been all right - but later he came between us. Will couldn't believe that I'd left John behind me. Perhaps I hadn't in every way. But it was Will I truly loved.'

'Was?'

'Is,' she said slowly, not looking at him. 'For all that, I'm marrying Tom. A mess, isn't it?'

'John Gale left his shadow hanging over us all, didn't he?' Graham said. 'Over you, over Will – and over me. I'm bringing up his child. You know that, don't you? Not that I mind. Johnnie's like my own kid. He was a terrific chap, Jessica. He cast a spell over us all, and, do you know what? Sometimes I think he still does.'

Ankle bound up with a piece torn off Will's shirt, Jeanette managed to hobble successfully the next evening with the help of a stick she cut from a tree.

Rain blew into their faces at every step, making the path muddy and treacherous. They passed the hut where the others had rested. 'We try to do this part in the *crépuscule*, dusk,' she said, 'because it is so narrow. *Très dangereux*. But we might catch the others up.'

'Will you be able to manage?'

'I manage,' she snapped. 'Just because you carried me yesterday, Captain Donaldson, do not think I am a little doll.'

'No one would make that mistake,' he said wrily.

'I am sorry,' she said reluctantly, and he grinned. For all her brave words, she was forced to accept Will's help in clambering over the rocks.

'*Voilà*!' She pointed after an hour to two huge mountain masses. 'That is Buztancelay, this is Aintziaga – and *there* between them is our path. That is the frontier, Captain Donaldson. The others rest the far side of the frontier in a shepherd's hut, and the last part of the journey is tomorrow night.'

'You can leave me at the frontier.'

'I do not leave you,' she snapped. 'It is as dangerous on the mountains the other side as this. You need to be shown the path – to go to the right village. It is not easy in Spain always.'

That he knew. It was better now but there were still plenty of horror stories, of months spent languishing in Spanish jails once the evaders reached the other side. Neutrality had a variable meaning in Fascist Spain, the treatment meted out there initially being worse than that afforded by the Germans. Now, as the Allies gained the upper hand, things were better. British evaders still had the long journey to Gibraltar to make for vetting by MI9's agent before return to the UK, but Americans were normally home more quickly, with the Embassy arranging pick-up flights.

At the thought of homecoming, his heart grew lighter. Still they climbed on up the path, though the peak they were aiming for seemed ever more distant. They passed a large solitary tree, standing starkly where in theory no tree should be able to survive. Jeanette greeted it solemnly as an old friend, and as they continued to climb the path to the frontier, miraculously the weather cleared.

'Here you stand on the frontier, Captain Donaldson – Will,' Jeanette whispered, her face white from strain. 'There lies Spain. There lies freedom. Take a step over this line.' She swept her hand in front of her.

Will ran forward, breathing the air of Spain. Suddenly delirious with joy he began to fling his arms and legs about in a wild dance.

'What is that thing you do?' she said, mildly disapproving.

'A cross between a Mohawk war dance and one of

those Basque fandangos I've been watching. Don't you recognise it?'

'Get a little further before you celebrate, Will. We travel for another day before it is safe. They are odd in their loyalties still, the Spanish. We show you the right village to declare yourselves, then we return, Joseph and I.'

He came back and took her in his arms, hugging her. 'I have a lot to thank you for, Jeanette.'

She stood still, face glistening. He wiped it dry with a corner of his truncated shirt.

'They are not tears,' she pointed out. 'It is rain.'

'Of course.'

'All the same,' she conceded, 'I am perhaps a little sad we say goodbye, Captain Donaldson.'

'How do I find you after the war?'

She hesitated. 'Will, if that girl of yours does not want you – you come right back, *hein*? We beat the Boche together. You'll find me, if you want to. Now I show her what she misses.'

She moved towards him and he took her into his arms again; this time he kissed her on the mouth, feeling the quick response as her lips parted and she relaxed into his embrace.

'Yes,' he said. 'I promise that's what I'll do.'

'Like a blinking pied piper he was, dancing over the mountains, us following behind like a load of rats. I tell you, I felt like a pissing – begging your pardon, miss—'

Jessica grinned to herself, mentally rewording this

vivid debriefing: 'We then proceeded over the mountain following our guide . . .'

Her mind wandered: a pied piper, Will in piper's gear, playing his clarinet, leading an enchanted brood. Herself following far behind, lame, hobbling, desperately trying to keep up, until he disappeared through a door in the mountain and the children after him. And only she was left outside, beating in vain at the rock.

Chapter Eighteen

Will drew a deep breath of satisfaction at a dream realised. He'd feared an anti-climax, this homecoming to England after so long away. He could see why they wrote songs about the White Cliffs. For him, they'd been Cornish cliffs, the cliffs he'd sat on with Jessica so long ago. He could see the Lizard clearly as the plane prepared to land. He'd bring Jessica back here, just as soon as he met her. Sweep her off to relive that night of eighteen months ago. And here on the cliffs, he'd ask her to marry him – as if there'd ever been any doubt. Here on the cliffs . . .

Even his usual impatience with stolid British officialdom vanished, evaporating in his relief at being back. An immense gratitude welled up in him at the thought of the risks his rescuers had taken, and he resolved that as soon as possible after this damned war he'd go back, find out what had happened to Maman and Papa after their arrest, even perhaps see the girl in the cave, and – he grinned – Lillette, Joseph and Jeanette. Already she and France were receding in his mind as the overriding urgency to find Jessica took over.

Debriefing by the USAAF was a much more casual affair than those he remembered from the RAF. 'Say, you're kidding. Really? A whore-house? Luck sure was a lady for you, Captain.' And then he was free. Those weeks at the Embassy waiting to get home had been luxurious with hot baths and much better food than he'd had in France. No more goat stew! But the frustration was as bad. Now he had one week to find Jessica. She'd have received the last message from the Embassy, even if the Debden one went astray. He'd addressed it to Dave Prince to make sure of its reaching her. Yet he was uneasy. He'd been puzzled when he rang the Uxbridge number to hear it answered by a strange voice. No one had heard of Jessica Gray or Art Simmonds. Still, Dave would know where she was. She might even be with him if Will were in luck.

But Dave Prince was alone and goggled as Will walked through the door. 'Where the hell did you spring from, you old bum?' he yelled, throwing his arms round him. 'I thought you'd run out on me for good. Gone back to Uncle Sam. Not a word in five months. And all that lovely dough I've got in the bank for you.'

'Didn't Jessica tell you I'd been on a walking vacation in France?'

'You what? Are you kidding me, Will? I haven't heard from Jessica, either. Not for five months – no answer to letters, no phone calls, nothing. I don't know where she is or what she's doing. I thought maybe you could tell me?' He broke off as he saw the look on Will's face. 'You can't.'

'You haven't seen her? But who's arranging concerts, broadcasts and so on? Has she gotten herself a new agent?'

'You don't understand, Will. When I say disappeared I *mean* it. She's not singing any more.'

Will stared at him blankly, unease turning to fear. 'How long, Dave? How long since you heard from her. *Exactly*.'

'Back around October – early October, it was. Just cancelled all outstanding arrangements. I thought she'd gone elsewhere, but there's been nothing, Will. She's given up. I thought maybe you could tell me why.'

Will's head swam. The false hope that had sustained him through France had been punctured. In sick horror he began to realise that he had been living a dream.

Dave looked at him compassionately. 'I'll ask around, Will. Someone must know. You see, we all thought you'd moseyed off and left her. I guess she did too.' There was a pause, then he said reluctantly: 'There's just one rumour – that she's been ill.'

'Ill?'

'I never got to the bottom of it,' Dave said apologetically. 'You have to move on in this business, Will. You know that.'

The London streets were cold and uninviting, a chilly March wind blowing. Without lights, Piccadilly was a sad place, the people shabbily dressed, shops displaying meagre goods, mostly Utility. No one would think the Allies had got the upper hand now. Why had he assumed everything would be fine when he got back? Will thought bleakly. That he'd find Jessica, marry her, take up life again where they had left it. Something had happened to Jessica and he had just six days to find out what before he reported back to Debden.

At Wilton Park, a newly-arrived WAAF officer stationed at Jessica's former desk, was sifting information from MIS-X on the St Jacques Line. The information had been newly acquired from returning American evaders. They added some interesting details to MI9's knowledge of this valuable link. The line was being reconstructed in the North, now that the traitor, a former courier, had been weeded out. She recalled that Wing Officer Gray had asked to see any information on the St Jacques Line that might come through, so she put the sheet to one side to send on to her. But at that moment the latest information from the Middle East Command arrived, and the single sheet from MIS-X was buried and forgotten – and with it the report from Captain Will Donaldson.

In London Jessica tried to concentrate on her work, preparing for the debriefing of 'parcels' newly arrived from the Comète evasion line, but the details swam in front of her. She hadn't slept well. Her mind whirled with lines from the Rattigan comedy at the Globe which she'd seen with Tom last night, thoughts of the invitation list for the wedding, the fittings for her dress, the bombed-out Shaftesbury theatre which she and Tom had talked about on the way home, and whether London would ever look the same again.

Perhaps Tom was right and they should just run off and get married by special licence. Suddenly it seemed a wonderful idea. Easter was looming all too near. She'd talk to him about it at the weekend. No, she had to rehearse the Bluebirds this weekend, ready for their first engagement. Perhaps she was trying to do too much, yet if she stopped she'd start thinking again about – no, she must go on. Mixed up with her jumble of thoughts she suddenly heard Will's voice, quite clearly. Impatiently she tried to push it away, but it would not go. It became louder, that characteristic humming he always did when trying to get her to grasp the essence of a new melody. She reached after it. That last phrase, where did it come from? She grasped at it, but it eluded her . . . No, it was not something she had known before. This was a *new* song.

Ridiculous. Or was it? Perhaps somewhere Will was thinking of her, composing a new melody. But if he'd wanted to see her, he'd had plenty of opportunity. Still the melody would not go away. It was coming to life in her mind, capturing her senses. It must be something she'd heard elsewhere . . . No, she mustn't think back. She was overtired. Yet the stupid thought persisted that Will was trying to reach her. She eyed the telephone on her desk. Should she try Debden just once more? Suppose it had been a mistake and he hadn't been posted after all? It would be so easy to pick up that receiver, give the operator the number . . . And then if he weren't there, she'd know once and for all that he had gone out of her life. Filled with sudden excitement at the possibility of action, she picked up the receiver.

The orderly room clerk was as ever courteous. 'No Captain Donaldson here, ma'am.'

She replaced the receiver ruefully, trying to laugh at herself for her own stupidity. No Captain Donaldson at Debden. Perhaps he'd gone back to the States without even bothering to let her know.

So that was that, she decided, trying to banish that pit of sick despair within her. He wasn't going to hold this power over her any longer. Thank goodness she was getting married – and soon.

It was like a nightmare, moving through a city preoccupied with its own concerns, reaching out only to find each handhold knocked away as he clung. The meeting with Don Field was as inconclusive as the one with Dave Prince.

Mutual friends had been posted, or else had not heard from Jessica. Officialdom in Whitehall pointed out he was not related and therefore no information might be given, etc., etc. So much for the returning hero, he thought bitterly. He was more on his own in these crowded London streets than he had been in France. Now there was only one thing left to do. He'd hoped to avoid it, but there was no alternative. He went back to his hotel and picked up the telephone receiver.

'Captain Donaldson, how very nice to hear you.' After a slight pause Bubbles' practised charm vibrated over the line. She was apparently full of joy at hearing his voice. Then another pause as he explained. 'Evaded in Occupied France? How thrilling! But you were asking after Jessica?'

'I heard she's been ill.' Was it his imagination, or was there a fractionally longer pause?

'Ill? Whoever gave you that idea? Now you come to mention it, she did have flu very badly last autumn. Perhaps it was that you—'

'Is she living with you? Where can I reach her?' he cut across urgently.

'Well, no, Captain Donaldson.' Righteous surprise in her voice. 'We don't *know* her whereabouts. She's a serving Waaf, you know, and doing a very hush-hush job. We don't know where she is. She just turns up from time to time. She may even be abroad. I expect you could write to her care of Whitehall—' brightly '—you know the address.'

'Yes,' he said quietly. 'I guess I do. Mrs Gray – why isn't she singing any more?'

'Isn't she?' Bubbles replied vaguely. 'I don't know, I'm afraid, Captain Donaldson. The BBC keeps finding new people; off with the old, on with the new . . .'

Slowly Will replaced the receiver.

Cicely Gray, almost alarmed at the ease with which she had lied, trembled very slightly as she put down the telephone receiver. But she had had no choice. She couldn't bear for it all to begin again. Not now Jessica and she were getting on so well. It was only that stupid singing thing that had come between them. Jessica was much happier now, more settled and soon she'd be marrying dear Tom.

Will went down to the bar and ordered a drink, watching the crowd around him. Only just over a year ago he'd been one of them, arm round Jessica, the future before them. Then, because of his damn stupid pride – for that was what it boiled down to – he'd left her. It had stung him to feel that some memory of John Gale might still be between them. Now he couldn't imagine why he'd minded. What mattered was that a man and a woman should be together. Wasn't it a kind of arrogance that demanded perfection, that things should be just so between them? Jessica hadn't demanded anything of him – why the hell should he have been so overbearing as to demand the impossible of her?

' "The dog it was that died," ' he quoted bitterly. Jessica was making no attempt to contact him; she had obviously made another life for herself while he was left alone. In frustration his fingers closed tightly round the stem of the glass. Jessica, he willed, *listen*. If you're happy, fine. If not, *remember*. The song he'd written in the aeroplane on his way back filled his head, its melody flooding over him. 'Remember', he'd called it.

What the hell to do next? As if by a miracle, his brain cleared. The solution was so obvious. Jessica would know he was safe and coming back, but not when – for the message he'd sent through Dave never reached her. So she would have written to Debden. That's where he should be, not monkeying around in London. To hell with leave. He was on his way.

The trains hadn't improved in six months, he thought wrily, fighting his way into the packed LNER train at Liverpool Street. Nor had the journey. The interminable stops and jerky starts drove him to a fury of impatience, the sound of the wheels seeming to mock him. Da, da, da dah, she might be there. Da da da dah, she won't be there.

The Dodge staff car was waiting for him, after he had cursed for the umpteenth time at the crazy British railway system that meant he had to change trains in the middle of the country and hang around, waiting for the toy train to chug him the last few miles to Saffron Walden. The two or three miles to Debden through the lanes seemed endless till they reached the South Gate and Station HQ. The hedgerows were beginning to show first signs of spring, catkins and wood anemones, even an early primrose, and as the base came into sight his spirits rose. He was certain now his quest was at an end.

'Good to see you, Captain. We weren't expecting you for another three days.'

'I'm kind of eager to get at those new Mustangs. I couldn't keep away.'

'Whoa, feller. These bucking broncos take some handling. You're outa practice.'

'Give me twenty-four hours, Adj.'

'I guess you'd better see the CO about that.'

There was another thing he had to do before seeing the CO. As if echoing his thoughts, the Adjutant rummaged in a drawer. 'Been holding this mail, Captain.'

Will looked at the well-known handwriting, not taking in the implications of the Adjutant's words: 'There was a balls-up when you were missing, Captain. Hell, we all thought you were on leave. The 355th kept sending through requests for information on a fella called Byng or Hamburger, but no one knew you were flying, Captain, so it took us a while to figure out it was you; and we still hadn't figured it out when Whitehall put through this request for confirmation you'd been flying that day. Some dame was calling too . . . Came up here once. Told her you was on leave. Wasn't till you didn't show after leave we figured out what might have happened. I guess the CO'll have a few things to say to you, Captain.'

Will had ripped open the envelopes and seen with sinking heart that the letters were written in late September and early October. The CO could wait. 'Nothing else?' he asked the Adjutant.

'Nope.' The Adj eyed him curiously. 'Anything wrong, Captain?'

Wrong? She'd never known he'd been shot down, the admin had gone wrong. And it was his own damned fault. The one thing he hadn't reckoned on. None of the messages had reached her. She'd left the Uxbridge house, stopped singing. Why? Hell, because she thought he wasn't coming. Later he'd read the letters. Later, but not now. He couldn't take it. Instead he walked into the mess. There were twenty or so pilots lounging there. Strange faces, familiar faces. One looked up.

'Hey, if it ain't the cat-house ace.'

In a moment he was enveloped in an exuberant embrace of a dozen pairs of arms as they swooped on him.

Molly heard heavy footsteps approaching down the corridor outside. This time? Would it be this time? In the pitch-dark of the cell, she reached out and took the hand of the other girl kept with her.

The footsteps stopped.

'*Heraus*!'

Their eyes, unaccustomed to light, took in three silhouettes, deeper black than the black that surrounded them. There was no need to ask any questions. This was no interrogation.

In silence, she embraced her cellmate, then they went, hand in hand, along the corridor to the small yard in Ravensbruck concentration camp. Girls in cells either side of the corridor listened as they went by. It had happened often before; it would happen again. Next time it might be them.

Together the two girls knelt down in the yard, and were blindfolded, still holding hands. The butt of a rifle knocked their hands apart, but they clasped them together again.

Graham, Molly thought to herself, fixing her thoughts on their last meeting, on the love in his eyes, and in his words. Keep my love always, always, Graham.

Then the shots rang out.

The CO harangued Will for ten minutes on his sins, before relenting and welcoming him back to the squadron. 'And well done, Will, for making it back. Next time, don't take so darned long about it.'

'I don't plan to get shot down again, sir. Give me twenty-four hours on the new Mustang and—'

'There's no hurry. And no next time for you, Will,' said the CO, 'not till after the invasion. You know the rules. No flying over occupied territory for returned personnel.'

'But, heck, the invasion's coming right down the line. You need me. You need every pilot you can get.'

'I reckon you owe more to those folks that helped you over there than to put them at risk if you get shot down and captured.'

The thought of Jeanette came into his mind. He could see the sense of it.

'Can't I just—'

'No,' the CO cut in firmly, then relented. 'I'll give you permission to convert to the Mustang – other than that, you fly a desk till the invasion.'

Geoff Swift's voice was cool over the telephone, when Will finally tracked him down to a new posting in East Anglia, ready for the big day. The tone changed when he heard Will's story.

'I haven't the foggiest where she is, Donaldson, but you'd better find her quickly. She thinks you walked out on her.'

'That I've gathered. What the hell am I going to do? And where do I find her?'

'I haven't heard from her in six months, not since she cracked up.'

'Cracked up? What the hell do you mean?'

'Just what I say. Her voice packed up in the middle of a performance at my station. Hasn't sung since. I thought at the time—' Geoff sounded embarrassed '—it was probably linked to you. I tried to contact her afterwards, but . . .'

Will replaced the receiver, cursing fate. So that was Jessica's 'illness'. She couldn't sing. Where the hell was she? She couldn't be dead, could she? If she couldn't sing any more . . . if she thought he'd left her for good . . .

Blindly he began to run to the Mustang the crew chief had assigned to him. He had to get in the air, think things out, tell himself it wasn't so. He listened impatiently while the crew chief ran him through the cockpit and instrument checks.

After a few minutes only he could see why it was called the Mustang. This baby was pretty wild. You had to fight for mastery. The Merlin engine lurched, with odd explosions during deceleration. He'd been warned about them. The airplane seemed mighty small after the Thunderbolt – more like his first love, the Spitfire. The squadron was off on a bombing mission over northern France, target the mysterious sites rumoured to be secret weapon depots. There must be some way he could get to fly operationally.

Good to be in the air again, not running for his life like a hunted animal. Up here the anguish over Jessica clarified, left him able to think positively. Fly it *at maximum*, the boys told him. The Merlin doesn't take kindly to pussy-footing. *Fly at maximum*.

Okay, that's what he'd do. The Merlin responded with a roar that set his ear-drums throbbing. Jessica – there was something he was missing. Jessica wouldn't be defeated, she was a fighter. But there was still something not right. *Fly at maximum*. That mother of hers. She'd been keeping something back. That was it! The unexplained hesitation in her voice. He'd ring again. No, he'd go there – he was still officially on leave – and force the truth out of her.

Graham Macintosh ate his eggs and bacon slowly and deliberately, concentrating all his attention on them. If he didn't, he might go mad. There was still no word from Molly. No use hoping that it was simply the wireless out of action. She must have been arrested. He took another mouthful quickly. Eggs and bacon were good before you went on a mission. Sometimes he got two rashers if he smiled at the girl.

He was flying a lot of missions now. Invasion was in the air, and SOE agents were reporting the appalling lack of arms in the French Resistance, crying out for drops. There was more activity on the agent side too, many more being dropped in to prepare for the Second Front. Tonight he was taking supplies to the Bordeaux area, and picking two agents up. Men, he'd been told, and only when he'd asked if it were Molly. But you never knew. She *might* be there.

He climbed into the Lyssie, patted her affectionately and took off. The flight was uneventful as he droned over the Channel, the moonlight making the water a ghostly pool of dark and light. Every mile nearer to Molly, he told himself. Perhaps she would be there, perhaps she would be there. The hope drummed itself over and over in his mind. The Luftwaffe was rarely around now, but flak had to be watched over the coast. Not much longer now, surely, to the invasion. Then Molly might come back.

He circled the landing spot. No signal. Odd. Time was getting on, he'd have to turn back soon. He circled it for some time until he reached his limit of endurance. He hated to give up, but something had obviously gone wrong. He'd have to go back. No choice now. Just as he set course for home, he saw the light. Was that the signal? Anyway he hadn't the fuel to go down. Nor the time now. That wasn't the right signal, was it? But it was a signal of some sort. And Molly might be there. *Molly might be there.* He couldn't take the risk of letting her down. He turned back and began the descent. Better have a good field, he thought grimly. It was going to be tough getting up again with his fuel situation.

That signal *was* wrong. No doubt about it now. Too late, he hauled on the stick and the Lyssie began to climb. It couldn't be Molly there, could it? He had to survive till next time, in case she made it then. But he'd left it too late, and a battery of guns blew him out of the sky.

'Let's get married right away, Tom. As you suggested. By special licence.'

His eyes lit up. 'Would you really want to? Very well, let's do it. We'll talk about it afterwards.' He paused. 'Are you ready?'

'Yes, let's get it over with.'

They had come over to Rye together to bring the telegram to Vanessa, guessing its contents. She was serving in the shop when they arrived, her pregnancy obvious now, and her beauty made the more striking for it. She glanced up and saw them, her instant pleasure turning to apprehension that deepened when they gave her the telegram.

'Graham's dead,' she said flatly, 'that's what it will say.' With trembling fingers she opened the envelope. 'Yes,' she giggled hysterically, 'I was right. First Johnnie, now Graham. Who next? Barney? You, Tom?' She subsided into a storm of tears and Jessica rushed to comfort her.

'I expect you think I'm crazy,' Vanessa sobbed. 'I know I left him, but I was fond of him, and now he's dead and I'm a widow . . . oh . . .'

They sat with her for two hours, until Jessica had to get back on duty.

'Don't go,' said Vanessa, 'please, oh please.'

'I must, Vanny,' said Jessica gently.

'Then Tom. Tom, you'll stay?'

Jessica looked at him. 'Can you, Tom? I'd appreciate it.'

He nodded reluctantly and without comment.

Will drove up the well-remembered lane to Frittingbourne Manor. Three and a half years now since the Battle of Britain, and pretty soon Kent would be the focus of military activity again. But there were battles of a different kind ahead for him.

He rang the doorbell at the Manor, and was shown into the huge drawing room. Bubbles came in almost immediately, still lovely but perhaps a little more strained, as if the image were more difficult to attain.

'Why, Captain Donaldson, how lovely to see you. How nice of you to call. Michael will be so sorry to have missed you.'

'I haven't been able to find Jessica,' he said bluntly.

'What a shame.' She smiled brightly. 'She hasn't been in touch since you telephoned, I'm afraid.'

'Where is she, Mrs Gray?' he said steadily. 'You know, don't you?'

Her shoulders seemed to tighten as she bent over the tea-tray, pouring tea. Then she seemed to come to a decision, set down the tea pot and said, 'I'm sorry, Captain Donaldson, I lied to you. I wanted to save you pain. I'm afraid you returned too late, you see. It's very sad – for you.'

'Too late?' he whispered, fear creeping up.

'Jessica married two months ago.'

The room reeled round him. Her words made no sense. 'Jessica married?' he repeated meaninglessly.

'I'm afraid she thought you had deserted her. She's so happy now.'

'Who?' he blurted out.

'Why, dear Tom, of course. You remember how devoted they always were – till this beastly war came and distorted everything.'

Till this war came along. This bloody, bloody war, Will repeated to himself as he sat in the car. Married. It all fitted. No wonder there was no word at Debden. His messages never reached her, she must have thought he'd just disappeared. But he just couldn't believe it! Jessica was his. And, hell, he wouldn't – not till he'd heard it from her own mouth. He started the car viciously, driving it at break-neck speed to the village, and pulling up outside the cottage with a squeal of brakes that brought disapproving glances from Tom's neighbour. He knocked loudly, angrily, on the door. Nothing. He knocked again. Still no reply. Slowly the anger drained out of him.

'They've gone to Rye,' supplied the neighbour helpfully.

He said nothing, but got back in the car and drove off. *They've* gone to Rye. So it was true. Of course it was.

Life stretched before him, unwanted, unvalued, his reason for it gone. Bubbles had been trying to convince him war distorted, that it was Tom Jessica loved all along. He couldn't accept that – it made no sense – but she'd obviously settled now for being a country schoolmistress. No music, no song to life. Why the hell had he been fool enough to leave her? ' "Tomorrow to fresh woods and pastures new," ' he muttered. 'OK, fella, Milton said it. "Time to rise and twitch my mantel blue." ' Tomorrow . . . If it didn't hold Jessica, life didn't hold anything he wanted to know about.

'I've got some bad news, Jessica.'

'Oh, no, not *more*.' Tom could hear her voice rise over the telephone.

'I'm afraid it's Molly. A telegram came for you from her aunt. She's missing on active service. "Believed dead" is what they didn't say. It doesn't look good.'

Jessica was silent. 'Where are you ringing from, Tom? Can I see you?'

'I'm still in Rye. That's the other bad news. I'm afraid Vanessa has had a miscarriage. It's the shock, they said.'

'Is she all right?' Jessica cried in alarm.

'Yes, but no baby, I'm afraid.'

'I'll try to get a pass to get down.'

Molly dead. A sense of great emptiness came over her. One by one, those most dear to her were vanishing, some chose to leave her, some simply vanished without trace. All that was good and true in the world was dying in this bloody war. And what was she doing? Nothing. She couldn't go overseas, she couldn't sing any more. All she could do was train a quartet of singers. Perhaps she'd be more of a success at being Tom's wife. But the idea of preparing for a wedding so soon was unthinkable now. With two deaths to mourn, how could she think of marrying? They would have to leave it till June. She smiled sadly. At least her mother's problems over clothes would be solved.

Bubbles Gray examined her conscience uneasily and decided it was still clear. Jessica was about to marry Tom; she was happy again. If Will Donaldson came back into her life, she'd be thrown into turmoil. She'd start all that nonsense about wanting to sing. And suppose her voice didn't come back? She'd go through the unhappiness all over again. No, much better to have things as they were. Besides, all the invitations had been sent out now.

'Request permission to fly operationally, sir.' Will's face was like granite as he faced his CO.

The CO looked at him for a minute. 'I don't know what's eating you, Donaldson, but you know the answer. Negative. For reasons already given. Dismiss.'

'Christ, sir, you can't expect me to sit here on my backside doing nothing, watching others get shot to pieces,' Will exploded.

'Still negative,' the CO barked. Then he softened, drumming his fingers on the table. 'How would it be if I got you in the air again, nowhere near France? Not operationally, but you'd be flying.'

'I want to—'

'Either that or I get you posted back to the States where you won't so much as smell a Mustang.'

'I'm listening, sir.'

'Right. 458th Bombardment Group need a liaison. They've recently flown in to Horsham St Faith's, just gone operational, and our Big Friends are anxious to establish contact with us Little Friends. I'll allot you your own Mustang.'

Liaison – what a let-down. But he had no option. Then he began to think. He could always thumb a ride to the Ruhr or the Big City inside one of those Liberators . . .

'I accept – and thank you, sir.'

The CO watched him unsmilingly. 'Just keep your ass in one piece, Donaldson. I'll need you, come the big invasion.'

Perhaps they should have kept to the Easter wedding after all, and then this waiting period would be over, with all its doubts and anxieties. Jessica was half still dreaming that Will would return, half guilty that she should be marrying another when, try to repress it though she might, she knew herself in love with another man. She threw herself into the game of 'weddings' as layed by her mother, interesting herself in the replies to the new invitations that had gone out. No reply at all from Geoff Swift yet. Perhaps he'd been posted. He was the only one she had invited from her past service life, perhaps because she knew he'd understand. Otherwise it was a closed chapter.

'Happy?' asked Tom, his arms close around her.

'Yes. Very.'

'You sound very positive.'

'I am.'

'Are you sure you can't get more than two days off?'

'No. I think it's all about to happen, don't you? Look at the number of troops pouring in. US Air Force too. You can't move on the trains here at the moment. There won't be a square inch left in Kent. They reckon early June is the best guess.'

'I hope it's not our wedding day.'

'I'll ask HQ when it is, so we can change the wedding day if necessary.'

'Or they can postpone the invasion. That might be easier than facing your mother with another postponement.'

Jessica giggled.

A bomber station was sure different to the world of fighters. These B-24 Liberators carried crews of ten for a start – ten times the personnel walking around. And the losses – fearful, terrible losses. He'd flown one mission so far, got in with a good bunch. Four squadrons in the group under Colonel Isbell. On the 21st, they'd been on a mission to the secret weapon site at St Omer – odd to be on the bombing side, to the same target he'd flown fighter escort too. He'd thought it an easy one till h heard the flak on the aircraft. They went to the Big City the next day, but he was due back at Debden where he remained closeted with the CO for more than an hour, discussing mutual needs and tactics.

'I wouldn't ask an angel to fly through this weather,' greeted the CO, glancing at the fog outside. 'Stay here tonight, Will. And that's an order.'

In fact he was there for some days, kicking his heels moodily with the squadron waiting for the weather to clear. On the 5th April it did.

'Make sure you're back here by the 11th, Will,' was the CO's parting shot. 'Ike's coming down, in person, *and* a whole wad of the Big Brass. I've got me an invitation to say my piece – and I want you there too. Ike wants to hear about France, for some reason. Maybe he's thinking of taking a vacation.'

'Okay.' Sure, he'd like to meet Ike. Sure, he'd like to talk about France. And more than talk about it. He'd got past the stage of wanting to consign himself to oblivion. Now he just wanted to get his revenge on the bastards who started this damn war. He was aiming to get back to France just as soon as he could. To France – and to Jeanette. He'd promised he'd go back if things went wrong with Jessica. And it was a promise that held some kind of future for him.

To his way of thinking, the invasion, wherever it began – in the Pas de Calais or elsewhere – would be aiming to continue north up to the Low Countries and across to Germany. Southern France could be left for a subsidiary invasion or even to troops coming up from Italy. So if after D-Day he were still flying from Debden, there'd be precious little chance of helping Jeanette with the Resistance war. There had to be some way he could get to France himself. Over here, he was constantly reminded of Jessica, of what he had irrevocably lost.

He hadn't seen as much Brass since his mother's old kitchen. A huge table filled with high-ranking officers of all the US services, and he a lowly captain. It was some sight. He had a notion the CO's eye was on him, though. He'd best take care. He hadn't been able to listen in on all the meeting, but to this part – on tactics on arrival in France – he had been summoned.

'Okay, Captain, let's hear what you have to say about France,' Ike growled.

Will spoke eloquently for ten minutes about the Resistance, about the Maquis, about the atmosphere he had encountered. 'Most of the Resistance are okay, sir, the best, but there are some hotheads who'll go wild the minute the troops land. You need to ensure they don't, or there'll be a civilian massacre – another Lidice – and that won't help your cause.'

Ike regarded him silently for a few moments, then impatiently muttered a few words to the Adjutant. Will caught the words – 'de Gaulle' and 'broadcast'.

'Anything else you can tell us about France, Captain?'

'They've been through a battering sir, emotional and physical. They won't like it if their towns and villages get bombed.'

'This is war, Captain. We try our best,' Ike said quietly, stopping Will in the tracks. 'Anything else?'

Will hesitated, then plunged on. 'One more thing, sir. I guess when we go it won't be to the Pas de Calais.' It was a bold step, and the room was deathly quiet. H might as well go on now. 'So if we land some way away, Brittany or Normandy, and the USAAF continue flying from England for a while, it might be a good idea to have an on the spot idea of what's going on there. I'd like to volunteer as liaison, sir, to go as soon as the first RAF squadrons fly in to a French base. I've been in the RAF. I understand them. I know France—' He broke off, quelled by the thunderous look on his CO's face.

But Ike didn't seem put off. 'RCAF, Captain, in fact, is first in. That's not bad thinking.' He turned to Will's CO. 'Okay by you, Major? Could you go with that? General?' He turned to General Spaatz, CO of the 8th Air Force. Two nods. The CO was fair, thought Will gratefully. He'd pay for it, but if it was in the squadron's interests, the CO would go along with it. So, hell, he'd got his way. He should have felt jubilant, but he didn't, merely tired, anti-climactic. He had thrown the dice and turned up a six. Tomorrow he would relax, think positively of his life ahead, of the search for Jeanette and rainbow's end, but tonight it seemed of small comfort.

Chapter Nineteen

'Jessica, it will be wonderful to have you living here again . . .'

Her mother's warm sugary voice broke in on Jessica's thoughts. They were sitting in the Manor garden. June was here now, and the garden was in full bloom, the flowers if nothing else benefiting from the poor weather. Only in the country could you appreciate the coming and going of the seasons, Jessica thought. In London one simply marked off dates on the calendar, measuring out the next rounds of battle against wartime restrictions. Here in the Manor garden there was another world, where it was possible to listen to birds sing and draw pleasure from a flower. Here in such a world she would spend her life. This claustrophobic world . . . Fleetingly, she was afraid. Would her marriage involve a return to the values she had hated so much at the Manor? No, surely not. She was her own woman now. Independent. She had made her choice. That made her decision not a capitulation, but a victory.

Besides, her married life would be different. She need not see much of her mother – Tom would see to that; he had no great love for Bubbles, though he got on well enough with Michael. June 10th was her wedding day.

Nine days to go. She firmly pushed away a wave of trepidation and instead began to think of her plans for the oasthouse once it was hers again. She'd use it to train the children's choir, perhaps. Yes, that was a good idea.

'I said the cake's here, darling. Do you want to look at it?'

A cake with a cardboard surround for icing. How farcical. She would have been happier had the wedding been a plain one, with her in her best cotton frock, but her mother had insisted on creating something out of butter muslin and parachute silk, for all the world as if she were the starry-eyed bride of John Gale. This was where it had all begun – and this was where it would finish on June 10th.

'Darling Vanny!' Bubbles shrieked, and as the village taxi driven by old Stebbins drew to a halt, Vanessa, still managing to look like a fashion plate, climbed out, helped solicitously by Tom.

'She insisted on seeing you before she went home,' he explained. 'I tried to get her straight back.'

One thing was different, however. She was very pale, and Jessica realised that for the first time in years she was not wearing make-up.

Perhaps she's run out of her American stores, thought Jessica, then reproached herself for her cattiness. Vanessa's face looked almost plain, without her usual sparkle. Concerned, once she noticed the strain around her cousin's eyes, Jessica ran to her and embraced her in a rush of affection.

'You won't go off again, will you, Vanessa? You'll stay this time?' she asked anxiously.

'Oh, yes, this time Frittingbourne's got me for goo

How're the wedding plans going?' she asked casually. 'Tom's been telling me as much as he could, but you know what men are.' It was said without her usual flounce.

He came over and kissed Jessica on the cheek. 'Sorry we're late. I had to keep proving I wasn't a Fifth Columnist before they'd let us on to the train for Kent. Something tells me invasion's in the air. You can almost smell it.'

'That's just June you can smell – or marriage,' she laughed.

'Yes.' He gave her a quick affectionate smile. 'That must be it.'

The CO weighed in without preamble.

'Give me one good reason why I shouldn't ground you forthwith, Captain.'

Taken aback, Will could only reply: 'Due back at Horsham St Faith's, sir.'

'Liaison, Captain, liaison. That means talk, Will. Discussion. It does not mean unauthorised flights in B-24s to dangerous targets.'

Will opened his mouth and shut it again. It was hardly surprising it would come out, but six weeks or so later, he'd thought himself safe.

'How many more?'

'Two or three, sir,' Will said reluctantly.

'Any reason I shouldn't kick you back to sergeant?' the CO said grimly. 'Any reason I shouldn't put you on a flight to Idaho? Any reason I shouldn't have you on a court martial?'

'No, sir, but—'

'Well, I've got one. I need you, Captain. I need to know what gives at Bomber HQ. I need to know what gives in France once the RAF's flown in – and so does General Spaatz.'

'Yessir. Thank you, sir.'

'You're out of order, Captain. Thanks not required. I don't know what's eating you, but if you're trying to get yourself shot down, you can damn well do it for 336th, not for our Big Friends.' He paused. 'I need you for the big day, Will. I need every Mustang, every pilot. Even you.'

The full sense of the CO's remarks was not clear till he spoke to the squadron later that evening. From now until further notice the camp was virtually sealed. No one could leave or enter without special permit. A buzz of excitement went round the room, for all the restriction had been expected. So this trip to Horsham St Faith's would be *the* one, thought Will, the final tactics for D-Day. It must be days away now. They'd been expecting it for the last week. A sense of excitement swept over him. He'd be flying the Mustang on D-Day, a part of the big picture again. He had nothing but respect for the bombers, but being cooped up in a Liberator, part of a team, wasn't his idea of fighting.

He'd been damn lucky to get out of the Hamm trip alive. It had been a disaster for some bomber groups, and it was only by luck that 458 hadn't been annihilated. The same old story, the German fighters waiting to pounce on the return journey, this time only ten miles from their base. He'd felt like a sitting duck, unable to do a thing himself in that vast unwieldy flying horse, the Liberator. In a Mustang he was his own master.

When they'd got back to base safely, he'd been trembling; and it was more to prove he could than from desire to fly another bombing mission that he had ever climbed into a Lib again. It proved something else to him too. He was going to stop this maniacal drive to get himself killed. That was no way out. If he was going to die in this conflict, he'd die the way he knew best – in a Mustang, and in France, where he might conceivably be able to strike one tiny nail in the vast coffin of the Third Reich.

Another few days, and he'd be in France. Then somehow he'd contact Jeanette, and help all those folks who had risked their lives for him. Maybe he'd make some kind of go of a permanent life with her. She was as different as could be to Jessica, and that was good. He could plaster over the void in his heart, the ruined hopes, and make some kind of life in which music played no part, for music was Jessica.

He stared up at the Station HQ as he passed it on his way to the underground command post. Roses covered the walls. How incongruous that they should bloom in the midst of war. Roses in Picardy. Wasn't that a famous song of World War I? 'But never a rose like you.' No rose like Jessica. There was a song there too. Not a sentimental one, but a contact with war, with pain, with everyday living. And suddenly a rose. No rose like Jessica. No, dammit, he wouldn't think of her. She was just Tom's wife now. Get out of my mind, dammit, keep out of my thoughts! But she wouldn't.

Before she left for London, it seemed important to Jessica to walk round the Manor garden again, almost as if she were saying goodbye. She'd be back in three days to prepare for the wedding; this would be her last moment of quiet.

Overnight rain had left pockets of water on the flowers; with the bad weather weeds were gradually advancing over the garden. Gardeners were at a premium now, and her parents more given to admiring than cultivating flowers. Like everyone else's, much of the garden had been given over to vegetables, and these alone were well tended, Michael having decided to ensure their food supply. Of the flowers only the roses flourished, disdainfully ignoring the weeds. Even the rain today could not diminish their beauty. When she went to bed last night she had lain awake, thinking of roses. Why, she did not know, but she seemed surrounded by them, their smell filling her nostrils in her imagination. She supposed she was thinking of her bouquet. Yet these roses didn't remind her of Tom. They seemed bound up with Will somehow. And, even odder, she could think of him without pain surrounded by those dream roses. Finally she drifted off to sleep, lulled and comforted by the scent.

She'd fill the house with roses after they were married, she and Will, she thought idly, looking at the pink rambler roses on the red-brick walls. Will? How stupid. It was Tom she was marrying. She felt stirrings of unease which she dismissed impatiently. Of course she wasn't over Will. She'd never be over Will. She loved him and that was that. What she felt for Tom had nothing to do with her love for Will. Nothing to do with the kind of love she'd always thought indispensable between man and wife. But now she knew that it was not, didn't she?

* * *

June 3rd, and the rain continued. Rain and a low cloud base. Will grimaced. No D-Day today – or yet awhile. The Channel would be rough, the visibility for the air armada nil. He'd only just made it back from Horsham St Faith's; it had been touch and go whether he got clearance. He'd probably have taken off anyway, the way he felt. The CO had told him if he didn't get back today he could kiss D-day goodbye – the camp was likely to be sealed off completely tonight. No way was he going to miss D-day. He'd got his posting orders now – report to Ford near Arundel on D-Day plus 1 at midday. That meant he could with luck fly missions on D-Day, leave for London in the evening, put up overnight and then push on to Ford – and France.

He'd been almost sorry to leave his faithful Mustang war-horse now, but the prospect of flying a Spit again more than compensated. Ike had been right. It was the Royal Canadian Air Force Spitfire Wing of 83 Group that was going to be first in France. With reasonable luck the 83 Group would go in on D-Day itself to act as liaison between RAF and the Ninth Air Force. He would pick up a Spit at Ford and fly in just as soon as an emergency landing strip had been laid on D-Day plus 1 or 2. It couldn't have been better – this was obviously why Ike had acceded so easily to his request. He knew Canada, he knew the RAF, he knew Eighth Air Force – he knew France. But Ford as a departure point intrigued him. Why Sussex? Why not a Kentish airfield? It was another piece in the jigsaw puzzle of D-Day that they were speculating on in every mess in England. Troops were constantly on the roads between East Anglia and Kent which hummed with activity. Barges and landing craft choked the Thames Estuary. New airfields had sprung up in Kent over the last year, now full of tented accommodation; vast army encampments were surrounded by a mass of barbed wire to keep out – or attract? – the curious. The King visited Dover to inspect new highly secret dock workings, Montgomery's HQ was at Dover Castle; tanks filled fields throughout Kent and East Anglia.

Things seemed to be moving in Kent. But that was the curious thing. Everything and everyone *moved*. Yet the numbers of troops didn't seem to increase, nor the number of squadrons. And even more curious, most of those tanks and barges were made of inflatable rubber. In Whitehall, the planners of Operation Fortitude, the deception ploy for D-Day, had done their work well.

In MI9 too, attention was focused on D-Day. It was now 3rd June. No point now taking evaders to the Pyrenees. No point encouraging them to stay where they were either. The last thing the Allies wanted was to have a mass of escaping servicemen behind enemy lines after D-Day, complicating the advance. So a plan had been evolved to keep all evaders in one vast forest camp south of Paris. For weeks any shot-down airman had been sheltered there, awaiting liberation under strict watch. Operation Sherwood, they had code-named it, with rather too much relevance for common sense.

To Jessica, with a sense of irrevocable destiny preparations for D-Day were bound up in her mind with her wedding. It was all going to happen, the climax of the war and this milestone in her life. Her work had not stopped, however. Far from it. In increasing numbers after the bombing campaign had intensified, men wer-making their way back, by diverse routes from many parts of the world. This morning she was due at the Air Ministry for last minute briefings on security, and not unexpectedly found Gerry Rhodes one of the officers there.

After the meeting she caught him up in the corridor, steeling herself to tell him about Vanessa.

'I am honoured by your eagerness for my company,' he murmured.

'Let's forget all that, Gerry,' she said impatiently. 'I haven't the time. I wanted to talk about Vanessa.'

'How pleasant. How is sweet-natured Vanessa?' His tone was much as usual, but his eyes were cold and steely.

'Not well, Gerry. She's had a miscarriage – you heard Graham had been killed?'

'Dear me, I hadn't heard that. The gallant sergeant. So she's a beautiful widow without the unfortunate encumbrance of a bastard.'

'She needs friends, Gerry,' Jessica said bluntly. 'You used to be fond of her.'

'I think dear Vanessa made her feelings for me fairly clear at our last meeting.'

'But you turned her out!'

'What the hell did you expect?' He turned on her savagely. It was the first time she had ever heard Gerry Rhodes speak other than in his affected drawl. 'I think,' he said reflectively, calming down, 'that little episode at our last meeting brought to an end my relationship with dear Vanessa – and therefore, sadly, my acquaintance with you, Wing Officer Gray. Don't weep too hard.'

'The little episode.' So she had been right. He would

never forgive Vanessa for those words – or Jessica for hearing them.

'By the way,' his eyes flickered, 'you were friendly with Will Donaldson, weren't you?'

She stiffened and said nothing.

'Poor devil,' he went on.

She went white. 'Why?' she blurted out.

'Bad luck to go that way.'

'Go?' She stared at him blankly.

'He's dead. You did know, didn't you?'

'*Dead*?' she repeated numbly.

'Shot down. Dead. Just like that. Pity, isn't it?'

The room started to spin round. 'When?' she asked faintly.

'Ages ago, darling. You must have heard. My, you are out of touch. Didn't anyone tell you? Last autumn sometime. The end of September. I remember noticing because it was near my birthday. Mind you, news only got to me recently. I say, are you all right?'

'Perfectly,' she said stiffly. 'Perfectly all right.'

He gazed after her reflectively. 'Missing believed killed.' That's what it said. No need to tell her there was a later list, giving his name as at large in enemy occupied territory in the charge of an evasion line. After all, it could be argued, it was in the girl's best interests. He smiled. She was getting married in a few days. No point upsetting apple carts. And he owed Will Donaldson that one. The fat lady had sung now all right, for Donaldson not him. See how you like that, *fella*.

She should be at rehearsal, but she wasn't. She was going to Kent. She'd tried to carry on as normal, then collapsed.

First she must wrestle with the near-certitude that Will had been killed on perhaps the very day he did not come to London as promised. Empty inside she forced herself to face the fact that all that time she had anguished, because of his betrayal in leaving her, he had been dead. Why hadn't they known that at Debden when she rang? Why had she been told he was on leave? Perhaps Gerry was wrong . . . No, her own intuition had told her that Will would not have left her without a word. Now she could trust it again. He had to be dead. There must have been some kind of administrative muddle at Debden. All these months of wasted agony. For the grief she should have had was that of loss, of separation, of waste, of a life snuffed out. Not that grief of betrayal and treachery that had seemed to invalidate all she and Will had had together.

What a fool she'd been. Of course he wouldn't have gone away without a word. Two emotions tore at her: agonising grief and a kind of triumph that now her love for him was vindicated. Side by side with them came the realisation that on Saturday she would be marrying another man. A man whom she was free to love without that tearing knowledge that somewhere Will walked free. That was how the world would see it – but there was something she must do.

'Tom, do you know what I'm going to say?' Jessica asked quietly.

'Yes,' he answered matter-of-factly. 'I think I realised some time ago. When you started training the Bluebirds.'

'It has nothing to do with that.'

'I realised you'd never be happy stuck down here. You

see, I don't want to go rushing around the world and you do. I don't share your passion for music. I'd always be either trailing behind you, or away from you. It wouldn't have worked, Jessica.'

'It isn't just that, Tom. It's knowing Will's dead. I can't explain why, but it changes things.'

He reached out a hand. 'I'm sorry, darling.'

'I'm beginning to make a habit of calling off weddings, aren't I?' She tried to smile.

'Third time lucky, perhaps,' he said lightly.

'Perhaps I'm a Jonah. First John, now Will.' She was silent. She couldn't yet come to terms with it. 'He doesn't seem dead, Tom,' she said quietly. 'He seems so alive, it's as though he's trying to make music through me. Can you understand that? Perhaps there are such things as spirits and he's trying to get through to me. Is that possible?'

'Jessica,' he said sharply, 'take care, take care. He's dead. What you hear now is the memory of his love. And that's going to send you onward, not back.'

'It seems an odd way to go forward, by breaking my engagement to you,' she said quietly. 'Are you really not too upset?'

He hesitated. 'Listen, Jessica.' He took her hand. 'It may seem odd, but I'm almost glad you've called it off. What you and I shared was a comfortable togetherness, something known and tested.'

'That's what we wanted.'

'Yes. Now you've found out you were wrong. And—' he hesitated '—I'm just beginning to think perhaps I have too. There's someone needs me, Jessica, more than you do.'

* * *

Telling Tom had been easy compared with telling her mother.

When she took it in, Cicely's face became almost ugly. 'You must, you must, you must go through with it!' she raged. 'No one else will want you. Why? What's happened to make you change your mind?' Rage and fear mingled on Bubbles' face.

Something held Jessica back from telling her mother about Will. How could she explain to her that his being dead had made her see she couldn't marry Tom?

'We agreed we weren't suited,' she said steadily, and would say no more. She couldn't tell her mother Tom had found someone else. Her mother would weigh into that delicate situation like an elephant trampling down corn. And her rage when she discovered it was Vanessa would be terrible to see. She'd calm down eventually, even be glad for Vanessa's sake, but the damage would have been done. I owe Tom more than that, thought Jessica. So she merely repeated in the face of her mother's barrage of questions that they weren't suited.

'It's no use, Mother,' she said wearily at last. 'I know you think you have my best interests at heart, but we'll never, but never, understand each other.' It was a lie, for she understood her mother very well – or thought she did.

Despite the persistent showers, she went for a walk on the downs before going back, for some reason taking not her favourite path but one that she and John so often took, down through Stedehill Woods and on to the Pilrim's Way with its views over the Weald. John was much in her mind. Why that should be she did not know. She stopped at the old oak tree where once he had carved their initials. 'JG loves JG.' The carving was weathered now but the initials still distinct. It seemed another age. She could not recall how it felt to be in love with John. Perhaps her love for Will too would pass in time? No, that would never happen. Her love for him would abate and lie down to sleep, blanketed by the needs of everyday living. But it would not die. Even if she eventually married someone else in years to come, it would always be there, lying dormant, ready to be looked at from time to time, and laid back with gentle loving care.

The wild roses were blooming on the hillsides now, glowing even in this overcast evening. Everything seemed still, suspended, as though waiting, waiting. For invasion? For the first sure sign that victory was possible? Or was it in her, this feeling of expectancy, that something hovered near? Will was dead, she told herself, yet inside her was not numbing grief but an odd feeling that something had been exorcised forever.

Was her love so selfish that his death took second place to the fact that he had not betrayed her? No, she couldn't believe that. The grief would return, reopen the wounds. But for this evening she was at peace. Here once she had declaimed that Britain would always be free, here stood to wonder at the view with John, lain with him in the long grass, here held back her love from him. And now she understood why. 'Forgive me, John,' she whispered.

She looked round, absorbing all the details of the place carefully, imprinting it once more on her memory. As she stood in the twilight, clouds scudding across the sky, she could hear the birds singing their songs of evening – and, yes, surely one was a nightingale. Perhaps it was even Lind's voice, carrying up to the hill. No, that was foolish. But a nightingale it was. She closed her eyes to listen, the songs floating up through the trees.

'Please, please open your eyes,' she heard Will say again. But she kept them closed as the nightingale sang. ' "As she sings in the valley below . . ." I could do something with that,' she heard him say. Swing it . . . 'The Sweet Nightingale' was where it all began so long ago.

The bird sang on; she picked the sounds out from amongst the other birds, straining to catch it. 'I heard a nightingale sing one night,' she whispered. 'His sweet sad song of love . . .'

'Open your eyes,' she heard Will say. If she opened them perhaps she'd see his face full of love above her, his body on hers, feel his hands caressing her, himself within her. If she opened her eyes. Their song swirled round inside her head, till she was giddy with it, the words taking over, whispering them. 'Open your eyes,' he murmured. 'Open, *please*.'

'. . . In my arms,
And our song began.'

Her eyes opened and she heard the words. Not whispered as she'd imagined but the song, full and glorious, soaring out in triumph. She cried out, clutching a tree for support. Then it happened again. She had no power to stop it, even if she'd wanted to. Music soared in her head, then poured from her throat in a triumphal stream. Tears of joy stung her eyes as she stood on the hillside looking at the valleys of Kent below her. Then she threw her arms wide and addressed them.

'I can sing,' she yelled at the top of her voice. 'I can sing, sing, *sing*. Are you listening to me, sparrow? Can you hear me, nightingale? I can *sing*!'

Monday the 5th had been earmarked as D-Day. The weather as predicted thirty-six hours earlier was windy, rainy and overcast. Not flying weather. The evening before General Eisenhower had tossed a coin with fate and set the new date as the 6th. They could wait no longer than that, whatever the weather. There was a chance it would clear sufficiently for the invasion to have a chance of success. Surprise – the major factor, in their thinking – might well be lost if they delayed further. Everyone was ready, men aboard ships, briefed and keyed up. There could be no second shot. The 6th it would be.

Jessica hurried back to London for her postponed rehearsal of the Bluebirds. Should she tell them what had happened to her? No, it was something she should keep to herself for the moment, something to think about carefully, to decide how to use once she had come to terms with Will's death.

At Debden they all turned in early. So it was tomorrow. The first mission would begin at first light – if it ever broke through that cloud bank. Keyed up, it was difficult to sleep. No fooling around tomorrow. This was going to be it with no second chances.

Will's kit was already packed. He'd fly most of the day, then leave for Sussex. And then he'd be out of this private hell of his; caught up whether he liked it or not in another kind of life – based in France not in England with its memories of Jessica smarting like an ever open sore. He tried to fix his thoughts on Jeanette, on the future – in vain. He drifted off into an uneasy sleep in which he ran after an ever-retreating Jessica, who was turning and shouting to him, but would not stop to allow him to come up to her.

A quarter of an hour after D-Day had officially begun, the first paratroops and assault forces dropped on to French soil. Already well on its way, the biggest invasion armada in history steamed its way across the Channel towards the Normandy coast.

And in the Pas de Calais the cream of Hitler's forces waited for an invasion that never came. Operation Fortitude, with its fictitious forces based in Kent, false radio traffic and dummy war material, had succeeded.

The Mustang bucked and roared its way across the Channel, the dawn just breaking now. Below him when the clouds cleared he could see a vast armada of black shapes dotting the ocean, steadily making its way to the French coast. Debden had a special rôle today; not escorting the bombers for once. The Group specialised in ground assault, and their role was to attack everything moving on the roads up to the beachheads.

It felt good to be back on ops again. And this time he wasn't going to be shot down. No, sir.

In France at 5 am the German Seventh Army watched the vast armada converging on the coastline with disbelief. Fifty minutes later the ships' guns opened up, and forty minutes after that American troops began to land. Further round the coast the British and Dominion

Armies set foot once more on French soil. Above them the sky was full of bomber fleets bombing from the Pas de Calais round to the whole of Normandy. German reinforcements were rushed up, clogging the roads to the beachheads – and then the strafers of the Eighth Air Force swept in.

In the Pas de Calais the Fifteenth Panzer Division, the pride of the Wehrmacht, still waited for the main invasion fleet, convinced that Normandy was a mere sideshow. Where were the other fifty Allied divisions their intelligence had convinced them were waiting in Kent?

Up in the Norman skies there was no sign of the Luftwaffe. Only later that day did a small force strike. But Will, lining up his Mustang on the road to Omaha Beach, saw none of them. The only opposition was anti-aircraft fire. The squadron was flying continually, coming back to refuel twice. By then Will was flying like an automaton, the early exhilaration gone with exhaustion. Firing, firing, firing. The Mustang was in its element now, sturdy and strong, seeming almost part of him as once the Spitfire had. Soon he'd be back with Spits. Meanwhile, he'd done it – he'd been a part of the greatest invasion in history.

'Okay, let's show 'em, pal,' he cried out in determination, drawing a bawdy comment from his wingman, listening in on the radio. 'Let's show 'em good.'

At eight o'clock that morning Jessica had switched on her wireless. Even then she could not quite believe it. The announcements were only taken from German reports, not British. But it must be true, it must! She hurried to he office where smiles and laughter replaced the phlegma anticipation of the last week. Everyone was talking. Everyone believed it. When they turned on the radio at 9.30 to hear John Snagge give the official British confirmation of the landing, it was almost an anti-climax.

Someone let out a whoop as they switched the radio off. A minute or two, then the hubbub broke out afresh, so loud that the sound of the telephone went unnoticed for some moments. Then someone answered it. 'You and your blessed Bluebirds. It's for you, Jessica. The BBC.'

By the time he left Debden, Will didn't feel like celebrating. It was a job well done, that was all. It meant at last they were getting somewhere in this damned war. For once the train, though packed, was not full of airmen, but of troops still making their way south. He managed to fight his way to the lavatory through celebrating passengers and on his way out bumped into one blue uniform. He recognised its occupant: Geoff Swift. He was drunk.

'Come and have a snifter, old chap.'

Will shook his head. 'I'll save it till I get to London, thanks. I'm maybe flying to France tomorrow.'

'Ah, well, I'll have one anyway. Here's to the lovely mademoiselles. Save a few for me.'

'Sure. Here's to them.'

'That reminds me . . .' Geoff frowned in concentration. 'Something odd. Meant to ask you – rang you up at Debden, but you were away. What's happened to Jessica?'

Will blenched. 'How the hell should I know?' he retorted angrily. Be damned if he was going to be forced to think about Jessica now. He went to move past Geoff but, drunk, he persisted when otherwise the sight of Will's face would have deterred him.

'Have a tiff, did you?'

'No.'

'Just parted again, did you? I say, old boy, you did find her, didn't you?'

'*Find* her? For Christ's sake, she's married. What the hell do you think I did? Barge up and say, "remember me?" '

'Married?' Geoff concentrated, hanging on to Will's lapels as the train lurched. 'When?'

'Just after Christmas, I think,' Will said through gritted teeth. 'Does it matter? She's married, that's all that counts.'

'She wasn't last week when she rang me,' said Geoff, trying to work it out. 'Must be some mistake. I'm going to her wedding on Saturday. Invitation chased me round and never reached me. Been moving around a bit.'

'But her mother—' Will stopped, the sickening truth sweeping over him. Bubbles Gray would stop at nothing. She'd never liked him. She wouldn't want her plans for Jessica's marriage upset a second time. And besides, suppose – oh God, suppose she thought the shock of seeing Will again, would bring back her daughter's voice, that music would re-enter her life . . . ? White to the lips, Will cried out, 'This Saturday? Christ, and I'm leaving the country tomorrow! I've got five hours or so to find her, and I don't bloody well know where to begin. Where the hell *is* she?'

Geoff looked at him compassionately. 'No use looking at me, old chap. I've no idea. You could try Bubbles, of course. She might help.'

Bubbles help? He'd stand more chance of help from a piranha.

* * *

All day she'd been battling with grief. Will's death was the harder to bear on this day of national happiness. And this evening she had to forget the one in the interests of the other. For she had an appointment to keep and somehow, some way, she'd make it Will's triumph too.

London, until recently so full of uniforms, was suddenly given back to its civilians. The pubs were crowded out as London drank to the success of the invasion, already laying bets on how soon the war would be over. The Kit-Kat Club, on the other hand, was almost deserted, and Will wandered out into the streets, simply so that he should not go over the agony again. It was 9 o'clock. He'd rung Bubbles. 'Can I speak to Jessica?' He gave no name, but she must have recognised his voice from the accent. The receiver was put down firmly.

He sat and looked at that damned instrument. He could hardly ring Tom Ackroyd, could he? Hell, there were limits . . . No, there were none so far as Jessica was concerned. He got the number from the operator and listened to that fateful ringing. Ringing into an empty house.

'No reply, sir.'

They must be out. Well, that was it. Short of flying back from France in a Spit and seizing her at the altar like Young Lochinvar there was nothing he could do. He'd even do that, if he thought she was marrying unwillingly. But he forced himself to acknowledge she was not. She'd chosen to marry. What right had he to come barging back into her life? If she'd made any effort recently, she'd have discovered he was still alive, even though she got the wrong information first time. But she'd given up. She no longer loved him, she loved Tom.

In sudden despair he turned into a pub in Piccadilly, packed with people. A drink. God, he needed a drink. Another hour before he could go to bed with any hope of sleeping. And then with the racket outside he wouldn't stand much chance of oblivion. And he needed that to keep away the nightmares.

He sat down in a corner, squeezing on to a bench. Above him a wireless was on. The song was familiar.

'It's those new Bluebirds,' said the woman next to him incomprehensibly. He could only hear 'You're my tea rose in the desert . . .'

'Ain't heard that for a long time, 'ave you, Jack?' she continued. 'Used to be our song. Remember?'

Will remembered. It was his song too. It finished, and they sang another. 'Don't let them ration you . . .' What the hell were those girls trying to do to him? He got up blindly. He had to get out of here. The man next to him pulled him down again. 'You've got to hear this one, mate. It's the Singing Waaf back again. Remember her? She's been off the air a good long while. Come back to sing for D-Day, that's what they said. Special broadcast.'

The Singing Waaf? Will stared at him. Not *his* Singing Waaf. Her voice had gone. They'd said so. It was someone else, it must be. And then he heard her.

'I sing this song for Will, who wrote it. Will, as dear to me today as all your sweethearts and dear ones fighting over there at the moment. Will, who died in action eight months ago. Will, the man I'll always love.

'I heard a nightingale sing one night,
His sweet sad song of love . . .'

Her voice, husky, mellow and true, rang out over the air, pinioning his heart once more. No other voice, no other woman. She was half a mile away and clarinets would play him to her.

'And our song began . . .'

'Ain't she got a lovely voice,' sighed his neighbour complacently. But Will did not hear. His heart began to sing, and all the music of the world came together to greet the sunrise in one glorious song of joy.

'Dead,' he shouted, laughing out loud. 'Dead! She thinks I'm *dead*.'

He rose shakily to his feet, oblivious of the staring faces, seeing only one, hearing but one voice.

'Lady,' he breathed, as he pushed his way through towards the telephone, 'have I got news for you!'